BEAUTIFUL
ASSASSIN

ALSO BY MICHAEL WHITE

Soul Catcher
The Garden of Martyrs
A Dream of Wolves
Marked Men
The Blind Side of the Heart
A Brother's Blood

MICHAEL WHITE
BEAUTIFUL ASSASSIN

uercus

First published in Great Britain in 2010 by

Quercus
21 Bloomsbury Square
London
WC1A 2NS

A CIP catalogue reference for this book is available
from the British Library

ISBN (HB) 978 1 84724 660 8
ISBN (TPB) 978 1 84724 661 5

10 9 8 7 6 5 4 3 2 1

Printed and bound in Great Britain by Clays Ltd, St Ives plc.

For Caitlin and Wesley, with love

BEAUTIFUL ASSASSIN

PROLOGUE

Colorado, 1996

Elizabeth had driven several miles past the dirt road before it occurred to her that it might have been the one the old woman had told her to take. After glancing once more at the directions, she decided finally to turn the rental car around and head back along the same parched stretch of eastern Colorado road. The August afternoon was scorching, the blacktop ahead undulating like a snake trying to shed its skin. Her eyes ached from the glare off the pavement, and even with the air conditioner on full blast, her blouse clung damply to her back. On either side of the road, the brown, desiccated plains stretched out to the harsh blue of the sky. The sheer relentlessness of the landscape called to mind a train ride she'd once made to Kiev for a story. She'd been traveling from Moscow, where she was the bureau chief for an American newspaper, and was on her way to interview one of the leaders of the Rukh nationalist movement. This was back in the eighties when the idea of an independent Ukraine was still a pipe dream. She remembered seeing out her compartment window the Russian steppes unfurling endlessly, their vastness giving her vertigo. Now, halfway around the world, she was, ironically, going to see another Ukrainian, one who'd declared her own independence a long time ago.

There was no mailbox or marker, but she took the chance and turned down the narrow dirt road. She drove over a cattle guard, then up a bumpy incline. The washboard road kicked up stones against the car's undercarriage, the pinging sounding eerily as if someone were shooting at her. When the road leveled off, it appeared headed straight for a windbreak of cottonwoods off in the wavy distance. In the shelter of the trees stood a weather-beaten barn and several outbuildings, a windmill listing precariously, a small white farmhouse. That had to be her place, Elizabeth thought.

She wondered if the old woman would look anything like the person in the newspaper photos. Every picture Elizabeth had come across, as well as everything she'd read about Tat'yana Levchenko, only confirmed that she had been a striking-looking woman. "A real knockout," one reporter had called her in that hard-boiled journalistic slang of the times. Dark hair done in those pin curls of the forties, short enough to tuck beneath the forage cap she sometimes posed in. The strong features, the high, Slavic cheekbones and slightly aquiline nose, the smooth, porcelain complexion. A full mouth that, for the cameras at least, was always made up with lipstick and smiling as buoyantly as a Girl Scout, an image that her uniform, with its cluster of impressive medals, only enhanced. Yet it was the eyes that drew the viewer: a lucid dark, wide and serious, exuding the innocent gaze of an ingenue having just arrived in the big city. But that image, of course, belied the facts, what she'd accomplished in the war (one newspaper article had dubbed her "the doe-eyed executioner"). Elizabeth sensed something else lurking beneath those innocent eyes. She'd seen that look before, the masklike expression in the faces of the Muscovites she passed in the streets, the old babushkas cautiously avoiding eye contact with strangers, the young trained to be wary, as if their very thoughts were being monitored by the government. Elizabeth felt that if she could get beneath the public face of Tat'yana Levchenko, she would get a glimpse of the real woman who lay beneath and the story she'd been guarding for more than half a century.

The American press back then had had a field day with her. A Communist, war hero, scholar, poet, and on top of everything, movie star good-looking, a figure right out of central casting. They'd fawned over her, eager to introduce her to an American public largely ignorant of their newfound ally, that notorious Russian Bear, and of a European theater of war that, in 1942 at least, was still just a distant rumble. She would have appeared to many a kind of Rosie the Riveter but with a rifle instead of a rivet gun. Today, her story would have commanded a seven-figure book deal; she'd have been on the talk show circuit and had a flood of movie offers. But today, of course, the woman would be almost eighty, and, as she herself had obviously preferred it, a largely forgotten figure. As Elizabeth drove along she thought of that odd photo of Tat'yana Levchenko up in a tree, one the Soviet press had reenacted for propaganda purposes, just as they had the blowing up of the Nazi eagle over the Reichstag days after they'd already taken Berlin. An obviously staged publicity shot with her wearing a camouflage poncho and holding a rifle, her face quite clearly made up, staring prettily through the scope at an imaginary enemy—all the while perched in a tree! Elizabeth had read the accompanying article in the *Saturday Evening Post,* about her near-fatal duel with the German sniper. How much of it was true, though? How much simply Soviet propaganda? In fact, how much of the woman herself was to be believed, Elizabeth wondered, and how much was just an agitprop creation, that cold war tendency to distort reality for some desired political advantage?

As she neared the house, Elizabeth grew excited at the prospect she was finally going to meet the woman she'd been hunting for years. She felt the sort of nervous anticipation she always did when covering a story that had consumed her so completely. But then she wondered if she should continue the subterfuge she'd started when she first called, that of being a distant relative of the woman's dead husband. She didn't like having to lie, felt her job as a journalist was to find the truth and tell it. But sometimes a small falsehood was the only way to get your foot in the door to a greater truth. She knew the woman would never have agreed to meet her if she'd confessed her real intentions up front.

"Who are you?" Tat'yana Levchenko had asked over the phone. Her English was fairly good but heavily accented, her labored breathing punctuated by raspy coughs.

"Elizabeth Meade. I'm related to your husband, Mrs. Bishop." Elizabeth used the woman's married name, not Andreeva, the alias she'd assumed more than fifty years before.

"He never spoke of . . . ," the woman began, but then paused for an intake of breath. "Any Meades."

"My mother was a Bishop. May I call you Irina?"

"How did you find me?"

"Through some old letters of my grandmother's," Elizabeth lied.

"What do you want?"

Elizabeth could hear the wariness in the old woman's voice, the caution of one who'd spent years in hiding, first as a sniper and later a lifetime looking over her shoulder, waiting for someone to come for her. Just as they had for Trotsky. Or Walter Krivitsky, who was murdered by KGB agents in a Washington hotel room. Or like Juliet Stuart Poyntz, a Barnard professor and high-ranking American Communist Party member, as well as a Soviet agent. Poyntz had been invited to Moscow in the thirties, but after seeing the brutality of Stalin's purges firsthand, she'd turned on the Communist Party. Fearing she might betray important information, Soviet agents were rumored to have kidnapped her in Central Park, and she was never heard from again. In those days, no one was safe from the long reach and even longer memory of Stalin, or his brutal enforcer Beria.

"I'm a writer," Elizabeth explained. "I'm writing a family history. I'd like to find out about your husband's side of the family."

"What's to tell?" the woman said. "My husband was not very close to them."

"I'd just like to talk to you. It would mean a great deal to me."

The woman fell stone silent on the other end for several seconds, so that Elizabeth thought she'd hung up. But to her surprise, the woman finally conceded. "It is a long way to come for nothing. But if you insist."

The next day, Elizabeth left New York on the first available flight for Denver. And here she was, about to meet Tat'yana Levchenko, a figure whose sudden disappearance a half century ago had caused headlines.

She pulled up in front of a white two-story house whose paint was badly blistered. As she cut the engine, the dust that had been trailing behind her finally had a chance to catch up. It swirled around her in an ochre cloud, and even inside the car she could taste something like chalk dust. When the air cleared, Elizabeth made out a squat figure standing behind the screen door gazing out at her. As she got out of the car she was immediately confronted by the yapping of a dog.

"*Fu!*" the old woman called sharply to the animal. The dog, a border collie with a grizzled muzzle, gave off a few halfhearted growls before slinking off toward the shade of a cottonwood.

"Irina?" Elizabeth called to her.

The woman nodded. "And you are Elizabeth, no?" She pronounced her name *E-leezabet*.

"Yes. Sorry I'm late."

Elizabeth reached back into the car for her briefcase, then headed up toward the house. As she approached, the woman opened the screen door and Elizabeth offered her hand in greeting. She was surprised that the old woman's grip was so vigorous, the palm callused, the fingers cracked and hooked like talons. Her hair was short and puffy-white, accentuating a ruddy complexion. She wore a shapeless flowered dress that hung on her, and she was thick through the body, with a large bosom that Elizabeth had not noticed in the old pictures, no doubt camouflaged by the bulky military jacket and Sam Browne belt. Hanging from around her neck was a pair of reading glasses. She was shorter than Elizabeth had assumed, not much more than five feet. Perhaps she had shrunk with age. Still, in all the photos she had projected an image of height, of substance. Her skin was badly wrinkled, her once pretty mouth hard and sunken. She looked nothing like the woman in the photos, just like some old lady who had lived a difficult life. Nothing about her suggested she'd had such a remarkable past. In fact, for a moment Elizabeth wondered if it could be a mistake, if she had the wrong person. But then the old woman's gaze met Elizabeth's. From this close, her eyes bore an unmistakable resemblance to those of the young woman in the photos. They were still clear and wide, darkly intent as a hawk's searching for prey. Elizabeth could imagine those same eyes fixing a target in her crosshairs. She remembered reading something about how the woman had said that the trick was to silence one's breathing, to kiss the trigger. That killing was simply a matter of controlling one's breath.

"*Zdravstvuyte. Bol'shoye spasibo zato, chto soglasilis' vstretit'sya so mnoy*," offered Elizabeth by way of greeting.

"*Rada poznakimitsya*," replied the woman. "Where you learn Russian?"

"I studied it in school. And I worked as a newspaper correspondent in Moscow."

"How come you no say you work in Moscow?"

"I used to," replied Elizabeth, catching the hesitant note in the woman's voice. Suspicion that someone from the old country had finally tracked her down? Or merely nostalgia for her homeland, for her past? Hoping to dispel the woman's fears, she quickly changed subjects. "I'm so glad to finally meet you."

"It is hot out here. Come," the woman said, inviting her inside.

As she held the door for Elizabeth, the dog slipped by them, into the house, its nails clicking on the wood floors. The place had an old-person smell to it, a stale and leathery odor like a pair of old shoes. There was also a vague smell of vegetables boiled and meats fried over a lifetime, the sort of earthy stench Elizabeth associated with Russian households. The woman walked with a cane, her other hand out to the side, touching the wall for balance, moving gingerly like a blind person. She led Elizabeth toward a small screened porch off to the right. A fan coaxed tepid air into the room, bringing with it, too, the same chalky smell Elizabeth had experienced before. Somewhere a fly buzzed noisily, stubbornly crashing into the screen. The room was plainly furnished—in the corner a bureau upon which sat a small portable TV, in the opposite corner a metal card table with two folding chairs. In the middle of the room was a well-worn recliner, in front of it a wicker coffee table with a Plexiglas top, and against the outside wall a metal glider for a couch.

The dog lumbered over to the couch, jumped up onto it, and was about to curl up.

"Get down!" the woman commanded. When the animal didn't budge, she whacked it firmly with the end of her cane. With a desultory slowness, the creature slid off the couch, walked a few feet, and collapsed on the floor with a loud exhalation of air.

"Please, sit," she instructed Elizabeth, indicating the couch.

The woman was nearly out of breath from the short walk from the front door. "May I . . . offer you something to drink?"

"If it's not too much trouble."

The woman turned and shuffled out of the room. The momentary break was just what Elizabeth needed—a chance to clear her head, to plan out how she would approach the interview. She glanced around the room, trying to get a feel for what she thought of as her "subject." She had interviewed many subjects in their elements, in their homes and offices and places of work. One time it had been in a prison cell where she'd interviewed a noted Soviet dissident writer. Another time it was in a T-62 tank with soldiers stationed in Afghanistan. Most of the time, Soviet citizens were wary of opening up to her, fearful of the repercussions, and Elizabeth had found that the objects they surrounded themselves with sometimes told her more than they themselves did. She'd once interviewed Yuri Andropov. The leader of the Soviet Union and former KGB head was a reticent subject. Both awkward and aloof, he kept fidgeting during the interview, checking his wristwatch. Elizabeth happened to notice a framed photograph of a tabby cat on his desk. She steered the conversation toward cats, and suddenly this hard-line old Communist who'd ordered the arrests of thousands became as chatty as a schoolgirl gossiping among friends.

Yet as Elizabeth glanced around the house, she saw little that hinted at the life of its occupant. The room had that frugal midwestern efficiency, neat and plain and anonymous as a budget motel room. A few insipid landscape pictures on the walls, some plastic flowers in a vase on the coffee table. On a bookshelf to the right of the recliner sat some knickknacks, as well as an assortment of books, a number, she noticed, in Russian. Elizabeth leaned forward to read their titles. There were several by Akhmatova and Esesin. From her research, Elizabeth recalled how Tat'yana Levchenko had written poetry (she wondered if she still did or was that another part of her that she'd had to leave behind). Sitting on the bookshelf were two framed photos. Both were black and white, one a picture of a tall, lean man wearing a straw cowboy hat. He had a long, angular face, and his expression was one of bemused annoyance. The husband, Elizabeth concluded. Her research had turned up little more than his name—Walter Bishop. The other was of a young blond woman in her twenties, though the hairstyle—bangs, with a large bouffant—suggested the picture had been taken back in the fifties. She was thin, sharp-featured, pretty in an austere sort of way. A daughter, Elizabeth wondered.

The idea for the story had come to Elizabeth quite by chance. The late eighties and early nineties had been heady times for a journalist covering the Soviet Union. It was the place to be for a reporter trying to make a name for herself, and Elizabeth had wanted to be at the epicenter of it. History was unfolding right before her eyes. Reagan's evil empire was imploding, everything in a dangerous state of flux. Each day brought something new, a threat or rumor, the end of the cold war or nuclear apocalypse. Yeltsin standing on a tank, defying the military. Nuclear missiles for sale on the black market. Old women waiting in long lines to pawn silverware so they could buy a little food. Some story hidden since the war just coming to light—like the one about Hitler's skull suddenly turning up in Moscow. Revelations and scandals and long-buried secrets unearthed. In short, a journalist's dream.

At a cocktail party Elizabeth had attended at the American ambassador's residence, the buzz was all about whether Gorbachev would resign peacefully in favor of Yeltsin or if there would be actual civil war. She happened to run into an acquaintance named Reynolds, a retired British diplomat. He'd worked with the Reds, as he called them, ever since the war, and still did something of a vaguely clandestine nature that he would allude to only with a self-important wink. He liked to give the impression that he was well connected. She found him vaguely annoying, a boozy blowhard with that patronizing manner that Brits often assumed with Americans. But for some reason he liked her, and while mostly he was just a big talker, occasionally he'd toss some newsworthy item her way. It was he who'd tipped her off that the Reds were about to allow Sakharov to return to Moscow. She was the first to break the story.

Reynolds was holding court with a small group of men when Elizabeth came up. The subject was Vasily Zaitsev, a famous sniper at Stalingrad whose recent death had been largely overshadowed by all the political upheaval in the country. Reynolds, however, claimed that the most famous Soviet sniper wasn't Zaitsev at all, but a woman.

"She killed hundreds of krauts," he said.

"What was her name?" Elizabeth ventured.

"Tat'yana Levchenko."

Elizabeth shrugged, used as she was to Reynolds's big talk.

"Now there's a story for you, my dear," he said. He went on to lecture in that supercilious manner of his that this Levchenko had fought during the siege of Sevastopol, had recorded the most kills of any Red soldier up until that point in the war.

"It just so happens that I met her personally. Right in this very room, in fact. Quite the looker," he said, winking at the other men. "But cold as ice."

"Are you making all this up?" she chided him.

"The God's truth," he said. "She was as well known over here as your own Audie Murphy in the States. Quite the darling of the big shots at the Kremlim, too." Reynolds went on to say she'd become so famous that Eleanor Roosevelt heard about her and invited her to visit America. "She toured the States with Mrs. Roosevelt, speaking on behalf of the war effort. Made a pretty big splash on your side of the pond."

"How come I never heard of her?" she asked.

"You ought to read your history, my dear," replied Reynolds.

"What happened to her?"

"Let's get another drink, shall we, and I'll tell you all about her," he said, slipping his arm into hers and leading her over to the bar.

Later, when they were alone, he said, "Some say she worked for the NKVD."

"She was a spy?" Elizabeth exclaimed.

"That was the word on her. Supposedly, she passed along information she got through her relationship with Mrs. Roosevelt."

He smiled at her evasively and sipped his drink.

Elizabeth wondered how much of this she could believe. Still, she had to admit the story intrigued her. A female war hero who spied on Mrs. Roosevelt. "Where did you hear all this?"

"Around," Reynolds replied, twirling his glass in the air so that some of his drink sloshed onto the bar.

"You still haven't told me what happened to her."

"Disappeared," he said, hooking his fingers as quotes around the word.

"What does that mean?"

"There was a big brouhaha for a time when she vanished. Some say the Yanks sent her into hiding. Others that they eventually caught up with her."

"What do you mean, 'caught up with her'? Who?"

"For a smart girl you can be bloody naïve, Elizabeth. The KGB. You know how these thugs used to operate. Still do, for that matter," he said, glancing over his shoulder, as if someone might overhear him.

"What did they do with her?"

Reynolds put his index finger to his temple and went, "*Tfff.*"

"I think you've been reading too many James Bond novels," she joked.

Nonetheless, her curiosity piqued, Elizabeth decided to do some digging on this Tat'yana Levchenko. Right away she learned virtually nothing was to be found regarding the woman in the Soviet records. As with that of so many other personae non gratae Soviets, her existence had been purged, wiped clean, like those ghostly blanks of individuals who'd been painted out of the group portraits with Stalin. So Elizabeth turned to American records, and there she found that the famous female sniper had, indeed, existed. She uncovered dozens of references to her, articles and photographs of the Soviet soldier in newspapers and magazines from her wartime visit to the States. And the more she learned about the woman, the more fascinated she became. Before the war Tat'yana Levchenko had been a scholar and a budding poet; a skilled marksman with a youth shooting club; a young wife and new mother; then with the German invasion, a sniper extraordinaire and sudden international war hero, someone who toured the States giving speeches with Eleanor Roosevelt, and with whom she'd become close friends. And all the while perhaps acting as a Soviet spy, passing secrets along to Red agents, though none of that was alluded to in the press. Elizabeth thought it would make a great story, maybe even that book she'd always been meaning to write. But she kept running into a dead end. She could find nothing about what became of the woman, beyond several sketchy newspaper reports of her "disappearance." "Soviet Hero Defects to U.S." read one front-page headline. Another article, a smaller one on page two of the *New York Times*, reported that the Soviets had lodged a formal complaint with the United States, insisting that their famous citizen be returned to them. Yet another article said simply: "Female Sniper Disappears." And then slowly the news about her faded, and Tat'yana Levchenko simply vanished, a footnote to history.

Over the next several years Elizabeth ran into more dead ends, and her research added little to what she already knew of the woman. But then, with the collapse of the Soviet Union, there were suddenly plenty of people who were, for a price, willing to talk. Reynolds arranged for Elizabeth to meet with a purported former KGB agent who apparently had direct knowledge of the woman. They met in a seedy strip bar on Prospekt Mira. The man, who must have been seventy, wore mirrored sunglasses and a threadbare coat that stank of cigar smoke and fried fish. As she spoke to him, he kept looking over her shoulder at the girls dancing on the stage behind the bar. Elizabeth could see their snow-pale, writhing forms reflected in his glasses. He asked for the agreed-upon payment—a thousand dollars; he wouldn't accept rubles. Elizabeth had withdrawn money from her own savings—she wanted this to be her story alone. Only then did the man remove a piece of paper from his coat pocket and slide it across the table. When Elizabeth looked at it, she saw a name scrawled in Cyrillic: Irina Andreeva. She asked him what this had to do with the woman she was looking for.

"That," he replied in broken English, a long, dirty fingernail tapping the name, "is same woman. Tat'yana Levchenko."

"That's the name she assumed?"

He nodded.

"What happened to her?" Elizabeth asked.

The man shrugged. "She defect to America."

"Did the KGB get to her?"

"*Tsh*," he scoffed. "Those fools couldn't find a turd in a toilet bowl."

"Is she still alive?"

He lifted his hands inconclusively in the air. At which point he started to get up.

"Wait," Elizabeth said. "If they didn't kill her, what happened to her?"

Rubbing his thumb over his first two fingers, he said, "Cost more."

"How much?"

"Thousand."

Used to the Soviet ways of bargaining for information, Elizabeth withdrew from her purse three hundred-dollar bills.

"Three hundred," she said, waving the bills at him.

As if he was going to strike her, he shoved five fingers at her face. "*Piat.*"

"Forget it."

Now Elizabeth made as if to get up to leave.

"All right. Deal," the man said.

He swiped at the bills, but she pulled her hand back. "First tell me what happened to her."

"I told you, she defect."

"Is she still alive?"

"Maybe yes, maybe no. Who can say?"

"You're lying."

"Is truth, I swear. People die. Now pay me."

"One more question. Was she a spy?"

He smiled mockingly at her. "If you find her, you can ask her yourself."

Holding out the money toward him, she said, "You had better not be lying."

He snatched the bills from her hand and stood. "*Shlyukha*," he said under his breath, then turned and hurried out into the streets of Moscow. In her gut she feared she'd just thrown away thirteen hundred dollars. But it would, in fact, prove to be her most important lead.

She decided to take a leave of absence from her newspaper duties and fly back to Washington, where she started to do research. By this time, countless wartime documents had been declassified, and Elizabeth was able to find out more about Tat'yana Levchenko. She spent months, which turned into an obsession of years, pouring through dusty government boxes filled with papers, old documents and files, newspaper articles, photos of the woman in Washington and New York and Chicago. Her next big break came when they released the Venona papers, part of Senator Moynihan's Commission on Government Secrecy. They included more than fifty years' worth of Soviet encrypted cables that America had been secretly collecting and decoding from as far back as 1941. At the NSA library, Elizabeth came across several telegrams, sent in early September 1942, from New York and Washington to Moscow, alluding to the "Captain's Wife" (the known code name for Eleanor Roosevelt, the Captain being Roosevelt himself). Mentioned with Mrs. Roosevelt was someone whose code name was simply "Assassin." Elizabeth wondered if that could be the Soviet sniper she was looking for.

Some months later, quite by chance, she stumbled upon a slender FBI file labeled simply ASSASSIN. Much of the information within it had been deleted, blacked out, with the words CLASSIFIED MATERIAL stamped in the margins. But from the photos it became readily apparent that this "Assassin" was actually the same woman Elizabeth had seen in the American newspaper photos—Tat'yana Levchenko. From what Elizabeth could piece together, it seemed that Hoover's Feds had had Levchenko under surveillance. In addition to the old newspaper photos, there were pictures of Tat'yana Levchenko giving speeches at large rallies, getting into and out of limousines, leaving a hotel lobby, talking with various people, candid photos taken from a distance, like those a private detective might snap of an unfaithful wife. There were several of her conversing with a heavyset man in a dark suit. There were also a number of Levchenko and a young man in uniform, an American soldier. In one photo this soldier and Levchenko were captured embracing in a doorway. And there were several of her and an older woman, a tall, gangly person with saggy jowls and buck teeth. It took Elizabeth a moment to recognize Eleanor Roosevelt. As Elizabeth perused the contents of the file, which seemed to stop in the late forties, she came across the name Irina Andreeva, the same one the KGB agent had given her back in Moscow. Even with all of this information in hand, it took Elizabeth another year before she was able to track down Irina Bishop, née Andreeva. Whose real name was Tat'yana Levchenko. Code-named Assassin.

The old woman shuffled into the room carrying a glass filled with iced tea. Unsteadily, she placed the glass on the table between them, then seemed to collapse into the recliner opposite Elizabeth. The woman's face was flushed, and she was obviously having difficulty breathing. Her shoulders heaved with the effort, and in her eyes there was the panicked look of one trapped under water.

"Are you all right, Irina?" Elizabeth asked.

The woman casually held up one finger, as if she were used to this routine. She was a tough old bird, Elizabeth thought. In some ways she reminded Elizabeth a little of her own grandmother, a feisty woman in her eighties.

"Emphysema," was all she said by way of explanation.

Elizabeth sipped her iced tea and waited for the woman to catch her breath. Finally, pointing at the picture of the man in the cowboy hat, Elizabeth asked, "Is that your husband?"

"That is Walter, yes," the old woman replied. Then she added, "He passed away six years ago. How is it you are related to him again?"

"His mother and my grandmother were cousins. Do you still farm?"

The woman put her hand to her ear. "You will have to speak up. I am hard of hearing."

"Do you still farm?"Elizabeth said, glancing out at the land surrounding the house.

The woman shook her head. "After Walter died, I sell everything but the house and barn. I keep a few chickens for eggs."

"You're pretty isolated out here."

She stared out the window, at the isolation. "One gets used to it."

"Do you have someone to look in on you?"

"My daughter checks in on me."

"Is that her?" asked Elizabeth, pointing at the photo on the wall.

The woman nodded.

From her briefcase on the floor, Elizabeth removed a pad and pen, as well as a small tape Recorder. "Do you mind if I tape our conversation?"

"Eez up to you," the woman replied.

Elizabeth pressed the Record button and placed the machine on the table.

"Where did you originally come from?"

"The Ukraine."

"How did you meet my cousin?"

"I came to America after the war. Was refugee in German labor camp. A Ukrainian group here help me to get settled. They arranged for a job in Colorado Springs. It is there I met Walter. At a dance." Then she added with a wistful smile, "He was only second man I ever danced with."

"Who was the first?"

"You would not know him," she replied, her eyes taking on a sudden pensive look.

Elizabeth nodded. "So you were a refugee?"

"Yes."

"But I thought the Yalta agreement mandated that Soviet refugees had to be repatriated to their homeland. How did you end up in the States?"

The woman stared curiously across at her for a moment, but then, almost without missing a beat, she replied, "I had connections. Was able to get visa to come to America."

"I see. Why didn't you want to return home?"

Elizabeth watched as she picked at a loose thread on her dress. "That was no longer my home."

"It must have been hard, though. Leaving your family, everything you knew."

"It was not my home anymore," she repeated. "And my family, they were all killed in the war."

"I'm so sorry."

"It was long ago," she said, with a shrug of her shoulders. Her brows furrowed as she looked out the window, squinting intently, as if trying to make out something at a great distance. Elizabeth pictured just such a look when the woman was aiming at an enemy soldier. After a while, she turned her gaze on Elizabeth. "I thought you wanted to find out about Walter. Not me."

She decided the time had come, that there was no point in pretending any longer. She reached into her briefcase again and removed a folder. She opened it on her lap and took out a sheet of paper. It was a copy of an old newspaper article. The blurry headline read, "Girl Sniper Credited with 315 Kills." Beneath it was a grainy black-and-white photo of a young, pretty woman in uniform, flanked by several men. She was smiling broadly for the camera, beaming like someone who'd just won a prize. Elizabeth placed it on the coffee table, facing the old woman, as if it were a piece of evidence in a court trial. The woman gave it a cursory glance, then stared across at Elizabeth.

"What eez this?" she asked coolly.

"Take a closer look," Elizabeth insisted.

The woman put her glasses on and leaned forward, picked up the paper, stared at it carefully for several seconds. Elizabeth watched her closely. The woman's expression hardly changed, save for a muscle in her jaw that knotted itself and released several times. Elizabeth had to hand it to her, she was a cool one. Finally, the old woman looked over her glasses at Elizabeth and dropped the paper onto the table.

"Do you recognize her?" Elizabeth asked.

Tat'yana Levchenko pursed her lips with something like scorn. "Why, should I?"

"What about this one?" Elizabeth handed her a second article. Similar to the first, the article's heading read, "Soviet Hero Meets First Lady." Below it was another photo showing the same uniformed woman, this time standing beside a grinning Eleanor Roosevelt. "Or this one?" Elizabeth said, passing her another picture of the woman soldier, this time speaking at a podium on an outdoor stage. The headline: "Red Hero Addresses Central Park Crowd." Again the old woman looked at it, though this time she gave it no more than a cursory glance before tossing it on the table with a disdainful flourish. By now her mouth had hardened into a thin, furrowed line.

Elizabeth tried to hand her another article: "Beautiful Assassin Wishes to Kill Even More Nazis" read the headline. The same young woman appeared below it. However, the old woman wouldn't even accept this last sheet, pulled her hand back so that Elizabeth had to place it on the table with the others. The woman didn't look at the photos in front of her but rather stared silently, steadily, across at Elizabeth for several seconds, her dark eyes narrowing. Then she leaned forward and picked up the tape recorder, fumbled with the buttons until she had turned the thing off. Elizabeth could see that she was angry now.

"You are not Walter's cousin," the woman hissed at her.

Elizabeth shook her head. "No, you're right. I'm not."

"What is your real purpose for coming here?"

"You *do* know who that is, though, don't you?"

"You lied to me. Who are you?"

"The real question, Mrs. Bishop, is, who are you?"

As the woman stared at her, yet another change came over her features. Elizabeth could see the anger in her eyes slowly leach out, replaced by something Elizabeth thought at first was fear. But then she realized it wasn't fear at all but a kind of weary resignation, as if the fate she had been waiting for all those years had finally arrived at her doorstep, was seated across from her. Her shoulders slumped with acquiescence, her body relaxing like a wild animal accepting its capture.

After a while Tat'yana Levchenko asked, "Are you with them?"

"Who would that be?"

"Don't play games. You know. The NKVD. The *chekisty*. Or whatever those swine call themselves now."

Elizabeth shook her head. She was surprised that the woman would actually think the KGB had come for her after all these years, as if what she'd done a half century before mattered anymore to them. But then again, she knew the fear the old regime had instilled in people, the insidious, all-encompassing terror of the Soviet state, its seemingly endless desire for, as well as the means to exact, revenge. "No, I'm just a journalist."

"You're lying."

"No, it's the truth. I doubt they even know you exist anymore."

"But you found me. They could too."

"Even if they could, they no longer care about you. There *is* no Soviet Union anymore."

The woman gave out a dry, sardonic chuckle that quickly segued into a cough. The cough grew worse, and soon she had worked herself into a paroxysm of hacking, her face turning bright red, her eyes straining with each breath. A terrible rasping sound echoed from within her chest.

"Can I get you anything?" Elizabeth asked.

With her free hand the woman made a drinking motion. Elizabeth hurried off toward the kitchen. In a cabinet she found a glass and filled it with water.

"Here," Elizabeth said, squatting in front of the woman and holding out the glass to her. After a while, the woman's coughing slowed, and she finally was able to take a breath. As she did so, Elizabeth gently rubbed her arm.

"Are you all right?"

"It doesn't matter anymore," the woman said with a resigned wave of her hand. She looked up and held Elizabeth's gaze for several seconds. In Tat'yana Levchenko's eyes, Elizabeth saw that young woman again, the one from the newspaper photos, a look both innocent and yet filled with a terrible knowledge, as if she'd had a glimpse of hell. "So why *are* you here then?" she asked Elizabeth.

"I want to tell your story."

"What story is that?"

"Tat'yana Levchenko's story."

"*Ona umerla davnym davno.*"

"But she didn't die."

Tat'yana Levchenko shook her head. "You are wrong. That woman perished in the war."

"No. *You* are that woman. People need to know your story."

"You should go, Miss Meade. Or whatever your name is."

Elizabeth paused for a moment. Then she asked, "Is it true that you spied for the Soviets?"

"That's a lie," the woman scoffed.

"The FBI had you under surveillance. They said—"

"I don't care what they said. I was . . . *soldat*," she replied, pointing a crooked finger at Elizabeth. "Soldier. I fought for my country. Can you understand that?"

"Are you denying you passed on information to the Soviets?"

"You know nothing," the woman exclaimed, her eyes suddenly flaring up.

"If you didn't spy for them, what did you do?"

"I told you. I was soldier. I did my duty. I was ordered to go to America and I went. That is all."

"Then people should know that. They should know the truth."

"The truth—*huh!* What do you know of the truth?"

"People should know who you are, what you did. You were a hero."

"Hero," she scoffed. "It is not a world of heroes anymore, Miss Meade."

"I think you're wrong. No woman has ever done what you did. People would want to know about you."

The old woman pursed her lips, then once more fell to staring out over the dry plains. Elizabeth could see her chest rising and falling, a dry rattling sound faintly reverberating from her lungs.

"It was different then," the woman said.

"What was?"

"Everything. The world. Your country and mine. You wouldn't understand."

"Make me understand then."

"Ach," Tat'yana Levchenko said. "I wouldn't know where to begin."

Elizabeth turned and reached for the folder again, took out another picture. This one showed the same pretty woman, though now she was up in the branches of a tree, holding a gun and aiming it off to the left.

"What about there?"

The old woman looked at the photo and shook her head, a scornful smile playing about her lips. "That was a lie, too."

"Then tell me the real story."

She could see the old woman debating, wondering if she wanted to do this, if she had the stamina, the courage to dredge up those times. Finally, she glanced down at the tape recorder. "All right. But leave that thing off," she said. "I shall tell you what really happened. And you can believe it or not, makes no difference to me."

Elizabeth went over and sat on the couch, got her pen and pad ready. The old woman closed her eyes again, leaned her head against the back of the chair. She remained like that for a long time. It was as if she had to reach down deep inside herself, to a place that was dark and had been sealed shut for ages, a place of war and of death, of intrigue, of memories she had to pick up and dust off. After a while, with her eyes still closed, she began to talk, softly, slowly at first, but then, as if her voice was a pump that needed only a little priming, in a swift torrent, the words spilled from her. She started in English, but after a short time, she lapsed into Russian, and her native tongue seemed to carry her along faster and faster. Elizabeth could almost sense that the story had been sitting there inside her, just waiting for this moment.

PART I

★ ★ ★

Let him who desires peace, prepare for war.

—VEGETIUS

1

Sevastopol, 1942

Imagine a woman in a tree, a silly, foolish young woman holding a gun and preparing to kill a man she does not even know. There she sits, waiting, hopeful of the smallest of lapses that will spell death for her opponent. She is fearless. She has on her side the vanity of youth, the blindness that comes from a righteous sense of revenge. She believes herself on a sacred mission, that each death she inflicts on the enemy brings her a little closer to peace. She doesn't yet know that she could kill every single German in the Third Reich, and she would not find peace. She has yet to learn this. But she will.

That time in the tree was mere luck. Nothing more than that. In war, you cannot count on luck. You can only avoid making mistakes. If you make one mistake in battle, you pay for it, usually with your life. That day I had made not one, but two mistakes. The first was hiding in the tree. The second was that I had let myself daydream. It was so unlike me to let my thoughts drift when I was in position, rifle at the ready, all of my senses heightened like those of a wolf stalking its prey. Such an indiscretion often ends badly, let me tell you. But there I was, recalling a summer morning before the war, remembering a way of life that seemed unreal, as gossamer as a fairy tale. In the memory I lay in bed alone. Kolya, my husband, was already off to his job working for the city of Kiev. I recalled that the bedroom window was open, the yellow curtains I'd made the first year of our marriage ballooning like a bellows. The cool air from the Dnieper was wafting into the room, and from the apartment below ours drifted the wistful cello notes of the music student who lived there. Mostly, though, what I remembered of that morning was the feeling, that strange and altogether wondrous sensation somewhere deep down inside a woman when she feels—no, when she *knows*—she is carrying life within her. I lay very still, feeling that life beginning in me, taking hold, filling me, knowing already that I loved the tiny creature that was sharing my body, loved it with all my heart and soul, loved it so much that the tears welled up in my eyes as I listened to something hauntingly beautiful by Rachmaninoff. I thought to myself, This is love. This feeling. This moment. I had never felt it before, not even with my husband, but I knew right then what it was.

At that moment, the war had faded far, far away.

But sentimentality is a luxury a soldier cannot afford. That's when the first bullet murmured softly behind my left ear. Its passage was no more than a feather over my skin, a warm breath along my neck, yet it was enough to yank me back to the present. I knew that breath all too well: it carried the foul stench of death itself. Its wake caused the hairs on my scalp to stand at attention, and the leaves surrounding me to jingle like a wind chime. I noticed a single leaf, prematurely aged, detach itself and spiral lazily toward the gravestones below. The ground was already littered with its comrades. Though only late spring, the leaves had begun to turn color and drop. Perhaps it was due to the general disruption in things— the gritty ash that rained constantly from the skies, the pounding of the big siege guns the Germans had brought up by train, the fearsome shuddering from the nightly air raids, the intense heat and smoke of the fires that had scorched the earth all the way to the hazy mountains west of Yalta. Whatever it was, it seemed even nature itself was in full-scale retreat, like the people in the city who'd taken to the sewers, trying to get to a place of safety, a place that no longer existed. And certainly not to be found in a lone apple tree in the middle of a cemetery.

Dura, I cursed to myself. For I was a fool, an arrogant fool. You see,

I didn't fear death, that was my biggest mistake of all. My life had long ago stopped mattering to me. It was but an instrument of my revenge. I was like Hamlet. For me the readiness was all, ready to spill my blood at the drop of a hat. Yet I didn't want to squander my life by a foolish mistake, didn't want that German *sobaka* across the way to beat me.

I pressed against the tree's slender trunk and froze. I waited five, ten, thirty minutes or more, not allowing so much as the twitch of a muscle to give away my position, though obviously that was a question already in doubt. When I thought enough time had elapsed, I slowly grasped the field glasses hanging from my neck, brought them up, and cautiously scanned the valley to the northwest. Once it had been rolling farmland, green and fertile and verdant, but now it resembled more a lunar landscape than any place on earth. An apple orchard, most of whose trees were broken and splintered as if by a giant's angry fist. Grazing land pockmarked by the Germans' 88s. The blackened remains of a farmhouse, in the yard of which lay the rotting corpse of a cow, its belly bloated obscenely in the heat. To the right of the house was the barn, curiously still intact. I inspected the upper and lower doors closely, then the stone wall that ran behind it, but instinct told me the shot had not come from there. About a hundred meters to the north was a stand of alder trees and dense undergrowth that lined the banks of a stream. Is that where he is? The *gitlerovets*. My fascist adversary. The one I'd been stalking and who, in turn, had been stalking me for the past several days. That strange dance we'd been engaged in, that terrible act of intimacy which is at the heart of killing. Yesterday he'd hidden in the loft of the barn. Knowing him as I'd come to, it should have been obvious, but then again, in my attempt to get inside his head and outwit him, I'd thought the barn would have been *too* obvious, *too* pedestrian for someone as clever as he, and so I'd ignored it. And because of my oversight, he'd managed to pick off three of my comrades and seriously wound a fourth before I was able to locate his position. By then, of course, he'd moved on, slithered away in that reptilian fashion of his to blend in somewhere else and kill again—two more times. A good day for him, a bad one for me. From the vantage point of the tree, I felt I'd have the upper hand. It looked right down the valley, on the German lines below.

Wherever he would take up today, as soon as he fired, I would have him in my grasp. I would kill him. But I should've known he'd counter my move, and now *he* was the one with the advantage. Wherever he was.

It was early, but already the sun exploded into my hiding spot. What had seemed before dawn to be the perfect position, now appeared for what it was: a trap. Too many leaves had fallen, making the upper branches of the tree resemble the head of an old man going bald. Sunlight from the east streamed into my sniper's nest through a hundred gaping holes. I felt suddenly naked and vulnerable. I should have listened to Zoya, the young corporal who was my spotter. We worked in teams, a sniper and a spotter. Zoya, always the cautious one, had warned me against taking up a position in the tree, especially one off by itself. The first thing we'd been taught in sniper training was that you must always have an escape route. You must move often, so that your position couldn't be discovered. Shoot and move, that was how we were taught. But now it was too late to move. I'd been discovered, my position known by my foe. So I did the only thing I could—I adjusted my feet on the branch below me, shifted my weight a bit, and accepted whatever slight protection the tree's narrow trunk offered.

Save for the raspy cawing of a lone crow somewhere in the distance, it was quiet for a long while. Then I heard Zoya calling me.

"Sergeant," she whispered hoarsely. Zoya had hidden in the foxhole over at the cemetery's edge, behind a hedgerow. Where I should have been. "Jump and run for it."

Yet I remained silent, unmoving.

I mulled over my options. It was four or five meters to the ground, which was a small cemetery. Beneath the tree, the earth was flat and clear, save for a few gravestones, most of which were small or composed of wooden crosses, and they offered little cover. It was a tiny village cemetery on the outskirts of the city. The closest cover was behind the small hill at the western edge of the cemetery where Zoya was dug in, some thirty meters off. If I landed cleanly, I could make a run for it. I was swift of foot, had won medals in track back in school. I figured with my pack and rifle I could cover that distance in five, perhaps six, seconds. Maybe I could make it. But that, I told myself, was wishful thinking. Before I reached safety I would have to surmount the small hill, then make it through the hedgerow. At this distance, in broad daylight, I would present an easy target. I wouldn't make it two steps up that hill before a bullet tore into my back. Then he'd have won, he'd have beaten me. In some ways that thought was more bitter than death itself. To lose to the fascist dog, to have him put me down in his kill log as another notch. No, I thought. Better just to stay put and hope that something else presented itself. Maybe I would get lucky.

Before dawn that morning, Zoya and I had crawled to the cemetery's edge, a half kilometer forward of our front lines. As always we had scouted out the position the day before and had planned on digging in, getting concealed and set up before first light. A sniper's life is one of careful planning, of concealment, of surprise, of infinite patience, and of course, of much luck. Behind that little hill at the edge of the cemetery was a good position, one that commanded much of the valley to the north where the German lines were. Yet as Zoya removed her entrenching tool and began to dig our foxhole, I happened to notice, in the middle of the cemetery, the darker, jagged outline of the tree set against the lighter blue of the predawn sky. I'd seen it the previous day, a single apple tree set off by itself amid the graves. Long ago, somebody visiting a loved one must have tossed an apple core, and the thing took root and sprouted there among the dead. I imagined its roots reaching down, entwining with the bones of those who lay sleeping. From its branches, it offered a tantalizing view of the valley, one even better than where we were now. A perfect sniper cell, one which *he* would never think to look in, exactly because it was too risky.

"What of that tree?" I whispered in the darkness. The spot where Zoya was digging offered shelter from the German lines, so we felt free to talk, at least in measured whispers.

"What about it?" Zoya asked.

"What if I took up position there?"

Zoya gave her usual humph when she felt something undeserving of comment, and kept digging.

"It looks right down at the barn," I explained. "From there you can see the entire valley. It's a good position."

"*This* is a good position," she said.

"But that is a better one."

"*Vot cholera*," she said, one of her odd, Ossetian curses. "Sergeant, you and I both know that would be foolishness."

"I would have a clear shot at him."

"And he of you," said the young woman in her heavy accent, one that sounded as if she had smooth tiny pebbles in her mouth.

I felt her hesitation was partly owing to the fact that she didn't like the idea of crawling through the cemetery in the dark. Zoya Kovshova was very superstitious. A mere girl of eighteen, she'd come from some tiny village way up in the Caucasus where the women were married off at thirteen and wore black for a year when their husbands died, and where a hare hopping across your path was considered an ill omen. She was forever crossing herself and uttering some oath against bad luck. Facing the Germans she was as fearless as any soldier in the entire Chapayev Division. During the evacuation of Odessa, for instance, when we were savagely fighting the German advance street by street, Zoya had remained behind in what was left of Birzhevaya Square, firing her machine gun until she'd run out of ammo. And only then did she leave her post when Captain Petrenko ordered her to do so. But if a crow lighted in a tree and squawked three times, she would mumble something in her strange mountain tongue and throw a handful of dirt over her shoulder; otherwise, she worried she would never be able to bear children after the war. And what man would want a bride whose womb had been dried up by a crow? But she was, I knew, also just watching out for me. Zoya was as protective as a mother hen. In fact, as a joke I sometimes called her "*malen'kaya*"—little mother. Now and then when I would shoot an enemy soldier and I'd lie in wait to claim a second one I could sense was nearby, she would touch my arm. "Don't get greedy, Tat'yana. It's not safe here," she would caution me. "Yes, little mother," I would reply.

"The sun will be in his eyes," I had said this morning.

"But if you're spotted, you cannot get out of it."

"I won't be spotted. He's a clever one, this German, and I have to outfox him."

Zoya straightened and turned to face me. I could feel her gray eyes fixing me even in the darkness.

"This is madness. You take too many risks, Tat'yana Levchenko." When it was just the two of us, she still called me by name, though I had by now been promoted to sergeant. I didn't mind. We were good friends as well as comrades. The fighting had brought us close in ways that only danger and the letting of blood can. During brutally cold winter nights, when we were in a foxhole, we sometimes used to sleep in each other's arms for warmth. Other times, when I would make a difficult shot she would throw her arms around me and kiss me on the cheek. So I usually permitted such familiarity, especially when we were alone.

"We are at war," I said. "Everything we do is a risk."

"But you take too many."

"Wait here then," I told her, picking up my rifle to leave.

"Has all the talk gone to your head?" she said.

I turned on her and said sharply, "That will be enough, Corporal." I had only recently been promoted to sergeant and wasn't used to pulling rank on her. For months as corporals, we'd worked well as a sniper team, sharing the demands and discomforts and dangers of our profession—sweating under the hot summer sun, freezing in the snow and cold of winter, shivering in the rain, many times coming within a hairsbreadth of catching a sniper bullet. And always taking equal credit for the kills. Sometimes, however, friendship had to take a backseat to duty, to the necessity of command. Besides, I knew the potential danger I was courting, and yet I wanted so very much to get this German, and I was willing to do almost anything, risk anything. But I couldn't permit Zoya to sacrifice her life for my prideful need for vengeance.

She picked up the bulky Degtyaryov automatic and the ammo pouches and started to follow me.

"Where are you going?" I asked.

"I am coming with you."

"No, you're not."

"But we are a team, Sergeant."

"Not this time."

She shook her head in annoyance. "Well, you'd better take this," she said, offering up her own canteen. I tried to refuse it, but Zoya was adamant, so I accepted it with thanks.

As I turned to leave, she touched my wrist. "Be careful, Tat'yana. This German has a powerful gift." More of her superstition. Still, it unnerved me a bit.

"He's just a man," I replied. "And like any man, he can be killed."

"So far no one has. Watch yourself," she said, getting in the last word.

The notion that this kraut was something more than an ordinary man had begun to spread through our lines. Like a fever it had permeated our troops, undermining our spirit. But then, realizing these could be my last words to Zoya, I softened my tone: "Don't worry. I shall be careful, little mother."

I crawled through the cemetery until I reached the tree. Quietly, I started climbing it, my rifle slung over my shoulder. I got into position, remained motionless, and waited for the dawn. From there, as the darkness melted slowly away into the folds and creases of the valley, I scoped the territory to the north, searching for some sign of the German, a clue as to his position. Some movement. The glint from a gun barrel. A portion of the landscape that had been disturbed from the previous day—a branch that had been moved, a section of overturned earth, a piece of wood that didn't look natural. As clever as these Germans were, the one thing they lacked was patience. They had the impulsiveness of spoiled children, the privileged sort who'd grown up in luxury and were used to having their every desire met instantly. Also, from the tree I had the advantage of the sun over my shoulder, which meant *he* had it in his eyes, at least until noon, when the tables would slowly be turned. I hoped to catch it flashing off his scope as he searched for me. I was excited by the prospect of getting him, of having my comrades cheer me when I returned to our lines. Yes, I must admit that I looked forward to that moment as an athlete does to the laurel crown of victory. And yet I knew when the moment of truth came, I would have to still my heart, keep my thoughts, my pride, my burning vengeance under control. I wouldn't pull the trigger until I was sure to send him to his Valhalla.

You see, in that strange communion that develops between snipers, this German and I had come to know the other, each one's habits and instincts, the other's preferences and idiosyncrasies. For instance, I knew that he liked to scope the terrain right to left, instead of the other way around, as most snipers did. That he sometimes took up positions in what would appear to be the most obvious, and therefore the least likely. That he had a tendency to shoot too quickly, which resulted in a wounded target rather than a kill. That he preferred flashy head shots to the safer torso strikes that most snipers aimed for. We had been playing a kind of cat and mouse game for the past several days, of move and countermove, a complicated dance. Before this day, he had fired at me several times, barely missing me once at twilight when I was changing my socks, soaked from a day of rain. And one time I had squandered a difficult but clearly possible shot at five hundred meters. Zoya had spotted him hiding in a hollow tree trunk at the edge of the woods. In my eagerness to take him, I had jerked the trigger instead of "kissing" it, as my first shooting instructor in the Osoviakhim, Sergeant Tarasov, had termed it, and the Mosin-Nagant had shot high, as it had a tendency to do. The tree, I felt, would give me the edge I needed. I'd convinced myself that with my camouflage poncho, I could blend into my surroundings. Besides, I had one important advantage over him—patience. People in my unit told me I had the patience of a saint, though I doubt there are any saints in war. I would wait him out, I thought. I would let him make a mistake and then kill him. I could even picture the surprised look in his eyes as my bullet caressed his heart.

But no sooner had the sun spilled over the mountainous country to the east than I'd begun to wonder if I myself had not made the first mistake. Had I convinced myself of the safety of the tree not because it *was* safe, but because I was beginning to think myself invincible? Perhaps Zoya had been right. Maybe all the talk about my successes—the 287 kills, the medals, surviving three wounds, the articles in the military newspaper, even those newspapers from as far away as Moscow—maybe all that *had* gone to my head. Maybe I'd acted out of pride, instead of cold calculation, as I normally did. It was cold calculation, you see, that had made me not only the sniper with the highest kill total in the entire southern front of the Red Army, but had kept me alive as well. Since the war began I had learned that the most important lesson of sniping wasn't marksmanship, a technical skill; in fact, it had very little to do with one's expertise with a gun. It was something inside, controlling one's emotions. You could hate the Germans with all your heart and soul, but you had to kill them with dispassion, with a cool head and a steady finger. That was the key. You had to turn your hatred into ice.

Still, I'd wanted this particular *gitlerovets* so badly. I burned to defeat him. Over the past week, he'd scored some two dozen kills against my comrades—dispatching machine gunners, a female medic, a mortar team, two officers, a cook, a radioman, even several wounded soldiers being evacuated to a field hospital. The Red Cross sign meant nothing to him. He killed without discriminating, as one would crush ants beneath his boot heel; he seemed almost to take a capricious delight in his selection of targets, not out of military necessity, but like some arrogant god striking down whom he wished simply to show that he could. But the one that disturbed me most was a fresh recruit from Kiev University, where I had been working on my thesis before the war. I'd spoken to him once or twice. A pleasant, boyish-faced youth named Gorobets. Bookish and retiring, he was studying philosophy. Like myself, he wanted to be an academic, to teach and write, to spend his evenings quietly pouring over books. Foolishly, he'd crawled out of the trenches to get a page of a letter that had blown away. The story went that it had been a letter from his sweetheart, and because he was so far back of the front lines and therefore believed himself in no danger, he'd gone over the breastworks to retrieve it. The German had killed him with a head shot from fifteen hundred meters. Which was, of course, utter nonsense. No one killed with a Mauser from that distance. It was impossible, even for someone as good as this German. The first time I'd heard the story back at camp it had been only a third that distance, but it had grown with each successive telling and with each soldier the German chalked up, as did his reputation among our troops. Some were beginning to call him Korol' Smerti—the King of Death. He had begun to get under our soldiers' skin, to plague their thoughts, their dreams. They would speak of him in those hushed and nervous tones little children use when talking of the *buka* hiding under their beds. In the evening, I could see the haunted look in their eyes as they discussed the troops he'd dispatched that day. Even my brave little Zoya had been affected. I thought if I could get him, it would put an end to such nonsense. They would see that these Germans were just men like any other. That they could be killed. That we could beat them eventually, and drive them from our soil.

I thought I even knew this King of Death's voice, could pick it out from the other Germans who called across the lines at night. Sometimes the Germans would call things across the divide of no-man's-land between our two lines, hoping to trick us, to goad us, to undermine our morale. They were good at propaganda, these Aryans, good at getting into one's head. With me it had started months back when my kill total had reached first one hundred, then two hundred. I began to get something of a reputation, not only on my own side but on theirs as well. Somehow they'd learned my name. It wasn't a hard thing, finding out my identity. Perhaps they got it from a tongue, what we called a captured soldier, or from one of the army newsletters that had fallen into their hands. Some of the things the Germans called were of a flirtatious nature, only what a brash Ukrainian boy back home might have said to me. "Tat'yana Levchenko, why don't you come over here," they'd say. "I have some schnapps and we can get to know each other." Their cockiness made me almost smile in spite of myself. Others, though, called out crude epithets, threats or taunts, aimed at provoking me into acting rashly and giving away my position. "You had better keep out of our way, Flintenweib"—"gun woman," the term the Germans used, part contempt, part awe, for female snipers. "If we catch you, we will tear you into two hundred little pieces and scatter them to the winds." Two hundred pieces—for the number of Germans I had at the time tallied. Once or twice, I'd heard a voice that for some unknown reason, I assumed to be that of the King of Death himself. He'd call out in crude Russian, "Put down your gun, Tat'yana, and I let you live. You can be my *shlyukha*." His whore. But I never let him—or whoever it was—get to me. I never lost my temper. Let them say what they would, I thought. I would let my gun speak for me.

Still, it was sometimes hard to ignore them, the personal things they said. Occasionally they would call out about one's mother or father, even one's children. Those despicable bastards would even stoop to that. They were good at finding a person's weakness. "How are your little ones, Tat'yana Levchenko? Are they getting enough to eat?" And, "What sort of mother leaves her children alone to go off and fight?" I knew they did this to other women soldiers too, said things of a general nature to make them feel guilty for going off to war. But unlike me, most of the women soldiers were actually unmarried, didn't even have families. That didn't stop the Germans. Of course, I realized the krauts knew nothing about my little girl. Nothing at all. How could they? Nonetheless, when I heard such things, they were like a dagger in my heart. If I could, I'd have gladly killed them with my bare hands, slowly, painfully, taking pleasure in it.

There, caught in my apple tree, I decided I would just have to remain still and wait for darkness—some eight hours hence. The bright day stretched out flat and thin and brittle, each second exaggerated, seeming to last an hour. My watch had been damaged by shrapnel several days earlier, so I had to estimate the time by the sun's passage. I picked out a gravestone below and marked the movement of its shadow across the ground.

By midday it was scorching. I felt the sweat soaking my shirt and tunic, running down my back. A bee buzzed near my head, drawn by the sweet fragrance of last season's apples rotting below. I watched an ant crawl up my sleeve, across my chest, onto the skin of my neck. Then I could feel it moving down between my breasts, tickling me, teasing me, as if knowing it could do whatever it pleased with impunity. A little German sympathizer, I thought to myself. Of course, I dared not move to crush it. To do so could spell death, so I bit on my lower lip to create a pain to neutralize the other. In the distance there was the sporadic *pock . . . pock* of small arms fire, the occasional *tat-tat-tat* of automatic weapons, but other than that the day was eerily still. For weeks we'd heard that the Germans were getting ready to attack, a final offensive to take the city. Supposedly they were bringing up reinforcements, two more divisions, as well as tanks and heavy artillery for the last thrust that would push us into the sea. The fine spring day unfolded like a ripe flower raising its head toward the sun. Now and then I caught a whiff of salt in the air from the sea just a few kilometers to my back. It would have been a wonderful day if not for the war.

When a second shot didn't follow the first for what I estimated was four hours, maybe more, I began to wonder if the danger I was in was real or imagined. Perhaps he didn't have a clear shot after all. Otherwise, why wouldn't he take it? Or maybe he hadn't even spotted me. Maybe the first shot wasn't even his, just a stray that happened to come close. It was, after all, a battlefield. I wasn't the only object of their guns.

My right leg had gone numb, so I chanced shifting my position ever so slightly. I moved one foot on the branch below, started to shift my thigh. That's when the next bullet thudded into the tree trunk: *whht.* I could feel its impact through the wood, a firm tapping against my cheek, a knock on the door of my mortality. And then another—*whht.* And two more after that. *Whht, whht.* The last grazed the bark at an angle, flying past the tree but spitting fragments of wood into my face. Was the German simply toying with me? Did he intend to savor his advantage for a while, prolong my agony before dispatching me?

Moving my head cautiously, I saw the last bullet's mark along the side of the trunk. It came from a Mauser 98k, the standard weapon of my enemy. The Mauser was bolt action, had a five-round clip, and shot a 197-grain, steel-jacketed bullet at 840 meters per second, if loaded with high-velocity machine-gun ammo, as I knew this King of Death did. The rifle had an effective kill range of five hundred meters, not as good as our Soviet rifle, but with a scope and in competent hands the Mauser could kill well beyond that distance. And this kraut was much more than competent. He was good. He was very good. I studied the angle the last shot had made along the bark, and using its trajectory I followed it to a point about three hundred meters east of where I'd previously assumed him to be. There the land fell abruptly away toward what had been a quarry. It ran for a half kilometer along the Soviet right flank. I'd passed it when our Second Company had been ordered to fall back and take up positions along this high ground overlooking the city. So, I thought. That's where you are. He was moving clockwise, to my right, getting out of the sun's rays and trying to outflank me, to put the sun in *my* eyes and get in position for a clear shot. And yet, if I kept moving to maintain the trunk between us, soon I'd be exposed to other German snipers and machine gunners to the north and west. I was vulnerable one way or the other.

Time was running out for me. I felt I had to come up with a plan quickly, before I became a sitting duck. Finally, I decided what I must do. I'd tempt him into shooting again and then pretend that he'd hit me and fall from the tree. This strategy, I knew, had only a slim chance for success, but it was better than waiting to be killed. I worked things out, trying to design my "death" so that it would look real. When I fell I wanted to make sure I was facing in the direction of the German's position, and that my rifle landed within reach. Cautiously, I removed the scope, not wanting it to get damaged, and put it in my rucksack, hanging over my shoulder. I also had to make sure to avoid hitting any branches on the way down. That might spin me out of control and I could very well break my neck. But at the same time my fall had to appear natural to be convincing—that I'd been hit and killed.

I took off my forage cap and placed it on the end of my bayonet and extended it ever so slowly just a little ways beyond the trunk, just enough so as to lure the German into thinking it was still sitting atop my head. He didn't disappoint me. In a moment the bullet's impact flung my cap backward into the leaves. As if hit, I released my grip on the tree and let myself go, plunging earthward.

I slammed into the ground, the back of my head striking painfully against something hard. Luckily, my right side took the brunt of the fall, so that it was diffused along the entirety of my body. Still, the impact knocked the wind out of me, and for a moment I couldn't breathe because of a stabbing pain in my side. I thought perhaps I'd broken some ribs. I could also feel a hot wetness inching down along my scalp behind my right ear. I didn't think that I'd been hit, but I couldn't be sure. Fortunately for me, the German, who was down below in the valley, didn't have a clear shot of where I now lay on the ground; otherwise, he'd have put another round in me just to be certain. If the tables had been turned I'd have done nothing less. I figured he'd probably come closer to make certain. So I had to lie perfectly still and pretend I was dead. That was my only chance.

I tried to gain control of my breathing, but each breath sent a new wave of pain knifing through me. I hoped that my act was convincing. From somewhere behind me, I could hear Zoya calling. She couldn't see me where I lay, not without leaving the safety of the foxhole and exposing herself.

"Tat'yana! Tat'yana, are you all right?" When I didn't answer, Zoya called again. "I'm coming for you."

"Don't!" I hissed through clenched teeth.

I would wait until dark and then crawl back to safety. However, the pain in my side was fierce, and coupled with an intense throbbing that commenced at the back of my skull, I felt my head reeling. I saw a flickering shadow pass overhead, crossing between myself and the sunlight. I thought of that poem by the American poet Dickinson that one of my teachers back in school, a Madame Rudneva, had had me recite in English: *With blue—uncertain stumbling buzz—between the light—and me.* I thought at first it was a plane or a bird, but then I realized I was losing consciousness. I shivered, feeling cold creep suddenly over my limbs, as if I were slipping into frigid water. My eyesight began to fail. After a while, darkness stole over me completely. In that darkness I remember calling out Masha's name.

When I came to—minutes? hours? later—I felt a burning thirst. My tongue was swollen and dry in my mouth, like an old piece of leather. It hurt to swallow. After a time, I chanced opening my eyes a crack, the light which poured in scalding my brain. Was I in the land of the dead? I wondered. When my eyes had had a chance to adjust, the first thing I saw was an old, weathered gravestone. It was that of a woman—Elyzaveta Fedutenko. Next to hers was another headstone, what I assumed was her husband, and next to that, two others, their children, I guessed from the dates of their births. They had all died in the same year: 1932.

Doubtless they'd perished in the Holodomor, the great famine that had swept across the Ukraine when I was a girl.

As I lay there looking at the stone, I thought again of my own child, my Masha. Perhaps because my head was still dazed, for a moment her memory came as a thing of undiluted joy. I pictured her in the park near the Dnieper, not far from where we'd lived. I saw her running toward me, her hair, blond and fine like Kolya's, bouncing as she ran, calling out to me, "Mama, Mama." As I lay there, I felt the sun's warmth waning, saw that its angle had changed. It had slid off toward the western horizon, beyond the sea. From the lengthening shadow of the nearby gravestone, I guessed it to be six, maybe seven o'clock. If only I could make it a little while longer. More time passed. Who could say how much? When you are lying half dead, waiting for your executioner to come, time has little meaning.

But as twilight settled in over the cemetery, out of the corner of my eye I caught the faintest movement toward the northeast. A figure in khaki detached itself from the woods and approached stealthily over the uneven terrain, moving up the hill through the now sparse orchard. Moving toward me. I could make him out only from his chest up. He carried a rifle and moved quickly but cautiously in a crouch. I wondered what to do. Where Zoya waited, she might not see him approach from this angle. I remained still until the German dipped momentarily out of sight, then I grabbed my rifle and rolled behind the headstone of Elyzaveta Fedutenko. I flicked off the safety and fixed my sights on the general area where I'd last seen the kraut. It was barely a hundred meters, so I wouldn't need the scope.

I didn't spot him for a while and panic seized my chest. He was a clever one. What if he were trying to outflank me, come around from the side? But just at that moment, I saw the top of his head bobbing as he approached from the northeast. He was flitting from tree to tree, moving cautiously. He waited at the last tree, surveying the cemetery. From this vantage point, he still couldn't quite see the ground beneath the tree from which I'd fallen. He paused there for a moment, and I found myself doing that odd thing I sometimes did—entering my enemy's thoughts, trying to imagine what he would be thinking. *The Rus-*

sian whore thought she was so clever! The Germans were a prideful lot, I'd come to understand. They did not like to be bested, and certainly not by a mere woman. It brought out in them a boyish bravado, a recklessness that made them vulnerable. If I had been a male sniper he'd have been satisfied, I'm quite sure, to leave things as they were, simply to chalk me up in his kill log and call it a day, go back to his German lines and celebrate with some warm food. But my being a woman compelled him to want to stand over my dead body, to take something that was mine. My cap, my Red Banner medal, my leather case containing my personal effects, the letter from Kolya, the lock of hair of Masha's. Something to possess, to show his mates.

So this led the German to make his own foolish mistake. Without seeing my body, he took several quick steps into the cemetery, out into the open. When he could finally view the ground beneath the tree and he didn't see me, he froze. Nervously, he scanned the area, his gun swung up to his shoulder, his knees bent in a position to fire. It took him only a moment to understand the full measure of his error, but when he did, he whirled and started to run back toward cover. He and I shared one thought: he was a dead man. Before he'd taken three steps, I had him in my sights. Quickly but calmly, I aimed the rifle and kissed the trigger. As always when a bullet strikes true, I could feel it before I saw its effects, could feel it in my right shoulder and in my trigger finger, in my bowels, in some part of my brain, too. I could usually tell as soon as I fired, the sweet certainty of putting a bullet exactly where I'd meant to. The impact spun the German halfway around. He staggered sideways and dropped to one knee. His rifle had fallen to the ground before him, and he struggled to get to it. Even now he was a soldier, and I felt a grudging admiration for that, despite the hatred I bore him. Without thinking, I worked the bolt and chambered another round. I was prepared to put a second bullet into him, but he suddenly collapsed onto his face and lay still. As our ammo was becoming scarce, we Soviets knew to be frugal. This one was dead. Then I told myself what I always did after killing a German: *For you, Masha. For you, my love.*

I got up and trotted to where he lay, keeping my rifle trained on his prone figure, my head low so as not to be exposed to the enemy lines below. Up close I nudged him with my boot, ready to shoot him again if he showed any sign of life. He didn't move, so I rolled him over. The bullet had entered through his left shoulder blade and exited the middle of his chest, tearing away his NCO's breast eagle and leaving a jagged, bloody hole in his tunic. A dark, wet stain had spread out over the front of his uniform. His eyes were closed, his lips slightly parted and forming what looked like a vague smile. Up close, I saw that my adversary was younger than I by a few years, perhaps only twenty-one. Good-looking in that frugal, Aryan sort of way, with angular features, straight white teeth, close-cropped, light brown hair. At his neck he wore the Iron Cross, which he'd no doubt won for his marksmanship. I could just imagine this King of Death in some beer hall back in Berlin or Munich bragging to all the pretty fräuleins about how he'd got the better of some Red whore who was supposed to be such a deadly sniper. And yet, lying there, he didn't look much like a king now. Merely a cocky boy who needed to be taught some manners. *Am I your whore now?* I thought with a prideful anger. What surprised me about war wasn't the fact that killing had become so easy. No. It was that one grows to actually enjoy it, to savor it, as you would any other hard-earned skill. Writing poetry or winning a footrace.

I knelt and lay my weapon down and began riffling through his clothes. I found some letters, one or two pictures, which I tossed aside. I didn't want to know his name, his past, anything about him. He was just a cipher to me: *288*. Nothing more than that. Another number to chalk up in my kill log. In one pocket I came upon a half-eaten piece of chocolate, his teeth marks scalloping the edges. Zoya loved chocolate, so I stuffed it in my tunic as a gift to her. Next, I stripped him of his ammo pouches and his bayonet. A comrade of mine named Kolyshkin, a radioman, liked to collect German souvenirs, so I leaned down to take the Iron Cross from about his throat. The pin was fastened tight, and I struggled getting it free. That's when an odd thing happened—the dead man opened his eyes and stared at me.

Startled, I was forced backward onto my heels. I grasped his bayo-net and brought it toward his throat, prepared to finish him off. But for some reason I paused, curiously watching him. He didn't move, just stared up at me. It had been a definite kill shot and by rights he should have been dead. And yet he wasn't. His breathing was shallow and labored, a sucking noise rattling from lungs slowly drowning in their own blood. A fine red froth began to gather at the corners of his mouth. He lay there looking up at me, a peculiar expression in his light-blue eyes. It wasn't hatred or fear or even desperation. He seemed well beyond such earthly concerns. His eyes were almost calm, and there was in them a kind of resigned understanding, the sort that sometimes—though not always—comes to one about to die in battle.

I wondered what to do. This had never happened to me before. Should I just turn and leave him there to die, as I knew he would shortly? Or should I use his bayonet to give him the coup de grâce? Even a German should not die such a death, I felt. As I made a move with the knife, though, he reached out and grasped my wrist. For a moment I thought he intended to fight me. So I switched the bayonet to my other hand, was about to plunge it into his throat, but I realized he had no fight left in him. The color had already left his face, and while I thought to pull away, I didn't. For some reason, I permitted his hand to remain locked on my wrist. I don't know why. To this day, I don't know why. Perhaps I was just too startled to do otherwise. His lips came together, and he appeared to be struggling to say something.

"What?" I asked, my tone impatient. I wanted him to get on with this business of dying. I was hungry and tired, my body aching from the fall, and I wanted only to get back to my own lines. To warm food and the comforting banter of my comrades around me, and to the oblivion of sleep.

He tried again, but nothing came out save for that rattling sound in his chest. So I leaned down and placed my ear near his mouth. His breath had the metallic odor of blood on it, the stink of the grave.

This time he said something. It sounded like a name: "Senta."

"What?" I asked.

He said it again, staring up at me, his eyes pleading. "Senta."

I knew only a few German expressions, so I decided to try the little English I possessed. "Your wife?" I asked.

But I could see the humanness rapidly ebbing from his eyes, the pupils seeming to relax, to widen, as if to allow his soul room to exit through them. He repeated the word a third time, staring up at me imploringly. "Senta."

"What do you want?" I cried.

He stared at me silently. I brought the bayonet to his throat, unsure whether it was to put him out of his misery or to end my own discomfort. But his eyes glazed over and his end on this earth came.

Only then did I realize that his hand was still locked on my wrist. I had to pry his fingers off. Freed of them, I could see their imprint still in my flesh. I stood then, staring down at my dead foe. I didn't exactly feel remorse, but something closer to anger, a sudden, inexplicable anger. *Don't blame me,* I felt like saying to him. *You brought this on yourself.* But he merely continued to stare up at me with his dead, accusatory eyes, like the stony eyes of a statue.

It was getting dark, and I didn't want to be mistakenly shot by my own sentries, so I collected his rifle and the other spoils of the victor, and trotted quickly back toward where Zoya was waiting.

"It's me," I called as I approached.

"Mother of Jesus," Zoya replied, crossing herself. She threw her arms around me and hugged so hard my bruised ribs hurt.

"Easy," I said.

"What is it?"

"I injured my side when I fell."

"For a while there I thought you . . ."

"That's what he thought too," I said with a nod of my head back toward where the German lay.

"Did you get him?"

By way of answer I handed her the Mauser.

"Wait till they hear back at camp!" she exclaimed. "You killed the King of Death, Tat'yana! You got him."

"Yes," I replied. "I got him."

"Are you sure you're all right?"

"Yes, little mother, I'm fine."

As we headed back to our lines, though, something didn't sit right with me. Though I should have been exalted and proud of what I'd pulled off, that I was still alive, I couldn't get the image of the German out of my mind. The way he'd stared at me, how he'd insisted on telling me the name of his wife or sweetheart or whoever the hell it was. I could still feel the pressure of his hand locked on my wrist, a cruel reminder that even the Germans were human.

2

That night when we got back to our lines, word quickly spread that I'd gotten the King of Death. The news buoyed our company's spirits immeasurably, so little had we to celebrate over the past several months. Many of my comrades came by to offer their congratulations. Kolyshkin, the radioman, thanked me for the Iron Cross I'd brought him as a memento, and some looked at the German's Mauser, touching the rifle reverently, as if it were a religious relic. Our company commander, Captain Petrenko, even broke out a bottle of vodka he'd been saving and toasted the two of us.

"To Levchenko and Kovshova," he said. "For getting the son of a bitch."

The troops whooped and hollered, and gave us a cheer, which embarrassed me a little but also made me feel quite proud. I bathed in the sweet afterglow of victory.

Zoya delighted in relating the story of how I'd managed to pull it off. The way I'd fallen from the tree, how I'd tricked the King of Death into believing he'd shot me, then lured him into my trap and sprung it when he got close enough.

"You should have seen the look on that Fritz's face," she said, mimicking the surprised expression of the German. A number of us were in an underground bunker, the ceiling of which was reinforced with heavy timbers and several meters of earth against the Germans' bombing runs. It was lit by several smoky lanterns that made the eyes burn. Zoya held the Mauser and pretended she was the King of Death sneaking up on me, taking exaggerated steps, like a character in a dumb show. She was quite the little actress. The other soldiers laughed heartily at her antics. Even I couldn't help but smile, this despite the fact that the image of the German continued to sit uneasily in my thoughts. I kept seeing his blue eyes staring at me, his whispering that name to me. Of course, I hadn't told Zoya about any of that. The fact that she hadn't even seen my shot didn't stop her in the least from embellishing the story. She was always bragging about my marksmanship, which made me a bit uncomfortable. Though I worked hard at being a good soldier and was proud of my accomplishments as a sniper, I didn't want my comrades to feel jealous about the acclaim I'd received, especially from the higher-ups.

"The kraut comes walking toward the sergeant and realizes he's fucked," Zoya explained. She'd come to the unit a simple country girl, modest and plainspoken, in some ways as pious as a nun. But now, especially in front of the others, she swore like a fishwife. With me, though, she was still the same innocent girl. "And the German takes to his heels. The sergeant here"—she glanced over at me, winking—"puts a round in the kraut's back from three hundred meters. Three hundred meters, without a scope!"

"She exaggerates," I said. "Not a third that distance."

"It's the God's truth," pleaded Zoya, crossing herself.

And so it went.

Over the next several days, each time she would retell it, the difficulty of the shot as well as the distance grew. Nonetheless, the troops enjoyed hearing the story about the killing of the German, and so I thought, let her tell her story. They could use some good news for a change. There was a collective sigh of relief that the King of Death could kill no more. It was as if we'd won a great battle, instead of defeating just one stinking fascist. Several of the other snipers in the unit came up to me to offer their congratulations.

"Good shooting, Sergeant," said a young man named Cheburko, who came from Donetsk after that city fell to the Germans. There was among the other snipers and myself a friendly sort of competition. We joked and chided one another, playfully bragging among ourselves of our exploits, the difficulty of certain shots, the number of our kills. In the first months of the war, when I'd started to make a name for myself as a sniper, some of them, I must say, begrudged my success. *What does a woman know about sniping*, I knew they sneered behind my back. But as time went on, most grew at first to accept, then to respect, me. Among snipers there is a certain camaraderie, as among members of a football squad.

"Thank you, comrade," I said. "Our team was successful."

"What team?" scoffed Zoya. "I didn't do a thing. It was all the sergeant's doing. Such shooting you would not believe."

Later, Yuri Sokur, the company medic, tended to the laceration along the back of my scalp.

"I guess congratulations are in order, Sergeant," he said to me. Yuri was a small, wiry man with a pinched and contemplative face that reminded one of a very brooding monkey. Before the war, he'd been an undertaker, and with his knowledge of the body they had sent him for medical training. He was known for his poor bedside manner, perhaps owing to the fact that his previous patients weren't able to complain very much. But for some reason he liked me, looked out for me like an older brother.

"You have yourself a nasty wound," he told me as he cleaned and began stitching the cut.

"Just a scratch," I replied.

"Scratch nothing. You could have a fractured skull for all I know."

"Ouch," I cried as he roughly drew the sutures through my scalp, as if to make his point.

"This big killer of Germans, afraid of a little needle?" he teased. "You need to take better care of yourself."

"I did what I had to."

"This makes, what, the fourth time you've been wounded?"

I shrugged.

The first two injuries I received were minor shrapnel wounds. The other, a bullet to my thigh, was more serious. It came during the evacuation of Odessa. My unit was pulling back toward the harbor. I was running for cover to a bombed-out building when a round ripped through my thigh. I would have bled to death if Zoya hadn't tied a tourniquet around the wound and pulled me to safety.

"Even a cat has only nine lives, Sergeant," Yuri warned me.

"That kraut needed to be stopped."

"Does the captain know about your wound?"

I shook my head.

"If he got wind of it, he'd probably have you shipped off to a field hospital just to be on the safe side. They don't want anything to happen to their star."

He said this not out of jealousy or sarcasm, but out of concern.

"I'm just doing my duty," I replied. "But you won't tell him, will you?"

Yuri paused and came around so he could look me in the eye. "You have done the one thing that we've not been able to do to those kraut bastards."

"And what is that?"

"You have pricked their Aryan pride. A woman has humbled the mighty Reich. And you've given us something to be proud of. So take care of yourself, Sergeant. We need you to stay alive."

That night, we sat listening as the Germans made their usual bombing sorties over the city. Sometimes fifteen hundred a night, the steady drone of their planes like a horde of angry bees. Even from this distance the explosions made the ground quake. Occasionally one of their big thousand-kilo bombs would strike close enough that the dirt above us was shaken loose and fell upon our heads. And yet, we'd almost gotten used to it. Some soldiers occupied themselves cleaning their weapons, others with making tea or playing cards or darning socks. A few wrote letters or read mail by the frail lantern light.

A short distance away, a sergeant we called the Wild Boar and a few of his friends were passing around a bottle of vodka and talking about the Brits and Americans. They were debating when our supposed "allies" were going to open up a second front we'd all heard so much about.

They used the disparaging term *Amerikosy* for the Americans, whom we thought of as spoiled capitalists fearful of the Germans. Occasionally we'd see the things the Amerikosy sent us through lend-lease— canned meats and radios, tires and trucks, barbed wire and guns and ammo. Most of us just wanted to know when the capitalists were actually going to get their hands dirty, when they were going to fight and die as we Soviets had been doing by the tens of thousands since the war began the previous year.

"What need have we for those capitalist dogs?" boasted Drubich, a bony man with gray skin and the large, flat eyes of a carp. He was one of the Wild Boar's cronies, a boot-licking sycophant. A cowardly man in battle, he liked to boast when the bullets weren't flying. "To hell with those bastards."

"I think we can use all the help we can get," replied another soldier named Nurylbayev, a dark-complected man who spoke with a Kazakh accent.

"Fuck the Yanks. And the Brits too," added Drubich. "By the time they get their britches on we'll have the krauts running back to Berlin. Ain't that right, Sergeant?" he said, looking over at the Wild Boar.

The sergeant only grunted. He was staring at Zoya, I noticed. She sat on the floor a few feet away, cleaning her machine gun.

"But they are supposed to be our allies," said Nurylbayev. "Why are we doing all the fighting, while they get to sit on their asses?"

"The Brits are too busy drinking their fucking tea," Drubich said, pretending he was sipping from a cup, his little finger raised in an attitude of high society. "And the Americans with their cricket."

"The British play cricket, you ignorant bastard," explained Nurylbayev. "In America they play baseball."

"And how the hell would you know?"

"I had a cousin who moved to Boston. He wrote me about the Boston Red Stockings baseball team."

"Red Stockings?" joked Drubich, sipping vodka from the bottle. "I didn't know they had Communists over there."

A few laughed at his joke.

"Gimme that," grunted the Wild Boar, wrenching the bottle away from Drubich while he was still drinking, so that some of it spilled down onto his pants. "It's that goddamned Jew-loving Roosevelt. He only cares about the Jews anyway. As long as they're making money from the war, they could give a shit about who's winning. Hitler had that part right. Too bad he didn't finish the fucking job before he took us on."

As he said this, the Wild Boar glanced over at me. Of course, I thought. Like the rest, he'd heard the rumor that I was a Jew. Because I had the dark hair and eyes of a Gypsy. Most of all, I guess because I killed the krauts with such cold intensity, such that only a Jew could have for the Nazis.

"Still, the capitalists ought to be fighting with us," replied Nurylbayev. "Not hiding like frightened children."

"Fuck 'em," added the Wild Boar. "Besides, when we get to Berlin, that'll leave more pretty fräuleins for the rest of us."

"That's right," said Drubich, wiping his mouth on the sleeve of his tunic.

I'd heard such talk before. How we were taking the brunt of the Wehrmacht while the Americans hung back, testing the waters of war with their big toe in North Africa. My own feeling was that we needed help, the sooner the better. We all knew that America was a big and wealthy country, one that could well afford to build bombers and tanks and battleships, a country that had plenty of young men to fight, soft and well-fed pampered boys who played baseball and watched moving picture shows and drove big automobiles. Yet in truth, all that I knew about America came from what I'd read—how it was a lazy and decadent land filled with lazy and decadent people. That and what a former teacher of mine, Madame Rudneva, had told me about it.

From his rucksack, the Wild Boar took out a large sausage, hacked off a piece with his knife, jabbed it with the point, and stuck it into his mouth. His real name was Ilya Gasdanov, but behind his back everyone called him the Wild Boar. Partly because he was thickset with a coarse beard that covered most of his face, and because he had small feral eyes and a broad, upturned nose that resembled the snout of a pig. But mostly we called him that because he acted like some wild beast—in the way he ate, the way he fought, the way he treated the soldiers under his command, especially the way he treated the women soldiers. He was always in possession of such rare delicacies as sausage. He had connections, knew people in the black market who could get whatever you wanted, at least for the right price—real cigarettes, German schnapps, Black Sea caviar, even silk stockings, which he would dangle like bait in front of the dozen or so women in the company.

"Would you care for a piece, Corporal?" he said to Zoya. She had the Degtyaryov spread out in pieces on a section of canvas in front of her. With the pan off, she was loading it with copper-plated 7.62 mm cartridges, her movements nimble and precise, and I could just imagine how, before the war, her hands would have worked using a needle and thread to darn a sock or hem a dress. In front of her too lay a letter she'd gotten during mail call. I'd watched her as she read it, saw whatever news it brought from home fill her eyes with that familiar distant longing that such letters always bring. Even good news tended to make one sad, because you were away from those you loved. She glanced up at the Wild Boar, then across at me. I sat with my back to the earthen wall of the bunker, working on a poem in my journal, a small leather-bound notebook I kept in my pocket. I guess I still clung to the notion that I was a poet. Before the war I had dreamed of being the next Akhmatova. Now I wrote just to occupy my time, to keep my sanity.

"You are far too skinny, Corporal," the Wild Boar said. "How are you going to kill those fucking krauts if you don't keep up your strength?" With his knife, he hacked off another large chunk of sausage, speared it with the point, and shoved it into the hairy cavity that was his mouth. The weapon, a dagger he'd taken off a dead SS officer, was a delicate-looking thing with a fancy engraved handle, something that resembled an expensive letter opener. "Uhm," he said, making an exaggerated show of the pleasure it gave him. His lips smacked as he chewed and his throat made the guttural sounds of a dog eating. He cut another piece and extended it on the end of the dagger toward Zoya. "Have some. Don't be shy, little one."

At first she shook her head.

"Go on. Take it. There's plenty more where that came from." He smiled at her. "Think of it as a reward for your good work today, comrade."

"For getting that kraut," chipped in Drubich.

Hesitantly, she reached out and accepted the proffered piece of meat.

"*Spasibo*," she said as she tore hungrily into it.

"Is good, no?"

She looked over and met my gaze, then turned away, embarrassed.

I went back to my journal. Each day I wrote something in it: random thoughts, observations, lines of a poem I never quite seemed to finish. It also served as my kill log, where I kept the official record of the men I dispatched as a sniper. Ironic, I knew, that between the same covers I both wrote poetry and recorded the number of Germans I shot. Creation and destruction in one book. My journal, though, was one of the few places that was private, a thing I didn't have to share with anyone else. And it was the one part of my old life that I hadn't lost, the one part of me that had remained constant. I sometimes felt that privacy was the worst casualty of war. I don't mean by this personal modesty. The year of fighting had nearly purged me of that. Although it had been awkward at first, I'd long since ceased to worry about bathing or changing clothes or attending to personal needs in front of a company of mostly men. And they hardly batted an eye at seeing a woman pull her trousers down, squat, and relieve herself. The war had made modesty a luxury no one could afford. No, for me at least, it had to do with the absence of any privacy of mind, the time and silence to be alone with one's thoughts, without being interrupted or pestered, without having to listen to a hundred other people jabbering or laughing, eating or farting, or snoring in their sleep. I missed the quiet evenings alone with a book, doing research in the musty-smelling stacks of the university library, sitting by myself along the river and working on a poem, allowing one line to open up an entire sonnet I hadn't even known dwelled within me.

"And what about the sergeant?" the Wild Boar asked, as if he could read my thoughts and wished to disrupt them on purpose. "Would she care for a piece of my sausage?"

I looked up from my journal. "No," I said flatly, then returned to my writing.

Despite already having eaten the watery gruel, the stale hunk of black bread, and the meager piece of dried meat or salted fish we all were given for our evening meal, I was still hungry. I was always hungry, as were we all, having been reduced to half rations since the Germans had tightened the noose around the city. All that is, except for the COs and commissars and the Party's blue hats—those feared political officers— and those like the Wild Boar who knew how to take care of themselves. With the revolution, we were all supposed to be equal. But the war only proved what we all knew already—that a select few got plenty while the rest got the scraps. It was just like before the revolution, only now we called it communism.

Though my stomach growled from hunger, I wasn't about to accept food from the Wild Boar. I didn't like him, found him repulsive. The Wild Boar was old school, a battle-hardened career soldier who'd been in the czar's army and didn't think they should let women fight. He thought we *"shlyukhi"*—cunts—as I'd heard him refer to us, just got in the way and were bad for morale. To him, a woman belonged in the kitchen or the bedroom, not the battlefield.

Early in the war, there had been many such men, men who didn't accept the notion of having women on the front lines. They felt defending the Motherland, killing Germans, was a man's job. I could still recall my experience at the recruiting station where I'd gone to enlist, in a small village west of Kharkov. My face haggard and hair a mess, my dress still covered in blood. I stopped by a farmer's water trough and asked if I could clean up. The woman there kindly gave me a bar of soap and some rags. I cleaned up, washed my face, tried to look presentable. From a wild cherry tree beside the road, I picked a couple of cherries, crushed them between my fingers, and rubbed their juice into my cheeks. I didn't want to give the appearance of being pale and weak. I wanted to show them I was healthy, that I was strong and capable of fighting.

The country was in utter chaos, with thousands fleeing eastward before the fascists and their "lightning war" machine. There were long lines at the recruiting office, which was set up in an abandoned factory. I noticed one or two other women, not many. They'd just begun the call-up for women to fight, the very fact suggesting just how desperate the situation had become. A couple of men whistled at me, and they spoke in those leering undertones that men do in the presence of a woman they find desirable. I hardly felt desirable. I hardly felt like a woman even. More simply a vessel filled with anger, with hatred and the compulsion to do violence, so filled with it I thought I would burst. When I finally reached the front of the line, there were two officers seated behind a table. They looked me up and down, traded smiles.

"Yes?" one of them said. He was a skinny man with a red face scarred by smallpox. He used a matchbook to pick at his teeth.

"I wish to sign up to fight," I explained.

"To fight?" he said with a laugh.

"Yes. For a combat unit."

"What do you think war is, pretty girl? A dance?" He and the other officer chuckled at this.

"I want to fight," I repeated.

"We have openings for nurses. If you want to be a nurse, I can get you in."

"I am trained as a marksman."

"Marksman!" he said in a mocking tone.

From my pocket I took out the certificate I'd received from the Osoviakhim, the paramilitary shooting club that my father had had me join back in Kiev when I was a girl. I had qualified as a marksman with a Mosin-Nagant rifle. At one hundred yards without a scope, I could put five shots within a five-centimeter pattern. I had won competitions throughout the Ukraine. I was a quite a good marksman.

"See," I said, presenting the certificate to him.

He gave it a cursory inspection and tossed it back across the table at me. "I told you, we need nurses."

"But you see there, I am good with a rifle."

"Do you think shooting Germans is like shooting targets, pretty girl?" he huffed at me. "Come here," he instructed, waving me to approach him. I hesitated, then leaned down toward him. "Closer," he said. "I won't bite." I leaned still closer. When I was close enough that I could smell the leeks on his breath, he aimed his finger at my face and went *bang* loudly enough that it startled me. I jumped backward, almost into the man behind me. Both officers laughed again, as did a few of the others standing in line. I felt like a fool, felt my face grow hot, the familiar burning sensation beginning again at the corners of my eyes, as it had for so many days past. But I was not about to let the idiot get the better of me. So I squinted hard, tightening the flesh around my eyes. I think it was then that the change in me really began, when I became something other than just another victim of the Nazis. You see, our Motherland had rapidly become a nation of grieving mothers, so much grief and mourning and heartache that it hung in the air, palpable as smoke, choking the lungs.

"I want to enlist in a fighting unit," I said firmly, struggling to control my voice.

"Don't be silly. Consider becoming a nurse."

"I don't *want* to be a nurse. I want to shoot Germans."

"Go home. Killing's a man's job," the red-faced officer exclaimed. Glancing past me he said, "Next."

But I didn't budge. I stood there, staring down at him. At that moment, I hated the red-faced officer almost as much as I did the Germans.

"You're right," I said, and then, despite my best efforts, I felt sudden hot tears pushing out of the corners of my eyes. But they were tears of vengeance, of a mother's love, fierce and irrepressible, tears that could singe anything they touched. Staring down at the officer I pointed a finger at him, all of my sadness turning to rage, boiling up in my breast. "Yes. Killing *is* a man's job," I cried. From the pocket of my dress I got out the leather case in which I had all of my worldly possessions. I removed the picture of my daughter and Kolya, my husband, and laid it on the table before them. "That's my little girl," I said, pointing at Masha. "I want to kill those Germans for her. If I have to, I will join the partisans and fight with them. But I *will* fight. Do you understand me? One way or another, I *will* fight."

I had spoken loud enough that those behind me heard what I'd said.

A few started to grumble. One voice said, "Let her fight." I turned and looked at the men behind me. Then another called out, "Yeah, give her a chance." And another: "We need every fighter we can get."

Finally, sensing the tide turning against him, the red-faced officer relented. "Fill this out and come back tomorrow," he said, thrusting a form at me. "Just remember, when you are getting your pretty ass shot at, don't say I didn't warn you."

In the Red Army we women had to prove ourselves, not once but over and over. If a man was afraid, if he cried or recoiled from the horrors of war, it was viewed as a momentary failing, something he could overcome with willpower or determination, or experience, or by a gun placed to the back of his head. But such a thing from a woman only proved what they already knew, that she was by nature weak, not cut out for war, for killing. We women had to push those natural emotions that all soldiers have deep down inside us. We had to deny not only our womanhood but also our common humanity. We had to be cold and remorseless. We couldn't cry, couldn't show fear or sympathy or tenderness. We had to become as cold and heartless as those Germans we fought against.

Only when I'd proved that I could kill as well as any man did my comrades begin to accept me. Still, there were many like the Wild Boar, who treated the women soldiers with contempt. He would give us menial jobs like digging the latrine or carrying the pails of soup to the front lines, or stripping the German dead of ammo and rations. The Wild Boar scorned our fighting ability, questioned our courage under fire. He cracked jokes about us and made condescending remarks. He called us *shlyukhi*. Except the pretty ones. With them he was friendly. Too friendly. When I first arrived in his unit, I'd heard the stories about him and was warned to keep my distance. Despite the lectures by the political commissars and the NKVD officers warning against fraternization between the sexes, how such things could cause problems and would therefore be dealt with harshly, that still didn't stop some from having affairs. In the loneliness of war, relationships inevitably formed between men and women. You could not stop it with government decrees. But there were some men like the Wild Boar who used their influence to pressure or lure women into doing their bidding. He would especially befriend the new recruits, who arrived weekly to replace those that had been killed, with small favors—a piece of cheese, a cup of vodka, a pair of silk stockings many liked to keep in their pockets to remind them what silk felt like against their skin. A few of the women in my unit would respond to his advances, out of fear of how hard he could make things for them or from simple hunger, or even out of the gnawing loneliness the war had brought into our lives, a loneliness that made even the Wild Boar's company seem appealing.

When I'd first arrived with the Second Company, he used to come sniffing around me, too. He would tell me how pretty I was, offering me things, chocolates and tins of sardines, bragging how he could get anything I wanted, *anything* at all. It didn't matter to him that I was married. When I told him, he laughed. He said we were at war and could die at any moment. I'd managed to keep him at bay, sometimes using cleverness, other times with not-so-veiled threats of going to Captain Petrenko, or even to the NKVD officer, Major Roskov. Then when my work as a sniper during the siege of Odessa got me promoted to sergeant and I was, at least technically, his equal in rank, he left me alone. Though, of course, I knew he was jealous of me. He didn't like the fact that I was educated, that I spent my free time writing in my journal, that I read. That I wasn't intimidated by him. And he certainly didn't like all the attention I'd gotten of late. "What courage does it take to sit in a little hole and kill at three hundred meters?" I'd overheard him say once to another soldier. Lately, I had begun to notice how the Wild Boar had become friendly with Zoya, talking with her, offering her food and small treats. She was young and naïve, and perhaps he thought he could take advantage of her some night out behind the latrines. I had cautioned her about him.

The Wild Boar wasn't a man to have his authority questioned. He got up and came over toward me. He squatted on his haunches and waved the thick sausage in front of my nose tauntingly. To be honest, its smoky flavor set my mouth watering. When one is hungry, one will do almost anything for food.

"Go ahead, Sergeant," he said. "Think of it as a reward for getting that kraut."

"I am not hungry," I lied, this time without bothering to look up.

"It is a simple compliment I am paying you, Comrade Levchenko. Surely such bravery as yours deserves recognition," he said, his tone edged with sarcasm.

"I *said* 'I'm not hungry.' "

"I am only being generous."

"I know all about your generosity, Gasdanov."

At this he snorted. "And what the hell does *that* mean?"

"I think you know what it means."

"What is it with you, Levchenko?" he said, dropping any pretense of being cordial. "Has all the big talk gone to your pretty little head?"

"I just don't want your sausage."

"Is my meat not good enough for the likes of you?" he replied, dangling the sausage obscenely between his thick legs. Smiling, he glanced over his shoulder at Drubich and the others, to see if they thought his joke funny. Drubich, his lapdog, sniggered nervously, but the others were reluctant to openly choose sides. Both of us were, after all, sergeants. The Wild Boar, a decorated veteran who'd fought in the Winter War against Finland in '39, was known as someone you crossed at your own peril; and while I was a woman and only newly promoted, they'd seen the way the higher-ups had treated me with deference. And there was the official-looking document that Captain Petrenko had nailed to a beam in the bunker several weeks earlier:

> This is to certify that Senior Sergeant Tat'yana Aleksandrovna Levchenko, 25th Division, 54th Regiment, 2nd Company, is a sniper-destroyer of the invading German fascists. She has single-handedly eliminated 244 of the enemy. The Soviet people offer her their heartfelt thanks.
>
> Army Military Council

Closing my journal, I stared at the sausage, then eyed the Wild Boar coldly. "Your *sardel'ka,* Comrade Gasdanov, is far too small to satisfy my hunger," I said to him. At this, Nurylbayev and Drubich and a few of the others dared to let out a chuckle.

The Wild Boar stared at me with his gray little pig eyes. "The hell with you then," he said. Snubbed, he turned his attentions back to Zoya.

"Have some more, Corporal," he said, squatting in front of her.

This time, taking my lead, she told him, "No, thank you, Sergeant."

"Go on," he said, insisting. "Don't listen to *her*. You're skinny as a scarecrow."

"No," she repeated.

"Men like women with some meat on them."

"Leave her alone, Sergeant," I interjected.

"Butt out. This is not your business, Levchenko," he replied, pivoting on his heels and pointing the dagger threateningly at me.

"I can make it my business," I said.

"Is that so?"

"It is."

He leaned toward me so that the others wouldn't hear him. This close I caught a whiff of his sour breath, a strong metallic smell like diesel fuel. "The big hero," he said mockingly. "The famous kraut killer. Huh! You think I give a shit about all that, Levchenko?"

"I don't particularly care what you think, Sergeant."

"Wait till it comes to real fighting. When you have to look a man in the eyes and kill him. Then we'll see what you can do."

"If it's trouble you're looking for, Gasdanov, I can give you all you want."

"Do you think your threats scare me?"

"The major would be very interested to hear about your 'activities.' "

Major Roskov was NKVD, one of the blue caps, the Party's secret police among the troops. Along with the political commissars, the NKVD, or *chekisty* as many called the hated and feared secret police, saw to it that the Party's political will was carried out even at the front lines. They wielded much more power than the military officers, and they could countermand any orders given by the military. They also had spies everywhere and were well known for their brutality. Even before the war, we'd heard the rumors about what they'd done to the Poles in the woods at Katyn. And we'd seen firsthand how they would shoot anyone who dared retreat. They'd established what were called "blocking detachments" in the rear of our lines, machine-gun emplacements whose sole purpose was to shoot, not Germans, but our own retreating troops. Everyone in the company gave Major Roskov a wide berth and was careful what they said around him. Even Captain Petrenko, who didn't take shit from anyone, was usually guarded around Roskov. The blue hats would come around, disciplining those who had spoken out against some action of the military or handing out medals or giving political lectures to urge the troops on against the Germans. Though some of the blue hats were bold fighters, most led an easy, often pampered existence, usually far from harm's way, slinking back only when a battle was over to lap up whatever credit they could garner. But they could be brutal when it came to discipline. While I detested men like Roskov, I realized that sometimes they could be useful. Like now.

"The devil take you both," cursed the Wild Boar, who stood and spat on the ground near my boot. As he stomped off, he muttered under his breath, "Fucking *shlyukha*." Whore—what the German had called me. Drubich got up and followed the Wild Boar through the canvas door of the bunker and out into the night.

I looked over at Zoya.

"Remember what I told you about him," I said.

"I know," Zoya replied. "But I was hungry."

At this, I recalled the chocolate I'd taken off the German. I removed it from my pocket and tossed it to her. "Here."

Zoya got up and came over and sat down beside me. "We'll share it," she said.

She was a small woman, with thin wrists and the delicate bones of a sparrow. She was pretty in a peasant sort of way, with a broad, heart-shaped face and the high cheekbones and hooded eyes of a Kalmyk. Though she cursed and fought like a hardened veteran, she was still just a girl, naïve and unworldly, especially when it came to men.

"How is your head, Sergeant?" she asked me.

"Not so bad," I lied, touching the bandage. "What's the news from home?"

She nodded thoughtfully. "I received word from Maksim that our mother was still the same. The doctor doesn't know if she will recover. My brother blames me for her falling ill."

"How was it your fault?"

She shrugged. "He is angry that he had to stay and take care of her. Help out with the little ones. While I get to go and fight."

"You're the oldest. You don't have a family of your own. It was your duty."

"He thought my duty was to stay home. That as the eldest boy, it should have been he that went off to fight for the Motherland."

"But your brother is only fourteen."

"Not even. It doesn't matter though. He still thinks a girl's place is in the home."

"Ach," I scoffed. "Too many men think like that." I glanced around the bunker. The air raid had stopped, and that unnatural glasslike stillness had taken over as it always did after their bombing runs, where it seemed that every noise had been sucked away, leaving the earth with the feel of an empty cathedral.

"Let's get some air," I said, shoving my journal into my pocket. I wanted to be able to talk freely.

Outside we made our way along the trench for a while, passing a sentry. It was Corporal Nurylbayev, a tall, potbellied man with bowed legs.

"Evening, Sergeant," he said. Nodding toward the west, he added, "Looks like the krauts hit something."

The usually darkened city below us burned brightly. A tire plant near the wharf was engulfed in flames, sending up dense plumes of tar-black smoke. A sweet, chemical stench was already wafting up into the surrounding hills, one that made your stomach retch.

We picked a private spot and sat down, our backs against the dirt walls of the trench. I took out my pack of cigarettes and offered one to Zoya. That was another change the war had produced in me. When I was single, I'd have the occasional cigarette, mostly as an affectation. At university I used to wear a beret and smoke brown Turkish cigarettes, and think myself quite the bohemian, a kind of wild-spirited Akhmatova. After Masha was born, I put aside my bohemian ways and stopped. Now it was something I did without thinking, something I needed as one does air or food. This despite the fact that most of the cigarettes we got were ersatz tobacco, made from chicory or dried potato peels or roots.

The evening was warm, oddly quiet, not a breeze stirring.

"Too many of them still think that all we are good for is to cook and clean and make babies. Like that pig Gasdanov. What we do in this war will change things, Zoya."

"Do you really think so?"

"Assuredly. We will show them women can do anything we set our minds to."

"Including killing?" she said uncertainly.

"Yes, even that. You have heard of Anka?" I asked.

She was the famous machine-gunner who'd fought with the great patriot Chapayev in the civil war after the revolution. Over the years her story had grown into mythic proportions. Whoever she'd been in reality, she'd long ago crossed over into legend. But it was a myth a young girl could latch on to and hold as a model of womanhood.

"Of course," Zoya replied. "What schoolchild hasn't read of her?"

"Well, we shall become modern-day Ankas, you and I."

Zoya shrugged her narrow shoulders. "I fight only to drive those devils from our soil."

"Do you think I want that any less than you? But we are fighting and dying just like men. And after the war, shouldn't we take our rightful place beside them, not as their maids or whores?"

Despite all the talk that the revolution had given women the same rights and opportunities as men, we knew the truth—that we were still second-class citizens. It was men who made the decisions, who had the real power and control. They were the ones who decided what everyone would do, how we women would live our lives, what choices we would have, if and when we had children, even what we would think. But sometimes I let myself believe that the war might actually change things. That if we showed them we were as strong and brave and tough and valuable as they, perhaps they would allow us the same freedoms and opportunities. The women I fought with made good soldiers, as good as or better than the men. We had more endurance and more patience, and with us the fighting had less to do with ego. Men fought out of pride, to show off in front of their comrades. Women fought to protect their home, their children, their loved ones.

"Yes," Zoya said, but I could tell she was unconvinced. Zoya was old-fashioned, a simple country girl with backward notions. "But a woman should be a woman, and a man, a man."

"And yet we are doing things now that only men used to do."

"You know what I mean. When I get married, I want a man who is strong. Who has broad shoulders. I wouldn't want to be with someone who is weak."

"Nor would I," I said. "But there are different kinds of strength. There is the strength to be gentle. The strength to be kind and generous. Those are the qualities of a real man."

Zoya nodded.

"And your husband, he has such qualities, Tat'yana?" she asked.

Her comment caught me a little off guard. "He is a good man."

"I bet he must be very handsome."

"Why do you say that?"

"To have a wife so pretty and smart as you. Do you have a picture of him?"

I reached into the inside pocket of my tunic and removed the small, worn leather case in which I kept my personal effects—a photograph of my parents, a poem I'd had published in a literary magazine before the war, a ticket stub to a symphony Kolya and I had gone to in Kiev, my wedding band, a locket of hair I had clipped from my daughter's head before we laid her to rest. The lone photo I had of Kolya, Masha, and myself. It had been taken at the park Vladimirskaya Gorka in Kiev, down near the river, the summer before the war. In good weather, a man would set up his camera there on Sundays and take your photograph for a few kopeks. In it Kolya was holding Masha in his arms while I stood next to him. She was two. She wore a blue cotton dress I had made for her, and I'd put a matching blue ribbon in her fine blond hair. It brought out the blue of her eyes. Though I'd told Zoya about Masha, I hadn't shown her the picture. Hadn't shown anyone. Perhaps because I didn't want to go anywhere near that terrible place inside me. Nonetheless, I carefully extracted the photo and handed it to Zoya. I removed another cigarette and lit it, then held the match so she could inspect the photo.

"That's him. Kolya," I said.

"He is quite handsome," Zoya remarked.

While I knew she was being kind, Kolya did have a certain boyish charm despite being over thirty in the picture, with his blond hair that fell casually in his face, beneath which his blue-gray eyes stared soberly out at the camera like a diligent student listening to a teacher's lecture.

"Have you had any word from him?" she asked.

I shook my head. I'd had only one letter from him since the previous summer. He had gone north to fight in the defense of Leningrad, and we all had heard how badly things were going there.

"I'm sure he's fine," she said, trying to reassure me. "You must love him very much."

I took a drag on my cigarette.

"What is it like to be in love, Tat'yana?"

What could I say in answer? How does one explain one's life to another, make sense of the convoluted longings of the heart, or those longings that are stifled? That I was fond of Kolya. That I respected him. That he was a kind and gentle man, a good friend, a wonderful father. But that I didn't love him. That I'd never loved him. I felt almost embarrassed to admit what seemed now, during such difficult times, a petty and selfish notion—love!—a feeling that I had put too fine a point on.

"Have you heard of the poet Tsvetaeva?" I asked.

I wasn't surprised that Zoya, who could hardly read, shook her head.

"She said this about love: 'Ah! is the heart that bursts with rapture.' You will know that you are in love when your heart feels about to burst."

"I have never been in love," my young friend replied.

"Surely you must have had a crush on some boy in your village, Zoya," I said with a smile.

"No," she replied.

"Not even once?"

"My parents were very strict. Now with the war, I fear that I will die and not know what it is like to love someone."

Suddenly I shared her fear: to die without ever having truly loved. What a waste of a life, I thought.

"You will live to find out what love is about."

Then she stared at the picture again. "May I ask you a question, Tat'yana? If it's not of too personal a nature."

"Of course," I said.

"What is it like to, you know . . . be with a man?"

I glanced over at her, smiled. "That would all depend, I suppose."

"On what?"

"The man."

"My mother told me that it hurts the first time," she stated.

"A little perhaps. Not too much."

"How do you know what . . . to do?"

Here she could kill men so coldly, and yet she'd never been with one. Was I any more experienced, though, at her age? I thought of my own wedding night. Kolya and I were both virgins. Nervous, I lay there in my nightgown waiting for him to make the first move. Then when he did, there was an awkward fumbling of cloth and hands, a frantic pushing and shoving, a last grunting and shudder by my new husband. It was over before I knew what had happened. That was my first time. I had expected more, but life never gives you what you expect, and the trick is to learn to accept what you get. That's what I told myself, anyway.

"When the time comes," I explained, "your heart will guide you."

"Did it with you?"

Sometimes it is better to lie. "Of course."

Before handing the picture back, Zoya glanced at it again.

"Is that your daughter?"

I nodded.

"How old was she there?"

"Two." Then I shared with her the pet name I used to call Masha by: *moy krolik*. My little rabbit.

She touched my shoulder with her hand. "When this is over, you will go home and you and your husband will have many more children."

"Perhaps."

"No, you will. We must all have large families."

I shrugged. I couldn't imagine bringing another child into this grotesque world. It hardly seemed right or fair. And yet, another part of me knew it was exactly what we needed to do. I knew that we must all have children, lots and lots of children, not to forget those who had died but to begin anew. To rebuild our country. To rebuild ourselves. And deep down I knew that I secretly hoped I would have another child, that I would feel life growing in me again, filling the vast hole the war had torn in me. It was a thought that both saddened me and gave me a strange glimmer of hope. There would be plenty of time, when the war was over, for me to consider being a mother again. But now I had to harden myself and be a soldier still. I could not yet think of bringing forth another life. I could concern myself only with the taking of it.

"I will pray for your mother," I said to her.

"Thank you. And I will pray for your husband."

"And after the war, you must come to Kiev and visit us."

"I don't like big cities. Too many people."

"But you'll make an exception for me, won't you?"

She smiled and said, "Well, all right."

"Don't worry, I won't turn you into a city girl."

"We should try to get some sleep," Zoya said. "We have to be up in a few hours."

"You go on. I'll be in soon."

The truth was I wasn't tired. My body was exhausted, but my mind rambled on. After fifteen or sixteen hours hunkered down in a sniper's nest, concentrating on killing, most nights as soon as I closed my eyes, I slept a dreamless, leaden sleep, like someone drunk on strong *gorilka*. Even the nightly bombardment by the Luftwaffe or our own howling Katyushas didn't keep me up. Tonight though, was one of those nights when my mind seemed to drone dully with random thoughts like a bottle filled with horseflies.

I took out my journal and turned on my electric torch. I opened the small notebook and read a poem I'd begun earlier:

> A naïve girl I left for war
> In a filthy railroad car
> With men grasping guns,
> Grunting and swearing,
> The world turned upside down
> All my hopes undone.

I had hundreds of such snippets of poetry. Scattered lines, isolated verses. I'd managed to finish only a handful. The more I killed, it seemed, the less I could write. It was as if killing sapped me of my muse, robbed me of my inspiration. Or perhaps it was that killing had become my new poetry, the new expression of my imagination.

Below the poem was the entry of my last kill.

26 May 1942. Number 288. Taken three kilometers northeast of Sevastopol. One shot to the chest. Recovered a Mauser in good working order. Witnessed by Z. Kovshova.

I needed only twelve more to reach my personal goal of three hundred. I couldn't say why exactly this arbitrary number was important to me. Still, I couldn't deny its significance. No male sniper had that many, and no female Soviet sniper had reached a third that number. I preferred to tell myself that I was doing it for noble reasons, began to believe what the newspapers and the Party propaganda had said about me—that I was a hero, that I was doing it for my country, for the Soviet people, giving them something to lift up their hearts in these dark days of retreat and humiliation, death and defeat. Even for my fellow women. I liked to think how young girls would see my picture in *Pravda* or *Izvestiya* and say to themselves, If Tat'yana Levchenko could do this, perhaps I could, too. My work, like that of the thousands of other women just like me in this war, was a bold and defiant act of liberation for our sex. To show not only the Germans but also our own Soviet men that we were their equal. But killing is never an answer to anything, and even when it is necessary, it is never something noble, never something to be admired. For all my fancy talk to Zoya of fighting to liberate women, my own reason was far more simple and selfish—hatred. Yes. I killed simply because I hated the Germans. Hated them for what they'd done to my country, to my loved ones, to me. And once I'd started to kill, to give in to that hatred, I found I was no better than the Germans. I enjoyed it, took a perverse pride in my skill at killing. I wasn't satisfied with just being a good sniper. I wanted to be the best, the very best sniper in the entire Soviet Army. I wanted the Germans to hear my name and tremble at it. I guess I thought that if I killed enough, that if I were, as Macbeth said, "in blood stepp'd in so far," then I would be able to let the hatred and rage and need for revenge go, and acquire some measure of peace.

Sometimes, though, it seemed that hatred was the only solid thing inside me, the only thing that propped me up and kept me going. Every other emotion seemed to have dried up in my breast. All the death, all the unimaginable suffering I'd seen or been a party to—all of this had numbed me, had made my heart like a piece of polished stone, smooth and impenetrable. Once, passing a bombed-out building in Odessa, I caught a glimpse of this woman staring out at me. I paused, struck by the likeness of her to someone I'd once known. But this woman was older, with a stiffening of the flesh around the mouth, sunken cheeks, the haggard look in the eyes of one who'd gazed upon some terrible thing. I was captivated, even more so when I realized I was looking in a broken mirror at *myself*. Before the war, I had been an attractive woman, or so I was told. Young, filled with, as my mother used to say, silly romantic notions, an aspiring poet. And now I was . . . what? A cold-blooded killer. I felt myself changed in ways I could hardly even fathom. Was I the same woman who had given suck to my little girl? Who had so loved the feel of her mouth against my breast, the smell of her skin, the sound of her voice? What had become of *her*? Sometimes I wondered if all the killing, all the death and bloodshed, had altered something so fundamental in me that when the war was over, I could never return to the person I'd been. Could I ever go back to enjoying such simple pleasures as a cup of tea in the evening, reading a book, a Sunday afternoon stroll along the Dnieper? Above all, in that other world after the war was over, when the dead were buried and the guns silenced, when the blood had had a chance to seep deeply into the stained earth, would love even be possible again? Could I love another ever again?

Still, now and then, the meaning of those numbers in my journal would creep into my consciousness. The numbers would become more than the immutable facts of war. I thought of the German sniper again. How he'd stared at me, gripped my wrist so desperately, as if to keep himself among the living. Who was Senta? I wondered. What was he trying to tell me? Was it his wife? A girlfriend? What if it were *his* daughter? I had brought life into the world, had loved and nurtured it, and knew what it was to lose it. I knew that those I killed, like the one today, had wives and sweethearts and, yes, even children, had dreams of returning home to family someday. If now and then a momentary tremor of remorse did begin to flower in me, I would normally resist the temptation to feel any humanity for those I dispatched. I'd only have to conjure the sweet face of my darling child. That usually was enough to stanch any misplaced sympathy.

I got out the solitary letter I'd received from Kolya. From handling, it was dog-eared and brittle as an old leaf. It was just a few lines, the only word I'd had from him since we'd parted at the railroad station. It had come eight months earlier, and there had been nothing since, despite the fact that I must have written a dozen letters to him. I felt I was throwing my words into a storm, that they were scattered and cast away. We'd heard that the mails were sporadic along the entire front, but especially in the north at Leningrad where his Twenty-third Army had been sent. Kolya's normally careful and precise handwriting was messy, as if written under duress, in a wobbling freight car or as bombs fell from the skies.

My Dearest Love

I miss you and my darling Masha dearly. I long to see you both again. Keep yourself safe, my dearest.

Yours, Kolya

Sometimes even, during quiet moments like these after a long, hard day of battle, I'd try convince myself that what I felt for Kolya *was*, indeed, love, at least a form of love, that the war had somehow distorted everything, twisted my feelings all about, drained me of my ability to feel *anything*. Or sometimes I wondered, what *was* love anyway? Hadn't my mother warned me about my silly romantic notions, that love didn't put a roof over your head or comfort you in old age? What would its absence really matter after such a terrible thing as this war? Kolya and I had been good friends, we would be good friends again. We would comfort each other. I would read my poetry to him, and we would listen to the music student Kovalevsky's cello strains floating upward into our apartment (though, of course, all that was gone, our apartment building, all of Kiev). We would take long walks along the river, both of us secretly imagining Masha holding our hands, our love for her and our shared pain over her absence binding us together as love never had. At night, I pictured Kolya and I clutching each other like a pair of frightened children, until we fell asleep. For each, the presence of the other would soften loss, would help us to forget all the death that we'd seen, all the death we'd caused. I'd promised myself that I would remain loyal to him and his soothing love would sustain us both. Perhaps, I told myself, I hadn't really known *how* to love before the war. Perhaps whatever I'd thought was missing from our life together then would somehow seem inconsequential after all of this. And perhaps, as Zoya said, some night we would come together in our terrible loneliness and need, and begin another life.

3

I f you are to understand me, why I did what I did during the war and later, you should have some idea of who I was before, so that you can know in what ways the fighting changed me, made me the sort of person who could kill with such dispassionate ease.

Though I was raised as an only child, my parents did have another baby before I came along, a son named Mikhail. Still in a crib, he went to sleep one night and, as my mother put it, "God decided he was needed in heaven." In one corner of our home she'd erected a small shrine to him—a pair of his baby shoes, a blanket from his crib, a lock of his hair, a single photograph showing a pretty, dark-haired boy who bore a striking resemblance to me. Though I never knew him, I sometimes resented my brother for leaving behind an unspoken sadness that pervaded my childhood, that hung palpably over our family. I could sense his ghost, the presence missing from the dinner table with the extra plate my mother always set out, could feel it in my mother when she tucked me in at night, her possessiveness, the fear that it would happen again. How my father looked at me with a barely concealed expression of displeasure. And I felt too, as all those who have lost siblings, the oppressive weight of responsibility that sits on those left behind—not to disappoint one's parents, not to cause them any further pain, to live, not one's own life, but that of the dead sibling.

My father's work for the *kolkhoz*, the government's farm collectivization program, caused us to move many times when I was growing up. We lived all over the Ukraine, in small villages and large cities. I was always having to get used to a new home, a new town, new schoolmates. I never felt a part of anything, never felt I had a home in any conventional sense of that word. And there were many Ukrainians who hated apparatchiks like my father, whom they felt were responsible for taking away their lands, dividing up their farms among the peasants, for the famine that eventually swept over the land like a plague. That and the fact that my father's government position permitted us to enjoy a certain status and financial security that most of our fellow Ukrainians did not—all of this only caused our family to be even more isolated and, in many cases, despised. We usually had a car, always a modest but pleasant home, plenty to eat—this at a time when most families were crammed into a single room or small apartment and had to stand in long lines with food vouchers to get a loaf of bread or a few potatoes. And in my native Ukraine, tens of thousands were starving during the Holomodor, when there were dead bodies in the alleys and scattered across the country-side like so many grains of wheat left after the harvest.

My father was a Russian, an educated and urbane man, handsome and remote in a nineteenth-century sort of way, with his high collar and pince-nez, his dark, wavy hair and bushy mustaches. An atheist, he came from a well-to-do family in St. Petersburg before the revolu-tion, though he'd taken an active part in the brave new world after the overthrow of the czar, even fighting with the Reds against the Whites in the civil war. A distant and reserved man whose capability for love, I think, was forever stunted by the death of his son, a man who seemed reluctant to allow himself to get close to another child. And yet, in his own way he tried to be a good father to his one surviving child, and I suppose he loved me in his own fashion. At night I remember him reading Turgenev or Gogol to me, or some Pushkin (it was from him that I developed my love of poetry). He took me to the opera and the symphony. He would listen to Mozart in the evening as he smoked his pipe, though later, after the German invasion, he would smash all of his "Nazi music," as he put it. He taught me to play chess and to swim in the sea. To throw a javelin and run the hurdles. (Later, it would be he who instructed me on how to shoot a gun.) Sometimes he would relate to me stories from his experiences in the civil war, fighting with the famous Chapayev, the sweet odor of his pipe intoxicating. While the peasant in my mother believed in the need to feed the people, she was naturally suspect of abstractions, both fearful of and bitter toward the government. My father, on the other hand, looked upon the Party as a benevolent if sometimes necessarily stern parent that wouldn't spare the rod because of its love of its children. He had placed his complete faith in socialism. It was his god, his religion, his heaven on earth.

I could recall at night, my parents sitting at the kitchen table, bickering about the government. My mother calling Stalin that *ublyudok*— mongrel dog—though she would always, as did most citizens even in the privacy of their own homes, instinctively lower her voice when saying something the least critical about the government, fearful that neighbors would overhear and inform on her. She detested Stalin and his cronies, feared and hated the *chekisty*, the dreaded secret police that came and took people away in the middle of the night. And she blamed the Holomodor directly on him, on his paranoid fear of and hatred for Ukrainian independence. On the other hand, my father took the position that the famine was merely an ugly rumor spread by traitors and reactionaries, or, if some few had actually starved, blaming it on drought or those selfish kulaks. For my father, the blame for any and all of communism's ills was never laid at the doorstep of Stalin himself, who was, in my father's eyes, the country's savior, pure of heart and beyond reproach, nor on the Communist system itself. And he had tried to indoctrinate his daughter with the same dialectical fervor. As I grew older, though, and saw for myself the glaring inequalities and hypocrisies, the failings and atrocities of our system, and later the grotesque circus that was Stalin's show trials, I couldn't help but question the government and its leaders, the twisted means to arrive at their perfect ends. But I never questioned my love of country or of my countrymen, which was also something I learned from my father. He instilled in me an undying love of my homeland, a love for which I would gladly give my life.

My mother was as different from him as night is from day. A Ukrainian, she came from a poor family of farmers, and she never shook her fear of poverty. A simple woman, with broad hips and a sturdy peasant body, she was always saving kopeks in a tin can she kept in her bureau for a rainy day, using milk long after it had gone bad, watering down the soups she made, patching and repatching clothes. Like many Ukrainians, she was shaped by necessity, fashioned by the memory of actual hunger, something I myself had never experienced. And yet she strove hard to make whatever house we stayed in feel like home. We'd hardly get settled in when she would be busy cleaning and scrubbing, making curtains for the windows and putting out our few possessions, including setting up the small memorial in the corner to my brother. I remember her making *nachynka* and *golubtsy*, her hands smelling of onions and cornmeal. I loved her hands, blunt, the nails broken, hands fashioned for work, but they were, nonetheless, gentle and loving; I remember them combing my hair or wiping the tears from my eyes when I'd scraped a knee. She tried to establish routines, to forcibly nurture a family life even in the most barren of places. For Christmas, she would place the *kolach* bread on the table with candles and dishes of salt and honey, and she'd dip the bread in each and repeat the prayer about Christ's coming—*Khristos rozhdayetsya*. This despite the government's view on celebrating such a bourgeois holiday. She was a good mother, whose loss of a child, unlike that of my father, only made her love me all the more fiercely, all the more protectively.

As I mentioned, my father, the former soldier, got me interested in shooting. He said that in this new world women too would need to take up arms to defend the revolution. But I think it was as much that he'd secretly wanted to fashion me into the son he'd lost; and I suppose I took to it for the very same reasons, to give him back that son, or perhaps, become one. When we lived in Odessa, he would take me to an abandoned quarry not far from the Black Sea where he taught me to shoot a heavy old Cossack rifle he'd used in the war. He would set up cans and have me shoot them from progressively longer distances. When I would miss, he would shake his head in disappointment, and I would feel the sting of having failed him and work all the more diligently. Then he would wrap his arms around me, about the only physical contact I'd ever had from him, and adjust my elbow and my head. "You must make your rifle an extension of your will, Tanyusha." That's what he called me, Tanyusha, his attempt at tenderness. I practiced hard, hoping to please him, to be what he wanted me to be. Later he had me join the Osoviakhim, the paramilitary shooting club that all Soviet youth were encouraged to participate in. I soon realized that I had a natural aptitude for shooting a gun. I wasn't afraid of the kick of the rifle or the noise. Instead, I found in it a wonderful symmetry, a synthesis of mind and eye and target, of a will made manifest.

When I was fourteen we finally settled for good in Kiev. It was both strange and comforting to have a place I could finally think of as home. In school I was but an average student, bright but undisciplined, lazy except in those subjects that struck my fancy. I could excel when it came to something like literature or athletics, but in class, I would often daydream, staring out the window onto the playing fields, thinking of how I would perform at an upcoming track meet or scribbling in the margins of my notebook some lines of poetry. From an early age I had become an inveterate scribbler of verse. I fashioned myself something of a modern-day Pushkin. One time in my mathematics class, I was working on a poem instead of doing the assignment. The teacher, a shrill-voiced, stolid woman named Comrade Borovechenko, crept up behind me and caught me in the act.

"What is this, Comrade Levchenko?" she said, snatching the paper I was writing on out of my hands. "Aha. It seems we have a poetess in our midst," she said sarcastically. Then, to my utter mortification, she proceeded to read the poem aloud to the entire class. It was on a favorite topic of mine at the time—love. The class tittered and taunted me.

At school I kept to myself, an introverted girl who hadn't many friends. I didn't seem to fit in anywhere, except on the athletic fields. A good athlete and one who enjoyed a challenge, I loved competing, enjoyed outdoor pursuits. I took great satisfaction in pushing myself, the feel of my body in motion. I ran track, competing in the hurdles and the javelin. I also loved to ski and hike, to swim in the Black Sea when we went on holiday. Growing up, I'd never had a boyfriend. I suppose all the moving around hadn't helped, but mostly I wasn't particularly interested in boys, at least not the ones that I found myself surrounded by at school. They were immature or coarse, strutting vainly around like roosters. The good-looking ones were usually brainless and conceited, the bookish ones too dull or homely or passive to strike my fancy. Or at least, so I told myself—the lies every insecure young girl learns to tell herself. For they weren't particularly interested in me either. Until I was thirteen, I was this awkward, ungainly creature, with skinny legs and big feet, a flat chest, a mouth too broad. And with my dark hair and serious dark eyes, which tended to look directly upon the world with a kind of challenge, some even took to calling me "Tsygan"—Gypsy. Others called me Jew, though I wasn't. (My father, for all of his many flaws, harbored no anti-Semitic views; when he heard this, he told me, "Go ahead and tell them you are a Jew. That I'm a Jew. That we're all Jews in this country.")

Despite being so physical, I also loved to read history and books on travel, anything I could find about the rest of the world, which seemed a fascinating and forbidden mystery to me. I loved to read about Paris and London and New York, the Andes and the Great Wall of China. I also enjoyed reading novels and poetry. The classics like Pushkin and Lermontov and Turgenev, as well as more modern writers like Tsvetaeva and Yesenin. I read whatever I could get my hands on, which, given the state's censorship, was often quite limited. As I said, I'd always written poetry, something to take up the long hours of a lonely young girl whose parents moved from town to town. I wrote in a journal, though I was too shy to show it to anyone, not even my parents. While most of my teachers thought me lazy or simply not particularly clever, a few saw beneath the sometimes prickly, disinterested surface I presented to the world.

One was Madame Rudneva, my literature teacher. Middle-aged, with a head of wild reddish hair sprinkled with gray, she had large brown eyes, sharp features, an inviting smile. Not so much pretty as striking. She smoked Gauloises and dressed differently from the frumpy way the other teachers did, in bright flowing dresses and exotic jewelry and a beret. She spoke half a dozen languages fluently, including English. It was rumored she had family money she had somehow managed to retain even after the revolution. It was also rumored that she was part Jewish, which made her suspect in the eyes of many and formed a bond for us. ("We're a couple of Gypsies, we two," she used to joke with me.) While the other teachers insisted they be called "Comrade," she preferred "Madame," in the European tradition. In class she would sometimes make satirical comments about an article in *Pravda* or *Izvestiya*, or some new policy of the government's she thought idiotic. She believed that women were the equal of men, that the revolution had preached that, and yet in practice, the role of women in the country was limited to teaching or working in a factory or on a collective farm driving a tractor, or worse, relegated to being merely someone's wife. Though we were supposed to read only the Russian masters and those tedious contemporary works by "approved" writers, which meant plodding stories about factory workers overjoyed about reaching their quotas, often she'd bring in something by Shakespeare or Keats and read it to us in class, translating as she went. Occasionally she even slipped in some banned book by a contemporary Soviet. At the front of our classroom was the mandatory picture of Stalin that every classroom had. His cold, snake black eyes seemed to stare down upon us students like the fearsome gaze of some slightly annoyed god. Right beside his picture, though, Madame Rudneva had put up that of Shakespeare, at least until the headmaster removed it.

I was just emerging from that awkward period of youth, when a girl magnifies her every flaw into some tragedy. Madame Rudneva, though, must have seen some spark in me, one I didn't even know existed myself. She found some excuse to have me stay after school once. At first I thought I was in trouble, as I sometimes was with other teachers. But instead we just chatted, about poetry, about life, about *my* life.

"What do you want to be when you grow up, Tat'yana?" she asked me. It was the first time anyone had ever asked me such a question. The other teachers, my parents, I guess even I, all assumed I would be like any other girl, no better or worse. Work in a factory, get married, make meals, produce healthy children, in short, silently accept what life had selected for me.

I shrugged. "I like to read," I told her.

"Reading is an avocation. It's not a vocation," she said to me. "What do you want to *do* with your life."

I paused, then blurted out, "I would like to write poetry."

"Poetry?" she said. I feared she'd said this with irony, but I couldn't detect the slightest trace of sarcasm, as other teachers would have responded to such a bold statement. My own mother, for instance, viewed my poetry writing as just a silly childhood hobby, like playing with dolls. Something that I would eventually grow out of.

I nodded to Madame Rudneva.

"May I see some of it sometime, Tat'yana?"

"I don't know," I replied shyly.

After school the next day the woman handed me a tattered copy of a poet I had never heard of.

"You have not read Akhmatova?" asked Madame Rudneva.

"No."

"She's our greatest living poet. Though her works have been banned by Old Whiskers," she said, tossing her head toward Stalin's portrait.

"Why do you call him that?" I asked.

"It's what they call him in the camps." She paused, then whispered cautiously, "I spent some years in one of his camps."

"My God!" I cried, startled. "What did you do, Madame Rudneva?"

She let out with a sardonic sigh. "I wrote a letter in support of my fifteen-year-old cousin who had been arrested for making a joke about the Party. For this, I received five years' hard labor." She glanced again at the picture of Stalin, then said, "'Old Whiskers' is too nice a name for that filthy swine." Madame Rudneva stared at me suspiciously, as if she only then realized she'd spoken out of turn and now didn't know if she could trust me. In those days, one had to be cautious of what one said. Fear and treachery were everywhere. The walls themselves seemed to have ears.

"Don't worry," I reassured her. Looking over my own shoulder, I whispered, "My mother calls him a mongrel dog."

We shared a conspiratorial smile at this, knowing then it was safe to talk openly.

"Listen," said Madame Rudneva as she opened the slender volume and began to read:

> "He told me, 'We're the best of friends!'
> And gently touched my gown's laces.
> Oh, how differs from embraces
> The easy touching of these hands.

"Lovely, isn't it?"

I nodded.

"Here," she said, handing me the book. "Just don't let anybody see you carrying it about."

I promised that I would be careful.

After that she would bring me other volumes to read, sometimes a frayed edition of a banned poet or a book smuggled into the country by an exiled writer living in Europe. I didn't let anyone see them. Especially not my father who, though he appreciated poetry, liked only the older poets, not the subversive modern ones who wrote "decadent bourgeois drivel," as he put it. Madame Rudneva encouraged me to show her some of my own poems, and while I had previously shared them with no one, I found myself letting her read them.

"These are very good, Tat'yana," she told me.

"Just some scribblings," I replied defensively.

"Nonsense. They need polish, of course. Nothing of beauty comes except with hard work. But they are good. They show real promise."

"Do you really think so?"

"Yes, indeed. You have the seeds of poetry in your soul, Tat'yana." Then she leaned close, as if the portrait of Old Whiskers might overhear her. "Yet I fear they will never bear fruit in this soulless country of ours."

Never before had anyone spoken to me like this, so frankly about our country and its failings, or about my passion for writing. Until then, my poetry had appeared to me as little more than a youthful romantic notion I felt compelled to keep to myself, an oddity I would, as my mother maintained, grow out of. As I came to trust Madame Rudneva, I found myself opening up to her, staying after school to talk about all sorts of things—poetry and philosophy, politics and history. The revolution. The Party. The rights of women. Even about love. Unlike most of my other teachers, Madame Rudneva was not closed-minded, not provincial or dogmatic in her thinking, and unlike the rest of my teachers, she was not afraid to express herself, despite the very real danger such things might bring to one who was so outspoken. She had traveled widely, to Europe, studying in England, at Cambridge. She'd even been to the United States, back in the twenties, before such travel was forbidden. She read Donne and Blake and Keats to me in English. She would spend afternoons teaching me to recite the words in English and then translating them for me. Once, she brought me a volume she'd purchased years before when she was in England, by the American poet Emily Dickinson.

"'There is no frigate like a book,'" she would read from Dickinson, and have me recite it after her. "'To take us lands away.'"

Slowly I began to pick up a little English, and with it a curiosity about America.

"What was it like?" I asked her once.

"In New York, the buildings are so tall the tops reach the clouds. And automobiles everywhere. Going this way and that. Zoom, zoom," the woman said, waving her hands rapidly about, as if shooing away flies. "And there is more food lying in the gutters than is on the tables of the wealthy here."

"No," I replied in astonishment.

"It's true."

"What sort of clothing do the women wear?"

"They dress in very bad taste. Flappers, they are called. They dance like this." At which point Madame Rudneva got up from behind her desk and demonstrated how the American women danced, kicking her legs up and moving her body wildly around the front of the classroom. "Come," she said, inviting me to dance. I shook my head, never having danced before. But she insisted. "I shall show you."

Madame Rudneva held my hand and spun me about in dizzying circles. After a while we both stopped and began laughing uncontrollably.

"Are they all as decadent as they say?" I asked.

"They are spoiled from such soft living," she replied. "But the Americans are not so very different from us."

"But they are capitalists."

At this time I still believed in some of the things my father had taught me, and he said the Americans were the epitome of capitalist greed and corruption, a society doomed to the "garbage heap of history."

"You mustn't believe everything those fools tell you, Tat'yana. The

Party tries to fill everyone's head with lies and deceptions. Because the truth would make everyone angry. And when some brave few try to tell the truth, the government uses fear to shut them up."

"My father says the Party exists only to carry out the will of the people."

"Huh." She laughed. "I once believed heart and soul in the revolution. I was young when we overthrew the czar, just a little older than you. I thought we could change the world. But those in charge wanted to change things only for their own betterment."

"Did you like America?" I asked.

"In some ways very much. There you are free to do many things we could not even imagine here. You can read whatever you want and write what's in your heart. People aren't afraid to say what they think. And American women aren't pigeonholed into this or that category. They can be anything. Do anything."

"Really?"

"Yes. You would like it there, I think."

"If you liked it so much in America, did you ever think of . . ." I asked, my voice trailing warily off, as we'd been trained when speaking of forbidden topics.

"Defecting?" replied Madame Rudneva. "I did actually. I gave it serious consideration. But this is my home. It's my country as much as it is those fools' who run things. Besides, there was the small matter of a man back here." She smiled at this, her thoughts drifting off for a moment. "I was young and in love. He lived here and I thought I would die if we were not together."

"May I ask what happened?"

"Like you he was a writer. A journalist. He wrote the truth, and when they told him to stop and he refused, they came and took him away. I never heard from him again. It broke my heart. I have had many lovers, but he was the only man I ever truly loved."

She let her gaze fall to the floor. I didn't know what to say. Here was a teacher sharing her intimate personal life with me, as if I were a friend, an equal.

"I'm sorry," I offered finally.

"I consider myself fortunate to have been in love with someone of such courage," she explained. "Have you ever been in love, Tat'yana?"

"Me?" I said, shaking my head.

"A pretty girl like you must have many admirers."

"Hardly," I replied. "I don't think boys are much interested in me, Madame Rudneva. They call me Gypsy because of my dark hair."

"You have lovely hair."

I shrugged.

"They are imbeciles!" she said, laughing. "But that will soon change. You are a beautiful young woman, Tat'yana. Someday you will have lots of men interested in you. And you will meet a handsome young man and you will fall in love just as I did."

"I doubt that."

"Believe me, you will. Do you know what Tsvetaeva wrote about love?" Of course, at the time I had never even heard of such a poet. "'Ah! is the heart that bursts with rapture.'"

Secretly, I hoped someday my own heart would burst with such rapture. You see, despite my competitive nature, my seeming disdain for boys and for matters of the heart, I hoped that I would someday fall in love, that I would meet a man who would stir the sort of passion in me that only my poetry or my shooting did now. I pictured someone tall with broad shoulders and an easy smile, a man who would not begrudge my wanting to write poetry, to think independently, who would accept me as I was and not want to make me into some coarse and dull babushka. As I began to devour Akhmatova as one would an exotic and heady fruit whose sweet nectar made the throat clutch with passion, I would see in her poems my own imagined lover. Someone whose touch was gentle and tender, who wasn't afraid to love fully and completely, even dangerously. Of course, life never works out as one imagines. Sometimes I think our dreams are there only to make us taste the bitter regret of how far short we fall from them.

After I graduated secondary school, I took a job for a while at an arsenal factory. I worked a lathe, making artillery shells, as unpoetic an occupation as there is. I recall coming home one evening, and over dinner my father casually telling me that my former teacher Madame Rudneva had been arrested. "Arrested!" I cried. Despite knowing the danger she'd always put herself in by her candor, I was shocked. I begged my father to use his influence, to try to find out where she'd been sent, to see what he could do on her behalf. But he told me that that was impossible, that he wouldn't put himself or his family in jeopardy for such a person. That night I remember crying myself to sleep.

When I grew bored with factory work, I decided to go to the university, where I studied Russian history and literature. I also shot competitively in the Osoviakhim, even winning many medals for my shooting, including being the best marksman in the entire Ukraine. In my spare time I read whatever I could get my hands on. A group of us shared books smuggled in from the West, rough, handwritten translations of T. S. Eliot and Walt Whitman and D. H. Lawrence, as well as banned volumes of our own countrymen, Pilnyak and Pasternak, and the great soul herself, Akhmatova. I also continued to write my own poetry. I showed it among my friends and even managed to publish some poems in small underground newspapers and in anonymous samizdat literary journals circulated in manuscript and read by a handful of like-minded people. Though, of course, you had to be extremely careful about what you wrote and with whom you associated. The editor of *The Workers' Voice*, which published one of my poems, had his apartment broken into by the secret police. His mimeograph machine and typewriter were smashed to pieces. Like Madame Rudneva's lover, though, he stubbornly refused to take the hint and continued to publish articles and poems against the government until finally he was arrested.

Still, it was good to feel a part of something important, a community of kindred spirits who wanted to think and speak and write freely. My father and I grew more and more distant, divided politically as well as emotionally. While I still deeply loved my country, believed in what the revolution had promised and the aspirations of the people, I had grown discouraged, even angry, with the Party, which I came to see as oppressive as any czar. My father and I began to argue, sometimes so heatedly that my mother would have to intervene. He thought I was associating with a decadent crowd, and that if I wasn't careful I would find myself like Madame Rudneva, which would reflect badly on him and my mother. I didn't want to hurt them, so I moved out and got a room near the university. I supported myself by working nights in the factory and going to school during the day. I gravitated toward a small circle of bohemian friends. We wore outlandish clothing and smoked and frequented a café down near the river where students and intellectuals and artists gathered. I struck a pose that suited me, fostered a romantic notion of myself as a poet. I liked to believe I'd be the next Akhmatova. That I'd write fearless and daring poems that would touch the heart, that would make people stand up and take notice. Like her, I would write the truth no matter the cost. Like her, I would live a life filled with intensity. I would live dangerously, love passionately. I was young and foolish and thought that one could control one's destiny.

Then I met a man named Nikolai Grigorovich. Nikolai—Kolya to those few friends he had—would sometimes come by the café and sit in the corner with a book and sip a cup of tea. He was older than I by some dozen years. He wasn't handsome, at least not in the traditional sense, but there was something about him, a seriousness of purpose, I found appealing. Those brooding, blue-gray eyes of his, a neatly trimmed beard, the complete focus with which he read his book so that he was oblivious to anything else around him. I had heard his name bandied about, an important Party member, they said. I would sometimes sit in the café, a volume of Akhmatova in front of me, and glance over at him.

"What is it you are reading?" he asked me one time out of the blue. I was startled actually that he even noticed me. After I told him, he said, "Oh, a shame what befell her."

"The shame is on those who persecuted her," I said.

He smiled, stroking his beard. "Your father works for the *kolkhoz*?"

I nodded.

He sat and introduced himself, in that formal way that he had. To my surprise we spent a pleasant evening conversing. Unlike so many of the dolts who were Party members, Kolya turned out to be bright, open-minded, well-read. We discussed history and philosophy, politics and poetry. I recall he even quoted some lines from Pushkin, which impressed me no end.

> I loved you silently, without hope, fully,
> In diffidence, in jealousy, in pain;
> I loved you so tenderly and truly,
> As let you else be loved by any man.

He told me he was an engineer, one whose specialty was building bridges. Such a vocation, I would come to learn, suited him perfectly. He liked connecting objects, bringing disparate sides together. He talked about the revolution, the new world order that would in time emerge from it. When he spoke, his voice wasn't that of the zealot or an ideologue, one of those who could kill in the name of the revolution. No, his voice was soft and calm, filled with gentleness, though at its core it had the strength of conviction, the passion of one who believed in helping his fellow man.

"What of the lives it has ruined to achieve this new order?" I said.

He nodded patiently. "Yes, many mistakes have been made," he agreed. "And many terrible things have been done in its name. But in the future, we will all be equal and no one will have power over another." Then, smiling, he added, "And poets will be our sacred priests."

"*That* I would very much like to see!" I replied with a laugh.

He was different from most men I'd known, and certainly most Party members. Quiet and self-effacing, not needing to prove something to himself or to others. He was generous and unselfish, almost without ego. He hardly ever began a sentence with *I*. A good listener, he would nod thoughtfully, even if he disagreed with you, his brows knitting themselves in concentration as I spoke. On days I didn't work, we would talk well into the night at the café or after going to the symphony or an art exhibit. We played chess, and while I thought I was good, he would drub me soundly each time, and then patiently try to show me my errors. Sometimes we would sit quietly reading, not uttering a word. Other times I would read to him, Pushkin or Akhmatova, sometimes even my own poetry. He took an interest in my poetry, read my work with the same seriousness that he perused his engineering textbooks. We took long walks through the city, with Kolya occasionally stopping near a bridge to admire its construction. He would bring a pad and sketch the bridge, its configuration, its trusses and support. Sometimes he would sketch landscapes or children playing in the park. He was a very skilled artist. Occasionally he would even draw me. Once when he showed me a sketch of myself, my breath was literally taken away.

"What's the matter, Tat'yana?" he asked. "Don't you like it?"

It wasn't that. Actually, the sketch was quite remarkable, showing just how talented he was. But it was as if he had reached into my very soul and pulled out a kind of wistful yearning, something I hadn't even been aware resided there.

"No, I think it's wonderful, Kolya," I said. "I just didn't recognize myself."

"You're lovely, Tanyusha," he said. It was the first time he had called me that, or said that I was lovely.

Looking back, I think he would misinterpret what that longing in my eyes bespoke. And for me, it hinted of something decidedly missing, something absent in my life or in my heart.

Still, for a while things between us continued along in this comfortable vein, a closeness and easy familiarity developing as with longtime acquaintances. In time I came to think of him as my dearest friend, someone whom I could trust, share my innermost thoughts with. That Akhmatova poem about friendship that Madame Rudneva had read to me made me think of our relationship: *Oh, how differs from embraces, The easy touching of these hands.* It was easy being with Kolya, the first time I'd felt such a feeling with anyone. In some ways, he seemed to me like the brother who had died.

Then one evening we were walking along the river. It was winter, the snow crunching under our boots. The Dnieper was frozen over and people were skating on it, carrying torches. It looked like something out of Brueghel, a still life in winter. We'd stopped along the way to admire the spectacle. Kolya was especially quiet, I'd noticed, seemed nervous about something. I asked him if anything was the matter, but he shook his head. After a while I couldn't help but notice that he was gazing at me in an odd fashion, as if I were a math problem he was puzzling over.

Finally, I grabbed his collar playfully and stared into his face. "For God's sakes, Kolya, what's the matter?" I cried, unable to keep from giggling.

Yet he continued silently to look at me with that odd expression. Then he leaned toward me and gave me an awkward, fumbling kiss on the mouth.

"Kolya!" I exclaimed. "What has gotten into you?"

Perhaps I should have seen it coming, but I didn't. In life, most of the time you see what you want to and are blind to the rest. We go about stumbling in the dark, until someone wiser than we turns on the lights.

"I love you, Tanyusha," he blurted out.

No man had ever said those words to me before, and I'd always thought that when they were finally uttered my heart would leap up with joy, that I would feel such wondrous bliss. But I did not. Instead, I felt my face flush, my stomach twist itself into knots. I didn't know how to respond. I cared for him, very much in fact, though now I realized not in the same way he did for me. I felt suddenly uncomfortable and was about to say something regarding my deep friendship for him, but he put a finger to my lips and told me I didn't have to say anything.

This, of course, changed things between us. Soon after this, he asked me to marry him. Trying to do the kind instead of the honest thing, which meant I would eventually be doing something very cruel to both of us, I didn't outright refuse. Rather, I told him I was too young, that at twenty I wasn't ready to get married, that we should, for now at least, continue just as friends. I thought by putting him off, he would understand that I didn't see the two of us in that way. He told me that he just wanted me to think about it, that he was patient and could wait. Kolya was extremely patient, but also persistent. He viewed me, I think, in the same way he did his engineering problems, as an obstacle to be overcome, a distance to be closed, that with a bit more bolstering here, a little more buttressing there, he could join us, put us soundly together so that our souls could cross over to the other. I don't say this to suggest that he was cold or unfeeling. Only that he saw problems and tried to fix them. He would ask me to marry him again, several times in fact. He told me he would take care of me, that I wouldn't have to work, that I could simply concentrate on my studies, on my poetry. Each time I told him as gently, as kindly, as I could that I wasn't ready to get married.

My father thought Nikolai Grigorovich had a very bright future in the Party, and my mother had become very fond of Kolya. Always the pragmatist, she said he would make a favorable match and that it was both foolish and wrong of me to keep him dangling on a string, that I should either tell him yes or no.

"I *am* quite fond of him, Mama," I explained. "But . . ."

"But what?"

"I'm not sure I love him. Not as a wife should love a husband."

"Ach, *love*," my mother scoffed, waving a blunt finger of scorn in my face. "You sound like a silly girl, Tanyusha." To my mother, a good match was something only a foolish woman turned down. And Kolya was, to her mind, a decidedly good match. He was educated, had a wonderful career ahead of him. "Look at all the rivers this country has. At how many bridges we are going to need. How can you refuse a man who will be such a success someday?"

"But is that enough? That he will be successful."

"You and Kolya are friends, no?"

"We are."

"Friendship is a start. Many couples do not even have that." She looked toward the kitchen, where my father sat reading.

"What of love, Mama?"

"You can learn to love," she said to me. "And if not, you can't eat love. It will never put a roof over your head or food in your belly. Besides, Nikolai's a good man, one who will make someone a good husband. And he won't wait around forever while you're dillydallying." Then, her tone softening, she took my face in her callused hands and said, "Tanyusha, don't think so much, or your life will be very hard."

I couldn't disagree with what she'd said about Kolya—he *was* a good man and *would* make someone a good husband. And the other thing was that he adored me, loved me unconditionally, as I had always dreamed one day of being loved by a man.

I felt an unstated pressure from my father to agree to the marriage, since Kolya was an important Party figure. And my mother was right, I couldn't just keep Kolya hanging on. That wasn't fair. If I'd been more honest with myself and with Kolya, I would have said no. Harder at first perhaps, but less painful in the long run. But I didn't want to hurt him. I told myself, I *was* very fond of him, liked his company, his friendship. Maybe my mother was right, that I was being naïve, hoping for too much. What was more, a part of me, a selfish part I must admit, was attracted to the notion of someone taking care of me, allowing me to write my poetry and not having to worry about getting by in life. So, when I couldn't find a good enough reason to tell him no, I took the coward's way out and surrendered finally—and it felt very much like a surrender. My mother hugged me, my father nodded at the rightness of my choice and went back to reading his newspaper.

We were married in the beautiful Andreyevskaya Church in Kiev, on a sunny autumn afternoon. Though neither Kolya nor I were particularly religious, we decided to have a traditional Ukrainian ceremony. I wore the dress my mother had worn for her wedding, and since we didn't have much money, Kolya and I exchanged simple gold bands and then our hands were joined by the customary *rushnik,* an embroidered cloth signifying our union. As I looked at Kolya, his face aglow with happiness, I told myself I'd made the right decision. That happiness could be achieved in making others happy. For our honeymoon, we went, ironically, to Sevastopol, the same city that would, in a few short years, lie in ruins. We strolled on Primorsky Bul'var. We walked hand in hand along the Grafskaya Quay. We went to the symphony. We talked and enjoyed each other's company. At night, we made love pleasantly, in the dark, with restraint and with a certain formality, with Kolya's head buried into the pillow next to mine, almost as if he were embarrassed by his own passion. That first time, I told myself it was not unpleasant, and besides, as my mother had reminded me before the wedding, it was my duty to my husband. Afterward, I turned and fell asleep in Kolya's embrace. In some ways I found marriage to be a comfort—the companionship, the conversations in the evening, his loving attentions, how he would prepare me a cup of tea, give me a back rub after a long evening of study, do anything he could to make me happy. Above all was the fact that Kolya would let me have my own space within the marriage, my time to write and read and be alone. He was not one of those possessive husbands who had to have my complete attention, thank God. However, from the very first, I realized that while I cared about Kolya, deeply in fact, my feelings for him were those for a cherished friend and would never grow into love. At least not the sort I felt should exist between a man and a woman.

After we returned from our honeymoon, we settled into our life, one filled with the slow but inexorable blunting of dreams but which most of us insist on calling an acceptance of reality—our life became our millstone. We moved into a small apartment not far from the Dnieper River. During the day he'd be off working, sometimes having to travel to distant construction sites where he'd be away for weeks on end. In some ways, I actually looked forward to his absence. I would attend classes or do research at the library or write in the tiny room off the kitchen. When he was home we would share a bottle of Massandra wine and chat about our days. Afterward we might go for a walk along the river or to our usual café or stay in and read to each other. He lavished on me small gifts, presents and things that few in the Soviet Union could afford. Below us lived Kovalevsky, who was studying cello at the conservatory. Sometimes, a few of his fellow music students would get together in his apartment, and they would invite Kolya and me down. We would talk and drink vodka and listen as they played. Later, back in our apartment, we would make love to the lilting sounds of Rachmaninoff or Prokofiev floating upward through the floorboards—sad, wistful music that filled me with unmet longing. Even then, when I was physically closest to Kolya, I would find my thoughts drifting off, seeking to be elsewhere.

"I love you, Tanyusha," Kolya would whisper to me before we fell asleep each night.

He was so earnest and sweet when he said this to me, so tender and caring, that my heart welled up in my chest, not because of what I felt for him as much as because of my nagging guilt. I would smile and stroke his face and tell him that I loved him too. And I tried hard to believe this, and in some fashion I succeeded in convincing myself I did love him. Though I suppose some part of me always knew it was a conditional love, not as he loved me, with all of his heart and soul, but only narrowly, as a dear friend. Yet as the weeks turned into months, and the months to years, I slowly came to resent his touch, and when we made love, I would close my eyes and go off to my own private place. Occasionally, I would be unfaithful to him. No, I don't mean that I took on lovers. But in my mind. I would pretend I was with someone else—a student I'd seen at the library, one of my instructors, a young man I saw in a café, even the lover in some poem by Akhmatova. Sometimes, when I couldn't endure his touch, I would tell him I was tired and turn away. "Is anything wrong, Tanyusha?" he would ask, never in anger, only with genuine tenderness for me. To which I would reply that I was merely fatigued from my studies. The truth was, I wasn't a good wife. No, I was never unfaithful, except for those transgressions in my mind. But I wasn't truthful with him, wasn't fair with him or, for that matter, with myself. I felt as if I were in a beautiful gilded cage, but a cage is still a cage nonetheless. I wish he would have gotten angry with me, wish he'd have yelled and screamed, even struck me, said he'd had enough. It would have made things much easier for me, for both of us. Or I wish I'd simply had the courage to tell him the truth. But it was equally true that he was my dearest friend, such a kind and gentle soul, and as such I had vowed never to hurt him. He seemed content enough with our unspoken "arrangement," with that small part of me that he had access to. He was a man, as I have said, of great patience and of modest needs, and his work took much of his time. Perhaps he was just waiting for me to come around, as my mother said I would.

And I? What was I waiting for? I was not unhappy with our arrangement, or at least I told myself this over and over, knowing that one can convince oneself of almost anything. Besides, when I compared my lot with that of my fellow Ukrainians, so many of whom were suffering terribly, who were starving by the tens of thousands or being shipped off to gulags, what right did I, with my bourgeois romanticism, have to complain in such a world? No, I'd made my bed, so to speak, and now had to lie in it.

Yet just when you think you have life figured out and can see it all the way to the grave, something happens to surprise and amaze you. In my case, it was two things. The first was Mariya, who came like a glorious ray of morning sunlight after a night of bad dreams. Kolya and I had talked vaguely of having a family, someday, "down the road." He wanted children more than I, but I knew it was something expected of me. After all, every good Soviet wife was called upon to produce children, healthy workers for the state. But there was my poetry, my studies to think about. And secretly, I wasn't sure if I wanted children, not yet, perhaps not ever. I had seen what the loss of a child did to my parents. Besides, I guess I looked upon children as a kind of period to the end of my sentence, a final gesture that would forever lock me in the life I was trapped in. But how wrong I was! As soon as Masha, as we came to call her, entered my body and my soul, she became my entire existence, my joy, my passion, my poetry. I loved her with the unconditional love I hadn't been able to find with Kolya. As I've said, I could almost tell the moment she entered my body. That warmish summer day, I was lying on the bed, the breeze lifting the curtains, and suddenly that tiny presence attached itself deep inside me, swelling me with life. From that moment on, my *moy krolik*—my little rabbit—completely captivated me, stole my heart and ran off with it. Both of ours. I remember Kolya had been away for a few weeks working on a bridge project near Zaporozh'ye. When he came home that night, I excitedly threw my arms around him and told him the good news. "We're going to have a baby, Kolya," I cried. He looked stunned. I wasn't sure if it was more due to the news itself or to the way in which I'd reacted to it.

Our daughter turned out to be blond like him, to have his thin, soft hair and blue-gray eyes. We put her cradle in what had been my study. After I nursed her, she would fall asleep in my arms, her rose-petal mouth pressed against my breast.

"Isn't she just the most perfect thing, Kolya?" I would say.

"She looks just like you," he would reply.

Kolya made a wonderful father. He was kind and loving, patient and gentle, and watching him with her, I felt this newfound tenderness toward him, found myself drawn closer to him, the way parents, even those not in love, will sometimes be brought closer because of their mutual love for a child. I would watch with bemused adoration as he swept her up and placed her on his shoulders, and carried her squealing with laughter about the apartment. She formed that missing link between us, a link that held us fast together.

When Masha would grasp my hair with her chubby pink fingers, I felt my heart so swollen with love, I thought it would burst into a thousand tiny pieces. Sometimes in the middle of the night, I would get up from bed and go into her room and lean down, close enough to make sure I could hear her breathing, that fear no doubt inspired by the example of my mother's loss of her firstborn. I loved the smell of her, of her hair and skin, the sweet hoppy fragrance of her breath after she'd taken suck. The way her eyes would dart beneath her closed lids, as if watching butterflies in her sleep. I would whisper into her ear "My sweet love" and "My little rabbit." When I was at school, I would take her to my mother's. Later, when she could walk, she'd scurry up the path from my parents' front door and throw her arms around my neck, crying, "Mama," as if she'd not seen me for ages. It was the most precious of feelings. My chest would ache with love, a love I could never have imagined before. I came to realize that what I had lost by marrying, I had more than gained with the gift of my daughter. I was happy at long last, prepared—no, eager—to spend the rest of my days like this.

But then the second change came into my life.

22 June 1941

It fell like a fiery comet from the sky, scorching everything in its path, obliterating everything. It was the day that monster from Berlin invaded my country. We were walking in the park, the three of us. A warm, bright summer day, the sun gleaming off the buildings, the smell of roses in the air. That's when a boy came running by, yelling that Germany had invaded. We couldn't believe it. Just two years earlier, Molotov had signed a nonaggression treaty between our two countries. War had been averted, we all thought. When we got back to our apartment, we heard the foreign minister on the radio saying that we'd been attacked by Germany and that a state of war existed between our countries. Later we heard the pleas of Bishop Sergey, one of the few clergy who hadn't been arrested or executed by Stalin, asking for all to help fight the invaders. We were shocked and dismayed, though in hindsight it should not have surprised anyone. Not just because of what Germany had been doing—the military buildup along our borders, the Nazi rhetoric that had openly called for Lebensraum, the need for the land of the Untermensch for their superior race—but also because of our own country's complicity. The treaty with Hitler, permitting us to chop up Poland and the Baltic states as if they were pieces of meat, was a deal we'd cut with the devil himself. Then there were Stalin's own purges, which had liquidated most of the military's top brass, replacing them with sycophants and incompetents. But now all that didn't matter. Our country was under attack. We were all Soviets, all patriots united against our common foe.

Kolya and I talked things over. He said he wanted to enlist straightaway, that the Motherland needed every available body to fight the fascists. That day he went down to the recruiting office and signed up, and the next day, Masha and I accompanied him to the station where he was to board a train heading north, to Leningrad he'd been told. The station was utter chaos. Thousands of new recruits and their loved ones had gathered there, hugging and crying, exchanging packages and saying their good-byes. Over the loudspeaker an announcement was made that the Germans had crossed the Dvina River and were pushing toward Leningrad.

"We must stop these fascist bastards," Kolya said to me. I found it surprising because he hardly ever cursed, and never in front of Masha.

I took his face in my hands and said, "You listen to me, Nikolai. You be careful. Don't be a hero."

"You will move in with your parents?" he asked.

"Yes."

"I love you, Tanyusha," he said.

"And I love you too," I replied.

I hugged him tightly to me, not wanting to let him go. I felt closer to him at that moment than I ever had. A tenderness, the sort, I suppose, one would feel for a brother going off to war. He kissed Masha, then, taking my face in his long, slender hands, he said to me, "Don't let anything happen to my girls."

His girls? I thought. The expression would come to haunt me. He was entrusting our safety and our love to me. I would come to feel as if I had betrayed him. Was I his girl? And hadn't I let something happen to Masha? He boarded the train with the other soldiers and waved as it pulled out of the station.

"Wave good-bye to your father," I told Masha.

"Where's *tato* going?" she asked.

"To fight the Germans," I replied.

"Why?"

How do you explain to a child the reason why adults kill one another? How would I ever have been able to tell her of all the men I aligned in my sights and sent to their deaths?

"Because he loves us."

"Will he come back?"

"Of course," I said.

As we walked home I told myself over and over that Kolya was a good man and that I would remain loyal to him, that I would love no other and that I would be waiting for him when he came home. But I saw through this flimsy pretense. In my heart I held the blackest of secrets, a maggot devouring my soul. Some part of me hoped that he wouldn't come back. Yes, it's true. I thought that if he died in the war, I could grieve for him publicly, honor him by wearing widow's weeds for a year. But then I would be free from my cage, free to live my own life as I chose, and not that which others had chosen for me or to which I had with cowardice surrendered. Only later would I understand the harsh wisdom of being cautious of what you wish for.

4

During those long, terrible months at Sevastopol, the lone joy I had was the occasional dream of Masha. It was as if because I tried so hard to banish her from my waking mind, like any child she craved her mother's attention and would come rushing up to me as soon as I fell asleep. "Mama," she would cry. And how could I deny her. In one dream we were on holiday at the seashore. I was sitting on warm sand, gazing out at her playing along the water's edge. She would follow the breaking waves, fleeing from them like a sandpiper as they chased her up the shore, squealing and laughing with delight. She scampered about, her wet, lithe body filled with a magical energy. Even in the dream I carried with me that vulnerability a mother has with her always, as if she is holding a small candle against a strong wind, fearing that sooner or later its flame would be extinguished. I called to her, "Come, my little rabbit."

"Sergeant."

A hand roused me roughly from sleep.

"Masha?" I mumbled.

"Sergeant, it's me," came Zoya's voice. "Time to get up."

I sat up, the sun and water suddenly vanishing, replaced by the murky dankness of the bunker. Masha's face turned into that of Zoya's. She squatted next to me, holding a lantern. Rubbing my eyes, I asked, "What time is it?"

"Three hundred hours, Sergeant. Would you like some tea?"

"Please."

Zoya headed over to the far side of the bunker where someone was boiling water over a small gas stove. She returned in a moment and handed me a metal cup.

"Here," she said.

As the steam rose up before me, I could still smell Masha's wet hair. Sweet, like rose petals just beginning to rot.

Zoya pursed her lips. "We have a little time yet." Then leaning toward me, she whispered apologetically, "I've gotten my monthly. I have to go change."

I took another sip of tea, a substance as unappealing as bathwater but which at least warmed the belly. We had an hour before we had to be in position, two hours before sunrise. Rubbing the sleep from my eyes, I glanced around at my comrades sprawled on the bunker's floor. The Second, dubbed the Shock Company because of its reputation for toughness in battle, was made up mostly of young troops, nineteen, twenty, with a few older veterans like Gasdanov and Captain Petrenko, who was in his mid-thirties, and Yuri Sokur, the medic. At twenty-five, I was one of the senior ones. We came primarily from the Ukraine, but there were some replacements mixed in from as far away as Stalingrad and Yakutsky in Siberia, and from all walks of life—teachers and students, factory workers and scientists, tailors and shoemakers, miners and peasants. There was even a concert pianist, a young man named Nasreddinov, who had played all over Europe before the war. There were about a dozen women in our company. A machine gunner, a radioman, several riflemen, a mortar team. We used to have a medic named Yana Marianenko, a good-natured girl who always had a pleasant smile on her face. But she'd crawled out into no-man's-land to tend to a wounded soldier, and that's when the King of Death picked her off with a shot to the head. Zoya and I were the only female sniper team in the Second.

I tossed the rest of my tea on the ground and stood, my head almost touching the timbers of the low-ceilinged roof of the bunker. It was now a couple of days after I had killed the King of Death. I gathered up my things—a canteen of water, enough to last me the sixteen hours

I'd remain in my sniper cell, some cheese and hard bread and a tin of kippered herrings I'd taken off a Romanian I'd shot several days earlier, and stuffed it all into my rucksack. I threw on my camouflage poncho and then checked the clip of my Tokarev pistol before sliding it into my holster. I grabbed a couple extra magazines for my rifle and the two grenades snipers always carried—one for the Germans, the other for myself and Zoya if it came to that. We'd been trained not to be taken prisoner. The Germans were especially brutal on captured Soviet snipers, more so even with females. Months earlier we'd counterattacked just outside a small village north of Odessa. Hanging from a tree were the mutilated remains of a young woman, a sign dangling from her neck: *Flintenwieb*. Gun-woman. She'd been stripped naked, her breasts cut off by the filthy bastards. That's why the second grenade.

Finally, I threw the strap of my rifle over my shoulder and headed for the door, stepping carefully over the sleeping forms on the floor. Outside the bunker, I shivered in the cool, sharp morning air, though I actually welcomed the change from the fetid atmosphere belowground. Above, the predawn sky was speckled with stars like fragments of mica in dark rock. At different points along the trench sentries stood watch behind the breastworks, facing north and east toward the German entrenchments below in the valley, in some places only a kilometer away. Nearby, Captain Petrenko sat on an empty ammo case, smoking a cigarette and talking with Zoya, who was squatting and arranging things in her pack.

"Good morning, Comrade," he said to me. "And how many will you get today?"

"That all depends, Captain," I said.

"On what?"

"On how foolishly the Fritzes behave."

The captain chuckled. He was a lean, muscular man, with a dusky complexion, broad face, and high cheekbones. Before the war he had been a chemist back in a factory in his native Georgia. I liked and respected Captain Petrenko. Soft-spoken, a man who never lost his temper or his composure, never complained, though he was a brave fighter and a good but cautious leader. He kept to himself, never shared much about his personal life. He wouldn't order his troops to do something he himself wouldn't do. And he refused to wantonly sacrifice their lives, unlike some of the field commanders who would do anything to curry favor with the higher-ups. Each death of one of his troops affected the captain deeply, and every time he had to write a *pokhoronka* letter home to the family of one of his soldiers, he would agonize over it. He not only supported my promotion to sergeant but had put my name in for the Order of the Red Banner.

"There's talk of another big push for the city," Captain Petrenko said to us.

"We've heard that before," I replied.

"There may be something to it this time."

"What have you heard?"

"That they've called up two more divisions. One armored," said Petrenko, taking a long drag on his cigarette.

"More big rumors."

"Not this time. Roskov said they captured a German officer. The NKVD boys got him to talk, the poor bastard."

I'd seen firsthand the *chekisty*'s methods of interrogating German prisoners. Back in Odessa, I'd had to report to the CO's headquarters once. Off in a corner of the room, they had a German soldier tied to a chair. He was a bloody mess, his wrists tied to the arms of the chair. Then I noticed several bloody hunks of what looked like sausages on the floor beneath him. They turned out to be his fingers, which had been hacked off, the pieces strewn about the floor like offal in a butcher's shop. His mouth had a gag stuffed in it, and his head was encircled by a belt and held immobile from behind by one of the two *chekisty* conducting the interrogation.

"This time," said Petrenko, "it looks as if the Germans are coming at us."

"We still have the navy to fend them off," I said. The Soviet Black Sea Fleet lay just twenty kilometers off the coast. It was their big guns that had largely been responsible for keeping the Germans at bay for the nine-month siege. Nonetheless, we were under no illusions. Von Manstein, the German commander, had nine full-strength divisions, plus three more Romanian divisions as well as heavy artillery and tanks. He had us completely surrounded, our backs to the sea. And we knew that Stalin had already written us off. We were fighting simply to give the Red Army elsewhere, in Stalingrad and Moscow, time to regroup, to establish defenses. We knew that Sevastopol was doomed, the army there merely cannon fodder to slow the German advance and to draw needed troops and matériel from other more important fronts. We knew this and yet we tried to believe it wasn't true.

"Sergeant," Captain Petrenko said to me, "you be careful out there. Anything happens to you, Roskov will have my neck."

"And here I thought you were just worried about my safety," I said.

"I'll make sure she's safe, Captain," Zoya offered.

"If those bastards didn't want anything to happen to her, then they should've pulled her from the front," Petrenko added.

"They want it both ways," Zoya said.

"Then they should've put her in some cushy desk job back in Moscow."

I found it odd how they spoke about me as if I weren't there, as if I were gone already. Or dead.

"But I don't *want* a cushy desk job," I interjected. "I want to stay here and fight."

You see, Zoya was right—they did want it both ways. The higher-ups, the military brass and the Party big shots, liked the propaganda value attached to my success as a sniper, but they didn't want me to get hurt again. They considered me too important to morale for anything to happen to me. The captain had heard rumors that they had "plans" for me, whatever that meant. With my growing reputation as a sniper, I'd become something of a poster girl for the Soviet military, a figure to rally our countrymen around. However, I didn't want all the fuss and attention, didn't want to be pulled away from my job of killing Germans. I wanted to reach my goal of 300.

I'd been pulled from the front once already, back when I'd reached two hundred kills during the early siege of Sevastopol the previous winter. From the Presidium of the Supreme Soviet, I was awarded the Order of the Red Banner, one of the country's highest military

honors, and one conferred on only a handful of women. I was drawing notice, making a name for myself, something for which I was
proud but which also made me a little uncomfortable. They were
going to send me off for a few days to Stalingrad; this, of course, was
before the Germans had arrived and turned it into hell. I didn't want
to go, but Zoya had told me, "Tat'yana, do you know how many would
give their right arm to sleep in a soft bed and be able to take a warm
bath." In Stalingrad, I was paraded around, placed on display like a
ballerina for the Bolshoi. I was gawked at and fawned over, patron-
ized by elderly Party officials smoking expensive cigars and eating
caviar, and drinking Belaya Bashnya vodka simply because that's the
brand Stalin drank, and carrying on as if there wasn't a war on at all.
I had to put up with toadying sycophants and sleazy opportunists who
knew nothing of battle, who would trivialize the bravery and sacrifice
of our soldiers for their own ends. "Comrade Levchenko," they would
ask of me, "how does one so lovely become such an accomplished
killer?" One reporter from *Izvestiya* called me "The Ukrainian Lion,"
after the famous thirteenth-century prince Lev Danilovich, known
for his ferocity. They interviewed me and took pictures of me with
Party officials and high-ranking generals of the Red Army. There I
met Chairman Kalinin, whom as children we had been taught by our
teachers to call *Dedushka*—grandfather—as well as Foreign Secretary
Molotov, and General Zhukov, who was at the moment preparing for
the defense of the city. They had me tour the Red October steelworks
and the Barrikady armaments factory, places that in just a few short
months would be the stage for the infamous "War of the Rats."

Just before dawn that day, the Germans attacked, the big offensive we'd
been expecting for weeks. It was preceded by a massive artillery bar-
rage, which lasted two hours. Luckily Zoya and I had been able to crawl
back to our lines. The krauts had unleashed their huge 800 mm Big
Dora, lobbing its massive five-thousand-kilo shells at us. Each one that
stuck within a kilometer deafened you for several minutes. In its wake,
all sound seemed to have been sucked away, the remaining silence as

profound as that underwater. This was followed by heavy aerial bombing from their Junkers and Heinkels. Our own antiaircraft guns lit up
the early morning sky, while offshore, the Black Sea Fleet responded
with its own guns. With my head pressed against the dirt of the trench,
I felt the earth shudder.

"They're coming this time," Captain Petrenko warned all along the
line. "Fix bayonets."

And he was right. When daylight came, the ground attack commenced.

Though we fought bravely that day, outnumbered and outgunned,
we ultimately had to retreat down the heights toward the outskirts of
the city. I saw firsthand some of our troops shot by our own blocking
detachments, machine-gunning those retreating from the German
advance. Still, over the next several days, the Germans pressed the
attack, slowly forcing us to fall back into Sevastopol itself. The enemy
advanced on all fronts, supported by its Panzers and artillery. However,
we made them pay heavily for each inch of ground we relinquished.
We fought savagely along the entire front, from Balaklava in the south
to Bel'bek and Kamyshi in the north. The staunch resistance we put
up was partly due to the fact that we were fighting in defense of our
own soil. Most of us were Ukrainians, and many came from Sevastopol itself. We fought for our homes, for our families, for our pride. But
we fought also because of the fear we had for the *chekisty*, who shot
those falling back.

I hardly recognized Sevastopol, which lay in ruins from the nine
months' seige. Save for the post office and a handful of other structures
that had somehow miraculously been spared during the bombing,
everything had been reduced to rubble. Entire blocks were little more
than charred and empty shells. The roads were pitted with bomb craters
and strewn with debris from collapsed buildings. The smoke from fires
hung above the city, raining a gritty ash down on everything. The grand
old buildings along Grafskaya Quay, the House of the Pioneers, the Sea-
side Parkway, Nahimova Square—all the places I had once visited on
holiday were utterly demolished. The sight saddened me, no doubt
because of all the memories I'd had of the city, coming here first as a

child with my parents, then after I was married with Kolya and Masha.

The city's remaining inhabitants scurried through the bombed-out streets, pallid figures, lifeless as ghosts. For months, those Sevastopolians who hadn't been lucky enough to escape or die had eked out an existence in the cellars and sewers. They'd lived on scraps of food, on the garbage dumps of the troops, on dead fish that the bombing had washed up on shore, on pigeons and seagulls and crows, on rats, even on dogs. The summer temperatures had hit one hundred degrees, forcing people out into the open in search of water. As our unit moved through the city, several emaciated children emerged from a sewer and came running up, begging for food and something to drink. As it turned out, they were from an orphanage that had been bombed, and they had been huddled together underground for weeks without an adult's supervision. We gave what we could spare, which wasn't much, as we'd been on half rations ourselves. I saw the bodies of the dead lying where they'd been killed, rotting in the streets or alleyways or left among the wreckage of buildings. An old and emaciated man pushing a wheelbarrow passed by with a pair of shapes wrapped in winding clothes. He paused for a moment when he saw us. "Look what those whores did to my children," he cried. My heart, of course, went out to him. "We will make them pay, *dedushka*," I offered to him.

Down at the harbor we saw them frantically loading ships with vehicles and munitions and other matériel. It was obvious now that the higher-ups considered the battle for Sevastopol utterly lost. Most of us hoped that he or she would be one of the lucky few to get a spot on a ship leaving this hellhole. There were some who even purposely wounded themselves so they could get transferred out on a hospital ship. Though even that wasn't entirely without risk. Fewer and fewer ships were getting through the heavy bombing by the Luftwaffe over the Black Sea. We'd all heard of the sinking of the *Armenia,* a Red Cross ship carrying wounded and civilians, near Gurzuf. Over five thousand went to a watery grave.

Rumors, as they always do in war, circulated as to what would happen to those left behind. The optimists said there would be reinforcements coming from the Soviet Forty-fourth or Forty-seventh up north, and that we just had to hold out until they could reach us. Others said that the navy was sending transport ships to evacuate the remaining troops. After all, they couldn't just sacrifice the hundred thousand remaining troops, could they, this despite the fact that we knew that in Kiev they had let six hundred thousand troops fall into German hands? Everyone wondered how long we could hold out, with supplies and ammunition and food growing short. Despite hearing about units fighting to the last man, word also spread of entire battalions, sometimes even regiment or brigade levels, surrendering to the Germans. Soldiers debated whether it was better to die fighting or to take their chances as prisoners, and many had already written letters home saying their good-byes to loved ones.

After an intense day of fighting, what remained of my company had pulled back yet again and taken up position in the wreckage of a marine engine factory down near the quay. Though the roof had caved in, most of the walls were still relatively intact, providing us with enough cover to dig in and make a last-ditch defense. Not fifty meters behind us was the sea. The stench of burning oil hung heavily in the air from a tanker ship that the Luftwaffe had hit out in the harbor. Dense black smoke drifted in, stinging our eyes.

A half-dozen soldiers from my unit had dug in behind what had once been a loading dock of the factory. From there, two hundred meters to the east we could see where the Germans had taken refuge in a bombed-out building, and beyond along the hills overlooking the water.

To our rear, several four-wheel GAZ vehicles drove past, bouncing over the craters in the road. They passed close enough that we could see the officers inside. They avoided our gazes. All were being chauffeured down toward the docks and rescue.

"Sons of bitches," Drubich complained, waving a fist in the air. He was crumbling cigarette butts he'd scrounged from off the ground and using the tobacco to roll himself a cigarette. For paper he used propaganda leaflets the Germans had begun dropping from the skies, telling us in bad Russian that if we surrendered we would be treated fairly, be given food and vodka.

"If you could save your neck, wouldn't you do the same?" replied a soldier named Ivanchuk, a big man with a pink, swollen face like the udder of an unmilked cow. He was loading a captured *Maschinengewehr*.

"We have to stay and die, while those bastards get evacuated," said Drubich.

"They could give a shit about us," Ivanchuk scoffed.

"I heard the old man wouldn't even ransom his own son," said another soldier named Polevoi, a signalman.

The old man, of course, was Stalin. His son had been captured by the Germans, and Stalin had refused to trade a captured German soldier for him.

"So why would he care what happens to us?" added Ivanchuk.

Drubich glanced over his shoulder, then in an undertone said, "We could surrender."

"Do you know what the krauts do to those they capture?" replied Ivanchuk. He made his right index finger into the barrel of a gun, put it to his temple, and said, "Bang!"

"Kill all of us? I don't believe it," countered Drubich.

"Believe it."

"I have a wife and baby. I want to see them again. Even the krauts can't be such monsters."

"They're worse than monsters," scoffed Ivanchuk. "And if you're not afraid of them, you'd better be afraid of our own side. At least for your family's sake."

"What're you talking about?"

"Those that surrender, their families *fttt*," he said, making a slashing motion across his throat.

"What?" cried Drubich.

"They're sent to the camps. Or worse."

"That's bullshit."

"It's true. So before you go surrendering, Drubich, you ought to think about that wife and kid of yours."

"Let Roskov catch you talking like that, Drubich," said Polevoi, "he'll shoot you even before the Nazis have a chance."

Several of the soldiers laughed nervously, that sort of hollow gallows laughter.

Lowering his voice and glancing over his shoulder, Drubich said, "And where the hell is Roskov, anyway? Has anybody seen him lately?"

"Maybe he was shot," Polevoi joked.

"We should be so lucky," replied Ivanchuk.

"Why should we be sacrificed?" said Drubich, his tone that of a petulant child. "Besides, how could the krauts kill a hundred thousand prisoners. They couldn't kill that many. Not if we surrendered." He turned toward me. "What do you think, Sergeant?"

"Nothing the Germans do anymore surprises me," I replied.

"So we are to fight and die for those bastards?" he said, flicking his thumb toward the road where the officers had just passed.

"No, not for them," I replied. "We fight for ourselves."

"Why the hell should we?"

"Because no one else will, that's why."

"So they can give you more medals, Sergeant?" Drubich said bitterly to me.

"I never wanted any medals," I replied.

"The rest of us fight and die, and she's the one who gets the credit."

"All right, Drubich," said the captain, "that'll be enough." He glanced over at me.

"I don't mind fighting," Drubich offered. "But this is crazy."

"It's all crazy," said Ivanchuk. "The whole fuckin' mess."

"I have a family," Drubich continued. "I don't want to die like this."

"Stop your fucking bellyaching," said the Wild Boar, who had been sitting quietly a short distance away smoking a cigarette.

"I didn't sign up to be slaughtered like cattle."

"I told you to shut the fuck up," grunted the Wild Boar. He pulled his Tokarev from his holster and pointed it at Drubich. "I should shoot you myself and save the krauts a bullet."

Drubich looked warily at the Wild Boar, then at Captain Petrenko. "I was just talking."

The Wild Boar didn't say anything but kept the gun trained on Drubich. He had a crazed look in his eyes. For a moment I wasn't sure whether he would do it or not.

Then Captain Petrenko said, "Put it away, Sergeant."

Finally, the Wild Boar lowered the gun and stuffed it into his holster.

Thousands of our troops, though, *had* already made the choice to surrender as the Germans tightened the noose around the city. I certainly didn't want to die, but the thought of surrendering was even more abhorrent. I'd heard what the Germans did to those who surrendered, especially to women. I wasn't sure I wanted to take the chance. Still, like the others, I felt betrayed by the Soviet high command. That they were so willing to let us all die here. And for what?

During a quiet moment, I scribbled a note to Kolya, more words tossed into the howling storm.

> My Dearest Kolya,
>
> We have fought hard and with great determination in the defense of Sevastopol. But it is now quite apparent that we shall soon be forced to admit defeat. I do not know what will become of us, or if I shall ever see you again, but you are in my thoughts. If I die, at least I can hope we will all be reunited in heaven.
>
> I pray you are safe. Take care of yourself. Please remember me always.
>
> I remain your loving wife,
>
> Tat'yana

As I wrote these words, the distance that I felt toward Kolya seemed suddenly unimportant, even trivial. My heart welled up with emotion. I felt very much the loving wife I'd portrayed in the letter, a wife who, if the war had ended right then, would gladly have returned to her husband, would have considered myself fortunate to be able to live the rest of my days with him, sleeping beside him, reading to each other, growing old in his company. With death looming so close, everything appeared suddenly very clear. All the details of my past with Kolya came rushing back to me—his gentleness of spirit, his quiet intelligence, the way his blond hair fell into his face, the pale blueness of his eyes. How, as he left for work in the morning, he'd gently cup my face as I slept and say, "I love you, Tat'yana." His love was something I'd taken for granted in the past. Can love sit dormant in a heart like a seed, I mused, until a moment like this, when it breaks out of its shell and begins to grow? I recall thinking then that it had taken a war for me to realize this. Of course, the irony was that I realized this only when it was too late.

I managed to give the letter to a wounded comrade who was being evacuated by submarine.

As night fell, Captain Petrenko gathered the company together.

"I don't have to tell you the fix we're in, comrades," he said in his usual even tone. "But I've got orders to hold this position."

"For how long?" asked the Wild Boar.

"We are to hold it, period."

A low grumbling began among the troops.

Finally the Wild Boar said what was on everyone's mind. "So those fuckin' *predateli* can sneak out in the middle of the night."

Another soldier said, "Yes, they are traitors to leave us while they scatter like chickens."

"General Petrov should be held accountable," a third cried.

Petrov was the general in charge of Sevastopol's defense.

"All right, shut up," Petrenko said. "It doesn't do any good to whine about any of this now."

"When can we expect reinforcements?" I asked the captain.

"There won't be any."

"None?"

"That's right. Look, I don't like this any more than you do."

"We could attempt to break through the German lines," offered a corporal named Timoshenko, a slight man who had the dark glossy hair of a crow.

"To where?" Petrenko replied. "The entire Crimea has fallen into German hands."

"The only option then is surrender," Drubich called out. There was a momentary silence, the startled sort, like that after a plate crashes to the floor while people are eating dinner. Then several soldiers followed this up with "he's right" and "why not?" One man shouted, "Why should we just sit here and wait to be slaughtered by their Panzers?"

Petrenko looked around at the troops. "I have my orders," he said.

"Where's Major Roskov anyway?" one soldier shouted tentatively.

Another chimed in with "Yes, where the hell is he?"

"He's already been evacuated," the captain replied.

"Wouldn't you know it," Timoshenko cried.

Growing bolder, someone else cursed, "The gutless prick." Then a chorus of taunts ridiculed the once-feared *chekist* officer.

"I'm in charge now," Petrenko explained.

"Maybe Drubich's right," said another soldier. "To continue fighting is crazy."

A few shouted out in agreement, while others called the group advocating surrender traitors. They went back and forth, their voices growing heated.

"All right, quiet down," said Petrenko, raising his hands for silence. "If any soldier decides to surrender, I won't stop him. Each of you will have to make that decision for yourselves. But I should warn you, the krauts are as likely to shoot you as not."

That seemed to sober them. After a while the grumbling died down. One soldier, the young sniper named Cheburko, said, "We might as well die fighting the bastards."

Several followed this with "He's right" or "Let's die like soldiers."

Afterward, we sat in the growing darkness. Some cleaned their weapons or counted their rounds, while others scribbled letters by candlelight. All of us knew that we had reached the end of the line, that there would be no more retreats, no more tomorrows. That this was it. Then someone began to hum the melody for "Katyusha." Soon others joined in and they began to sing the words:

> *Apple and pear trees were a-blooming.*
> *Mist was creeping on the river,*
> *Katyusha set out on the banks,*
> *On the steep and lofty banks.*
> *She was walking, singing a song*
> *About her true love,*
> *Whose letters she was keeping.*

Petrenko approached me and whispered, "A word, Sergeant."

I followed him into a small room at the far end of the building, one that looked as if it had been a boiler room.

"They want you out," he said.

"What do you mean 'out'?"

"The higher-ups. They want you on the next submarine out of here."

"Why?" I asked, though of course I knew.

"They don't want anything to happen to you."

"I can't leave," I cried. "Not now."

I was neither a fool nor a hero. I didn't want to stay and die. But I also didn't want to abandon my comrades. I thought of what Drubich had said about my being given special treatment. To him and the others this would only confirm that.

"You don't have a choice, Sergeant. It's an order."

"When?" I asked.

Petrenko took a long drag on his cigarette. "Some time tomorrow. A sub is to arrive. You're to be on it."

"What of the rest?"

He smiled sadly. "We're fucked."

"What if I refuse to go?"

The captain shook his head. "This comes straight from the top. Hell, anybody else would give his right arm to be out of this shit hole. But you, you want to stay." Petrenko let out with a brittle laugh.

"I merely want to fight like everyone else."

"Don't worry. You've done more than your share of fighting." Petrenko's face glowed orange as he took another pull on the cigarette. He reached out and laid his hand on my shoulder. "Sometimes, Sergeant, we can serve best indirectly. They have big plans for you."

"Plans?" I said. "What have you heard, Captain?"

He smiled at me. Instead of answering my question, he said, "There will be other chances to fight them. And other means."

I nodded, though I didn't really believe it. You fought those bastards by putting a bullet into their flesh, by killing them before they killed you. Still, I couldn't blame Petrenko. I knew it wasn't his fault. He had been a good unit commander.

"It was an honor serving with you, Captain," I said.

"The same goes for you, Sergeant."

He offered me his hand. "Good luck, Sergeant," he said.

"Thank you, Captain. You too."

"By the way," he said, reaching into his jacket and bringing out a letter. "If you get out, could you see that this gets posted. It's to my wife."

"I will."

The submarine I was to depart on didn't arrive the next day or the day after that either. Few ships were getting past the Luftwaffe. On the third morning, at daybreak, the Germans launched what was to prove their final assault. They pounded us with mortars and artillery as well as with tanks they'd maneuvered up onto the high ground overlooking the harbor. Our company was pinned down beneath heavy automatic weapons fire, and a German sniper had taken up a position on our right flank, somewhere up above us in the rubble of buildings. From that vantage point he had already killed three soldiers. The second had been a runner Captain Petrenko had sent to the Fourth Company on our right flank asking if they had any ammo they could spare. He hadn't made it ten meters before the sniper cut him down. And when another soldier had crawled out to help him, the sniper had killed him as well.

"We must do something," Zoya said.

"We don't even know where he is," I replied. For hours we'd been scoping the bombed-out shells of the buildings above us, trying to locate him but without success.

Then I felt Zoya tugging on my sleeve.

"Look," she said. She was pointing at a shallow ditch that ran along to our right. Draining into it some fifty meters away was a narrow sewer pipe that angled sharply up toward the high ground above. "I wonder where that leads?"

I looked at the pipe, then glassed the area above it, all the way up the hill past the German lines. The landscape was mostly covered with debris from buildings destroyed in the bombing.

"If we could crawl through that pipe," Zoya said, "maybe we could flank him."

I considered it for a moment. We had to try something.

"Come on. Let's talk with the captain," I said.

We crawled over to Petrenko, who was talking with two of his unit leaders.

"Excuse me, Captain," I said. "But if we don't stop that sniper he'll cut us to pieces."

"So what do you suggest, Sergeant?" he said.

I told him of Zoya's plan.

"You don't know where that sewer goes," he said. "Besides, they might have mined it already."

"We have to do something. We can't just sit here."

His dark, broad face took on a brooding expression. Finally, he turned to Zoya. "Corporal," he said, "go find Cheburko and the two of you investigate it."

"No," I said.

Petrenko glared at me. "What?"

"Sorry, sir. But I should be the one to go."

"I'll say who goes."

"But I'm your best marksman."

He rubbed the stubble on his cheek. "You're supposed to be on that ship out of here."

"Captain, we don't know when it's coming. Or even *if* it's coming."

Petrenko mulled this over for a moment. Then he said, "All right. But be careful, you hear me?"

Under covering fire, we crawled down into the drainage ditch, with Zoya as always in the lead. Keeping low, we dragged ourselves through the slimy muck, our weapons draped over our shoulders. The ditch smelled rankly of sewage and raw earth. The foul smell sickened me, but I was able to push the sensation away and focus on the job at hand.

When we reached the pipe, which was two feet above the ditch, we cautiously pulled ourselves up into it. The sides were slick, and given the pipe's upward angle, we found the going hard. We kept slipping and had to wedge our boots or fingers in any crack or crevice we could manage to pull ourselves forward. The pipe was hardly wide enough to squeeze our shoulders through, and we had to crawl on our bellies. It was dark, and it grew progressively darker as we went along. After a while, Zoya had to take out her electric torch in order to light the way. Soon the sewer opened up a little so we could now move on all fours. We came to a Y where the tunnel divided to the right and left, and we had to decide which way to go. Zoya mumbled something, a kind of prayer. Finally she said, "This way," and took the route to our left.

We'd been crawling through the tunnel for a while when Zoya suddenly stopped. Up ahead, in the glare of the electric torch, we saw a sudden movement. With one hand, Zoya swung her machine gun around, but before she could fire, I cried, "Wait."

A pair of eyes nearly hidden behind a tangled mass of hair stared back at us. It was a little girl, perhaps six years old. Yet she was so filthy and bedraggled she hardly resembled a child at all. As we started toward her, she suddenly turned and began to scurry away from us.

"Hold on," I called to her. "We're Soviet soldiers."

The girl stopped and looked uncertainly over her shoulder at us. "It's all right. We're not Germans," said Zoya. The child still appeared ready to bolt.

"Come, little one," I pleaded. "You have nothing to fear from us."

Slowly, she turned and started crawling toward us. When she'd gotten to within a few feet, she stopped, her small, dirty hand trying to block the light of Zoya's torch. I saw that she had long hair whose color could not be deciphered because of its filth, hair that fell across her emaciated face in straggly lines. Her pipe-thin arms were befouled, her dress torn and soiled. Her shoes, far too big for her feet, were obviously some pair she'd scrounged up somewhere or other. And yet, beneath the filth, I could see that she was a pretty child, with large, dark eyes and white teeth, which glistened in the light. She huddled with her scrawny arms wrapped around knees scraped raw from crawling about the sewers. She was older than she'd first appeared, perhaps eight or nine, and yet she had the weary eyes of an old person.

Zoya asked, "What's your name, little one?"

The girl hesitated, then said, "Raisa."

"How long have you been down here, Raisa?" I asked.

In reply, she lifted her thin shoulders. "I don't know."

"Where are your parents?"

She brought her dirty hand to her face and pulled a strand of hair behind her ear. "Mama was killed early in the war. Tato went off one morning to look for food. But he didn't return. Then I went down here. There used to be others but they died."

I reached out and stroked her hair. "Are you hungry?"

The girl nodded. From my tunic I took out a piece of hard bread wrapped in brown paper and gave it to her. She tore into it.

Zoya turned to me. "What are we going to do with her, Sergeant?"

I thought for a moment. Finally, I said, "You bring her back to camp."

"What about you?"

"I have to try to get the sniper." Then to the girl, I said, "Go with her, Raisa." I turned back to Zoya. "Give me your grenade and your torch."

Zoya handed them over, then hugged me. "Don't be a hero," she told me.

"I'll see you back in camp."

Then to the girl, Zoya said, "Follow me, little one." She turned and started back the way we'd come.

The girl hesitated, though, staring at me.

"It will be all right, I promise," I said. I reached out and stroked the girl's cheek. At this, she literally leapt into my arms. I could feel the sharp bones beneath her clothing, her small, trembling body. She clung to me with such desperation, such need. And I, who hadn't held a child in so long, clung to her with equal desperation. I kissed the top of her head, remembering how I used to do that with my own daughter. And for a moment it was as if I *had* Masha back in my arms again. "It's all right, Raisa," I said as I rocked her.

"Perhaps you should return with us, Sergeant?" Zoya asked.

"No, you take her back. And don't let anything happen to her," I said, recalling what Kolya had told me that day at the train station.

"I won't. Good luck, Tat'yana."

Then to the little girl, I said, "Go now. You'll be safe with Zoya." Only then did she relax her grip on me and follow Zoya down the tunnel.

With that I turned and continued on my way. The sewer grew gradually lighter, so that soon I could turn off the torch. Rounding a bend, I saw up ahead a broad bar of sunlight streaming down into the sewer. As I neared the spot, I removed my pistol. Cautiously, I peered up. Overhead a dozen feet or so, I saw a piece of blue sky, bisected by a splintered wooden beam that lay across the opening. I climbed metal rungs built into the side of the wall. Near the top I waited for my eyes to adjust to the harsh brightness. Not far away, I could hear the incessant *tat-tat-tat* of machine-gun fire, the *thwonk* of mortars, the deafening blasts from their Panzers. More distantly I could make out a German voice, someone barking orders. Cautiously, I shoved the beam aside and inched my shoulders through and peeked over the top of the manhole. It was sheltered by debris, fallen timbers, bricks and plaster from a wall that had collapsed around it. I pushed some of the wreckage aside and climbed up farther. To the west, I saw the sea glistening under the midday sun, while to the northeast, well up on the hill, I made out the muzzle of a German tank poking out from beneath camouflage netting. Directly ahead of me, though, were the remains of a brick wall, which blocked my view of the German lines below. I carefully lifted myself out of the hole and crawled over the debris to it. Slowly, I peered over the jagged top of the wall.

To my surprise, I'd come out some fifty meters behind the enemy positions. Below me, I saw two Germans in a foxhole, their backs exposed to me. One was firing a machine gun toward our lines, the other feeding the belt. Beyond them I saw more Germans dug in all along the crest of the hill, what looked like an entire battalion. I made a quick scan of the area, looking for the sniper's position, then got out my field glasses and carefully glassed the area below me. Nothing. I continued looking. Still nothing. I could keep searching, hoping to find him, or I could take what was given to me. I decided on the latter course. Slowly, I slid the barrel of my rifle through a crack in the wall.

I shot the machine gunner first; then, before his assistant knew what had happened, I shot him too, both in the back. I moved down the line toward the other Germans in the trench. I shot a soldier smoking a cigarette. Then a man loading a mortar. When his companion reached for his rifle, I shot him too. I continued down the line and shot three more men. It was like shooting targets at the range. I wasn't thinking, just acting on instinct, a soldier's instinct. I had no fear. I figured my life was already over and I thought only of killing as many as I could before I died.

The Germans now were in a wild state of panic, scurrying about, trying to find the direction from which the fire was raining down upon them. I'd reloaded and was able to kill four more before the krauts finally realized it was coming from behind them, and then they swung around and began to return fire. I had to duck down behind the wall as rounds zipped overhead and sent fragments of bricks and red dust raining down on me. At least one machine gun had opened up on my position. I took out a grenade and tossed it down the hill, more simply to create a diversion. I used the explosion to crawl east along the wall for twenty-five meters, so as not to present the same target. Besides my remaining grenade, I had only four rounds left. Cautiously I peered through debris covering what had once been a window. With my field glasses, I scanned the area below and to the west. Still nothing. The Germans continued to lay down a murderous fire, and I was about to abandon the mission, turn and make my way back to the sewer, when something caught my eye. About seventy-five meters away, in what was left of a stairwell of a building, two stories off the ground, I saw the telltale glint of sunlight off metal. When I looked more closely I recognized it as a rifle barrel, then a scope. As I continued to inspect it, I was able to make out a hand attached to the rifle, next a finger wrapped around a trigger, and finally, behind that, the crest of a field cap projecting just above some bricks. *There he was. My sniper.*

Doubtless he'd heard the commotion and had swung around and was searching behind the German lines. Searching for *me*. In fact, the barrel seemed aimed right at me. Had he spotted me? I wondered. Should I make a run for it? Instead, recalling the time I'd been caught in the tree, I decided to take my chances and remain perfectly still. I waited for the bullet that would slam into me, but after a moment, I saw him move his scope to my right, up the hill, hunting. This gave me all the opportunity I needed. I slowly brought my rifle up and into position. He didn't present much of a target. Just the top half of his field cap. That would have to be enough. I flicked the safety off and took aim at a point just below the crest of the hat. I breathed in, blew out, breathed in again and held my breath. Then I fired. I could feel the bullet strike home even before I saw the spray of blood against the wall behind him, saw the rifle barrel drop from the hand that held it and fall to the ground below.

Though I didn't know it then, it would be my last kill.

The others now knew my position and started to fire on me. I returned fire until I ran out of ammo, then took out my pistol and shot until it was empty too. At that point, I got up and, in a crouch, started running back toward the sewer. That's when I heard the familiar, high-pitched scream of a mortar descending to earth. I didn't hear the blast—one never does—but felt myself pitched forward and then slammed headlong into the ground. I lay there momentarily on my side, dazed, my ears ringing, the coppery taste of blood in my mouth. My teeth felt loose from the impact. Turning my head slightly, I saw a jagged piece of blue sky off by itself, as if the sky too had been shattered by the blast. I stared at it with a vague curiosity. My right arm lay beneath me, at an odd angle. Yet I didn't feel any pain. I didn't feel much of anything, in fact. There was a burning low in my belly, the sensation of something warm running down along my side, soaking my tunic. Then I heard muffled voices. I couldn't tell whether they were speaking German or Russian, but I knew they were getting nearer. Get up, I told myself. Get up or you will die. Despite this warning, I didn't move. I felt so tired, so weary suddenly, as if all the fighting and killing, all the war, had only now caught up with me. I just wanted to close my eyes and sleep for a long while.

Yet I was aware enough to know I didn't want to be captured. I turned my head and searched the ground for my rifle, but with my right arm immobile the weapon, I knew, would be useless anyway. Then I remembered the remaining grenade. With my left hand I grasped it and brought it up to my mouth so I could pull the pin with my teeth. I would wait for them to come close, close enough so that I could take some of them with me. I found the feel of the grenade in my hand strangely comforting. Above, the segment of blue sky wavered and began to darken.

So this was how it would be, I thought. Oddly, I didn't fear death. In fact, in some ways I almost welcomed it. If there was a life after this, I thought, I would be reunited with my baby. And if not, at least I would no longer have to live without her. The last image I had was of her running along the beach, as in that dream. Her blond hair bouncing, her legs churning. *Mama,* she called to me. *Mama.*

5

I n the claustrophobic darkness, the first thing I became aware of was the moaning, the lonely terror of a body in pain. It came, I realized, from directly above me. A man's voice, though fragile and petulant as a child's. And then I recognized the odor. I'd smelled it back in Odessa, in the bombed-out buildings of Sevastopol, in all those places where they hadn't a chance to bury the dead. The rankness of corruption, the foul stench of flesh gone bad. It surrounded me in the darkness, made me almost want to retch.

I felt groggy, my thoughts sluggish and disoriented, my head aching dully. I glanced at my right arm, seemingly frozen from shoulder to wrist. A strange and heavy armor appeared to cover it. It seemed to glow in the darkness, white as a bone left exposed to the sun. With my free hand I reached over and touched the surface, which had a pleasing smoothness to it. As I moved my free arm I became aware of the long, slender snake whose fangs were sunk into the back of my left hand. Curious, I followed the snake to where its tail was attached to a bag dangling over my bunk. The movement brought about a stabbing pain low in my belly. I tried to lie still, hoping it would go away. As I lay there, I slowly became aware of another sensation—a feeling of being in motion, moving, gliding through the darkness. It was an unsettling sensation, like that of falling in a dream.

"Oaaah," came the moaning again. I heard someone pound the

bunk above me with a fist. "For Christ's sakes, I can't take it anymore," he called out.

From somewhere else in the darkness another voice cursed back: "Shut the hell up."

"Fuck you."

"We're all in pain. If you don't shut up, I'll come over there and wring your goddamned neck."

With that, the man in the bunk above me quieted down for a while.

Slowly coming to, I glanced around the narrow, cavelike room, with its low ceiling and concave walls, which seemed to press inward. As my eyesight adjusted to the darkness, I could make out double bunks lining each side of it, with only a small space dividing the upper and lower rows. Bodies lay on the bunks. I saw an arm draped loosely over the edge, a pale leg drawn up, the white incandescent glow of dressings. The armor on my arm, I realized, was merely a cast; the snake in my hand an IV. Occasionally someone coughed or groaned, while others snored. The man above me leaned over the side of the bunk, only the outline of his shaggy head visible.

"Ssp. Are you awake?" he whispered.

"Yes," I replied.

"Did they give you your meds yet?"

I had to think for a moment. "I don't know," I told him.

"My leg is killing me. Do you hear me, you bastards?" he cried out again.

"I'm warning you," came the other voice once more.

Besides the ache in my belly, there was a faint ringing in my ears, like frozen leaves making a tinkling sound in the winter wind. Things slowly, grudgingly returned to me. Every time I woke it was like this. I had to start from scratch, put what had happened back in place again—my memory like a large, complicated jigsaw puzzle I'd worked hard to piece together, only to find it scattered on waking. I remembered climbing through the sewer with Zoya. Finding the little girl down there. Shooting the Germans in the trench and finally getting the sniper. Then running and being thrown by the explosion. Lying on the ground, unable to move, the piece of blue sky hanging overhead. Clutching the grenade, waiting for the Germans to come. And then, right before I lost consciousness, thinking of my daughter. I remembered all that. The rest since then was just loose bits and pieces scattered in my head. Coming to for a few minutes, occasionally seeing the strangely familiar face of someone leaning over me, adjusting the IV, the cries and moans of those around me. Then more darkness and that odd sense of movement, of slipping through space and time.

"Christ, how do they expect me to stand this," the man hollered again.

After a time someone did come by to check on us. A small, thin man, he carried an electric torch in one hand, while in the other he had a metal box with supplies—dressings and bandages, syringes and vials of medicine.

"It's about time," the man in the bunk above me cried.

"Stop your bellyaching," the small man told him. His voice was one I'd heard before, but I couldn't make out his face behind the bright light of the torch. The medic checked the man's vitals, then drew him a shot of something from a small vial. "There," he said. "That should shut you up for a while."

Soon the man did quiet down, and in short order he was snoring lightly.

Then the medic squatted beside my bunk.

"How are you feeling, Sergeant?" he asked.

And then it came to me. "Yuri?" I replied. It was Yuri Sokur, our medic.

"That's right."

"You made it out?"

"By the skin of my teeth," he joked. "And how's our famous patient doing?"

"My stomach hurts."

He nodded. "You had yourself a very serious injury, Sergeant."

He took my pulse and listened to my heart, then fiddled with the IV.

"What's the matter with him?" I asked, pointing toward the bunk above me.

"Lost a foot. Now the leg's going bad," Yuri explained with the practiced callousness of those who'd seen a lot of suffering. He sniffed. "Can't you smell it? Let's have a look at you, Sergeant."

He carefully lifted the bandage on my stomach and inspected my wound, an ugly, jagged T that ran from just to the right of my navel down to the line of my pubic bone, then at right angles across my lower belly. On either side of the wound, the skin was bruised a dark wine color and puckered from the many stitches. There was crusted blood along the length of it. And it smelled too.

"This will hurt a little," he explained as he cleaned the wound with carbolic acid.

He was right—it did hurt. But not a little. I winced as he worked. "Jesus!"

"Sorry. I can give you something for the pain."

"Where are we?" I asked as he readied a syringe.

"In the Black Sea."

"How long have I been here?"

"Three days. Maybe four."

He explained how I was transferred to the sub with a group of wounded from a makeshift field hospital in Sevastopol. Now we were headed for the Caucasus.

"I think I recall asking you all this before."

"That's all right," he said, smiling good-naturedly. "You've been in and out."

He started to rub alcohol on my arm. Before he would shoot me up with morphine, I said, "Wait. How did I get out?"

"I don't know. All hell broke loose those last few days. I was pulled out to help with the wounded on the sub."

I tried to sit up, but he stopped me. "Easy. You don't want to open your wound."

"What happened to the rest of our unit?"

"Gone," was all he said.

"Gone? Did anyone get out?"

"Cheburko," he said.

"That's it. What of Corporal Kovshova?"

He shrugged. "I only know that the Germans took the city."

"How many were they able to evacuate?"

"A handful."

"Out of a hundred thousand troops!" I exclaimed. "What of the rest?"

Yuri shook his head. "You were one of the last to be evacuated. Count yourself lucky."

At this, I felt a great sadness settle over me. I thought of Zoya, of Captain Petrenko, of the others in my unit. All those with whom I'd fought and suffered and endured that hellhole for nine months—gone.

"My things?" I said. "I had a case with some pictures. Personal effects."

"I don't know about any of that."

Then I remembered the girl we'd found in the sewer.

"There was a little girl we came upon in the sewer. She returned with Corporal Kovshova. Do you know what happened to her?"

Yuri shook his head. I closed my eyes to keep from crying.

"You have nothing to be ashamed of, Sergeant," he offered.

"I should be back there with them," I said.

"What good would that do anyone?" Then, trying to cheer me, Yuri said, "You have made the entire nation very proud of you."

"What are you talking about?"

"The name Tat'yana Levchenko is on everyone's lips. Wait." Yuri held up a finger and hurried off. He returned in a moment carrying a copy of *Krasny Chernomorets*, the newspaper of the Black Sea Fleet. "See," he said, shining his torch on the front page. There was my picture. The headline read, "Woman Sniper Reaches 300 Fascist Kills."

"You are a national hero," Yuri exclaimed.

I'd forgotten about all that, my goal of reaching three hundred kills. At one time such an accomplishment would have made me proud. Now it didn't matter in the least. In fact, it seemed mere vanity. What I had done was meaningless, knowing that my comrades were prisoners, or worse. That Zoya was gone. And then I wondered how they'd arrived at that 300 figure. I'd talked to no one, and there had been no witnesses to my last dozen kills. Where had they got it? Probably, I thought, just made it up out of whole cloth, the way the Soviet propaganda usually did.

"When I am an old man," Yuri said, "I will tell my grandchildren that I knew the great sniper, Tat'yana Levchenko."

Then he rubbed my arm with alcohol and slid the needle into my flesh. I felt the prick, followed by the cool, intoxicating rush of the morphine. Soon I was drifting on a warm wave in a bright green sea. I dreamed of starfish and mermaids.

Except for once when we surfaced and were dive-bombed by German planes, the trip across the Black Sea was uneventful. Yet I was hardly aware of the passage of time, spending most of my days dozing fitfully in an unsettled world of shifting darkness. What sleep I did manage was continually interrupted by the cries of the wounded around me or by my own pain, which sometimes seemed like a large hand grabbing me around the belly and shaking me to consciousness. Yuri would then stop by and give me another shot of morphine, and I would sink back down into that darkness again. However, as I started to improve a bit, from somewhere he scrounged up a frayed copy of *Eugene Onegin,* hoping a book would prove a healthy distraction for me. Yet the story of the dilettante Onegin and the strange relationship he had with his beloved, ironically a woman named Tat'yana, held little interest for me now. My mind wandered, and the ringing in my ears distracted me. I felt depressed, filled with black thoughts. At odd moments, I found myself weeping. Through all the months of fighting, I'd never felt this way. The momentum of war, the simple acts of fighting, of surviving each day—those things had kept at bay what I was feeling now. But now I wept inconsolably—for my lost comrades, for Zoya and Captain Petrenko. For the little girl Raisa. For my parents. Most of all, I wept for my daughter. I guess because of the war I hadn't had a chance to properly mourn her passing. The hatred—and perhaps too my guilt—had so filled me that there wasn't room for anything else. Now in the darkness of my bunk, I felt her death as if it had happened only yesterday. I couldn't get the image of those last few moments of her life out of my head. Her calling to me, running toward me. The bullets tearing into her tiny body. How I had watched the spot that was her grave fade into the anonymous vastness of the countryside. Suddenly, I just felt so terribly sad.

Some of the wounded as well as a number of the sailors stopped by my bunk to see how I was doing. They treated me deferentially, as if I were someone famous. One of the wounded was Cheburko, the young sniper from my unit. With a mop handle, he hobbled about on one leg. He pulled up a stool beside my bunk and sat down.

"How are you feeling, Sergeant?" he asked.

"A little better. You wouldn't happen to have a cigarette?"

From his pocket he took out a pack and gave me one, then struck a match and lit it for me.

"Would you know what happened to Second Company?"

He shook his head.

"It was crazy. We ran out of ammo and were fighting the krauts with bayonets."

"How did you manage to get out?" I asked.

He shrugged, glancing down at his missing leg. From his coat pocket, Cheburko took out a small flask and handed it to me. I took a sip of watered-down vodka and handed the flask back to him. The vodka didn't even burn the throat going down, it was so weak. "*Za zdorov'ye*," I said.

"*Za zdorov'ye*," he said, taking a sip. "To a lot of good soldiers." He glanced over his shoulder, then whispered, "Good soldiers stayed and died while those fucking officers took to their heels. An entire army gone like *that*," he said, snapping his fingers.

Cheburko looked down at his missing leg, as if he couldn't quite believe it was actually gone, as if it might still reappear and he'd be whole again. "I guess it's a small price to pay. Now I can go home to my family. How about you?"

"I don't know. As soon as I'm well enough, I'd like to get back to my unit."

"There is no unit, Sergeant. They're all gone."

We reached port finally, a small town on the Georgian coast. As I was carried off the sub, I saw sunlight for the first time in weeks. An even stranger sight accosted me—a landscape that hadn't yet been touched by war. The town's streets weren't pockmarked with craters and the buildings were unscathed. Along with the other wounded soldiers, I was loaded onto a rickety twin engine Yakovlev transport plane and flown over the mountains to a hospital in the Azerbaijan city of Baku.

There I was treated like royalty. I had a sunny room to myself, with a window that looked out at the Caspian Sea. Instead of the ground, I slept between clean sheets on a soft featherbed with a pillow in place of a backpack. A tall, awkward nurse with a toothy grin would come by and give me a bath, then wash and comb my hair. And each morning she brought me an enormous breakfast of hot tea with cream and sugar, salami and goat cheese, eggs and oat porridge, *vareniki* and *dovag*. The irony was that while I'd been so hungry during the fighting, now when I could eat to my heart's content I didn't have much of an appetite. The nurse would cajole me with, "Eat! Eat!" She would even go so far as to pick up a spoon and try to force-feed me, as if I were a finicky baby.

A good-looking, dark-skinned doctor would stop by to check on me.

"How are we feeling?" he asked.

"Tired."

"It'll take a while for you to regain your strength," he said as he lifted my gown to inspect my belly.

For the first time in a long while, I felt the return of modesty, something I thought I'd lost forever. I was embarrassed as he nonchalantly poked and prodded my naked belly, had me sit up so he could listen to my heart. With my one good arm I tried to shield my breasts. I felt my cheeks redden.

As he took my pulse, I asked, "When can I rejoin my unit, Doctor?"

Ignoring my question, he took a light and looked into my ears. "How is the ringing?"

"Not bad," I lied. The ringing had continued, though I'd almost gotten used to it. "But I *will* be able to fight again, won't I?"

Then he said an odd thing to me. "Sometimes it takes a woman a while to adjust to such a change. Especially one as young as you."

I stared at him, not fathoming what he was telling me. "What do you mean?"

"Didn't they tell you?"

"Tell me what?"

"The wound you suffered was very severe. It damaged your repro-ductive organs. Infection set in. They had to do a hysterectomy on you."

I still didn't quite understand what he was saying to me. I stared at him dumbly, waiting for him to explain.

"You will not be able to have children. I'm sorry."

Then he turned and left me there with my sudden barrenness. I felt like sobbing, wished for the soothing balm of tears, but for some reason I didn't cry. Couldn't cry. I placed my hand over my stomach, where my Masha had lived with me for nine months. I felt a gaping hole in the center of me, as if they'd not only taken my female parts but had also amputated my very soul. I thought of what Zoya had told me—of the imperative of having more children after the war, of replenishing the lives the Germans had stolen from us. The vague desire that I had flirted with over the past year, of having another child someday, that too was suddenly stolen from me.

For weeks I lay in my bed in a fog. I ate and slept and slowly recov-ered from my wounds, but all I can recall of that early period in the hos-pital was thinking how alone I was, with everything I'd once had now stolen from me. Not only my past, but my future too.

Then one day I awoke to see on my nightstand some cards and let-ters. They were from various dignitaries, important figures of state. There was even a note from President Kalinin, expressing the nation's gratitude for my "heroic efforts in destroying the Hitlerites." A number of important Party officials as well as military top brass stopped in to see me. One of my visitors was General Petrov, the commander of the forces at Sevastopol. He had a shiny bald head which resembled a pick-led egg, and small dark eyes beneath gold pince-nez. On his chest was a cluster of bright medals. I thought how he and his staff had slipped out of the city, leaving behind tens of thousands of soldiers, sacrificial lambs to be fed to the German wolf. With him was a captain with the distinctive NKVD shoulder boards.

"It is a pleasure to finally meet you, Comrade Levchenko," General Petrov said to me. "How are you feeling?"

"I am fine, sir," I replied coolly.

"And they are treating you well?"

"Yes, sir."

He made a perfunctory attempt at small talk before turning to the captain. The other handed a box to the general, who opened it, removed a medal.

"Tat'yana Aleksandrovna Levchenko," he recited formally, "for your gallantry in fighting the fascist invaders of Sevastopol, on behalf of Secretary Stalin and the entire Soviet people, it is my great honor to present you with the Gold Star medal, honoring you as a Hero of the Soviet Union. Congratulations, Lieutenant," Petrov said.

Then he placed the medal on the flimsy material of my hospital gown. After which, he stood at attention and saluted me. The award, I must confess, came as a surprise, as did the promotion to lieutenant. But more surprising was the fact that I really didn't care about any of that now, the medals and honors, the number of Germans I had killed. Others in my unit had fought just as hard and as bravely as I. And so many had given their lives. In fact, it all felt hollow to me now. Just more empty propaganda from the big shots in the Kremlin. I thought of all the troops left behind in Sevastopol, abandoned by men like this Petrov, men who'd saved their own necks because they were too "important" to die for the Motherland. I told myself to let it go, that it would serve no point. Besides, I was a soldier, and it was not my place to question the decisions of my superiors. Still, I felt I couldn't remain silent. I had to speak for the others who couldn't speak for themselves.

"The soldiers left behind, sir," I said.

"Yes, Lieutenant?"

"What of them?"

The general nodded gravely.

"Yes, indeed. A terrible tragedy."

"They felt betrayed, General."

I saw my comment reflected in Petrov's startled expression. He stared at me, his thin lips pursed, his eyes inflamed by such impudence.

"It was a very difficult decision, Lieutenant," he replied curtly.

I hesitated, wondering how far I could go. How far I *dare* go. Yet then I thought of Captain Petrenko, Zoya, the others left behind.

"You betrayed us, sir."

"That will be—" began the captain harshly, but General Petrov stayed him with a hand.

Petrov turned toward me, his eyes softening.

"In war," he explained, "unpleasant decisions have to be made. Sometimes a battle must be lost in order for the war to be won." Then he reached out and took my left hand in both of his. "I understand how you feel, Lieutenant. Believe me, they are all on my conscience. Before I go," he said, "is there anything I can do for you, Lieutenant?"

"Yes, sir, there is. A soldier in my company, Corporal Zoya Kovshova. We were a sniper team. This medal is as much hers as it is mine. We were separated in the last days of Sevastopol. If it is possible, I would like to find out what became of her?"

General Petrov turned to the captain, who wrote something in a little notebook. "I shall look into it," Petrov said to me.

"Thank you, sir."

"Anything else, Lieutenant?" said Petrov, glancing at his watch.

"One more thing, sir. My husband, Nikolai. I have had no word from him for nearly a year. He was sent to Leningrad."

"I'll have Captain Meretskov here look into it. The people of the Soviet Union are grateful to you, Lieutenant. You have been a tremendous inspiration to all of us."

My recovery went slowly. The ringing in my ears lessened to a low drone, and the wound in my belly had healed enough to permit me to get up and walk a little. But I was exhausted after just a few steps. When I took a bath, I was startled by both the bright pink scar that slashed over my belly and by the weight I'd lost. My ribs stuck out, and my normally well-toned arms were thin. My face too had become gaunt, my eyes dull and sunken. Still, each day I pushed myself a little harder, walking farther up and down the corridors. I forced myself to eat despite having no appetite, hoping to get back to the front sooner—that was the one thing that inspired me, kept me going. Whenever I met the doctor, I'd ask when I could return to the war. He would always say something vague like, "Soon, soon."

I read books whose titles I couldn't remember, met people who came in to see the Hero of the Soviet Union but whose names and faces I quickly forgot. I wrote to Kolya, at first long, rambling letters talking fondly, nostalgically of our days in Kiev, a city that no longer existed, about a life that no longer existed either, letters I knew had little chance of finding their way to him. But then I began to write more truthfully, more honestly, of how I felt. Of how I'd always felt. Perhaps knowing that the letters would never reach him permitted me at last to be honest, knowing they were more for myself than for him. Perhaps too it had something to do with the fact that I could never have children, that if I returned to my marriage it would just be the two of us, forever. Without even the possibility of children to soften the loneliness that would enclose the two of us like a cell. I no longer felt as I had when I thought I was going to die. One's feelings are exaggerated, distorted at such extreme moments. I loved Kolya, but it was the love one has for a dear friend, for a brother. Not for a husband. And while I didn't say it in my letters—that would be too cruel—I knew now that if we were able to survive the war and meet again, that I would leave him. As much for his sake as mine. He deserved to have someone love him as much as he loved me. And I deserved to be honest with myself, to live a life *I* wanted and not one that others wanted for me. Writing truthfully of my feelings, I felt a heavy weight lifted from my shoulders.

As I walked along the corridors, I saw many of the other wounded, some much worse than I—soldiers missing limbs, others badly burned or in wheelchairs, some paralyzed and confined to bed. I befriended one young soldier who had been blinded in the fighting at Odessa, a private named Polyakov. His face and hands were terribly disfigured from burns. It was hard to look at him at first. He resembled a shriveled-up old man with a mummy's leathery face. I would sit by his bedside and read to him. When I finished reading, he would say, "Please. If you wouldn't mind, just a little more, Comrade." I knew it was mostly that he didn't want to be alone. So I'd read a few more pages.

"Does it look so bad?" he asked me once. "You can tell me the truth."

"No," I lied.

"Before the war I had a fiancée. Zhenya was a pretty girl. All the young men in my village wanted to court her." He paused for a moment, staring off with his sightless eyes. "I wonder if she will still want me now."

"Of course she will," I said to him. "You have sacrificed much for the country. What girl wouldn't want to marry someone like that?"

"But the war has changed me. I'm not the same person she knew."

"On the outside perhaps."

"I *feel* different too. Do you feel different inside, Lieutenant?"

"I suppose, a little. But it's the times that we live in. We're still the same people. When it is over, everything will go back to being the way it was."

"Do you really think so?"

"Of course," I replied.

Later, as I lay in bed staring out at the sea, I thought of what I'd told the young private. How everything would go back to the way it had been. A lie, I knew. *I* wasn't the same person anymore. I was as different from that woman as the burned man was from his former self. And I knew neither of us could go back to those former selves.

One day a soldier showed up in my room, carrying a burlap sack over his shoulder.

"You are Tat'yana Levchenko, no?" he asked.

"I am."

He dropped the sack on my nightstand. "This is for you," he said and left.

Inside, I found a pile of mail. Hundreds of letters, all addressed to me. I took out a letter, opened it, began to read.

Dear Lieutenant Levchenko,

I am fifteen years old. My family was killed at Korelitsy. My parents, three brothers and sister. I managed to escape and fled into the woods, where I joined the partisans. Hearing of your daring exploits against those monsters has given me new hope. Get well for all of us.

Sincere regards,

Lyudmila Bershankaya

I picked out another, this one in a thick brown envelope that had some heft to it. When I opened it, something solid and heavy fell onto my lap. I picked it up. It was a 7.62 mm bullet. On the side of the shell casing was written, FOR FRITZ.

Dear Tat'yana Levchenko,

    I want to personally thank you for every German you have sent to hell. My son was captured at Kharkov and I have not heard from him since. I have been working in a munitions factory in Voronezh. With each bullet I make I say a little prayer that it finds the heart of an invader. I send you one that I would be honored for you to use in your glorious work. May God bless you and keep you safe.

    Yours truly,

                      Nadezhda Sebrova

I read another and then another. They praised or thanked me. They spoke of my courage. They told me how proud they were of me. They said how much my bravery had inspired them, given them hope. Many offered prayers for my speedy recovery. A few sent photos of loved ones who'd died. Others enclosed small gifts, sweets or cigarettes or tinned food. In one there was a rosary. In several I found articles cut out of newspapers, articles about me. As I read them, I found tears welling up in my eyes.

Over the next few weeks I received piles of such letters, from all over the Soviet Union. Each day I would read some. They were mostly from women, mothers and grandmothers, daughters and sisters. But there were also a few from men. One man wrote a poem to me, expressing his undying love. A father sent a picture of his little daughter who said she wanted to grow up to be like Lieutenant Levchenko and kill Germans. I could read only so many before being overcome with emotion. Hearing of my countrymen's losses, of the deaths of loved ones, of their pain and suffering, of the fragile hopes they'd fastened to me—I found it nearly overwhelming. But at the same time, the letters also buoyed my spirits. I felt both proud and humbled. The depression I'd felt since being wounded began to leave me. Slowly I started to feel better, to regain my strength. Now I wanted only to get well so that I could rejoin the fight. So I could fulfill everything they'd said about me.

———

One day after I'd been there for almost a month, I was returning to my room after having read to the burned soldier. Standing at the window looking out was a small woman in uniform, her back to me.

"May I help—" I began, but I froze when the woman turned toward me. "Zoya!"

We rushed to greet each other and hugged fiercely. When I winced from my still tender wound, Zoya said, "I'm so sorry. Are you all right?"

"Don't worry. Come, sit."

We sat on the bed and held hands, and alternately cried tears of joy and hugged each other and giggled like a couple of schoolgirls.

"I heard you received the Gold Star," she offered.

"Yes."

"Such an honor," she said, squeezing my hand. "I am so proud of you."

"You deserve it as much as I."

"Nonsense. You did the shooting. I just served them up to you."

We laughed at that.

"I still can't believe my eyes," I said. "I thought you were dead."

"The last I saw of you I thought the same thing."

"So it was *you*? Who saved me."

Zoya nodded, smiling modestly.

"How? What happened?"

"When I returned with the girl, the Germans had already overrun our position. Our troops were retreating down to the harbor under heavy fire. There was no sense trying to help, especially since the girl was with me, so we stayed in the sewer. I headed back to see if I could help you. I found you lying there. The girl and I pulled you into the sewer. We dragged you until we heard friendly voices. The last I saw of you they were bringing you to a field hospital."

I hugged her again. "Once more I have you to thank for my life, little mother."

"Look," Zoya said, pointing to her shoulder. I hadn't noticed the three red stripes of an NCO. "For saving your neck, they promoted me to sergeant. How about that?"

"That's wonderful," I cried. "Tell me, how on earth did you find me?"

She shrugged her shoulders. "I was in Sumgait. They'd flown some of us there from Sevastopol. A blue hat came up to me and said I was to get on a plane at once and come. So here I am."

"What happened to our company?" I asked.

Zoya harrumphed in her usual fashion. "Only a few of us got out. Ivanchuk. Cheburko. The medic, what's his name? Yuri. The rest were either killed or taken prisoner."

"The captain?"

Zoya shook her head. "He stayed behind, fighting to the last."

I was almost afraid to ask. "And the little girl?"

"Raisa was evacuated with us."

"Thank God," I said.

"Yes, thank God," Zoya said, crossing herself. "They put her on a ship bound for Canada."

"Canada?"

"Yes. With other orphans from the Crimea."

I was pleased to learn not only that Raisa had survived but also that someone would take care of her, love her. She would become the woman my own Masha could not.

Just then the aid came in with my noon meal.

"Would you join me, Zoya?" I asked.

"No, you go ahead and eat. You need it. My goodness, you're skin and bones."

"Ach. They feed me so much I'll be fat as a pig," I said, puffing out my cheeks. Zoya laughed. "There's enough for two. Come, we'll share."

As we ate, we talked about what had happened to each other over the past several weeks. We spoke of Zoya's family, and she asked if I'd heard anything from my husband. I told her I hadn't. I didn't tell her the extent of my wounds, the fact that I would never have children. I guess I didn't want to blunt our joy. Zoya looked different to me. In the short time we'd been apart she no longer had the features of a girl. Perhaps it had been happening all along and I had just now noticed it. But the soft fullness of her face had become angular. Her cheeks were more prominent, and her mouth had the cynical edge to it of one hardened by experience. The change saddened me a little. When Zoya had first come to the unit she was hardly more than a fresh-faced girl.

She told me that her new unit was going to be shipped out soon.

"Do you know where?" I asked.

"Word has it we're headed for Stalingrad. Let's hope it doesn't end like Odessa or Sevastopol."

"I wish I were coming with you."

"You're crazy, you know that," Zoya said, glancing around the room. "They should make sure your head wasn't injured."

We both laughed again. A sausage remained on the plate, and Zoya looked down at it, then at me.

"Go ahead," I said. "I'm full."

She picked it up and began eating it.

"Besides," said Zoya, "you're famous now. They can't risk losing you."

"How long can you stay?"

"Not long, I'm afraid. I have to be back on the plane tonight."

"Remember your promise?" I told her.

"What promise?"

"You said you would come and visit me when this is over."

"Of course," she said, glancing away.

We both suspected, I think, that it would never happen. The war had brought us as close as sisters, had us sharing a foxhole and food and danger, had us killing men we didn't know, and when it was over we would go back to our separate lives. It saddened me to think that I would never see Zoya again. We sat there, looking out the window toward the sea.

"Oh," she said, fumbling in her pocket. "I have something that is yours."

She took out a small leather case that I recognized immediately.

"Dear God!" I cried. It was the case that held my personal effects, my wedding band, the only picture I had of Kolya and Masha, the lock of her hair.

"I wanted to hold on to it for you," she said. "I didn't want it getting lost. And then we were separated."

"Thank you, Zoya."

I opened it, looked at the picture of my daughter and Kolya, and began to cry.

Zoya put her arm around me. "It's all right, Tat'yana."

We talked for a long while. When it was time for her to leave, we hugged once again, and she headed for the door. But she stopped and turned toward me.

"You take care of yourself, Tat'yana," she said. "Allow yourself to be happy."

"Yes, little mother. I will."

"Good-bye."

6

One morning several weeks later, while I was lying in bed reading some of the get-well letters I received, two men showed up at my room. The first was an older man, tall and gaunt and pale as curdled milk, with bushy eyebrows and thick glasses that made the whites of his eyes appear exaggeratedly large and soggy-looking. He looked like death warmed over. The other was much younger, a red-haired man with dark eyes and pimples still on his chin. It was sweltering, and both were sweating profusely. NKVD, I thought as soon as I'd laid eyes on them. *Chekisty.* You could always tell their sort. They were dressed in those dark, standard-issue, badly tailored suits and wore the unmistakable air of self-importance of the secret police. They strode in and stared around my room, without even bothering to identify themselves.

"May I help you?" I asked.

"Are you Lieutenant Tat'yana Levchenko?" replied the older of the two. He seemed to be the one in charge. He had a brusque demeanor, someone used to giving orders.

"Yes," I replied.

"You are to come with us."

"What is this about?" I demanded.

"I am not at liberty to say. You are to get your things together."

They stood in the room while I packed my soldier's bag.

"Do you need help?" offered the younger one. He was nicer than the other one, trying to be pleasant.

Though the doctors had taken the cast off my arm, it was still in a sling and I wasn't much good for anything. Still, I didn't want these two touching my things.

"No, I can manage," I replied.

"Here's a new uniform," the younger one said, handing me a paper sack.

Even as I dressed the two didn't leave, so that I had to pull the curtain around my bed for privacy. I wondered what the secret police could want with me. I recalled how I'd spoken out with General Petrov, criticizing him for leaving his troops. Had that something to do with the presence of these two? I thought of all the stories of people who'd been taken away, never to be heard from again. Yet I was now a Hero of the Soviet Union. They wouldn't dare try anything with me, would they?

"What do you want with me?" I asked through the curtain.

"Move it. We have to be going," replied the older one impatiently.

The younger one carried my duffel bag as we walked outside into the blistering sunlight. They had me get in the backseat of an automobile. Another one of theirs drove. It was stifling in the car, and the two policemen sat silently on either side of me, pressed so close I couldn't move. I could smell the sweat on them and the unmistakably sweet tang of gun oil. They drove me to an airbase on the outskirts of the city. They escorted me toward a plane on the runway, its propellers already spinning. As we were about to board, I stopped and turned to the older one. "I demand to know where you're taking me."

"It would be better if you just got on the plane, Lieutenant," he replied.

I wasn't going to be cowed by these two. After all, I'd fought against the German Eleventh Army.

"I refuse to go unless you tell me."

"Just get on the plane," said the older one, growing visibly annoyed. "No!"

He drew his lips tight over his too-large teeth. I could see he was used to having people obey his orders without question. Finally he said, "We are taking you to Moscow."

"Why?"

"That is not for us to say."

"I won't go unless you tell me," I repeated.

The older NKVD agent glanced from me to the younger one and back to me again. I think he was considering just grabbing me by the hair and dragging me onto the plane. The Soviet secret police had never been known for their subtlety. Finally, though, he threw his hands in the air, mumbled something to his partner, and headed up into the plane, as if leaving this unpleasantness to his colleague.

"They wanted it to be a surprise," said the red-haired man.

"What do you mean, 'surprise'?"

"They want to honor your achievements. We were told to say nothing. Now please, Lieutenant," he said, extending his hand toward the plane with a kind of elegant bow.

I still wasn't sure I believed them, but finally I acquiesced and climbed aboard.

At sunset that evening as we approached from the south, I made out the colorful domes and spires of the Kremlin. I gazed out the plane's window, searching for the massive Palace of the Soviets. I'd read about it and seen sketches of it in newspapers. It was to be the tallest structure in the world, the grand expression of Stalin's vision for our new country. I thought it would have been finished by now.

"Where is the great palace?" I asked.

"What palace?" replied the younger of the two policemen.

"Why, the Palace of the Soviets, of course."

The younger one laughed. "See that big ditch down there," he said, pointing through the window at an excavated area that resembled a massive bomb crater. "That's what's left of it. They used the steel for making tank defenses."

We landed at Kuybyshev military airport and drove into the now-darkened city, where they brought me to a hotel on a narrow out-of-the-way street. I noticed that some of the hotel's windows had wood covering them, and here and there the bricks were pockmarked, no doubt from the German guns during the previous year's assault. I'd heard that the krauts had come within a few kilometers of Moscow before being driven back. My room on the third story was cramped and musty-smelling. They dropped my bag on the bed and turned to leave.

"Wait," I said. "What now?"

"Someone will be by for you in the morning," instructed the older one. "I hope everything is to your liking," he added, flatly, without the least sarcasm.

I listened with my ear to the door as they walked away, and when they were gone I turned the lock. In bed that night, I had an odd feeling. I felt naked without my rifle, vulnerable and defenseless. I'd not had it in the hospital, but that was different. For a year in the war I'd kept it with me constantly, when I ate and when I slept, even when I went to the latrines. It had always been within arm's reach. It had given me a feeling of security. Without my realizing it, my rifle had become a part of me, like an arm or a leg. That's what war does to one. I lay on the bed, still in my uniform. That night, I slept irregularly, tossing and turning in the strange room. The pipes clanged, and outside in the hall I thought I heard footsteps, though maybe it was just one of several strange dreams I had.

In the morning, a knock on the door woke me. I got up and answered it. There in the hallway stood a heavyset man with ruddy cheeks, his thick neck overflowing his collar. He was wheezing from the climb up to my room. He wore a dark, smartly tailored suit, and sweat beaded on his upper lip. In his hand he held a fedora hat by the brim.

"I am Vasilyev," he said, and without asking permission strode into my room. He stood there, looking disapprovingly about. "You'd think they could have done a little better than this for someone who has just won the Gold Star." Then, turning back to me he said, "Your picture doesn't do you justice, Lieutenant."

"Who are you?" I asked.

He smiled at me and gave an exaggerated bow, sweeping the fedora in front of him. He had a meaty face, with a dark shadow of a beard, and he was thick through the middle. About the only thing that wasn't abundant was his mouth, which was thin and severe, a sharp line separating his thick nose from his double chin. Despite his bulk he had a certain grace to him, a delicacy that was almost feminine.

"I told you, I am Vasilyev. I fear it is going to be unbearably hot again," he said, dabbing his forehead with an embroidered handkerchief. His movements seemed almost theatrical, those exaggerated gestures of a second-rate actor. "Oh, pardon me. Let me welcome you to Moscow," he said, extending his hand. When I offered my hand, instead of shaking it, he bent and kissed it, as if he were a figure out of some nineteenth-century novel. As he spoke, I caught a faint whiff of alcohol on his breath. "Vasily Vasilyev. At your service, madam."

"I don't need your service."

"Then think of me as your escort."

"To what?"

"To certain events they have planned for you." Then turning toward me, he said with disdain, "That uniform looks as if you slept in it, Lieutenant."

"As a matter of fact, I did."

He smiled and walked over to the window, pushed the curtains aside and looked out. "Your wounds," he asked, "have you recovered fully from them?"

"Yes," I replied. "I'm fine."

"I am pleased to hear that."

"So when can I return to the front?"

At this he smiled, his hands folded beneath his prominent belly, as if it were a basket of clothes he was carrying.

"Have you had breakfast yet, Lieutenant?"

"No."

"Neither have I. Come," he said.

We headed down and got into the backseat of a black Citroën and were chauffeured by a man with a sharp, narrow face like a wood chisel. We drove east along the Moscow River, with the walls of the Kremlin to our left. The day was warm and bright, with a light breeze coming off the water. We wound our way through the city, stopping eventually in front of a small café in an old neighborhood on Tverskaya. "The only good French restaurant left in all of Moscow," Vasilyev said as the two of us headed in. When the waiter came up, he said, *"Ah, bonjour, Monsieur Vasilyev. Comment allez-vous?"* The two spoke rapidly and fluently in French. My escort ordered a prodigious breakfast of eggs and sausages, blini cakes and *grenki* and porridge. Though he ate heartily, his manners were the refined sort of someone who'd come from a cultured background. Now and then he'd daintily wipe the corners of his mouth with his napkin, and once he removed from his coat pocket an expensive-looking silver flask. He offered it to me, but I shook my head.

"Ninety-proof bourbon from America," he explained. "Munitions can't get through the German U-boats, but booze can. It is a strange war, no?"

As he took a long draft, I noticed that he had a wedding band that creased the flesh on one fat finger and that his nails were perfectly manicured. His dark brown hair was thinning and combed straight back. His eyes were also dark, and beneath them the flesh was discolored and loose.

"When can I return to the front?" I asked again.

"Ah, the front," he said, taking a sip from the flask. "Where is it today? I have not read the paper. It keeps changing so fast."

"I want to get back to fighting."

"That is a very admirable sentiment, Comrade. But right now we have more important things planned for you. You really ought to try the blini. It is delicious," he said, eating heartily.

"What sorts of things do you have planned?" I asked.

"A little this and that," he said, waving his fork about in the air. Now and then he'd take the handkerchief from his coat pocket and wipe his flushed brow. On the one hand, he gave the appearance of a rough-hewn peasant who enjoyed his earthy pleasures. But he was, I would come to know, a complex man of many sides, many contradictions too—erudite, sophisticated, worldly, someone equally well read in Pushkin or Goethe, or in the subtleties of Soviet propaganda, but also someone who could be fiercely cruel. "We want to give a human side to the war," he explained.

"There is no human side to it," I snapped. "It's all brutish and vicious."

"Then let's say we wish to show you off."

"Show me off?"

"Yes. The capitalists call it marketing. We intend to market you as they do one of their motion picture stars."

He obviously thought this funny, for he smiled broadly. He reached into his pocket and brought out a silver case and offered me a cigarette. I took one, and he lit it for me and laid the case on the table. I noticed it had words engraved on the side: WITH ALL MY LOVE, O. His wife? I wondered.

Through the café window, I saw a second black sedan across the street from where our car was parked. Two men sat in it. The one behind the steering wheel wore glasses and had bushy eyebrows. I recognized him as one of the two *chekisty* that had brought me to Moscow.

After breakfast we got back in the car.

"I'm to show you about the city," Vasilyev said. "Have you ever been to Moscow?"

"No."

"Good. I shall be your tour guide."

We visited the Novodevichy convent and its famous cemetery, where we saw the graves of Chekhov and Gogol. Next we went to the Pushkin museum. After a leisurely lunch, where Vasilyev drank an entire bottle of Italian Barbera all by himself, we headed to St. Basil's Cathedral. After that we proceeded to Lenin's tomb. As we stood there, staring at the grayish figure of Lenin apparently asleep beneath the glass, Vasilyev leaned toward me and whispered conspiratorially, "Wax."

"What?" I asked.

"The real thing is in Siberia," he explained. "When they thought the Germans would take the city, they removed Lenin's body and replaced it with a wax figure. The NKVD sent an entire lab to keep his body preserved."

Even now everywhere I saw artillery batteries with Katyushas and howitzers and antiflak weapons, soldiers manning machine guns behind heavily fortified emplacements. Tanks nearly collided with trolley cars and horse-drawn carts.

"It still looks like a city under siege," I observed.

"They are not taking any chances," Vasilyev replied. "If that crazy fool in Berlin changes his mind, they'll be back."

Vasilyev seemed thoroughly to enjoy his role as tour guide, gesturing at places we passed, pointing out landmarks, laughing heartily at his own jokes. He was chatty, gregarious, making witty comments. He seemed at times even a little flirtatious, though I would come to learn that this was an affectation, him just plying his trade. He had no interest in me in that way. There was, nonetheless, something about Vasilyev that made me wary. Was he, like the other two, NKVD? Everywhere we went we were followed by the black sedan. When we went inside some museum or palace, the two secret police would follow at a distance, never really trying to hide themselves but never coming too close either. Several times, the younger red-headed man made eye contact with me, and once I thought he actually nodded and smiled.

It was late in the afternoon when we arrived back to my hotel. We sat outside in the car for a moment.

"You have a couple of hours in which to freshen up," Vasilyev told me. "I shall pick you up at seven."

"Where are we going tonight?" I asked.

"The symphony," he explained. "There will be a lot of important people there. You'll want to look smart, Lieutenant."

"Smart?" I asked.

"Presentable. You will find a dress uniform waiting in your room for you. By the way, do you have lipstick?"

"What?"

"You know," he said, mimicking the application of it to his own thin lips.

"Why must I wear lipstick?" I asked. "I'm a soldier."

"You are also a woman. Women wear lipstick."

"I don't see the necessity."

"It has nothing to do with necessity," said Vasilyev. "Please, just put on a little lipstick. Okay?"

"I don't have any," I replied, thinking that would be the end of it.

With this Vasilyev reached into his coat pocket, and like some magician performing a trick, he pulled out a small silver cylinder. "I suspected you would need some. And while you're at it, rub a little into your cheeks. You're far too pale," he said. "And be sure to wear your medals. They'll want to see them."

When I got back to my room, I found a vase filled with fresh flowers on the nightstand along with a bowl of fruit and a box of chocolates. I thought of Zoya, how she loved chocolate. Next to the chocolates was a bottle of champagne. And spread out over the bed lay a dress uniform, complete with a visored cap, Sam Browne belt, a skirt, as well as a pair of shiny new boots, none of which I'd gotten during the hasty westward rush to confront the German invasion the previous summer. I went over to the window and peeked through the curtains. Below in the street, I saw the same black car that had been following us all day.

In the bathroom I found a number of toiletries—soap, toothpaste, shampoo, a razor and blades, things I'd almost forgotten existed. I drew a bath, treated myself to some chocolates and an orange. Then I got the bottle of champagne and a glass and slid into the water. It was so hot it took my breath away as I eased myself into the tub. Yet even now in this room so far from the front, I felt the war's presence. It was as if I could never completely wash away its mark, the smell of it on me, the taste of it in my mouth. I noticed the tattoos of battle: the matching pair of knotted scars on my thigh where I'd been hit by a bullet—entry and exit wounds; the quarter-moon scar from shrapnel along my calf; the pale thinness of my broken arm; various other cuts and scrapes and abrasions, some of which I'd not even been aware of until now. Especially the long, still-pink, still-tender wound over my belly, the one that had robbed me of the ability to have life inside ever again. I thought of my comrades—Zoya off fighting in Stalingrad, Captain Petrenko and the others, either dead or in some German POW camp. Kolya in Leningrad. And here I was, drinking champagne and soaking in a warm bath, about to go to the symphony. Then I thought of my daughter, in an unmarked grave somewhere along the road to Kharkov. Though I knew it was foolish, I worried that she would be lonely there, afraid without me.

But after a while, the hot bath and the champagne eased my mind a little. It had been more than a year since I'd had a real bath. I scoured my skin hard, rubbing it raw, like some religious flagellant, trying to remove the stench of war. I scraped the dirt and gun oil and blood from beneath my nails. It was heaven, let me tell you. I felt like a new woman, like a girl going on her first date. I wanted only to lie there and savor the fact that I was in this warm tub, alive, getting a little tipsy from champagne, about to go to a symphony. It was a strange, strange world, I thought.

I got dressed and put on lipstick, combed my hair. I looked at myself in the mirror. Thinner than I had been, a little older about the eyes and mouth perhaps. But given all that I'd been through, I was pleased with what I saw. I thought I was still an attractive woman, a sentiment I hadn't felt in a very long time.

That evening when Vasilyev saw me at the door, he stood there for a moment looking me up and down, his hand rubbing his chin in a caricature of appraisal. Finally he gave a smile of approval, his fleshy cheeks pressing his eyes into narrow slits.

"Very nice, Comrade," he said as he entered the room.

"Thank you," I replied, with more than a trace of sarcasm, which he decided to ignore.

"The uniform fits well?"

"Yes."

"I wasn't sure what size. I could only go by what my wife wears. And she's a bit, shall we say, larger than you," he added with a smile. "Do try to be a bit charming tonight, Lieutenant."

"Charming?" I said.

"You know, smile a little. Be pleasant. We want to show everyone that our female soldiers can have a feminine side. Come, we mustn't be late."

As we drove along, he took out his handkerchief and said, "Turn toward me." When I did, he reached over and made as if to wipe my mouth with it.

"What are you doing?" I said, fending off his touch.

"You look cheap."

"Cheap," I replied, my voice sounding petulant even to me. "You said to wear lipstick."

"But I didn't tell you to make yourself look like some five-ruble *shlyukha*. I don't want them to get the wrong impression. Come here." Then he added, "Please."

I relented finally and let him wipe my mouth, feeling as he did so like a little child when my mother used to wash my face.

"There," he said. "Much better. And here," he said, handing me a pair of silk stockings he had removed from somewhere on his person. "Put these on."

"Now?" I said.

"Yes."

"I don't have a garter belt." I thought this would suffice, but Vasilyev, I would soon learn, did not take no for an answer. He was, if nothing else, resourceful.

"Stop the car," he called to the driver.

At this, the man put on the brakes. "In the trunk there's a first aid kit. Bring it to me," Vasilyev instructed the man. The driver got out and returned in a moment with a military first aid kit and gave it to Vasilyev. He opened it, took out a roll of adhesive gauze, and handed it to me. "Use this to hold up your stockings," he said.

"You're joking," I replied.

"Quickly. We don't want to be late." When I hesitated with him sitting there, he said, "Aren't we the modest one. All right, I shall be outside."

The entire episode would have struck me as comical if I wasn't so annoyed by his trying to control my every movement. Even then, I was beginning to chaff under his claustrophobic hand, his Svengali-like manipulation. I longed for the simplicity of battle, the clarity of knowing your role, which side was the foe. I felt I was entering an entirely new and subtle kind of arena, one in which your enemy, as well as your comrade, was much harder to distinguish.

Soon Vasilyev got back into the car.

"Are we all set, Lieutenant?"

"Yes, *we* are all set," I replied.

He glanced down at my legs. "You have lovely legs," he offered.

"Are you with them?"

"With whom?"

"Those two," I said, nodding my head toward the car that followed us.

"Those idiots!" he replied, indignant. "Hardly. I work in the Ideological Department."

"Never heard of it."

"It's not important. Your job and mine are similar, though."

"How so?"

"We are both trying to win this war, Lieutenant. It's just that you do it with your gun, while I do it with my pen."

"A pen doesn't kill a single kraut."

"That's rather disappointing to hear from a poet. Don't you believe the pen is mightier than the sword?"

"I don't like any of this," I said, motioning toward my new uniform. "Wearing makeup and silk stockings. Eating enough to feed an entire platoon. When our people are dying. I should be out fighting. That's where I'm needed."

"Your way, Lieutenant, is killing one German at a time. But if I write something that inspires a million more to join our cause and they each kill a German, that's a million dead krauts. Think of it."

"We've already lost a million soldiers in the Ukraine alone. Where are we going to get that many more?"

"That's where you come in, my dear."

"But I don't write. At least not your brand of writing."

"Yes, that's true—you are a poet," he said, his tone sliding toward something like sarcasm. "A poet and a killer in the same lovely person. What a lovely paradox."

We finally arrived at the Kremlin and pulled up in front of a long, pale-colored, brightly lit building, which Vasilyev explained was Poteshny Palace. Taking my elbow, he led me inside and toward a large room where a crowd of people were milling about. Music drifted from a small string quartet in the corner. There were tables set up with food—more food than I'd ever seen before. Large platters with sturgeon and smoked salmon, sides of beef and hams, pheasant and duck and quail, cheeses and caviar, fresh fruits and small pastries and various delicacies. On one table alone there was an entire suckling pig with an apple stuffed in its mouth. Waiters came through the crowd with trays of appetizers or champagne. I was intoxicated by the heady aroma of it all.

Vasilyev leaned in close and whispered, "Look over there." He pointed across the room at a group, in the center of which was a tall man with wild, dark hair, thick horn-rimmed glasses, and an expression that betrayed a look at once bored and full of disdain. The others surrounding him appeared to be journalists. Several had cameras, and some were writing on small pads as the man spoke. "That scrawny fellow," Vasilyev explained, "is Shostakovich."

"The composer?" I asked.

"Yes. He's back in the good graces of the Party, don't ask me how. His problem is he's all genius and no charm. When those journalists come over and start asking you questions about your experience at the front, be sure to tell them that morale among the troops is very high."

"But it isn't," I countered.

"We must give the people something to hope for."

"Even if it's not the truth?"

He scoffed at this. "The truth is, we are fighting for our very lives. If a lie will help us to beat those sons of bitches, then so be it. Wait here."

He walked over to the bevy of reporters. For a heavy man, he moved with a natural grace, gliding effortlessly across the floor with a dancer's lightness of foot. As he spoke to the reporters, they glanced over at me, and in a moment they had left the composer and approached me en masse.

"Comrades," Vasilyev said with the dramatic flare of an impresario, "I would like to present to you Lieutenant Tat'yana Levchenko, Hero of the Soviet Union." At this, there was applause and several flashbulbs exploded, blinding me for a moment. "The destroyer of over three hundred fascists. Our secret weapon. Our very own *la belle dame sans merci.*"

One reporter blurted out, "Lieutenant Levchenko, how do you feel about winning the Gold Star?"

I hesitated, nervously staring at the small crowd. "It is . . . a very great honor," I replied. "But I can only accept it on behalf of all my comrades in arms."

"She's just being modest," Vasilyev chimed in.

"What do you think makes you such a great marksman?" a second asked.

"Patience. A steady hand."

They continued to ask questions—what part of fighting I found hardest, did I think women fighters were as capable as men, was I ever frightened, how soon would I return to the front.

"Do you think we are winning the war?" one man called out.

"I am confident that we will, in time, defeat the fascists."

"What would you like to say to the Soviet people, Comrade?" asked another, his pencil poised for my answer.

I hesitated. It made me nervous to think that what I said would be read by millions of people, those same people who had written letters to me.

"I would tell them that our troops' fighting spirit remains high," I said. I saw Vasilyev nod approvingly at this, roll his finger for me to continue, to expand on that. "Our men and women are confident we will soon drive the invaders from our land. I would tell them that we must all be heroes to defeat the enemy. The factory worker making munitions no less than the farmer who feeds our soldiers."

At this, Vasilyev stepped in. "Thank you, gentlemen. Comrade Levchenko is still recovering from her wounds, and we don't want to tire her out."

Taking me aside, he said, "Excellent, Comrade."

"Was I charming enough?" I asked sarcastically.

"I particularly liked the business about the farmer and the factory worker. Had a certain poetic ring to it. Then again, I would expect no less from a poet."

I turned toward him. "How did you know I wrote poetry?" I asked.

Smiling obscurely, he said, "We know a great deal about you actually, Lieutenant. You ran the hurdles and threw the javelin in track and field. You used to associate with an undesirable element back in your university days. You published a poem in *The Workers' Voice.*"

I stared at him, wondering how he could have known that. Of course I hadn't signed my name to it.

"For what it's worth, I think your poetry is quite good. Though I would be more cautious about what I put my pen to from now on. You are a public figure now. Come, I want you to meet some people."

I noticed some women there. Mostly they stood off by themselves talking in small groups and eating hors d'oeuvres. Arrayed in furs and jewelry, they were the wives, I assumed, of the Party leaders. Stout-bodied women, with soft, flabby arms, they didn't look as if the war had caused them to miss a single meal. To formal events such as these, the men would bring their wives, leaving their mistresses behind at their dachas.

Vasilyev took me by the elbow and ushered me toward a small group of men who were sipping champagne and smoking cigars. As I walked I could feel the tape pulling uncomfortably against the skin of my thigh.

"Good evening, Comrades," Vasilyev said to them in his overly grand manner. "It is my great pleasure to present to you Lieutenant Levchenko, Hero of the Soviet Union."

Smiling, the men applauded politely.

"Over three hundred of the fascists have fallen to her deadly aim," Vasilyev continued.

Each one kissed me on both cheeks. When they thought I wasn't looking they stole a quick glimpse at my legs and chest.

"A pleasure to meet you," said one, an old man with jaundiced eyes.

"With brave soldiers like yourself we will soon have the fascists on the run, eh," added another, who had a large mustache.

I nodded. "I am grateful I was able to do my duty."

"And you are even more lovely than your picture," said the third, a slight, balding man with a large head and wire-rim spectacles. Behind his glasses, his eyes had the rapacious look of a wolf.

When I didn't reply, Vasilyev answered for me. "Thank you, Commissar General Beria."

Everyone knew Lavrenty Beria, the head of state security. Stalin's pit bull. The one who made up the daily lists of names for Stalin's signature, the ones who were to be shipped off to the camps or tortured in Lubyanka or straightaway taken out and shot. And we'd heard the whispered rumors of Beria's insatiable appetite for young women.

After we had moved off, Vasilyev said to me, "Now that wasn't so bad, was it?"

"How long do we have to stay?"

"Relax and enjoy yourself. Are you hungry?"

"A little."

He led me over to the food.

"Oh look, there's Alexeyev," Vasilyev said, waving to a man across the room. "I will be right back. Can I get you some more champagne?"

I shook my head. I still had the same glass he'd given me when we arrived. I stood there by myself, feeling awkward, with everyone watching me. I would rather be in a foxhole with Zoya than here with these sycophants and flatterers. I was thinking of her when I heard behind me a low voice, almost a whisper.

"Comrade Levchenko?"

I turned to see a man standing there. Older, wearing a plain khaki uniform without insignia, he was short, slump shouldered, with the thick body of a peasant and a head that was too large for his height. His hair was coarse and black with just a few gray strands in it, his bushy mustache resembling a small furry creature. But it was his eyes that were his most striking feature—small and not quite black, more really a complete absence of color. They were the eyes of something both primitive and yet cunning in its way. Where had I seen them before, I wondered.

"I am she," I replied.

"It is a great honor to meet you," he said, shaking my hand and nodding his great shaggy head. He spoke Russian with a thick Georgian accent. Though his hands were large and blunt as bricks, his handshake was surprisingly soft, almost effeminate. As he spoke he continued holding my hand. His gaze ran the length of me, from my calves to the top of my head, but unlike the other men, his interest wasn't in the least of a carnal nature. He viewed me coldly and dispassionately, more appraisingly, the way a farmer might look at a plow horse. I slowly freed my hand from his grasp.

"Thank you," I said. I assumed him to be some Party figure of importance with whom I needed not to say the wrong thing or Vasilyev would reprimand me.

"You have meant a great deal to our war effort," he offered. "You have lifted the spirits of our troops at a time when we most desperately need it."

"I only try to do my duty, sir."

He leaned in to me, as if to tell me something in confidence. "You and I know what it is to look into the eyes of a man before we kill him," he said, the slightest hint of a smile lingering beneath the bushy mustache. "These others"—he gave a wave of his blunt paw—"they chatter like a bunch of old women. But when it comes down to it, they are gutless creatures. You and I, Comrade, we are made of different stuff, are we not?"

I nodded, though I wasn't sure what he was getting at.

At this he turned and left me standing there.

Vasilyev returned shortly after this. "What did he say to you?"

I shrugged. "That he and I knew what it was like to look into a man's eyes before we killed him."

Vasilyev frowned, concern lining his face.

"What did he mean by that?"

"I have no idea. Who was that?"

He stared at me as if I had suddenly grown another head. "Surely you're kidding."

I shook my head.

"That was *him*," Vasilyev said.

"Who?"

"The general secretary."

I stared at him dumbfounded.

"Stalin," I blurted out. "You're joking."

"I would not joke of such a thing," Vasilyev said. "That was him. My goodness, you didn't even know it."

A shiver passed through me. To think that I'd actually met the man. The man my father revered, the same one my mother detested. I was surprised too that he was not bigger. All of the images we'd seen of him in the newspapers or film reels made him out to be this imposing figure, the Man of Steel. And I recalled the picture in front of the classroom back in school, the same cold, soulless eyes staring down upon us. Eyes that Madame Rudneva had called the devil's. Old Whiskers.

After a while, we moved off into a large hall where Vasilyev brought me up and had me sit at the front. A few seats away was Stalin, flanked by his toadies, Beria and Molotov. Before us was a stage, with an orchestra tuning their instruments. At the front of which was the man I had seen earlier, the composer Shostakovich. When all had been seated, Shostakovich spoke a few words to the audience. He explained that we were going to hear a new work, something called the Leningrad Symphony, which he had named in honor of the heroic defense being put up by the citizens of that brave city. Then he turned and began to conduct the orchestra. I soon found myself forgetting my objections about coming along. I was swept up by the intensity of the work, its initial martial drumbeat proclaiming that Leningrad was under siege by the Germans. The last movement began quietly, with the strings slowly rising in pitch until they were joined by woodwinds, before picking up the marchlike melody again. Finally, the woodwinds built until violins took over and carried the piece to its final rousing crescendo. I was mesmerized by the music.

Once during the symphony, I happened to look over and catch Stalin staring at me. It was a strangely enigmatic gaze, as indecipherable as that one might receive from a crow or a rat. I averted my own gaze for a moment, and when I looked back at him, he was still staring at me. I felt my blood chill in a way it had never done before, not even when a sniper bullet would pass within inches of me. This was something beyond mortal fear, beyond the potential harm he could do me, something that had to do with an elemental dread, the terror that strikes the heart when one recognizes that the world is run by forces one cannot even begin to fathom.

At the end of the symphony, there was utter silence, a tense, glassy stillness that left one almost breathless. All eyes, I noticed, were directed not at the stage but at Stalin, not the least of which were those of Shostakovich himself, who waited onstage, his baton hanging from his hand, anxiously peering down at the small, mustachioed man in the front row. Slowly, the secretary rose from his seat and directed the same impenetrable stare he'd given me at the composer now. Finally, he brought his blunt hands together in a modest, almost grudging show of appreciation. Only then did the crowd respond with a thunderous ovation.

As we passed out of the hall, Vasilyev suddenly clutched my elbow and said, "He wishes a word with you."

I was directed over to one side of the stage. Someone held back the curtain, and as I stepped past it, I spotted Stalin standing there, smoking a cigar.

"What did you think of the performance, Lieutenant?" he asked, an odd grin distorting his features.

"I thought it was quite good, Comrade Secretary."

He nodded, but without conviction, as if that wasn't the reply he wanted. He took another puff of the cigar, which he held delicately between thumb and forefinger.

"You will get them to fight, no," he said.

"Pardon me?" I asked.

"Those timid capitalists."

"I'm afraid I don't follow you, sir," I said.

Through the haze of smoke from his cigar, his eyes narrowed and he squinted at me. Right then a general came up to him and whispered something in his ear. Whatever it was, it wasn't good news, for his expression changed to one of mild irritation. With a flick of his hand, he dismissed the man, who withdrew a short distance away and waited. Turning back to me, Stalin leaned toward me, so close that I could smell cigar smoke and the rusted-iron breath of a man who habitually dined on rich foods and spicy meat. "Can I trust you, Lieutenant?"

I didn't quite know how to respond to this statement, what he meant by it, so I said, "Of course, Comrade Secretary."

"Good. Because you will have a mission of utmost importance to perform for the Motherland. Now you will have to excuse me."

Then he turned and walked over to where the general waited.

On the ride back to the hotel, we rode mostly in silence. Vasilyev seemed preoccupied. Finally, he said, "You did well tonight, Lieutenant."

"I'm glad I performed to your expectations," I said sarcastically.

"What did you and the general secretary talk about?"

"He wanted to know if he could trust me. And he said I would get them to fight. Get whom to fight?"

"Why, the Americans, of course."

"What are you talking about?"

We had by now reached my hotel. Vasilyev reached over and patted my hand. "It's late. You've had a long evening. We shall talk about this matter later. Get some sleep."

Over the next several days, Vasilyev would pick me up and show me about the city as if it were his own private amusement park. During the day we visited museums and art galleries and historical sites, while in the evening we attended elegant dinners or went to the theater or to the Bolshoi, where there were always crowds eager to see me. Before one ballet performance, I was asked to come onstage, where I received a bouquet of flowers from a ballerina in a tutu. Beside her, I felt clumsy and unfeminine in my uniform and heavy boots. Nonetheless, I received a standing ovation from the crowd. Wherever we went, Vasilyev paraded me around, often introducing me by some clever pet name— the Ukrainian Lion or the Queen of Fire. But his favorite was Krasavitsa Ubiytsa, which translated roughly to "Beautiful Assassin," a title that he was quite proud of having coined and one that I wouldn't be able to shake. One time, we showed up where a large group of people had gathered in the street. It was below Vorobyovy Gory. A small military band composed of old men was playing some martial theme. It turned out they were naming a street after me—*ulitsa Levchenko.* I toured hospitals, where I shook hands with wounded vets, and old people's homes and spoke to groups of schoolchildren. They had me go on the radio and tell of my experiences, though not before Vasilyev had coached me to "sound positive," to put our war effort in a good light.

Another time, accompanied by a man with a camera, we drove south of the city. We stopped at a farm and got out. From the trunk Vasilyev took out a camouflage poncho and a rifle, then we started walking across a field toward a grove of trees.

"What are we doing?" I asked.

"We're going to take your picture," Vasilyev said gaily. When we reached the trees, he said to the other man with the camera, "The light's good here, no?" The man nodded. Then Vasilyev turned to me. "Here," he said, handing me the rifle. "Get up in that tree," he said, pointing to a spindly looking birch tree.

"What for?"

"We are going to photograph your duel with the German."

"I would never try to hide in such a tree," I said.

"Poetic license," he said with a shrug. "But first put a little lipstick on."

Though I thought the entire episode utterly ridiculous, as I would so many that would come up in the next several months, I did as I was told. I shimmied up the tree to a small branch that felt far too thin to hold my weight. From below, Vasilyev called instructions, as if he were directing a film. "Now take aim and make believe you've got a kraut in your sights."

"But I didn't shoot him *from* the tree."

"Who's going to know?" he said. "Now turn this way more. Don't frown so much. And fix your hair. A strand has come undone. There we go. Perfect," he added.

Each time I'd bring up the question about what I had to do with getting the Americans to fight, he would somehow manage to elude the subject. Once, as we were driving to the Kremlin, I turned to him and said, "Now that I'm feeling well enough, when can I return to the front?"

Instead of answering, he had the driver stop the car. He jumped out and hurried with that odd nimbleness of his over to a nearby kiosk and purchased a paper. When he returned he showed me a copy of *Izvestiya* with my picture on the front page. "Female Hero Kills 300 Fascists" the headline read.

"*There*," he said, his fat forefinger stabbing the page for emphasis. "That's how you can best fight the krauts."

"That's not fighting. That's just show."

"But you are mistaken, Lieutenant. You are a student of history. You ought to know that bullets and bombs and tanks don't win wars. Wars are won here," he said, tapping his temple. "Do you know what you have done for the morale of our soldiers, for our people? They read what you have accomplished and you give them hope. What is more, you will buy us time for the West to get involved too."

"I don't understand," I said.

"Trust me, you will," he said, bringing his fingertips together to form a small globe in front of his face. That phrase—*trust me*—was one he would often use, and the more he did, the less I felt ready to trust him. "I understand why you want to kill them so badly."

Glancing over at him, I said, "Yes. They are the enemy."

"No. For you, it's quite personal." He reached across the seat and patted my hand. "You see, I know about your daughter."

I stared at him in surprise. How had he known that? Save for Zoya and those few people who were there when it had happened, I hadn't told anyone. Of course, that was not counting the letters I'd written to Kolya. Had they opened them up and read them?

"You have suffered greatly and you want your pound of flesh. But by helping us, you will have many more pounds of flesh than you could have your way. Besides, you will be thought a great patriot. You will go down in history as someone who helped the Motherland in a time of her greatest need."

After I was in Moscow for about a week, Vasilyev told me I was to meet a group from the West that evening. It was to be held at the Spaso House, the residence of the American ambassador.

"There will be important Amerikosy there," Vasilyev had told me. I noticed how he had used the demeaning word for Americans.

"What do they want with me?"

"They very much wish to meet you. Lieutenant, you are famous not just in our country, but all over the world now. The Yanks are fascinated by you. They can't get enough of you." Here he paused for a moment, brought his knuckle to his mouth in thought. "I must ask you one question, though. Are you a Jew?"

"What?"

"I heard that rumor."

"Why on earth does it matter if I'm a Jew?"

"It would just be better if you weren't. The Americans can be quite touchy about such things. But if you are, we can work around that."

"You mean, change it?"

"You could be a ravishing Georgian. Or a lovely Armenian."

I was struck by how fluid reality was for Vasilyev. I would find that nothing was so fixed, so permanent and unchangeable that he couldn't alter to his purpose with a nice turn of phrase, with a catchy line. Even the war—*especially* the war—was something he could manipulate. He had only to change a headline, reword a few sentences, take a couple of publicity photos, and voilà, the war was swung in our favor, the Germans close to being vanquished.

"I'm not a Jew," I said.

"Well, that simplifies things."

That evening when I got in the car, seated up front near the driver was another man I'd not seen before. He was smoking a cigarette.

"This is Radimov," Vasilyev said, indicating the man in the front seat. "He will act as your interpreter." The man in front looked over his shoulder and smiled at me, his lips drawing back to show teeth stained from smoking. He was thin, with a ruddy complexion. "I've read much about you, Comrade," Radimov said.

"Hello," I said, in English.

"So you speak English?"

"A little. Not very much, I'm afraid," I replied.

The ambassador's residence was in Spasopeskovskaya Square, not far from the Kremlin. As we pulled up in front of the impressive mansion, Vasilyev put his hand on my wrist and said, "Lieutenant, be mindful of what you say to the reporters. We don't want to alienate them. They are invaluable to us. Above all, be sure to tell them that we are winning the war. After all, they wouldn't want to bet on a losing horse."

Inside the embassy, I was greeted by the ambassador, a tall, gray-haired man named Standley. He wore wire-rim glasses and had about him a slightly distracted, professorial demeanor.

"I'm so pleased you could come, Lieutenant Levchenko," he told me through the interpreter Radimov. He shook my hand vigorously. "I've heard so much about you. I can certainly see why they call you the Beautiful Assassin."

"I am honored to meet you as well, sir," I replied.

"They tell me you can shoot the wings off a fly at a hundred meters."

"I think they exaggerate."

"And I think you're just being modest. Three hundred krauts! That's some shooting, young lady."

I was led into a palatial hall with a high, domed ceiling from which hung a huge chandelier. The ceiling was painted a pale blue, so that it reminded me of the sky on a clear spring day over the Crimea, before the war and all the smoke. When they spotted me, a small group of journalists, some holding cameras, rushed over, pushing and shoving to get close. Unlike the Soviet reporters, the Americans had little sense of decorum. Like unruly children, all at once they began yelling things out at me in English and waving and trying to catch my attention.

Vasilyev attempted to quiet them. "Gentlemen, please," he said through the interpreter. "Lieutenant Levchenko will be happy to answer your questions. But one at a time."

Their hands leapt in the air.

"You," Vasilyev said, pointing at one reporter.

He stared at my legs, then said something in English.

"He wants to know if you wear stockings while fighting," the interpreter explained to me.

The reporters guffawed as a group, much like a bunch of raucous boys at a football match. I glanced over at Vasilyev, who offered a smile that was meant to placate me.

"No, I don't wear stockings to fight," I replied.

"Is it difficult to sleep in a foxhole beside men?" asked another.

"It is difficult to sleep in war period," I replied. "There is much noise."

They asked many questions in a similar vein. If the men flirted with me. If my fellow soldiers treated me like a girl or like a soldier. How did I change in front of the men? What did I think of the sight of blood? At least the Soviet reporters had treated me with the dignity due a soldier. These Americans were fools, I thought to myself.

"We are at war," I explained. "We don't think of such things. We think only of defeating the enemy."

"Let's get some pictures, sweetheart," one American called out. He was dark featured, good-looking, with fine white teeth and hair heavily pomaded. He spoke rapidly, the words spilling from his mouth in the self-assured way I thought all Americans spoke, like gangsters in the movies. "Pretend she's aiming her gun."

"Smile," added another.

"Tell him I don't smile when I shoot my gun," I replied.

The interpreter, however, looked over to Vasilyev, who gave me a frown, then instructed me simply to go ahead and smile for the picture. Which I did, albeit stiffly.

"Atta girl," one journalist called out. "By next week, your face will be in every paper in the States."

"The boys back home are gonna eat you up, sweetheart," said another.

I felt like saying I didn't care in the least what those overfed and pampered capitalists who sat back and let my countrymen die while they went to their picture shows and drove their fancy automobiles thought of me.

"What would you like to tell the American people?" one called out.

I paused, then said, "I would encourage your soldiers to fight like men."

The interpreter again looked to Vasilyev, who sighed, then, turning toward the Americans, replied for me. "Comrade Levchenko said she is delighted to have the full cooperation of all our valued American friends. She desires only complete victory over our mutual enemies, and is sure that with your continued assistance we shall soon defeat the fascists."

"What does she think of Mrs. Roosevelt's invitation?" one reporter called out.

When the question was translated, I frowned, then turned to Vasilyev.

"Later," he whispered to me. Then to the group he replied through the interpreter. "Lieutenant Levchenko is deeply honored by Mrs. Roosevelt's invitation. She feels that the International Student Conference is a wonderful opportunity for our two countries to create an open dialogue that will ensure a lasting world peace after the hostilities are concluded." He then turned toward me and smiled, before saying, "She eagerly awaits meeting the First Lady in person."

As soon as we got into the car to head back to my room, I turned to Vasilyev and asked, "What do you mean, 'meet the First Lady'?"

"You are going to America," he replied bluntly.

"America?" I exclaimed. "I cannot go to America. My place is here."

Before he replied, he told the driver to stop the car.

"Gentlemen," he said to the two in front. "May I have a moment alone with the lieutenant."

We happened to have stopped beside the river. The others got out and walked down toward it, where I could see them light up cigarettes in the dark.

"Mrs. Roosevelt," Vasilyev began, "has heard about you and desires to meet you in person. She is organizing an international student conference convening in Washington and has graciously extended an invitation for you to come as her personal guest. The theme of the conference is peace among nations in the postwar world. You will attend as one of our country's representatives."

"But I want to return to fighting."

"You will do far more good for your country there than at the front."

"I am a soldier, not a diplomat."

"We feel it is important for the Americans to see you."

"Why?"

"You will present the new face of the Soviet Union," he said. "One that is intelligent, educated, brave." Smiling, he added, "And attractive too. It is our hope that your presence will inspire the Americans to get off their fat capitalist asses and open that second front they keep promising."

I suddenly recalled my conversation with Stalin, how he said I would get them to fight. Only now did I understand. They had all known about it. Everyone but me.

"So this isn't really about my going to a peace conference, is it?" I asked.

"That too. But we are at war now. Winning takes precedence."

"So let me go back to fighting."

"This is the best way for you to serve your country right now. You will go to the conference, and then when it's over, you can return home and go back to shooting Germans to your heart's delight."

"What if I refuse to go to America?"

He wagged his head so that his jowls quivered. "I'm afraid you can't, Lieutenant. This comes from the very top. You will do your duty."

"My duty is here."

"Your duty is whatever we say it is, Comrade Levchenko," he said, his dark eyes flashing with impatience and the muscles in his soft face tensing. It was the first time I'd seen him on the verge of losing his control. Yet in the next instance his face relaxed, and he assumed his usual congenial demeanor. "You will go and enjoy yourself. And as soon as the conference is over, I promise that you can go back to the front lines then. And your country will be deeply grateful for your service."

"Why didn't you tell me this before?" I asked.

"Certain details had to be worked out."

"When do I leave?" I said finally.

"Tomorrow."

"Tomorrow!"

"Yes. Think of it as a little R & R. A much deserved one."

"How long is the conference?"

"A few days."

"And then I can return when it's over?"

"You have my word," he said.

We drove back to my hotel in silence. I was a loyal soldier and only wanted to do my duty, to do all that I could to defeat the Germans. I loved my country and would gladly have given my life for it. If I could best help in this way, I was determined to do it, despite my own personal disappointment in not returning to the front.

As I was about to get out, Vasilyev placed his big paw on my arm. "Lieutenant," he said. When I turned to look back at him, I saw that he was holding something in his hand. An envelope.

"Here," he said, his tone hinting at something ominous. I hesitated taking it, sensing that something was wrong and that by accepting it I'd be authenticating whatever the bad news was that it contained. I glanced down at what he held, then back up at him. "It's about my husband, isn't it?"

He nodded.

Reluctantly, I accepted the letter but continued to stare at it for a moment. I thought how until I opened it, Kolya was still alive, still very much in the world with me. He seemed so real, so palpable to me then. I could picture his hands, the color of his eyes, hear his voice. He had been a good man, I thought. A doting father to Masha. Someone who had not only loved me but had done so unconditionally, even though he knew it wasn't returned. With the deaths of Masha and my parents, he was all that I had left, the only slender thread connecting me to my former life. I thought of what I had secretly wished for when we'd parted at the train station over a year before. Did I really want that?

As soon as I opened it and saw the military letterhead, I knew immediately that it was a *pokhoronka* letter, one of those formal missives informing next of kin of a death. As I read it, I learned that Kolya had been reported missing in action in the fighting at Leningrad. Not dead, but missing. Still, I knew what that implied. If he wasn't dead, he was a prisoner, which was just as good as dead. As I stared at the words on the page, tears sprung to my eyes and slid down my cheeks. I hadn't wanted to cry in front of Vasilyev, but I was helpless to stop. I had never felt so completely alone in the world, so utterly vulnerable. Kolya, I realized as never before, had been there for me, protected me, insulated me from the world. Now I was alone.

Vasilyev reached out and put his hand on my back and rubbed it in small circles. "My deepest sympathies, Comrade," he said. "Would you prefer company?"

I looked over at him.

"I assure you, my offer is quite benign. Just an ear to listen," he explained.

"Thank you, Comrade," I said. It was one of the few times Vasilyev would show a more human side. "But I think I'd rather be alone."

"Good night then. I shall pick you up at seven, Lieutenant."

Without bothering to get undressed, I lay on top of the covers, staring at the ceiling. Another part of my life had just come to an end. Some time during the night, sleep finally claimed me.

PART II

★ ★ ★

It is amazing how complete is the delusion
that beauty is goodness.
—TOLSTOY

1

nd so, I left all I knew behind me, my past, my homeland, my own identity. I had never been so far from everything I had known and loved. But it was much more than physical distance. I felt emotionally alone, isolated. My family gone. My comrades killed or taken prisoner, or off fighting the Germans, as I should have been. My beloved country under siege.

From the deck of the ship, I stared out at a sea that was a savage gray, riotous and unsettled as my own heart. A cold, driving rain out of the northwest pummeled the decks. The *Poltava,* a 25,000-ton dreadnought, slammed headlong into ten-meter swells, the ship's engines shuddering each time the vessel crashed into another wall of water. I had to fight just to remain standing. Everything toward the horizon appeared a leaden void, the sort of dim netherworld I imagined inhabited by the blind soldier I'd read to in the hospital at Baku. The weather had taken a turn for the worse shortly after we'd passed the Faroe Islands. The previous night at dinner, the captain, a gregarious, silver-haired man seemingly too old for war, had said we should be thankful for such weather. It shielded us against the wolf packs that prowled the North Atlantic. I hardly felt fortunate, though. I could still only pick at my food, having spent the first several days of our voyage hunkered down in my cabin over a bedpan. As I now stood on the deck looking out at the vast, roiling grayness, my knees weak, my stomach still churning uneasily,

I had the distinct feeling that this was a passage between worlds, like that which exists between the living and the dead.

We were six days out from Murmansk, the port we'd sailed from. The first four days I'd been confined to my cabin with sickness, until I'd gotten, as the sailors called it, my sea legs. Then we ran into weather, and the captain gave orders that we were to stay belowdecks, that it was dangerous to go topside. However, despite the wind and rain and rough seas, I finally had to get out of the stuffy, fetid air down below, which seemed only to make me sicker. When no one was watching, I slipped out of my cabin. I was able to get my hands on a poncho, which kept me from getting completely soaked in the lashing rain. I took cover in the lee of the ship's starboard gun turret. From here, I could gaze out at the tenebrous world we sailed through.

When I wasn't sick, I'd spend most of the time in my cabin reading, thinking about things. I'd found some books in a small footlocker beneath the bunk I slept on. A tattered copy of Turgenev's *A Sportsman's Sketches*, which my father used to read to me when I was a girl. Gogol's *Dead Souls*, whose title seemed almost a description of myself. Vasilyev had also given me a small American phrase book, with which I was to practice English. It had silly expressions like *My favorite baseball player is Babe Ruth*. Or, *Where is the Empire State Building*? Or, *Please hand me the ketchup*. Several times, Vasilyev would have Radimov instruct me. He turned out not to be a particularly good teacher. He was impatient and often short with me. "No, no, no," he would cry, exasperatedly waving his cigarette about. "Not *pleasant*. You say, 'It gives me great *pleasure* to meet you.'"

Or I'd pass the long hours of the voyage writing poetry. It was the first time since the war started that I was actually able to concentrate on writing without distractions. A strange calmness, that quiet introspection necessary for poetry, had seeped into my soul once more. You see, without realizing it I'd found myself changed again, altered in some incalculable fashion. These past several months—the weeks recovering at the hospital, the time in Moscow, the last several days aboard ship— had been an uncomfortable but necessary period of adjustment for me. I found I was no longer the person I'd been just a short time before, the warrior, the callous sniper who could shoot the enemy without batting an eye. Sometimes I would wake from nightmares about the German I'd killed in the cemetery in Sevastopol. I'd jerk awake as his hand gripped my wrist, his voice urgent. "Senta," he'd cry. "Senta." Then again, I certainly wasn't that other woman I'd been prior to the war either, the wife and mother. Especially with the news of Kolya, that part of me was gone forever. Another casualty of war. I was in a gray area, neither fish nor fowl. And now I was leaving all that I'd ever known and heading off to an alien land, for what purpose I had no idea but about which I felt a strange foreboding. I told myself I still wanted to return to the fighting, to the brutal clarity of battle. But another part of me wondered how I could ever go back to placing men in my sights and coldly killing them. As much as I still hated the Germans for what they'd done—to me, to my country—I didn't know if I could do that again.

One afternoon I had been in my cabin working on a poem. It was about Kolya.

> I should have loved you better—
> should have adored the quiet understanding in your eyes,
> the tenderness that was the gift of solitude
> you offered me like a bouquet of wilted flowers;
> should have cherished the forgiving touch
> on my naked shoulder those nights I turned away,
> leaving you to your own desert thoughts.
> Even now I hear the quiet sighs of rejection,
> can taste the salt of your unshed tears,
> can feel the broken heart beating inside your chest.
> Does that heart still beat in some faraway trench,
> or has it, too, been silenced by another sort of grief?

As I worked on the poem, I found myself rubbing the wedding band I had taken to wearing again. I don't know why exactly I'd begun wearing it. I didn't love him as a husband, of that I was certain. Perhaps it was out of guilt. Or maybe loyalty. Then again, maybe it was hope, the frail hope that if I wore it Kolya might still be alive. I wondered, had it not been for the war, if I would've stayed with him. Learned, as my mother had said, to love him. Or would I have turned into one of those old and embittered women whose frustration is visible in her eyes and mouth. Or would I have followed my heart and left him. But now with the news of his being missing in action, all that was just a moot point.

That's when a knock came on my cabin door. It was Vasilyev, who had brought me a bromide he'd gotten from the ship's infirmary.

"I'm told this will help your stomach," he'd said.

"Thank you," I replied, waiting for him to leave. He didn't, though. Instead, he stood in the narrow doorway of my tiny cabin, filling it with his bulk.

"What is it you are writing, Lieutenant?"

"A poem."

"I would very much enjoy hearing you read it."

"No," I said with more brusqueness than I'd intended. I could see his mouth take it as an insult. "What I mean is, it's not done."

"Of course," he said. "But when you finish it, I would be honored if you wished me to peruse it."

"Perhaps," I said.

He remained standing in the doorway. "Lieutenant, regardless of what you might think, I am not the enemy," he offered.

I stared silently at him.

"We are on the same side. We want the same things."

"And what would those be?" I asked.

"For one, victory over the fascists. For another, a better life for our people. A place where poetry can flourish."

I couldn't help but smile.

"You don't believe that?" he said.

"Not when our poets are thrown in prison."

He nodded ruefully. "Of course, some minor setbacks are to be expected."

"If you were one of them I don't think you would call being sent to the camp a minor setback," I scoffed.

"If it were up to me, poets would have much more freedom."

"As they do in America?"

"*Pfft*," he scoffed. "They have no poetry there. No *real* poetry, anyway."

"Have you been there?" I asked.

"Yes, several times. The last was shortly before the war."

"Did you like it?"

He shrugged. "It has, how shall I say, a certain appeal. They make excellent bourbon. And I enjoy New York. At least it has some culture."

"How did you find the people?"

"They are very self-centered. Like children, they live for the moment. They have no sense of history. No understanding of class struggle. Even the poor bow down to Mammon. They've been duped into accepting the lie that is the 'American dream.'"

I thought of what Madama Rudneva had told me about America. "But they have freedom," I offered.

"Freedom!" he scoffed. "For the wealthy few perhaps. Not for the millions of workers who live in poverty. Or for their Negroes, who are still enslaved."

"But they can live how they choose."

He had snickered at this. "It's all an illusion, Lieutenant. Marx said religion is the opiate of the people. For Americans it's the opiate of success."

To my right I heard someone say, "You really oughtn't to be out here." Startled, I turned to see Viktor Semarenko walking toward me, his feet splayed against the heaving of the ship, his legs rubbery as those of a drunken man. He was one of two other Soviet students headed to the conference in America with me. Viktor was tall and rawboned, with a long, equine face. A gaudy scar inched its way beneath his left cheek, where a German had cut him with a bayonet. The knotted scar drew his features to that side and gave him a slightly skewed expression.

"I needed some air," I replied.

"So you'd rather freeze your balls off up here?"

"I don't think I have to worry about that, Sergeant," I kidded.

"Not from what I've heard. You have more *mude* than most men."

Like me, Viktor had been a sniper, one who'd had over 150 kills to his credit. He'd fought at Kiev and Kharkov, was captured once and managed to escape. During the battle for Kharkov, he'd killed an entire platoon of Germans, for which he'd had his picture on the front page of *Izvestiya* and received the Gold Star and the Order of Lenin. And like me, he'd been paraded around, feted, accorded a hero's status. However, I'd heard that he could be difficult, that he drank too much and had an eye for the ladies. There was a rumor that he'd gotten into some trouble involving the wife of a local Party leader. Unlike me, he eagerly looked forward to going to America, anything to get away from the war. Now he was interested only in having a good time, and he looked upon this trip as if he were going away on holiday. He joked that when he was there he wanted to ride in a convertible with a "big-bosomed blonde" who looked like Betty Grable sitting by his side. I had never heard of this Betty Grable, so he'd taken from his wallet a frayed picture of a long-legged blond woman in a bathing suit. "Not bad, eh? You don't find legs like that back home."

Viktor was coarse and foulmouthed, but also funny. He made me laugh, and I liked him for that. He played cards and traded with some of the sailors on the *Poltava,* for cigarettes and booze and German souvenirs. Despite his peasant language, he was actually pretty bright. In fact, before the fighting, he'd been studying to become a veterinarian. To him the war was just a stinking pile of *der'mo,* as he referred to it, something we should be grateful to be out of for now. He hated the way the Soviet high command had sacrificed the lives of tens of thousands of soldiers while the big shots back in the Kremlin lived like kings. And he couldn't stand Vasilyev, called him "that fat swine." I'd warned him he'd better be careful or his mouth would get him in trouble. "Fuck him," he'd replied. "He needs us. What's he going to do in America if he doesn't have real war heroes to parade around?"

"How are you feeling, Lieutenant?" he asked me now.

"A little better."

"Here," he said, holding out a flask to me. "It'll warm you up."

"I don't know if I should," I explained, touching my stomach.

"It'll settle your guts. It's first-rate cognac. I won it off one of the sailors."

He removed the top and took a drink. "Go on," he said, offering me the flask. "You need to relax. That's your problem, Lieutenant."

Finally I gave in and took a small sip. At first, though, I regretted it, as I felt a new wave of nausea sweep over me.

"Give it a chance," Viktor said. He was leaning against the base of one of the big guns, his *ushanka* pulled low against the rain. Water collected in the furrow of his scar and ran sideways down along his face.

After a while, my stomach did settle down as the cognac's warmth fanned out throughout me. "That's good," I said.

"What did I tell you? I offered that little *khuy* Gavrilov a sip, and you know what he says?" Viktor asked me. "He says he doesn't touch hard spirits. That it weakens the will and we need to remain firm against our enemies."

As he repeated this, Viktor mimicked Gavrilov's high-pitched, pedantic voice, and he stroked an imaginary goatee, exactly the way Gavrilov did when he talked. It made me laugh. Anatoly Gavrilov was the third member of our student entourage, some sort of official in Komsomol, the Party youth organization. Viktor didn't like him and was always needling him. He called him that little *khuy*—a prick. I didn't much care for Gavrilov either. A slight, bookish man who always had his nose in some Party tract, he was arrogant and condescending, like a precocious child in school, the one who was always vying for the teacher's attention. He never just talked—he lectured, haranguing you about Party politics or Communist ideology.

"He *is* an annoying little bugger," I agreed.

"He's down there now, yakking with the fat swine. Christ, to hear Gavrilov tell it you'd think he'd seen all this action."

"Where did he fight?"

"Huh!" Viktor snorted. "That's just it, he didn't. He spent the last year behind a desk in Moscow, writing propaganda for *Komsomol'skaya Pravda*."

"Why is he going on this trip then?"

"My guess is he's a *stukach*."

A *stukach* was an informant for the government. Every factory or building or organization in the Soviet Union had them, and they curried favor of those above them by informing on their colleagues.

"You think so?"

"I'd bet on it. So watch what you say around him. Anything you say gets back to Vasilyev." Viktor looked out to sea for a moment. He was a good-looking man despite the jagged scar across his cheek. When he turned back to me, he said, "Besides, he has his eye on you."

"What do you mean?" I asked.

"He's sweet on you."

"Gavrilov?"

"You haven't noticed?"

Gavrilov and I had had only a handful of conversations, and in those he seemed only to try to annoy me. Several times I happened to say something about the war, how badly it had been botched in Sevastopol, and he would take me to task on it. "Lieutenant, it is not up to us to question the strategies of our government," he said to me once. "Ours is only to defeat the enemy." As if the little sycophant had killed so much as one lousy German.

"You're kidding," I said.

"No. He's quite taken by you," Viktor advised. "So watch yourself, Lieutenant."

"And Vasilyev?" I asked.

"What about him?"

"What's his role in all this?"

Viktor snorted, as if the answer was all too obvious. "He's secret police."

"He told me he wasn't. That he worked for something called the Ideological Department."

"Horseshit," he scoffed. He hawked together some phlegm and spit it over the side of the ship. "He's NKVD, all right. The other day, I happened to be passing his cabin, and I overheard him in there talking with those two *chekisty* pricks. He was giving them hell about something."

"Over what?"

"I couldn't make out what they were saying, but you could tell they were afraid of him. They don't fart unless he okays it."

"Why do we even need them along? We're just going to a student conference."

Viktor stared at me, the corner of his mouth twisted into that partial smile of his.

"Don't be so naïve, Lieutenant," he said.

"What do you mean?"

"I'm not sure what Vasilyev has up his sleeve, but this is not just about some student conference."

"How do you know that?"

"Think about it, Lieutenant. It doesn't make sense. They send three people halfway around the world, on a fully manned battleship when they need every fucking vessel to fight the krauts. Just to go to some peace conference?"

"I was told our presence might get the Americans to be more willing to open a second front," I offered.

Viktor rolled his eyes.

"Do you really think the Yanks are going to give a damn what we have to say? A couple of Russian *vanyas*. When they don't listen to the Old Man himself."

"Then what do you think our purpose is?"

He shrugged, took a final drag of his cigarette, and flicked it over the side. "I don't know. And to tell you the truth, I don't give a shit. They want to take me away from the front, let me sleep in a soft bed and give me plenty to eat, I say fine. But I tell you, they have something up their sleeves."

"Whatever their reasons, Vasilyev told me I could return to the front as soon as it's over."

"You can go back to the fucking war. Me," he said, "I just might decide to stay."

I glanced over at him. He stared out to sea, his brown eyes squinting, as if trying to sight something in the thick mist.

"What do you mean, 'stay'?"

"I mean, not go back. I could find myself a pretty little American *devchonka,* buy a big convertible automobile, and become a fat capitalist," he said, smiling.

I stared at him for a moment, trying to gauge whether he was kidding or not. He kidded around so much it was sometimes hard to tell.

"Joking like that could get you into hot water, Viktor."

His expression, though, turned suddenly serious. "Who's joking?" he replied. "My father was a good Party member until he crossed somebody, and they shipped him off to the camps. We've not heard from him since. I had a brother who fell at Smolensk. What do I owe those fucking bastards?"

"But you're a patriot," I said.

He laughed out loud. "I wouldn't expect such Party bullshit from you of all people. You fought at the front. You know what it was like. How we got fucked by those lying gutless bastards."

"All the more reason we have to remain loyal to our cause," I replied. "We're fighting for our country's survival."

"Listen, Lieutenant. Like you, I fought for my country. As did the soldiers I served with. You and I know the truth. Not the made-up bullshit those lying pricks like Vasilyev and Gavrilov write about. We were sent to fight and we were slaughtered like sheep. And for what? So that the big shots can dress in fancy suits and eat caviar, have their dachas in the country."

"But—" I began.

Casting a glance over my shoulder, Viktor quickly brought a finger to his lips.

"Speak of the devil," he whispered to me.

When I turned I saw Anatoly Gavrilov approaching us along the deck.

"Good morning, Comrades," he said. "I see you are taking the air, such as it is."

"Did you and Vasilyev decide on how you were going to win this war?" Viktor said, his sarcasm hardly contained.

Gavrilov glanced at the much taller man and drew his thin lips sharply together, as if he'd just bit into a lemon. He was short, with a dark, pointed face made all the more sharp by the Vandyke he trimmed to a fine point. Though he wore pince-nez to read, he didn't have them on now, and his eyes appeared startled, as if he'd just come from perusing a book with small print. On his head he wore a brimmed leather cap, of the type Lenin once wore. It was part of his image, the goatee, the pince-nez.

Ignoring Viktor, he offered, "The captain said if we make good time, we should arrive in New York in four days."

"If the U-boats don't get us first," Viktor said.

"Why such negative thoughts, Comrade?" Gavrilov replied.

Glancing at me, Viktor said, "I'm going to get something to eat." Then he turned and walked brusquely away.

After he was gone, Gavrilov asked, "What's the matter with him?"

I shrugged.

"I fear he drinks too much. That it's the cause of his pessimism."

"He served his country bravely," I said.

"I don't question his bravery. It's his attitude. Comrade Vasilyev would not approve if he knew of the questionable things he says."

"It isn't your place to tell him."

"Of course I would never tell on him," he said, suddenly indignant. "And how are you feeling, Lieutenant?"

"Better," I replied.

"I am glad to hear it. Let us hope you are fully recovered by the time we get to New York. It will demand much of us all."

"How so?"

He stroked his beard. "We must show the capitalists our resolve. Our iron will to defeat the fascists. As you have done with such bravery, Lieutenant. I personally am proud to know you." He stared at me then, smiling so hard that his gums showed. I thought of what Viktor had told me, that he was interested in me, and it turned my stomach.

"Good-bye, Comrade," I said, leaving him to the storm.

Two days later, the weather finally broke. I took the opportunity to walk along the deck, glad to be basking in sunlight for a change. The skies were a clear, flawless blue, the sea stretching out like a dark, polished tabletop. The sun felt good on my skin, warm and bracing, seeming to melt away the chill of the past week. I saw flying fish leap out of the water, their scales glistening like diamonds in the bright light. In the distance, a large convoy of vessels traveled eastward, a fleet of merchant ships being escorted by the United States Navy. On the third morning, off to the northwest at the horizon, I could make out a thin, uneven gray band that was neither sea nor sky, which I would later learn was the coast of Nova Scotia.

That afternoon the younger of the two secret police approached me as I stood looking out to sea. Viktor had found out that this one's name was Dmitri, with whom he played cards, while the older man was called Shabanov, though Viktor had taken to calling him *trup,* the Corpse, because he was so gaunt and deathly pale, and silent all the time. They didn't take their meals with the three of us students and Vasilyev in the captain's quarters. They seemed to flit about like shadows, standing in the periphery, watching us, spying on us, I felt. Once, returning to my cabin after dinner, I thought that my journal, which I kept beneath my pillow, had been moved ever so slightly, as if someone had handled it.

"I hear that we are almost there," the one named Dmitri offered.

"Yes," I replied.

"Are you looking forward to America?"

"I suppose I'm a bit curious about it."

I was surprised that he was trying to engage me in conversation. Up close, I realized he wasn't quite so young as I'd first taken him to be. Late thirties. He had the drowsy gaze of someone who'd habitually gotten too little sleep.

"By the way, the Boss wishes a word with you, Lieutenant."

I headed belowdecks to Vasilyev's stateroom. As I approached along the narrow passageway, I heard voices within his cabin. One voice actually, Vasilyev's. I glanced over my shoulder to make sure Dmitri hadn't followed me, then I leaned in toward the door. I couldn't make out much; it all sounded garbled to me. But I did catch a few scattered words. One word that Vasilyev repeated several times was *rezidentura.* Residencies? But what residencies? I wondered.

The room fell quiet, and I quickly stepped back a few feet, and made as if I were just walking toward Vasilyev's cabin. The door suddenly opened, and the Corpse emerged. He glanced at me, his large, wet-looking eyes beneath the thick glasses appearing chastened.

"He wants to see you," he said gruffly.

When I entered, Vasilyev was seated at a small table writing something. On the table were a bottle of cognac, some papers, an unlit cigar in an ashtray. Beside his chair was an expensive leather briefcase. He wore his wire-rim spectacles, and his hair was uncombed, a grayish stubble shading his cheeks. It appeared as if he hadn't slept well.

"Come in, Lieutenant." Without looking up, he motioned for me to enter. "Shut the door. Please, have a seat."

The only place to sit was the unmade bed, so I sat there. His bulky shape was still imprinted on the sheets. Vasilyev continued writing. The room smelled stuffy, of smoke and stale whiskey.

"I just finished writing up a press release for your visit, Comrade. Here," he said, handing it to me.

The first line read: "Senior Lieutenant Tat'yana Levchenko, the Soviet Union's 'Beautiful Assassin,' who has courageously destroyed 315 of the fascists, is the leading sniper in the entire Red Army."

"What is this?" I exclaimed. "I didn't kill three hundred and fifteen."

He waved the thought away, as if it were of little consequence. "Unfortunately, we've just learned that there's another sniper who has reportedly killed three hundred and ten. Some fool journalist already wrote a story about it."

"Then he should be acknowledged as the leading sniper. Not I."

"But you are here. And this other fellow is not nearly as pretty as you."

"First or second. What difference does it make?"

"You ran track. No one remembers who comes in second," he said. "Things will go much more smoothly if you just say you recorded three hundred and fifteen kills."

I thought how to men like Vasilyev facts were only a minor inconvenience, things to be manipulated to serve their purpose. As I was, a mere fact to be used. If I had not been considered pretty or a woman I'd probably still be fighting at the front. Or expendable, like those left behind in Sevastopol. But for now, at least, I was useful to them.

Beneath his spectacles, Vasilyev's eyes were puffy and unfocused, with a look in them I had not seen before—a harried look, of one who had much on his mind.

"Would you care for a drink?" he asked.

"No, thank you."

He picked up the bottle and poured some in a glass, downed the cognac in one swallow. Then he leaned forward in his chair, his elbows on his knees. He put his fingers together, as if in prayer, and tapped them against his lips, as I had seen him do before. "We should be arriving in New York some time tomorrow," he explained. "I wanted a word with you beforehand. To remind you that you will be representing the Soviet people, Lieutenant."

"Did you think I would forget that, Comrade?"

"It's just that we all have to be, well, extra vigilant."

"Vigilant?"

"Yes. About what we say and how we say it. The image we project. You see, America is a very undisciplined society. They are not very good at keeping secrets."

"What do you mean?" I said.

"Anything you say could find its way into the newspapers and have unintended consequences. Regarding the war, for instance. Berlin has only to read the American newspapers or listen to their radio to find out what these fools are planning next. The Amerikosy are not to be trusted," Vasilyev said with such uncharacteristic venom that it startled me. "They are like spoiled children. They are pampered with self-indulgence. A debauched nation that will collapse under its own corruption."

"I thought they are our allies."

"For the time being," he said almost glibly.

"What does that mean?" I asked.

"As they say, 'war makes for strange bedfellows.' I don't want you speaking to any of the Americans without Radimov or my being present."

"That would be rather hard, wouldn't it, Comrade, since I hardly speak the language?"

"Be that as it may, you are not to talk about the Soviet government, or say anything negative regarding the handling of the war."

"Certainly they will ask about my experience at the front."

"That is fine. You can tell them about all the fascists you killed. But you are to say nothing of a defeatist nature."

"Such as the hundred thousand troops we lost at Sevastopol?" I replied.

My sarcasm elicited from him a disapproving stare.

"You are an intelligent woman. Perhaps too intelligent for her own good. A simple view of things is oftentimes preferable. Or at least, safer," he said archly, with a glance in my direction. "Our job, Lieutenant, is to help persuade our reluctant American allies that ultimate victory is as much in their vital interests as ours. That this is not just some European conflict in which they have little at stake. We need them. At least we need their tanks and bombs and deep pockets. Anything we can do to further our mission is imperative. And anything that interferes with that mission would be frowned on at the highest levels."

"The highest levels?" I said.

"Yes, the very highest," he emphasized. "Do I make myself clear, Lieutenant?"

Vasilyev removed his glasses, put one hand to the bridge of his nose, and squeezed. "I am on your side, Lieutenant."

"My side?"

"Yes. In fact, I am your biggest advocate. I much admire you. There are others who would not be so understanding as I."

I thought of what Viktor had said about our reason for going to the States. I hesitated before asking, "Is there something else I should know?"

"Such as?"

"About this 'mission' of ours," I said.

He looked at me and said, "This is all you need to know for the time being."

"And after the conference, I can return home?"

"Of course. I'm sure there shall still be plenty of Germans for you to shoot," he said with a chuckle.

I sensed, even then, that whatever our "mission" was, that Viktor was correct—it wasn't just about some peace conference or sticking our hands deeper into the Americans' deep pockets. Perhaps it wasn't even just about getting them to open that second front. I sensed Vasilyev had something else up his sleeve, though it would take a while for that to become apparent. Everything about him was gleaming surface, smiles and subterfuges, wit and urbanity, with only hints now and then of something darker that lay beneath. I began to view Vasilyev as this very skilled puppeteer, working behind the scenes, pulling the strings, controlling all of us, including myself.

"Comrade Semarenko," Vasilyev said, "may present a problem for us."

"How so?"

"He's a loose cannon. He speaks too freely. Some of his comments I find troubling."

"He likes to joke."

"Still, I'm beginning to think we erred in bringing him."

I tried to protect my friend. "Viktor's a good soldier."

"His soldiering is not in question. It's his judgment I'm worried about."

"He'll be fine."

"Perhaps it might be good for you to speak to him."

"Me?"

"Yes. You and he have struck up a friendship, I understand. He might listen to you. Emphasize the importance of this trip to our war effort. That he is not to say or do anything that can reflect badly on our country. See that he doesn't drink too much. The liquor tends to loosen his tongue, so that he doesn't know when he oversteps himself."

"I am not going to be his nursemaid," I said.

"But perhaps you could save his neck," Vasilyev offered point-blank, smiling at me, though his eyes retained their sober look.

"I'll see what I can do," I offered. "Is that all?"

"Yes," he said. I got up and started for the door.

"Oh," he suddenly remembered. "I had a telegram."

For a moment I thought it might be something regarding Kolya. My heart leapt up at the possibility that he'd been located, that he was alive. I wasn't sure what the fact his being alive would mean for us, our marriage, but now I very much wished that, at least as my friend, he was all right.

"It's from Mrs. Roosevelt," Vasilyev replied. "She looks forward to meeting you with 'great anticipation.' Those were her very words."

The next day I was in my cabin when Viktor showed up.

"Come," he said urgently.

"What is it?"

"Hurry up."

I quickly followed him topside, thinking perhaps that the entire German Navy was waiting for us. We walked along the starboard side of the ship, heading toward the bow. The morning was cool and shrouded with mist, and in the distance I could hear the muffled blasts of fog-horns. For a while we could see nothing but fog, occasionally darker shapes looming in the distance.

"Viktor," I said, "Vasilyev asked me to speak to you."

"About what?"

"He asked me to warn you. To watch your tongue. Not to cause trouble."

"Fuck him."

"You'd better be careful. He's not someone to mess with." I started to say something else, but he was no longer listening. He was staring over my shoulder.

"Mother of God," he said. "Look!"

He pointed westward, and I followed where he indicated. At first I couldn't see anything because of the fog. But then, slowly emerging out of the mist like a photograph developing in a darkroom, I saw something gigantic gradually come into focus. Its greenish gray skin seemed to catch the light and radiate an eerie, incandescent glow. As we approached, I made out that it was the huge figure of a woman standing in the middle of the harbor, a spiked crown around her head, in one hand a torch held aloft.

"Now *there's* a woman," Viktor said, smiling lewdly.

8

America, I thought, as I stared out at the grand lady in the middle of the harbor. At first glance, her sharp features and aloof bearing made me think of some heartless Aryan valkyrie, cold and unapproachable. But the more I watched her, the more I realized it wasn't coldness at all that the artist wanted to convey but fortitude, an iron will. That arm of hers holding the torch had to be strong. She reminded me of the women I'd fought with, tough, determined, fierce. Exactly the sort of a woman this terrible age would need if the world were to survive. Gazing out at this strange new land, with its gigantic female symbol, with New York's massive skyscrapers in the hazy distance, I had an equally strange premonition that my life would never be the same.

Before we docked, Vasilyev called us to his cabin and gave us a last-minute lecture on how we were to conduct ourselves in America. We were to make sure we spit-shined our boots and that our uniforms were clean and well pressed, our medals polished and gleaming. We needed to pay close attention to our personal hygiene, as the Americans, he explained, were a people who did not like the smell of their own bodies. We should avoid any sort of profanity or coarse language, and especially when speaking to the press, to be certain that we smiled and were polite and courteous (as he said this, he stared at Viktor). He spoke to us as if he were the father of children he fully expected would embarrass him publicly. Instead of using the word *retreat* in reference to any battle in which we'd been forced to pull back, we were to call it *strategic redeployment*. Instead of *defeat,* we were to use the word *setback.* Instead of saying *capitalists,* we were to say *our American friends.*

As we were leaving the cabin, Vasilyev said to me, "A word, Lieutenant."

When we were alone, he approached and stood right in front of me. He inspected my uniform closely—adjusting the medals on my jacket, straightening my dress cap, checking to make sure my hair was in place, that I'd put on sufficient makeup and lipstick but not too much.

"You look nice, Lieutenant," he offered. It was only mid-morning, but he smelled heavily of alcohol, and he was sweating profusely. Lines of sweat ran down his neck, wetting his collar. "Don't forget to smile," he said, smiling exaggeratedly as if to show me what he meant. "At least pretend you're having a good time. Let's show these Amerikosy that our women are not all dour-faced babushkas driving tractors. And here," he said, slipping me a small bottle—it was something called Chanel No. 5.

I turned to leave.

"Oh, one more thing, Lieutenant," he said. "I'd like you to take off your wedding band."

"What?"

"I'd prefer that they not know you're married."

"That's ridiculous. Why?" I demanded.

"I would prefer them to think you are . . ." He paused, then said, "Unattached."

"*Unattached!*" I cried. "Whatever for, Comrade?"

"I'm only talking about the image you project."

"What image is that? I'm still a married woman, remember."

He reached out and laid a hand on my shoulder.

"Lieutenant, I don't have to tell *you* of all people, exactly what missing in action means in this war. Especially in Leningrad."

"Until I hear differently, I *am* still married. Besides, I don't quite get your point."

"We need to find a way to get these reluctant Americans to fight with us. Not in two or three years, but right now. Each day they delay, we lose tens of thousands to the German meat grinder. Their focus now is completely on their war with Japan. They could care less about what happens to us on the Eastern Front. Many in this country hate and fear us almost as much as they do the fascists. In fact, they would love nothing more than for the Communists and the fascists to slug it out for years."

"I still don't understand what all this has to do with my being 'unattached.'"

Vasilyev smiled that smile which explained so little, hid so much. What he said next momentarily left me speechless.

"I want every American man who lays eyes on you to fall in love with you."

When I'd recovered, I let a laugh slip from my throat. At first I thought he must be kidding, but then I could see that his gray eyes had that hard-edged gleam to them. "You what?"

"I want them to fall in love with you."

"You're serious?"

"Quite. What man would let his own beloved fight in his stead? I want every red-blooded American male to want to protect you from those terrible Huns. I want *you*, Tat'yana Levchenko, to put a face to the war, one they want to embrace."

"I'm a soldier. If they want to fight alongside me, let them. If not, to hell with them."

"But we can't afford to take such a cavalier attitude, Comrade. You better than I know what's happening at the front. It's our job to ensure that these spoiled Americans get off their asses and fight now. I want them to look at you and follow you into battle. Remember when I told you you can kill many more Germans by getting a million soldiers to fight with us? Now is your chance. Think of your comrades fighting back home. Think of your country." He paused a moment for effect, then added, "Think of your little girl."

I felt like slapping him for daring to use my daughter's name like this.

"Don't you dare bring her name into this," I said.

"But you fight for her, no? You kill the Germans so expertly in her memory?"

I shook my head.

"And what if they ask whether I'm married or not?"

"Tell them the truth."

"What is that?"

"I think we both know what that is, Lieutenant. I will see you topside."

Back in my own cabin, I sat on my bunk, staring at my ring, pondering what Vasilyev had asked me to do. I knew that he was probably right, that the chances of Kolya being found alive were extremely slim. Still, I felt uneasy about removing it, sensing a superstitious foreboding that if I did, it would somehow doom Kolya. Nonetheless, I slipped the ring off my finger and dropped it into my pocket. From time to time after this I would catch myself rubbing its warm smoothness with my fingers, a kind of prayer for him.

As we docked, I could see a small crowd of people gathered below on the wharf. One man held a sign which said in Russian, WELCOME ALLIES, and emblazoned with the hammer and sickle. The August day was sweltering, and my legs, unused as they were to being covered by stockings, itched terribly.

Once ashore, we were met by a number of officials and police officers; a contingent of reporters; civilians who'd somehow heard of our arrival; even a military band, which played "L'Internationale." As it turned out, the mayor of New York, a Mr. La Guardia, had had an emergency, and in his place he had sent a representative to greet us. He welcomed us to America and then gave the three of us students bouquets of flowers. After which, the reporters flocked around us, snapping pictures. Through Radimov, Vasilyev introduced us, first Gavrilov, then Viktor, and finally me, dubbing me, as he'd already done back in Moscow, the "Beautiful Assassin." Then they called out a few questions, which Radimov translated for us.

"Are the Germans as tough opponents as they've been cracked up to be?" asked one reporter.

Gavrilov jumped in with "They are formidable but hardly invincible."

At this, Viktor nudged me with his elbow. "If the weasel saw a German he'd shit his pants."

Vasilyev must have caught this, because he gave Viktor a stern look.

When it was my turn to speak, I said in stumbling, rote English something I had been practicing with Radimov's help for a while: "On behalf of the Soviet people, I wish to express deepest gratitude to the American people."

One reporter called out a question for me, which Radimov translated.

"Is it true you killed three hundred krauts?"

"Actually," I said, glancing over at Vasilyev, "it was three hundred and fifteen."

The reporter then whistled and exaggeratedly waved his hand in front of him, as if he were very hot.

Glancing above the heads of those surrounding us, I peered at the vast city stretching out in the hazy afternoon sunlight. Wavering miragelike, it struck me as something not altogether real, like some gigantic mural painted by a government artist hired to make it appear like a real city. Like those pictures I'd seen of the Palace of the Soviets.

After this short exchange, the seven of us from the Soviet contingent—Vasilyev, Radimov, and the city officials in one limousine, the three of us students and the two secret police in another—were driven across the city to Penn Station, where we were to catch a train for Washington. I sat between Viktor and Gavrilov. Outside in the street, there was a maddening rush of cars and trucks and buses flying every which way, a deafening cacophony of noises, of pedestrians rushing here and there. There seemed to be no rhyme or reason to any of it, almost as if a thousand lunatic asylums had suddenly thrown open their doors and commanded all of their inmates simply to go.

We were stopped at a light when a blond woman crossed in front of us. She wore a sleeveless white dress that barely reached her well-toned calves and black high-heeled shoes, the sort of impractical footwear you never saw on a woman back home. She strutted along, her hips sashaying back and forth.

"Look at her," offered Viktor, craning his neck to watch the woman. He rolled the window down and let out a long, drawn-out whistle.

"Don't act like a fool," Gavrilov said across me.

"Who's the fool? Are you blind, man? Look at those legs."

Viktor was about to whistle again when the Corpse reached over and rolled the window up. "That will be enough."

As we passed into the station, I saw an advertisement hanging on the wall. It showed a woman in an American naval uniform, smiling coyly, the top buttons of her blouse suggestively undone. It surprised me. Were Americans finally allowing their women to fight? Beside her were some words in English.

"What does it say?" I asked Radimov.

" 'I wish I were a man,' " he translated for me. " 'I'd join the navy. Be a man and do it.' "

I suppose it was the same sort of ploy Vasilyev was using with me, to taunt the American men into fighting out of some chivalric code of masculinity.

When we finally reached the train platform, we learned that there had been a mix-up and we'd missed our train to Washington. The mayor's representative, a balding man who smiled too much, apologized profusely, and then he and Vasilyev went over to the ticket booth to try and straighten things out. The rest of us headed into the high, cavernous lobby to sit on benches. The station was noisy with the whistles and hisses of trains arriving and leaving, and crowded with people rushing to and fro, many of them American servicemen.

While Vasilyev was gone, Gavrilov occupied himself by reading a small pamphlet entitled *Of Three Characteristics of the Red Army*. Viktor, on the other hand, spent the time studying the women who passed by, occasionally elbowing me and offering some comment about them. "They say redheads are very passionate," he observed about a buxom red-haired woman crossing in front of us.

The station lobby was an imposing room, with massive stone pillars and steel arches, a high-vaulted ceiling filled with windows from which the ponderous afternoon sunlight seemed to drift down like sifted flour. In several spots a large clock hung with a sign below it in English. As I was watching people rushing this way and that, I happened to spot a young woman seated a few benches away. She was petite, with dark hair and a plain, somewhat doughy face. Beside her sat a small child, a girl of perhaps seven, her brown hair fashioned in a single braid down her back. She wore a bright, summery dress with shiny patent leather shoes that didn't look very comfortable. Clearly bored, the girl kept fidgeting, shifting on the hard bench and squirming around, which obviously annoyed the mother. Every once in a while, the mother would lean toward the child and quietly reprimand her or pull down the hem of her dress. The little girl made me recall Raisa, the child we'd rescued in the sewers of Sevastopol. I wondered where she was. If she'd reached Canada safely. After a while, a young American soldier appeared, and the little girl rushed up and threw her arms around him.

I saw many American servicemen hurrying to catch their trains, duffel bags slung over their shoulders, their uniforms pressed and sparkling, as if they'd never gotten dirty. Some were dressed in brilliant white sailor's uniforms, others in the drab khaki of the army. There were enlisted men and NCOs, and a number of officers, even a pair of Negroes wearing corporal's stripes. The American soldiers walked with the confident strides of athletes who'd not yet entertained even the possibility of defeat. By the summer of '42, the Americans had just entered the war the previous December, and save for Pearl Harbor, they hadn't really tasted what war was like. And the horror of the Russian front was, I thought then, something unimaginable to them. Some turned to stare at me, perhaps because they weren't used to seeing a woman in uniform, especially one in a Soviet uniform and with so many medals attached to her chest. A few even stopped and made attempts at conversation, mostly through gestures, pointing to my medals and giving me the universal thumbs-up sign. They seemed friendly, gregarious, carefree.

After a while, Vasilyev returned with the mayor's representative.

"I'm afraid it's going to be a while," Vasilyev explained.

"How long?" I asked.

"A couple of hours."

"Can we at least get some grub?" Viktor asked. "I'm starving."

With surprising affability Vasilyev offered, "A very good idea, Comrade." He took out his billfold and removed some American currency and handed it to Dmitri, instructing him to go off in search of some food. "Radimov, you accompany him."

"I want an American cheeseburger, with lots of onions," Viktor said. "And a chocolate . . . what do they call it, Radimov? With ice cream."

"A milk shake," the interpreter replied.

"Yes, a chocolate milk shake."

After they left, Vasilyev said he had to make a phone call to the Soviet embassy in Washington. For some reason, he took Gavrilov with him. Viktor and I waited there with the Corpse, who sat opposite us, smoking a cigarette.

Finally Viktor nudged me with his elbow. "I have an idea," he whispered.

"What?" I said.

"Ssh. Just follow my lead," was all he said, giving me a conspiratorial wink.

"I have to use the can," Viktor said to the *chekist* officer.

"You'll have to wait until Comrade Vasilyev returns," replied the Corpse.

"I can't wait."

"Are you a child?"

"Something I had for breakfast didn't agree with me," he said, rubbing his stomach. "I have to go. *Now.* The bathroom is just over there." He stood and pointed off toward a doorway at one end of the huge lobby.

The Corpse glanced in that direction, then gathered his lips in annoyance.

"Or you can come along and hold my hand," Viktor joked.

"All right, go! But make it snappy."

Viktor glanced at me.

"I have to go too," I said.

"You'll have to wait until he comes back."

"She should come with me," Viktor said. "You don't want her going unescorted to the bathroom. This is New York, after all. Vasilyev wouldn't want anything to happen to our national treasure," he added, with a mischievous glance toward me.

The Corpse mulled this over. Finally he conceded. "Well, all right. But get your asses right back. And don't let her out of your sight."

I knew Viktor was up to something, and while I wasn't sure I wanted to be part of it, I went along anyway. We passed through an arched doorway, and then, instead of heading toward what were obviously a pair of lavatories—we saw men and women streaming into them—Viktor started for a staircase that led up toward street level.

"Where are you going?" I asked.

"We're in New York. I just want to see a little of the city."

"Are you mad?"

"You heard them. We're stuck here for a couple of hours. Besides, we'll be back before they even suspect anything. I'll say I had the runs."

"You know what Vasilyev told us."

"Big deal," he scoffed.

"I don't think you want to get on his bad side, Viktor."

"What's he going to do? He needs us. We're the war heroes."

"He could ship you home. He could . . ."

"What?"

"He could make serious trouble for you."

"Trouble?" he said with a laugh. "You and I just came from the front. We know what trouble is. I thought you had guts, Lieutenant."

"It's not a matter of courage, Sergeant. It's a matter of common sense."

"Stay then. I'll be back in a little while. Tell them I had the runs."

With this, he turned and started up the stairs.

I hesitated for a moment. I thought how Vasilyev had asked me to talk to Viktor, to make sure he stayed in line. Then I figured there would be less of a chance of his getting into trouble if I went with him. And Viktor was right, Vasilyev couldn't send us both back. He needed us.

"Wait," I called to him.

Halfway up he turned and reached out his hand toward me. "Hurry up then."

I rushed up the steps, my heart beating fast. I felt a little frightened, but more than that, I felt a giddy sense of exhilaration, of freedom.

"Five minutes," I said. "No more."

"Relax."

Out on the street, I was nearly overwhelmed by the city's teeming chaos, by its assault on the senses. Its sights and sounds and smells. Its noise and frenetic pace. By the crush of people surging along the sidewalks. The dizzying skyscrapers whose tops were lost in the afternoon haze. The gaudy colors of the clothing and signs and lights. The tempting fragrances that floated in the air like a stew. The babble of a million voices all seeming to talk at once. The dazzle and glitter of shop window after shop window offering any item imaginable, and some that were, quite frankly, unimaginable. Automobiles and buses zooming in and out, weaving lanes, as if it were all an intricately choreographed dance. In some ways, the pandemonium was like being in the midst of a battle—only the smoke and dead bodies were missing. I was reminded of what Madame Rudneva had told me about New York. But it was many times worse than I could've imagined.

"This beats the hell out of a muddy trench, eh, Lieutenant?" Viktor said, grinning.

We started walking, trying to negotiate the surging currents of humanity that flowed past. Viktor and I stumbled along, bumping into people who had gathered at stoplights or paused to gaze in a store window. Those New Yorkers, however, seemed to have mastered the technique for moving through the crowds. They darted nimbly like minnows in a stream, cutting this way, slashing that, speeding up or slowing down. We approached one building whose doorman was holding open the door of a long black limousine that had pulled up at the curb. I watched a couple emerge from the backseat. The young woman, tall and sinewy and lovely, was dressed elegantly, a diamond necklace about her swanlike neck. In her arms she cradled a small dog, no bigger than a rat in one of the sewers of Sevastopol. She was followed by a stout, gray-haired man in his fifties.

We continued on. I was amazed by the Americans' keen awareness of their own vaunted freedom. They moved about with such complete certainty, with an absolute assurance that the world had been fashioned exclusively for them and their desires. They walked and drove their autos and behaved without the least sense of restraint, or of order or propriety; they pushed and jostled and elbowed others in their way; they cut in front of people, even old babushkas shuffling along with canes; they yelled and called things out, from the tone both in anger and in jest. I was struck by how they lacked all manner of civility and politeness. How they spat on the sidewalks or tossed their chewing gum or cigarette butts, without the least concern for others or for the fact that a policeman might catch them. How loudly they conversed or laughed, without the slightest regard for someone eavesdropping on them. Back home, no one wanted his conversation overheard, so in public we spoke in cautious whispers or not at all. We who lived under communism kept things to ourselves. Something that Vasilyev had said occurred to me then. How the Americans were not good at keeping secrets. Perhaps he was right.

A few blocks away, in an alley, we came upon a disheveled man in a tattered military coat. He sat on a kind of mechanical creeper, in one grubby paw a tin can with a few coins sprinkled in the bottom, which he shook at passersby like a newborn's rattle. Both of his pant legs were rolled back, exposing the outlines of stumps.

"Do you think he's a real veteran?" Viktor asked me.

I shrugged. His uniform looked old, perhaps from the Great War. Viktor reached into his pocket and withdrew a couple of kopeks, and dropped them into the can.

"What's he going to do with kopeks?"

"Buy some vodka," he joked.

As we walked along, we saw similar examples of terrible poverty side by side with grand displays of unbelievable wealth. The poverty I well understood. It was the wealth I found hard to comprehend. I saw hungry-looking men gathered in alleys right beside fancy restaurants. The homeless sleeping on the sidewalk near elegant apartment buildings. No one seemed to notice, however, or if they did, to care. America, I was quickly realizing, was a land of glaring extremes, a vast spectrum of humanity.

Passing a fruit stand in front of a store, Viktor reached out and casually snatched an apple, slipping it into his coat pocket.

"Are you trying to get us arrested?" I whispered to him.

"They call it the Big Apple," he explained.

"Did you make that up?"

"No, it's true. A sailor aboard ship told me." When we were a ways away, he removed the stolen fruit from his pocket, rubbed the apple against his sleeve, then tore a bite from it. "Look around, Lieutenant. I think they can spare one stinking apple for one of their allies."

I had to admit, the sheer abundance of the city was astonishing. Everywhere there was food and more food, food beyond one's wildest imaginings—on street vendors' carts, in store windows, in displays before markets, on the plates of people eating in restaurants, hanging in butchers' and greengrocers' stalls, displayed on signs, in the hands of people passing by. Nowhere did I see long lines waiting for a loaf a bread, a piece of meat. In the garbage cans on the street I saw enough food to feed entire families back in Kiev. I recalled suddenly how hungry I had been at the front. Yet here there was such a dizzying profusion of food, more even than on the tables of the Party big shots back home. Where did it come from? I wondered. Who had the money to buy it all?

And everywhere, I saw people going about their business with such seeming nonchalance. No, it was more than that. Contempt. An utter contempt for the rest of the world, for the past or the future, for anything but right here and now. All else didn't matter in the least to these people. As I walked along I saw two well-dressed women my own age conversing in a small patisserie, someone waiting for a bus reading the newspaper, a man whistling as he made deliveries, a couple strolling happily arm in arm, a teenage boy bobbing his head to loud music that wafted out of a store. These Americans didn't seem to have a care in the world. It was as if for them there were no Kharkov and Kiev, no Smolensk and Sevastopol, no Babi Yar or Nikolaev. It was as if they hadn't heard about the millions already dead or starving in German POW camps. They were at war themselves, but it was as if it were just a distant rumor, something that didn't really affect them in any tangible way. Suddenly I felt such a righteous wave of anger rise up in me like bile. They are fools, I thought. Someone must tell them the truth. Someone must make them aware.

"Look at them," I said to Viktor as we walked along.

"What?"

"It's as if they don't know there was a war going on."

"What do you expect?" he replied, taking a final bite of his apple and tossing the half-eaten core into a garbage can. "They're spoiled capitalists."

"Then what the hell are we doing here?"

"Having a little fun."

"No, Viktor. I'm serious."

We had stopped at a busy street corner. A rush of traffic surged past us like an attack of Panzers, tires screeching, motors roaring.

Turning toward me, Viktor said, "That's your problem, Lieutenant. You take everything too seriously. Why not try to enjoy yourself a little?"

"It's hard to forget the war."

"No one's asking you to forget it. Just let yourself live a bit."

"But doesn't it anger you?"

"What?"

"That these people are so ignorant of what's going on in the rest of the world. The suffering. The danger we are all in."

"You think too much."

"That's what my mother told me."

"She was right."

At that moment, the light changed and the crowd surged forward. Viktor grabbed my hand and pulled me along.

"Are you hungry?" he asked.

"A little," I replied. "Perhaps we should be getting back though."

But we continued walking and soon found ourselves ensnared by the tantalizing smells of a bakery. We stopped and peered in the window at breads and pastries, frosted cakes and torts, strudel and puddings, something flat that looked like blini but was rolled and filled with some sort of cream. I felt my mouth water.

"Those look delicious," I said, pointing at the cream-filled dessert.

"Do you want one?" Viktor asked me.

"We don't have any American money, remember."

Viktor slipped by me and entered the store.

"Viktor," I said, following him. "Don't."

He ignored me.

"That's an order, Sergeant," I told him.

He looked back over his shoulder and said, "We're no longer on the battlefield, Lieutenant. I don't take orders from you anymore."

The store was crowded with people. Viktor got in line and slowly worked his way toward the front, a glass case behind which were more baked goods. A wide-hipped young woman in a filthy apron waited on him, saying in English something like "Can I help you?"

Viktor pointed at one of the cream-filled pastries behind the glass. When the woman reached to pick up something else, he shook his head and pointed again at the item he wanted. Once more she reached for a pastry, and once more Viktor had to shake his head. This went on several times. Finally, her hands on her hips, the woman straightened and said something harshly in English, which I didn't understand.

"*Zdes'*," Viktor said, meaning "here." He pointed again at the one he wanted.

The woman shrugged in annoyance.

"*Zdes', zdes',*" Viktor insisted, pointing into the case. Then he held up two fingers.

At last the woman picked up the right one and put two in a bag. She thrust the bag brusquely at Viktor and said something in English.

Viktor removed a fifty-kopek coin from his pocket and placed it on the counter. "Keep the change," he said in Russian, then turned to leave, grabbing me by the elbow and leading me quickly toward the door.

The woman called after us.

"Keep going," Viktor told me. I hesitated, so he gently shoved me ahead of him.

Outside, we hurried down the street. I turned back once and saw the woman standing in front of the store, shouting, waving a hand at us. At this we broke into a run and continued down the street for a ways before turning onto a side street. We ran down it for a while, and then Viktor pulled me into an alleyway. I felt suddenly winded from the exertion, the wound in my stomach aching dully. I didn't realize how out of shape I'd become since being hospitalized. And I couldn't believe what Viktor had just pulled.

"You're mad!" I growled at him.

"We're just having a little fun."

"Our first day in America, we end up in prison. Vasilyev would love that."

But Viktor had that disarming, lopsided grin on his face, like a mischievous boy who'd played a trick on his teacher.

I couldn't help smiling back at him. Here we were, standing in some alley in a foreign land, having already broken the law. More than that, I worried about Vasilyev's reaction to our going AWOL. Still, I had to admit that I felt an odd and exhilarating sense of . . . what? Limitless possibility? Of unbridled hope? The irresponsibility of hope. It was what I'd witnessed in the crowds of Americans that day. It was as if the feeling had somehow rubbed off on me.

"Here," Viktor told me, handing me the bag. "Enjoy."

I removed one of the pastries and took a bite. The outside shell was brittle and cracked as I bit into it. The cream inside was delicious, such sweetness as I had never tasted. My first meal in America.

"Delicious," I said.

We devoured our treats, laughing as we stuffed our mouths full of the sweet delight. After a while, I said, "Now we need to get back to the station."

We got lost and had to stop and ask a police officer in a blue uniform the directions. "Train station," was all I was able to tell him. Through gestures and pointing, he was able to show us where to go.

We finally made it back and hurried down into the station lobby. Vasilyev spotted me and came rushing over. He was followed by the others. Vasilyev's face was red, his mouth tightly pinched in annoyance. "Where the hell were you?" he cried suddenly. "We were looking all over for the two of you."

Viktor started to mumble something about being sick, but Vasilyev turned on him and struck him with the side of his hand. The gesture startled even me.

"I warned you, you idiot."

Then Victor did a foolish thing. He smiled at Vasilyev.

Vasilyev grabbed him roughly by the collar and shoved a finger under his nose. "Wipe that smile off your face, Sergeant," he hissed at Viktor. "Or you'll be sorry." Though Vasilyev's face was flushed and sweaty from the heat, his dark eyes held a strange glow to them, a razor-edged coldness, something as deadly as a bayonet sharpened on a whetstone. I recalled that time in the automobile returning from the American embassy, that sudden change that had come over Vasilyev. Yet I had never seen anything from him quite like this before, and frankly, this darker side disturbed me a great deal. Then again, I wondered if *this* side wasn't the real Vasilyev, and the other, the one who smiled and was jovial and charming, who enjoyed his food and drink—if that side wasn't just part of the façade he put on, part of his carefully constructed image.

"Don't blame Viktor," I interjected. "It was all my fault."

"What happened?" he asked me.

"You see, when I came out of the lavatory, I mistakenly went the wrong way and I got lost. It was Viktor who found me."

"We could have missed our train because of you two idiots."

Over his shoulder I could see Gavrilov enjoying this. He had a smug expression on his narrow face. "Comrades," he offered prissily, "you should behave yourselves."

"I am sorry," I said to Vasilyev, who glanced from Viktor to me.

"We will continue this conversation later," Vasilyev said. "Now we must hurry."

9

On the ride down to Washington, we shared a private compartment. We were all tired and irritable from the long journey, and rode mostly in silence. Once Dmitri fell asleep with his head on the shoulder of the Corpse, who woke and shoved him rudely off. For his part, Vasilyev seemed preoccupied with correspondence and perusing papers he took from his briefcase. Occasionally, though, he would glance over the tops of his spectacles and give me a look that suggested we hadn't heard the last of this.

I stared out the window as America raced by in the late afternoon sunlight. My last train ride had been a far different affair—a cramped and smelly cattle car hurtling toward the German advance. Now I sat comfortably in a spacious seat gazing out as cities gradually gave way to neat and orderly suburbs and then to long stretches of rural areas, with small towns congregated around a couple of church steeples, followed by farms and rolling fields, then scattered forests and lakes and swampy tidal flats followed by more cities. Used as I was to the Ukraine's flat, open expanses, there were more trees than I could have imagined, and all was green and lush, even in the summer heat. America too seemed far more crowded than I had pictured it. Every few minutes we passed another town or city, with people scurrying here or there. Save for a few squalid areas in the cities, the extravagant wealth I had witnessed back in New York continued unabated. Everyone, it seemed, had a house and an automobile, everyone had good clothes and shoes on their feet as they walked along. There were restaurants and petrol stations, markets and stores, parks and swimming pools and carefree children riding bicycles. Along the way, I saw the ubiquitous capitalist signs hung everywhere, displaying this or that product—cigarettes or shaving cream, liquor or washing machines, clothes or milk or cereal. All had happy, smiling people in them, presumably made happy by the product they used. I even saw one sign showing a happy dog eating food that came right from a can.

It was late in the evening when our train finally arrived at the station in Washington. A chauffeur in a large black automobile met us and drove us to the Soviet embassy. There we were greeted by two men, one older, stout, with gray hair, a wide affable face, and wire-rim glasses whose side pieces dug sharply into his fleshy temples. The other man was in his forties, brown haired, with sleepy-looking eyes.

"Vasily, you old scoundrel," said the older man, hugging Vasilyev heartily. He had a booming voice and an accent that was decidedly British. "You haven't changed a bit."

"There's a little more of me," Vasilyev joked, patting his stomach.

"Nonsense. You look well. How's Elena and the children?"

"Fine, fine," he said.

"Brilliant," the ambassador cried. "I assume you received my telegram?"

"I did, yes," replied Vasilyev.

"We shall talk about the matter later." Turning to the rest of us, he said, "Welcome. I am Ambassador Litvinov. This is Secretary Bazykin."

I had, of course, heard of Maxim Litvinov. He was a well-known figure in Soviet history. We had read about him in school. A close friend of Lenin's, he had been an early revolutionary and noted Bolshevik, and it was he who was largely responsible for getting Great Britain to become our ally (he'd even married a British woman), as well as for playing a role in the lend-lease program with America. As the ambassador spoke, his gray eyes lit up and his face broke into a broad smile, giving him an avuncular demeanor rather than that of a seasoned diplomat who could more than hold his own with the world powers. He warmly greeted each of us in turn. When he came to me, he glanced at the Gold Star medal on my chest and said, "Lieutenant Levchenko, your reputation precedes you. It is indeed a pleasure to meet you."

"Thank you, sir," I replied.

"Secretary Stalin sends you his warmest regards," he said. "So tell me, how do you like America so far?"

I hesitated, not knowing quite how to answer, and also without alluding to Viktor and my little jaunt in the streets of New York.

"What I have seen of it appears . . . very wealthy."

He let out a booming laugh, his substantial belly quivering.

"Yes, our dear American friends are blessed with many resources," he said in an overly loud voice, as if he were speaking to a large audience. The reason for this would very shortly become apparent. "But they are generous with their resources and wonderful allies in our fight against Hitler. Yet enough of that. Come in."

He led us down a hallway of the large mansion. We made a couple of turns and found ourselves in the kitchen, where a young, dark-haired girl wearing a maid's uniform stood at a stove preparing something. I noticed Viktor giving her the eye. The ambassador opened a door and led us out into a small garden area behind the embassy. We followed him over to a shed at the rear of the property, in front of which was a tall stone wall that surrounded the entire backyard. He took out a key and unlocked the door to the shed, then stepped inside and bade us enter. I wondered what we were doing, if perhaps he was planning on showing us something of interest. Once inside the cramped shed, I realized it was a place where various tools were kept. Shovels and rakes and saws hung from the walls, and on the floor rested a curious little contraption with wheels and curved blades that I would later learn was a machine to cut one's grass. The room smelled of new-mown hay. In one corner, however, there was a chair and desk. Upon the desk sat a telegraph machine with headphones. When we'd all managed to crowd into the confined space, bunched tightly shoulder to shoulder, the ambassador closed the door and turned on a light, a bulb that hung loosely from the ceiling. I found myself shoved against the far wall, perilously close to the tines of a rake, with Gavrilov's elbow pressed, I thought, needlessly hard against my breasts, his overpowering cologne making me almost nauseated. What on earth was going on? I wondered. In a whisper, Ambassador Litvinov answered my unspoken question.

"We have good reason to believe the Americans have put listening devices throughout the embassy. This," he said, with a smile, "is the only place we can speak reasonably freely. During your stay here, it is important that you take care. Remember, the Amerikosy can hear everything you say."

I pictured an enormous ear into which everything we said flowed. I wondered why the Americans would want to know what we talked about. Was I being naïve to think that Germany was the enemy, not us? But this was just the beginning of what I would come to think of as my "American" education.

"And how are things in Carthage?" Vasilyev asked the ambassador.

"As always, filled with petty intrigues," Litvinov said with a smile.

Carthage? Though I didn't know it then, I would soon learn that it was a code word for Washington, just as I would learn a number of other code words that the Soviets had devised in their language of secrecy and deception. The ambassador and Vasilyev spoke for a time, about things of which I had little understanding. Before we headed back into the main house, Ambassdor Litvinov turned to the three of us students.

"Comrades," he said, "I want to tell you that your dedication and sacrifice on behalf of the Motherland here will be of no less significance to our ultimate victory than that which you made on the field of battle. Much will be asked of you, and you must obey with the same unquestioning loyalty that each of you showed while fighting the Germans. A grateful nation will honor your actions."

What did all this mean? I wondered.

Before dinner, we were shown to our rooms in order to relax and freshen up. The toilet was down the hall, and as I was heading there, I happened to meet Viktor coming out of his room. He pulled me into his room and shut the door.

"What did I tell you?" he whispered into my ear. "They're cooking up something."

"What do you think the ambassador meant by all that?" I asked.

"Who the fuck knows. But whatever it is, it's a lot more than we're being told."

That evening the three of us students had dinner with the ambassador, his wife, and Secretary Bazykin, while the two *chekisty* and Radimov took their meal in the kitchen. I was seated next to Mrs. Litvinov, an elegant woman who spoke fluent Russian but with a decidedly British accent.

"It's such a pleasure to have another woman around," she offered, patting my wrist with a thin, bejeweled hand. She had a long, sharp face, high cheekbones, and a ready smile, and while not beautiful she had that English charm. "All my husband wants to do is prattle on about the war. This battle, that battle," she said, arching her thin, penciled eyebrows. "Frankly, I find it all quite boring."

"My dear," the ambassador said to his wife, "we have Comrade Levchenko to thank for bringing that boring war just a little closer to its conclusion."

"Can't we please just give it a rest for one night, dear?"

"Through our friends here in America we've set up something called the Soviet War Relief Fund," the ambassador explained. "We hope to raise enough money to—"

"Maxim! Enough!" Mrs. Litvinov chided with a smile. "These poor students have come all the way from the front. Let them relax and enjoy themselves for one bloody evening." The woman was not at all like the dour, plain wives of most of the big-shot Party members, no doubt in part because she was British. Then in a whispered aside to me she said, "My hairdresser is coming tomorrow. I could have her do yours if you'd like."

"Why, does it not look all right?" I asked, touching my hair self-consciously.

"It's fine for the front. But you're going to meet the president and First Lady tomorrow. You will want to look your best."

"I suppose . . . if it wouldn't be too much trouble."

"No trouble at all. It shall be fun, just us girls," she said, smiling benevolently. Then she reached over and picked up my hand. "And those nails certainly won't do. We'll have to get you a manicure too."

As we sat sipping wine, servants brought out platters of food. The ambassador and his wife proved to be gracious hosts, laughing and chatting easily, drawing each of us into conversation. They talked about the four-day student conference and the sights they wanted to show us around Washington. Vasilyev too was in rare form, swilling down the ambassador's wine and talking of old times before the revolution.

"This is very good," Vasilyev said, regarding the wine.

"It's Château Maresque, thirty-six."

"There is nothing good to be had anymore back home."

"That's the trouble with war," Litvinov lamented. "Hitler gets all the good French wines now."

At one point the ambassador stood and proposed a toast. "To our brave young men and women who have defended the Motherland in its darkest hour. And with our dear American friends," he added, rolling his eyes, "we shall have victory over the fascists."

When it grew late Ambassdor Litvinov told us, "Tomorrow will be a big day. A press conference at noon. Then meeting the president and First Lady at the White House. I imagine you are all quite tired from your trip. You should get some rest."

Mrs. Litvinov brought me up to my room.

"If you need anything at all, please don't hesitate to ask. Toiletries. Makeup." Then smiling confidentially, she added, "Feminine items. Heaven knows, these men wouldn't think of such things. Do you have a slip to wear for tomorrow, Lieutenant?"

"A slip?" I said. "Why, no."

"Come with me, dear. They can't expect you to look your best without a slip."

She led me down the hall to what must have been her room. She went over to a bureau and removed a slip.

"Here," she said, handing me the silk undergarment. "I think we are about the same size. You can use this until we have a chance to get you some clothes. I'll speak to Maxim tomorrow about seeing that we purchase a few necessities for you."

"Thank you, Mrs. Litvinov. You are very kind."

"We girls have to watch out for each other," she said with a laugh.

———————

After breakfast the next morning, Mrs. Litvinov showed me upstairs to a small sitting room off her bedroom. There an American woman dressed in a blue uniform arrived to do our hair. She brought her own suitcase filled with scissors and brushes and various other paraphernalia of her trade, and she began with the ambassador's wife. While I waited, the woman gave me a magazine to peruse, on the cover of which was a pretty, well-dressed woman holding a small white dog. "That's what they call a fashion magazine," Mrs. Litvinov told me in Russian. "You might get some ideas for your hair looking through that." I thumbed through the magazine, gazing at pictures of beautiful women sunning themselves beside pools or riding in large automobiles or seated at some elegant dinner table. It seemed that American women inhabited lives of mindless ease, unconcerned about the stark necessities of life. Like princesses in fairy tales, they never touched a shovel or lifted a single brick.

When it was my turn, I sat in the chair, and the American woman draped a cloth over my uniform. She said something in English, which Mrs. Litvinov translated. "She wants to know how you would like your hair done, my dear."

"I'm afraid I don't know," I said.

Mrs. Litvinov gave the woman instructions, using her hands to demonstrate how she wanted my hair to be cut.

"I told her to take a little off and put some curls in it. You have such lovely hair, a little curl will look good on you."

The ambassador's wife stood there looking on, occasionally giving instructions in English to the woman. We chatted while the hairdresser worked, as dark clumps of my hair fell about my shoulders like ashes in the war.

"Are you married, Lieutenant?" the ambassador's wife asked me.

I hesitated for moment, recalling Vasilyev's warning. But then I thought he had meant that only for the Americans. "Yes," I replied.

"Where is your husband?"

"He is at Leningrad." I paused before adding, "He's been reported missing."

"Oh, I'm so sorry," she said, her face wrinkling with empathy. "I'm sure he'll be found safely."

"Please don't tell anyone I'm married, though. Comrade Vasilyev didn't want—" but then I lowered my voice, thinking how the Americans might be listening to us. "He didn't want the Americans to know."

"Why not?"

"He wants them to think, well . . . that I am unattached," I replied.

"What!"

Whispering, I explained to her what Vasilyev had said to me.

"That's absurd. Who does he think he is?" Then, shaking her head, she added, "I'll speak to my husband."

"No, please," I said. "I'd rather you not."

"Well, if you insist. But watch yourself around Comrade Vasilyev. Beneath the smiles and bonhomie, he's rather an unpleasant sort of fellow."

Mrs. Litvinov didn't ask any more about my personal life, for which I was grateful. She spent the rest of the time telling me about life in Washington, the parties and dinners she'd recently been to, the best places to dine, where to buy clothes.

"Do you know Mrs. Roosevelt?" I asked.

"Of course. Ellie and I are good friends."

"What is she like?"

"She's something of an acquired taste," Mrs. Litvinov offered with a smile.

"What do you mean?"

"She marches to her own drummer. The woman wears the most dreadful outfits, especially for the wife of the president. Doesn't care a fig about her personal appearance. She goes out in public looking like a peasant." She laughed at her own joke. "But she's also the most sincere woman I've ever known. And completely fearless. Not afraid to speak her mind. Even with her husband. I fancy you and she will hit it off nicely."

When the hairdresser was finished, the woman held up a mirror for me to see her handiwork. I stared at myself, surprised but pleasantly so, to see the change my new hairstyle made in me. My hair was shorter and swept back in soft waves, framing and highlighting my face. It actually made me look younger, even pretty, like one of the women in the magazine.

"What do you think?" Mrs. Litvinov asked.

"I like it very much."

"It's quite flattering on you, my dear. Believe me, you will turn some heads at the White House tonight."

Later that morning, Vasilyev met me in the hall outside a large room on the first floor of the embassy where the press conference was going to be held.

"What on earth did you do with your hair?" he said, looking me over critically.

"Mrs. Litvinov suggested I have it cut. Why, don't you like it?"

He leaned in and whispered, "You look . . . too American."

"What does that mean?"

"They are expecting a soldier from the Soviet Union. Not Lana Turner."

I had no idea who Lana Turner was. "It is *you*, Comrade, who is always harping on the importance of my looking presentable."

"But I want you to look like a simple country girl. You should have cleared it with me first."

"I didn't know I would *need* your permission to have my hair cut," I replied crossly.

"Here," he insisted, taking my cap out of my hands and setting it on my head. He adjusted it, stuffing my hair up under the sweatband. He glanced over his shoulder to make sure no one was listening, then said, "They are broadcasting the press conference on the radio. Millions of Americans will be listening. This will be their first real contact with a Soviet citizen. Be sure to tell them how pleased you are to be in America. How much you are looking forward to meeting the First Lady. Also, try to work into your responses the importance of America opening a second front."

We then entered the room, which was crowded with reporters talking and holding cameras and little notepads. We headed up to the front and sat behind a table set up with a bevy of microphones.

"Good morning, Lieutenant," said Viktor, who was already seated next to Gavrilov. "Are you ready for the show?"

Gavrilov leaned across and said, "You look quite nice this morning, Comrade Levchenko. Have you done something different with your hair?"

"I had it cut."

"You look radiant."

After a while, three Americans—two civilians and a soldier who had the insignia of an officer—entered the room and proceeded up to the table. One of the civilians, a gray-haired man with a stern, deeply lined face, greeted Ambassador Litvinov, and the two conversed amiably in English, as if they were old friends. Litvinov, who spoke English fluently, then introduced us to the Americans. The gray-haired man was someone named Charles Bowen, an assistant to President Roosevelt. The other civilian, a slight, mustachioed man in a white linen suit, was Robert Swall, a reporter from CBS Radio, who would act as moderator. The soldier was a Captain Taylor. He was tall and fair, with short, receding hair. The most obvious thing about him, though, was that the left sleeve of his tunic was empty and pinned to the shoulder. He smiled as he shook our hands and welcomed each of us with "*Dobro pozhalovat' v Ameriku.*" He spoke Russian fluently.

Mr. Bowen said something to us, and the captain translated for him. "On behalf of the president, Mr. Bowen extends his warmest greetings. The president is very appreciative of your bravery on the field of battle and looks forward to meeting you all."

After this, the press conference got under way. The ambassador stood and in English briefly introduced the three of us students to those in the room. I watched as the reporters scribbled in their pads. Then Mr. Swall, with Radimov translating for us, explained how the journalists would go up to a microphone they had stationed at one side of the room, state what newspaper they worked for, and then ask their questions, which Radimov would translate for us. We would then make our replies into the microphones in front of us, after which the American captain, who sat on the other side of Vasilyev, would translate for both those in the room and those listening on the radio. It seemed needlessly complicated, and I didn't quite understand the need for two interpreters, but evidently each side wanted to make sure that they weren't misquoted.

At first the reporters put questions of a general nature to all of us. About what we thought of America, the upcoming peace conference, the prospect of meeting Mrs. Roosevelt, the war in the East. Gavrilov did most of the talking to start with, making it appear that he'd been in the thick of things. As he spoke, Viktor shot me a sardonic look. Viktor was asked a few questions—where he'd fought, how he'd gotten the scar on his face. I sat back, content to quietly observe the proceedings. After a while, though, I slowly became the focus of their questions. I was, no doubt, a curiosity to them, a woman soldier, a sniper, an oddity as interesting as a bearded lady in a carnival.

"Miss Levchenko," one reporter said, "can you tell us why you fight?"

The question, of course, struck me as patently absurd, but I did my best to answer it.

"As you Americans do, I fight because of a love for one's country. And because of my hatred for the enemy."

"Is it true that you've recorded three hundred and fifteen confirmed kills? The most of any Soviet sniper."

I glanced over at Vasilyev before answering. "I cannot say for certain if that is the most. But that's what I have been told."

One man went up to the microphone and asked if it was hard to pull the trigger.

"The key," I replied, "is to calm your breath and gently kiss the trigger, not pull it."

"What I mean is, is it hard to kill a man?"

I shrugged. "They are the enemy. It is my duty to kill them. One's skill at killing is merely a matter of controlling one's breath. Making the heart go still."

At this I heard a collective groan, as if I'd said something that offended them.

"But you are a woman," the reporter persisted.

With a masklike smile, I said, "I am glad you noticed, sir." This evoked laughter from the crowd. "No one takes pleasure in killing, not even Germans. But I do take pride in my job. In defending my country."

Another man said, "Some newspapers have called you the Beautiful Assassin. Do you mind being called that?"

"What woman would mind being called 'beautiful'?" I replied. Before translating my words, the American captain glanced over at me, and I could see that his mouth held a hint of a smile. The reply elicited more scattered laughter from those in the room.

One reporter asked me if I wore makeup or nylons into battle. When he asked this I noticed some of the men looking at my legs beneath the table. I replied, with as much politeness and decorum as I could muster, that such frivolous things did not concern a soldier when he or she was fighting, that all of one's attention had to be focused on the task at hand, otherwise one could be killed. Another wanted to know if the men in my unit watched their language in front of us women.

"No. We women are not such fragile things as you may think."

"But doesn't such coarse language offend the sensibilities of Soviet womanhood?"

"We can hold our own as far as cursing," I offered with a smile.

More laughter, this time loud and raucous. I could see that they considered me "interesting," a novelty that might help them sell their newspapers.

"Miss Levchenko, has the war made you any less feminine?" asked another.

"It has certainly toughened me, if that is what you mean. But beneath my uniform, I am still a woman."

"America doesn't permit women to participate as combatants," began one reporter. "What do you think about the Red Army allowing women to fight?"

"It is not a question of allowing us to fight. We *must* fight. Every available body is needed to defeat the Nazis."

"But do you think women are cut out for battle?"

"No one is cut out for battle," I replied. "It is something one has to learn. Both men and women. But I do think women have more patience than men."

This last comment brought a couple of whistles from the men. Another reporter wanted to know if I was married.

"No," I replied, again looking at Vasilyev, who gave me an imperceptible nod.

They asked many other questions, many of which were quite foolish. At one point the moderator asked of the three of us students, "What would you like to say to the American people?"

When it was my turn I said, "I would like to thank the Americans for their support. We soldiers in the field greatly appreciate it. But we desperately need more help. Not just guns and trucks. We sometimes feel we are fighting the Germans alone. We need you to open a second front. Not in a year or two. But now."

When the press conference was over, the captain approached me and offered his hand in greeting. In Russian he said, "I just want you to know how proud America's fighting men are of your bravery. You are really an inspiration for us."

"Thank you, Captain," I replied in English.

Smiling at me, he said, "So you speak English?"

"Just a bit."

He was about to say something when the ambassador interrupted us then to gather the students together for photographs.

After the press conference, the ambassador led Vasilyev, Radimov, and the three of us students out to a waiting limousine, where we headed off for the White House.

"You handled yourself quite well, Lieutenant," the ambassador said to me. I sat across from him, between Viktor and Gavrilov.

"Thank you, sir."

The day was sunny and clear, the city shining brightly. The foliage and flowers were in full bloom—a far cry from our own capital, with its dirt and concrete fortifications, its tanks and trenches and gun emplacements, the rubble left in the wake of bombs. Just as in New York, people were busily going about their business as if there wasn't so much as a rumor of war. As we wound our way through the city, I stared out the window at the various sights of the capital, its massive stone buildings, its broad, tree-lined avenues, its monuments and statues.

"The First Lady is a woman of the people," said Ambassador Litvinov. "She has championed the rights of workers, the poor, Negroes. She is someone we hope will be supportive of our aims."

"If I may ask, Ambassador Litvinov," I inquired, glancing across at Viktor, "what exactly are our aims in regards to Mrs. Roosevelt?"

The ambassador looked at Vasilyev before answering.

"The First Lady is very influential. Millions of Americans read her columns in the newspapers. She is a beloved figure. Besides which, she has the president's ear. She has been quite supportive of our struggle against the Nazis. That's where you come in, Lieutenant."

"Me, sir."

"From our sources in the White House, we know that she is quite taken with your accomplishments, Comrade. In fact, in her newspaper column just yesterday she said that you were an inspiration for all women."

"I am flattered," I replied. "But I still don't quite know what all this has to do with me."

Litvinov smiled condescendingly.

"For now, it's enough to know that Mrs. Roosevelt might be quite useful to our plans. Go out of your way to befriend her."

As we drove along I pondered what that meant, befriending the president's wife. I also thought about how the ambassador had said our government had "sources" in the White House. Of course, I should have known that the NKVD, which spied so extensively and pervasively on its own citizens, would be spying on the United States. Still, it came as something of a surprise to know they could be so close to the seat of American power.

At the White House we were warmly greeted by a short woman named Miss Thompson, who turned out to be Mrs. Roosevelt's personal assistant. She led us inside, past several guards, and into a large round room that had blue wallpaper and a massive chandelier hanging from the ceiling. She had us sit around a low table set up for tea.

"Mrs. Roosevelt will be with you presently," she said through Radimov.

Soon a tall, ungainly woman of middle age strode briskly into the room. She wore a dark shapeless dress with a white collar and clumsy black shoes that made her feet look enormous on her too-thin legs. Her reddish brown hair had streaks of gray in it and was held unceremoniously back with a white headband, the sort a factory worker back in Kiev might have worn. I recalled what Mrs. Litvinov had told me about her. Though she obviously didn't care much about fashion, there was about her a confident air as she made her way across the room, her shoulders thrown back, a barely withheld smile on her face. She was accompanied by her assistant and behind them the American soldier I'd met earlier at the Soviet embassy.

In well-rehearsed if somewhat mechanical Russian, she said, "*Ya rada, chto vy priekhali.*" She was pleased we had come. Then in English, which the American captain translated for her, she said, "Welcome to the White House."

After translating her words, the captain, smiling awkwardly, quickly slipped in: "Hello, again. She's been practicing that all week," he confessed. "I didn't get a chance to tell you I work here as an interpreter."

Following the introductions, Mrs. Roosevelt served us tea, chatting amiably with each of us in turn. Several times, Vasilyev jumped in to answer questions the First Lady had directed toward one of us. For instance, when she asked Viktor if he was eager to return to the fighting, Vasilyev replied by saying that as Soviet patriots we were all eager to return to the defense of the Motherland. After serving me, she reached out and rested her hand on my wrist. Her hands were plain and unremarkable, those of a common woman, save for one thing—a beautiful sapphire ring. "I've so been looking forward to meeting you, Lieutenant," she said, smiling. She had narrow, slanting eyes, a weak chin, and buckteeth that protruded from her small, eager mouth. Yet she was pleasant-looking, and when she smiled her entire face beamed with unbridled joy.

"It is a pleasure to meet you . . . ," I said, pausing, unsure of how I should address her. The captain, who was translating what I said, came to my aid. "She prefers Mrs. Roosevelt," he said.

"Thank you, Captain," I said to him.

"I had no idea you were so young," the First Lady exclaimed.

"Not so young. I am twenty-five, Mrs. Roosevelt."

"I find that hard to believe," she said with a mock frown. "You don't look a day over seventeen."

"I don't feel seventeen," I replied, forcing a smile. "In fact, I feel quite old."

"It's no wonder, after all you've been through. I must say, you've been an inspiration to all of us."

"Thank you."

"You've done more for the cause of women's equality in one year than I've managed to do in my entire life." Giving me what I would come to know as her characteristic grin, Mrs. Roosevelt then said something which the captain hesitated to translate. He stared at me, the merest hint of a smile on his own lips. For a moment I thought it was a joke between them, about which I was the object.

Finally the captain enlightened me. "Mrs. R thinks you're very lovely." When talking to me he would sometimes shorten her name to our "R." I wasn't sure if it was an expedient given the needs of translating or if he was on familiar terms with her. But as he said this about me, I felt my face redden. Not so much because of her compliment but because of the way the captain looked at me as he said this. His gaze lingered on me, as if he wanted to say something more.

"Tell her she's being too kind."

"No, not at all," Captain Taylor interjected. "In fact, I agree with her completely."

I happened to glance over at Vasilyev. He was staring curiously at the American soldier.

The First Lady chatted cordially with us for a while, asking about our trip and if we'd found America to our liking, and hoping that the oppressive summer heat wasn't too hard on us. "It's always so dreadfully hot here in August," she said. The captain translated for her while Radimov did the same whenever one of us spoke, except for the ambassador, who, as I've said, spoke English fluently.

"How is Moscow this time of year?" she inquired.

With a smile, Ambassador Litvinov replied, "Still standing, madam."

"Indeed," concurred Mrs. Roosevelt. "In London, I saw firsthand some of the devastation caused by the war. Let me tell you, it gives one an entirely new appreciation for what you soldiers have gone through."

"We merely fight for our homeland," replied Gavrilov.

Mrs. Roosevelt then shared an amusing story about Foreign Minister Molotov's visit to the White House.

"Your Mr. Molotov showed up with a loaf of black bread and a pistol in his suitcase," the First Lady said with a high, fluttering laugh. "I guess he thought we might not have food and that Germans were prowling the streets of Washington."

We all chuckled at this.

Soon Mrs. Roosevelt stood. "The president is about to give his radio address and would like to invite you all to attend."

She led us down a corridor, pointing out portraits and other things of interest as she went. She then escorted us into what she called the Oval Office, where the president would be giving his address. The room was filled with people.

"I would introduce you to Franklin," Mrs. Roosevelt said in an undertone to us, "but he doesn't like to be disturbed before he goes on the air."

We were given headphones so that the president's address could be translated for us. Mr. Roosevelt sat behind a large desk and spoke into a microphone, his head jerking this way and that for emphasis. He talked about the war effort and the strong unity that existed among America's allies. How together we would defeat the fascists and the Japanese Imperialists. And then he spoke of something he referred to as the "four freedoms"—freedom of speech, freedom of religion, freedom from want, and freedom from fear. Things that our enemies did not grant to their citizens. As I listened to him, I wondered how my own country was any different from those we were fighting against. I remembered my teacher Madame Rudneva, telling me that our government filled people's heads with lies and that they used fear to stifle anyone who disagreed, and I felt even more strongly now just how right she'd been. Then I thought about Vasilyev's comment, how the Americans were our allies now, with its dark implication for a future in which we might actually be enemies. Would the alliance between our two countries turn out as the one between Germany and my own country had? As I pondered these things, I thought how it was easier being a soldier, with your enemy so obvious, the dangers so clear-cut.

When the president was finished, Mrs. Roosevelt brought us up to meet him. From behind the desk one couldn't see the wheelchair he sat in. But now, seeing him in it, it took me a little by surprise, the fact that this powerful man was paralyzed, with stick-thin legs and a haggard look to him. Here was the great Roosevelt, Stalin's counterpart, whom I'd once seen in a Soviet newspaper sitting in the back of a convertible automobile, wearing a top hat and smoking a cigarette in a long cigarette holder, looking very much the epitome of capitalist success. Yet this man looked rather ghostlike, his face gaunt, his rather sad-looking eyes sunken with dark circles beneath them. He appeared almost a wasted caricature of himself. When he stood to greet us, he had to have support from two men on either side of him to help him out of the chair. Below his pant cuffs, I noticed the leg braces.

"Franklin, I'd like you to meet some brave soldiers," his wife said, introducing each of us. When he came to me, he took my hand and said, "It is a pleasure to meet you, young lady." His grip, however, was not that of an invalid but rather that of a man in robust health. He smiled at me, his features suddenly becoming animated. I could see the handsome young man he had once been. "Not only a deadly shot but the very picture of loveliness. Tell me, how did you like my speech?"

"I liked it very much indeed, Mr. President," I replied.

"Excellent! I'm delighted to hear that. Sadly, it is your generation that has inherited the problems of mine, and it's a pity that we ask for such terrible sacrifices from young people like yourself. I'm told you've just come from the Russian front."

"Yes, sir. We all have," I replied.

"Are things as grim as we've been hearing?"

I shot a quick glance at Vasilyev. He gave me the sort of circumspect look a music teacher might give to his prize student before some important competition, as if to remind him to hit certain notes correctly.

Right then, however, someone standing next to the president whispered something into his ear.

"Unfortunately, young lady, I'm told I have a meeting with your ambassador," Mr. Roosevelt said. "But my wife tells me you'll be joining us for dinner tonight. I'd love to continue our conversation. Cheers."

The First Lady led us back to the room where we'd had tea. She turned to me and, through Captain Taylor, said, "I've arranged for a private luncheon where you and I can have a chance to get to know each other better, Lieutenant Levchenko. Woman to woman." Then turning to Vasilyev she said, "Nothing that would be of much interest to you men."

Vasilyev paused for a moment, then said, "Of course, madam. I will send along our interpreter."

"That won't be necessary, Mr. Vasilyev," Mrs. Roosevelt said with a dismissive wave of her hand. "Captain Taylor will accompany us. Besides, you'll need your interpreter. Tommy," she said to her assistant, "see that the gentlemen are fed. They must be hungry. We shan't be gone long."

Then Mrs. Roosevelt linked her arm in mine and led me out of the room, with Captain Taylor following close behind. We headed upstairs to what turned out to be her sitting room. We sat facing each other on elegant wing chairs, with the captain seated to my right. On the low coffee table between us there was an assortment of foods, including several Ukrainian dishes—*kolach, mlyntsi, vareniky,* and *salo.* I hadn't eaten much for breakfast and found myself suddenly ravenous.

"I had the cooks prepare a few things from your country. Please, help yourself."

I took a plate and tried one of the *mlyntsi,* with sour cream on top. I hadn't had any potato pancakes in a very long time.

"I hope it's to your liking."

"It's delicious," I said. "My mother used to make them."

"Wonderful. I wanted to make you feel right at home. This place can be rather intimidating," she said, glancing around the room. "May I call you Tat'yana?"

"Of course, Mrs. Roosevelt."

"I would like us to be friends." She poured me some tea. "And eat some more. Heavens, you are so far too thin, Tat'yana."

Then she indicated for the captain to help himself to the food as well.

"There now. This is much better. Just us girls," said Mrs. Roosevelt, winking at the captain. He smiled sheepishly as he said the words to me.

"When I first read about you," Mrs. Roosevelt explained, "I told Franklin, now there's a woman I want to meet. Ready to get in there and mix it up with the boys. I think I would be just scared to death if someone were shooting at me. Aren't you afraid?"

"I must confess, madam, that many times I am afraid too."

"It's not the absence of fear that makes one truly brave," Mrs. Roosevelt advised as she sipped her tea. "It's confronting one's fears. You are just the sort of woman this world is going to need not only to win this war but in remaking the world afterward. I know Franklin is very much looking forward to talking to you."

"He is?"

"Yes. He wants to know all about what it was like at the front. A first-hand account. But I shall leave that to him. I'd rather know a little about you, Tat'yana."

"What is it would you like to know?"

"What are your interests? That is, when you're not shooting Germans," she said, with that same light, tremulous laugh I'd heard before. "What did you do before the war?"

As she spoke I thought she reminded me of someone, though I couldn't put my finger on who it could be. I told her how I had been a student, that I liked hiking in the mountains, skiing, running track.

"Sounds like you were a regular . . ."

Captain Taylor fumbled for a moment trying to find a Russian equivalent for what she'd said. "Mrs. R. says you are a *tomboy*."

"What is tomboy?" I asked.

"A girl who behaves like a boy."

I frowned, not sure I liked being called that. "You mean *lesbiyanka*?"

"No, no," he said, with a chuckle. "In our country a tomboy is a girl who is tough, unafraid to do what boys do."

"Where did you pick up a love for shooting, Tat'yana?" Mrs. Roosevelt asked.

"From my father. He taught me to shoot a gun when I was a little girl. He thought all Soviet girls should be able to protect our country from its enemies."

Mrs. Roosevelt tilted her head at an angle. "He sounds like a man ahead of his time. What are your other interests, my dear?"

"Poetry," I offered.

"Really? Who are your favorite poets?"

I hesitated, wondering if I should tell her that my favorites—Tsvetaeva and Yesenin, and of course my beloved Akhmatova—had fallen out of official favor. That was probably something Vasilyev would frown on. So instead, I replied with, "I've read a little of your own Emily Dickinson."

"You don't say. I just adore her work," replied Mrs. Roosevelt. "Let's see. It's been a while. 'Because I could not stop for Death/He kindly stopped for me.'"

"'The carriage held but just ourselves/And Immortality,'" I replied in English.

Mrs. Roosevelt laughed that high fluttering laugh of hers and clapped her hands gleefully. "Bravo."

"My English not so good," I said.

"No, you recited it perfectly. Didn't she, Captain?"

Captain Taylor glanced over at me and said in Russian, "You must have had a good teacher."

It was then, of course, that I knew of whom Mrs. Roosevelt reminded me. While she looked nothing like her, the First Lady had the same sort of vitality and charm, the same disarming candor, as Madame Rudneva, my old friend.

"I'm told that you write some verse yourself," Mrs. Roosevelt said.

I stared cautiously at her, wondering how she'd found that out, if, as with Vasilyev and the *chekisty,* the Americans knew all sorts of things about me, too.

"I dabble a bit," I replied.

"Good heavens. In addition to all your other accomplishments, you're a poet too. I must say, you're a very accomplished young lady. Well, I hardly consider myself a poet, but I manage to scribble a few words. I write a daily newspaper column. What I'd like to do is to have you write a piece about your war experiences."

"I don't know," I said.

"I think it would open the eyes of many Americans. We don't know much about your country or the war on the Eastern Front. They need to know how bad things are. To hear it firsthand. Besides, it would do wonders for our women to see what you've managed to do. What a woman is capable of when she's given the opportunity. Don't you agree?"

"Of course," I replied. "But I would first have to get Comrade Vasilyev's approval."

"Oh," Mrs. Roosevelt said, pursing her lips. "I see he keeps a rather tight rein on all of you."

I smiled uneasily. "I think he worries that we will say something . . . inappropriate."

"Inappropriate?" the First Lady repeated.

I took a sip of tea, hoping to give myself time to choose my words with care. Though I'd taken an immediate liking to this woman and felt instinctively that I could trust her, I still needed to be cautious. After all, what did I really know about her, or about Americans? Vasilyev had warned me to be wary around them, that they couldn't be trusted. Even at this point, I felt myself treading water that was much deeper, with far more dangerous undercurrents, than I could ever have imagined. I happened to glance up and catch a look pass between Mrs. Roosevelt and the captain. Their eyes met for the briefest of moments before they looked away, but I sensed in that moment something, a familiarity, the sort that passes between those who share a secret.

I put my cup of tea down.

"Comrade Vasilyev doesn't want us to say or do anything that might offend our hosts," I explained.

"I have little fear of your doing that, Tat'yana," the First Lady said.

Captain Taylor stared at me after he had translated this. "What are you so afraid of saying?" he asked cryptically. "You're among friends." Yet he had a look in his eyes that belied the smile. I wasn't sure if he was making fun of me or asking a question whose meaning I could not quite glean.

"I mean only that we are in a different country, with different customs," I explained. "I would not want to say anything that could be misconstrued in any way."

"That's understandable," Mrs. Roosevelt said. "And what of your personal life, Tat'yana? Are you married?"

"I . . . was," I replied stumblingly, feeling a sudden and terrible rush of disloyalty toward Kolya. "My husband was killed at Leningrad."

"I'm so sorry," Mrs. Roosevelt offered, reaching across and patting my hand. "And your family?"

"They are all gone, too, I'm afraid. They were lost in the bombing of Kiev." I thought of telling them about my daughter, but for some reason I hesitated. I wasn't sure if it was to keep them from feeling overwhelmed by my loss or to keep myself from it.

"You poor, poor dear," offered Mrs. Roosevelt. "And yet you've managed to carry on so gallantly."

"It was not a matter of choice," I said. "It had more to do with my hatred for the Germans."

Mrs. Roosevelt made a *hmm* sound. "It is, indeed, a vicious world we live in, Tat'yana. What gives me a little peace, however, is that I keep a prayer close at hand. It provides me with great comfort in times of need. Would you care to hear it?"

"Indeed."

Dear Lord, lest I continue in my complacent ways, help me to remember that somewhere someone died for me today and help me to remember to ask, Am I worth dying for?

"It is quite a beautiful prayer, Mrs. Roosevelt."

"Yes, I think so too. If this terrible war has taught us anything, it's that we owe so many for our own lives. But enough of the war for now. I'd love to see some of your poetry sometime, Tat'yana."

"Perhaps," I replied vaguely.

We talked for a while more. Mrs. Roosevelt was an affable woman whose agreeable demeanor and ready smile put people immediately at ease. Several times she tossed her head back and laughed out loud, girlishly and without the least self-consciousness. I noticed too how she'd often rub the sapphire ring on her finger, almost unaware she was doing it.

"That is a very lovely ring you have, Mrs. Roosevelt," I told her. "Did the president give it to you?"

She glanced down at it pensively. "No. A very dear friend gave it to me."

At the end of our meeting, she said, "Franklin and I are having a few people over tonight for dinner. He would very much like for them to meet you, my dear."

When I hesitated, she said, "Don't worry, we've already worked it out with Ambassador Litvinov. You're to come to dinner tonight and then stay over as our guest."

"I am to stay at the White House?" I said.

"Yes. Franklin and I would be delighted to have you."

"It is indeed a great honor."

As we were heading back downstairs to join the others, Mrs. Roosevelt was met by a balding man with glasses. She excused herself for a moment and went off to talk to this man.

Captain Taylor said to me, "I am deeply sorry about your losses."

"Thank you," I said.

"It's hard to imagine losing my entire family. You are very brave."

"Not so brave really. We all do what we must, no?"

He seemed as if he would say something more, but instead he nodded and smiled sadly. He was tall, well over six feet, with narrow, slumping shoulders and a lean frame that his crisp uniform hung loosely on, as on a scarecrow in a field. His slender face was boyish-looking with light freckles sprinkled over his cheeks like cinnamon. He had pensive, hazel-colored eyes, and a mouth that was almost too full for his slender nose, so that his lower lip bunched itself together and drooped just a bit, giving him a slightly pouty expression.

"Hopefully you'll have a chance to have some fun while you are here," he offered. "I could show you around a little."

"I doubt I shall have any time for fun, as you put it."

"That's a shame. If I can do anything for you, anything at all, please let me know," he said, smiling, but with a lingering look I couldn't quite read. Perhaps, I thought, it was just that I was unused to Americans' ways.

"Thank you, Captain," I said.

10

That evening, Vasilyev and I sat silently in the backseat of the limousine as we returned to the White House. Radimov had taken ill suddenly, presumably because the American food was wreaking havoc with his bowels, so it was just the two of us. The capital swept by in a blaze of golden light, monuments to America's history illuminated by spotlights in the growing twilight. It seemed odd to be in a city lit up so carelessly, so audaciously, as if there wasn't the slightest concern about the Luftwaffe. Through my open window, the warm, humid night smelled sweet, of honeysuckle and laurel. In the distance I could see the dark skin of a river, lights from the far side playing off its moving surface. On my lap I balanced a small overnight bag Mrs. Litvinov had lent me for my stay at the White House, since I had only my bulky soldier's duffel bag.

"Are you sure you left nothing out?" Vasilyev said to me.

"I believe I have everything," I replied, starting to open up my bag.

"No. I meant with your conversation with the president's wife."

"Oh. I told you everything." We'd already covered my conversation with Mrs. Roosevelt in detail. When we had gotten back to the embassy, he spent half an hour asking me questions.

"You were with her a long time. You must have talked about something."

"This and that. Nothing of importance."

"Did she ask about the war?"

"Not really," I replied.

"What does 'not really' mean, Lieutenant?"

"She said her husband was interested in hearing about the fighting in the East. That's all."

"Tonight if you speak to him, you'll be certain to mention the need for a second front."

"If the occasion presents itself."

"Yes, yes, of course. You want to be subtle. You don't want it to sound as if it's been rehearsed. But try to work it into the conversation." He removed his silver case, took out a cigarette, and lit it. "Would you like one?" he asked. "Camels. Real tobacco. Not like back home."

I took one, glanced at the dedication—WITH ALL MY LOVE, O. As he lit my cigarette, I asked, "Is that a present from your wife, Comrade?" Though, of course, I knew already that it couldn't be from his wife, as I'd remembered her name was Elena.

He looked at me with a blank expression. "What?"

"The cigarette case. Did your wife give you that?"

"No."

"I thought 'O' might have been your wife," I explained.

"My wife's name is Elena," he said, continuing to frown. "What are you talking about, Lieutenant?"

"Who is 'O' then? A lady friend, perhaps."

He turned and gave me a harsh look. "I have been married thirty-two years, Lieutenant. In all that time I have not been unfaithful to my wife. Not once."

"Congratulations, Comrade," I said. "You must have a very happy marriage."

"I like to think ours is," he explained, his tone both indignant and boastful. "Despite what you might think of me, I am a man of strong morals."

"I'm sure you are."

"I *am*," he said emphatically.

"Who is 'O,' then?"

"Someone I once knew," was all he said.

"Do you have children?" I asked. I don't know why I asked him this. It might have been to try to get under the surface, to see him as a person, instead of just another *chekist* agent, if that's what he was.

He nodded. "Three daughters and a son." He paused for a moment. "My son is a captain in the Sixty-second Army."

"You must be proud of him."

"Proud, yes. Concerned too. The Sixty-second has recently been moved to Stalingrad for the defense of the city," he said, his thin mouth puckering. I thought of his answer to the ambassador, that his family was fine. "You see, Lieutenant, we both have loved ones in harm's way." He turned to look at me. "Did Mrs. Roosevelt say anything else about her husband?"

"Like what?"

"She didn't happen to say anything about his plans for the next election? If he intends on running again for office."

"Why on earth would she tell me that?" I asked. "I just met the woman."

"Women talk about things. She might have said something inadvertently."

"She said nothing of the kind to me," I replied, drawing on my cigarette. The American tobacco tasted slightly sweet, but it was strong, and it made my head swirl. "Besides, what does that have to do with anything?"

"A great deal actually. These Americans are very fickle. They change with the wind. The same is true of their leadership. A promise by this president may be broken by the next. Our people are getting contradictory information about his intentions. If you can, Comrade, casually ask his wife if her husband plans on running again."

"How can I *casually* ask her that?"

"If it comes up in conversation. Did she happen to say anything about his health?"

"We've already been over this," I said.

"Listen carefully, Lieutenant. No matter how seemingly trivial or unimportant anything she tells you, anything you overhear—and I mean *anything*—I want to know about it. Do you understand?"

I sighed and looked out the window.

"She seems fond of you."

"I like her very much too. She's quite nice."

"It is good she has befriended you," said Vasilyev.

I hesitated for a moment, then said, "Ambassador Litvinov said Mrs. Roosevelt could be useful to our plans. What are our plans besides getting the Americans more involved in the war effort?"

He turned toward me, holding my gaze for a moment. In the darkness, his eyes gleamed but without the least illumination in them. No light or feeling seemed to leave them. They were glossy and polished, hard as opals. There was about Vasilyev always a certain inexplicability, something fundamentally elusive, unknowable, perhaps like the Soviet government itself. Sometimes I thought it had to do with the demands of his job, the secrecy entailed in working for the Ideological Department or NKVD or whatever it was he worked for. But other times, I thought that it was only him, his character. Even when he occasionally let his guard down, as he had with his wife and family, he quickly put up his walls again.

Instead of answering my question, he asked, "What did you think of her interpreter?"

"The captain?" I replied with a shrug. "I don't know. He seemed pleasant enough."

"He speaks Russian quite well. I wonder where he learned it. Perhaps he has Russian ancestors."

I took another drag of my cigarette and stared out the window.

"He seemed interested in you," Vasilyev offered.

I glanced over at him. "What are you talking about?"

"The way he looked at you."

"That's his job, to look at me. To read the nuances of what I say."

He nodded. "Remember, Radimov will not be with you tonight, so choose your words with care."

"Poets always choose their words with care," I said, somewhat flippantly.

By then we had arrived at the White House.

"I will pick you up tomorrow morning," Vasilyev explained. "Prepare a few words to say at the conference."

As I started to get out, he laid a hand on my wrist.

"Here, Lieutenant," he said, giving me an envelope. "Put that in your pocket."

"What is it?"

"Its contents don't concern you. Someone will contact you tonight. You are to deliver it to him. He will give you something in return. Of course, you are to let no one see it."

"How will I know who it is?"

"He will say the word *yurist*. It's his code name."

Lawyer, I thought. And I thought again of what the ambassador had said, that "they" had contacts in the White House.

I was met and escorted into the White House by Miss Thompson. When Mrs. Roosevelt saw me, she came right up and hugged me, as if we were old acquaintances.

"I'm so glad you could come, my dear," she said, the captain translating for her. She wore a long white dress with a corsage of flowers at her shoulder, and her hair was done up. She looked actually young and pretty, vivacious as a schoolgirl.

"Thank you for inviting me," I replied.

"Come. Everyone's just dying to meet you, Tat'yana," she said.

She escorted me into an elegant dining room where a couple of dozen people were milling about. Except for Captain Taylor and myself, everyone else was dressed formally, the men in suits, the women wearing long evening gowns and jewelry. Servants in white jackets carried trays of hors d'oeuvres. Mostly the men congregated in small groups, smoking cigars and laughing loudly while the women stood off talking among themselves. I didn't see the president yet. Mrs. Roosevelt, however, was eager to show me around, while the captain shadowed us, translating.

Mrs. Roosevelt brought me over to introduce me to three men standing near a fireplace, over which hung a large painting of a white-wigged man on a horse, waving his tricornered cap and seeming to address his troops before battle.

"I'd like you to met Mr. Stimson, Mr. Hopkins, and this cagey little fellow here with his pockets full of money is Mr. White, of the Treasury Department."

The others laughed heartily at Mrs. Roosevelt's little joke.

"You've certainly given those krauts what-for, young lady," said Stimson, who vigorously shook my hand. He was in his seventies, but lean and athletic-looking, with a long, narrow face, a stubby mustache.

"Mr. Stimson is our secretary of war," Mrs. Roosevelt explained to me. "He thinks we should attack Germany right now. Isn't that right, Mr. Stimson?"

"Indeed I do, madam. And the sooner, the better. We can't just sit back and let the Germans run roughshod over Europe." Then he turned toward me. "What do you think, Lieutenant?"

Smiling, I said, "I . . . I am just a soldier."

"But you've been in the thick of things. Who better to know what's going on over there than you?"

As Vasilyev had warned, I chose my words with utmost care. "We would certainly appreciate any additional help from our American friends," I said.

"See, Harry. That's exactly what I've been telling you," said the man standing to his left.

"Mr. Hopkins," explained Mrs. Roosevelt, "is one of my husband's closest advisers."

"It's a pleasure to meet you," said Hopkins, shaking my hand. He was thin, with a sallow complexion. I had seen this Hopkins before, in *Izvestiya*. He had met with Stalin and Molotov, beginning right after the German invasion. Back home he was viewed as a friend, more favorably even than Roosevelt, who many felt was only a reluctant ally. It was this Hopkins who'd pushed for the lend-lease policy for the Soviet Union. In person, he was a rather sickly looking fellow with tubercular eyes.

"If it wasn't for Harry here," offered Stimson, "your Red Army would be running on its tire rims."

"Then I should thank you," I said.

"Well, we want to give the Soviet fighting man—"

At this Mrs. Roosevelt interrupted him. "And woman, Harry," she said, smiling. "And woman."

"I stand corrected, Mrs. President," he replied affably, nodding his head in apology. "We want to make sure that every fighting man—and *woman*—has everything they need to beat those Germans."

The man named White was about to say something when someone formally announced the president's arrival. Everyone stopped in mid-sentence and all eyes turned toward one door, through which the president came in his wheelchair, propelling himself into the dining room. In his mouth was a cigarette in a long holder. He was smiling broadly and waving.

Mrs. Roosevelt led me over to him.

"There you are, young lady," he said, shaking my hand. "Just the person I wanted to see. Tell me, how many Germans did you kill again, Lieutenant?"

"Three hundred," I replied, then added, "and fifteen."

"My goodness." Turning to Secretary Stimson, he said, "Henry, we don't need more planes and tanks. What we need is a few more women like this young lady. We could whip those Germans in no time at all."

Everyone laughed at this.

"I don't think the Republicans will agree to let us draft women, Mr. President," replied Stimson.

"Then we ought to see that they're voted out of office," he said, winking at me. I could see that the president, despite his sad-looking eyes, was in good spirits and that he had a playful side to him.

Mr. Roosevelt then said something to his wife, who in turn spoke to the captain.

"The president wishes a word with you in private," Captain Taylor informed me.

I followed the president and the captain into a small pantry off the dining room. The room was narrow, and the president had a little difficulty negotiating his wheelchair. I felt nervous, wondering what he could possibly want to talk to me about in private.

"Let me begin by saying just how much I admire you, Lieutenant," the president said, with the captain translating. "Your courage is a shining example for us Americans in this terrible struggle we face."

"Thank you, sir," I replied in English.

The president smiled at my attempt to speak his language.

"No, it is I who should thank you for all of your sacrifices. But tell me about the situation on the Eastern Front," he said. "And I want you to be completely honest with me. Don't mince words."

"It has been difficult, sir. Nonetheless, the tide of victory is slowly starting to turn," I heard Vasilyev say through me, as if indeed I were his puppet.

"Our reports suggest otherwise," the president said soberly. "That the Germans have been routing the Red Army on all fronts."

"Indeed, we've suffered a few setbacks."

The president waved a dismissive hand in front of his face. "I'd call them more than a few setbacks, Lieutenant. I'm told you've just come from Sevastopol. What was it like there? What is the morale of the troops?"

I thought of all those we'd lost, all those the high command had abandoned to the Germans. But then I lied and said, "Our morale remains strong."

The president and Captain Taylor spoke for a moment, with the captain seeming not quite to understand what the president was telling him.

Finally the captain turned to me and said, "The president wishes to know if you personally believe that?"

"Pardon me?" I said.

The captain repeated it: "He wishes to know if you really believe that or if that's just the 'party line.'"

I looked down at the president in his wheelchair. His weary eyes probed mine. I didn't know how to answer. Here I was, speaking to one of the most powerful men in the world, and he was asking me if I were lying. Should I pretend to take offense? Should I continue to lie?

"What choice do we have, sir?" I asked. "We must continue to fight the Germans. To the last man or woman if need be."

"What can we do to help you, Lieutenant?" the president asked. "What do you most need?"

"Everything—ammunition, artillery, medical supplies, petrol. But most of all, we need . . ." Here I paused, wondering if I should tell him what I was thinking.

"Please feel free to speak candidly, Lieutenant. Don't be afraid of being blunt. You won't hurt my feelings."

"Well, Mr. President," I said, "more than anything we need for you to fight alongside of us."

"Rest assured, we are your strongest allies in this struggle," he said.

"With all due respect, sir, we need more than words. More even than the supplies you send us, for which we are greatly appreciative. We need for you to spill your blood on the battlefield. For you to fight and die with us."

"Is that what the troops in the field think of Americans, Lieutenant?"

I hesitated. "They think Americans are afraid to fight." I glanced at the captain as I said this. He sucked in his mouth, as if he'd taken personal offense at what I'd just said.

"Do they now?"

"Yes, sir. My comrades think that you Americans are spoiled and soft from living so well."

The president shook his head. "I can assure you, Lieutenant, our boys are just itching to jump into the thick of it. And believe you me, I'd like nothing better than for us to open up that second front your Secretary Stalin has been asking me for."

"Then why don't you, sir?"

"I'm afraid it's very complicated."

"What is complicated is that each day that you delay, tens of thousands more of my comrades die."

"I am not unsympathetic to your situation, Lieutenant. But my advisers tell me we're not ready yet. That we need more time to build planes and ships and tanks."

"Do you think we were ready when the Germans attacked? I am just a woman, but I took up a rifle and killed over three hundred fascists. If we are true allies, Mr. President, then we should share the sacrifice equally. It shouldn't be just Soviet blood that is being spilled to save the world from the Nazis."

The president nodded pensively. "I wish that you could speak to our Congress, young lady. Perhaps they would listen to you. But I give you my solemn word," he said, extending his hand to me, "I shall open up that second front just as soon as it's humanly possible. Not a moment later."

We shook hands.

"Thank you, Mr. President."

"I bet you're hungry."

"A little, sir."

"I can just imagine you didn't eat all that well at the front. You look a little thin, Lieutenant. Let's go in and eat, shall we?"

At dinner I sat between Mrs. Roosevelt and Captain Taylor, so that he could translate for us, and for those nearby. To the right of the captain was a chatty blond woman, wife of one of the President's advisers, while to the left of Mrs. Roosevelt was a heavyset woman named Lorena Hickok. Through the captain, she introduced herself as a friend of the First Lady's.

"It's such a pleasure to meet you, Lieutenant," she said. "I hear that you're staying with us tonight."

"With us?" I asked.

"At the White House, I mean. I live here," she explained, pointing a finger toward the ceiling. "I'm a reporter. I cover the First Lady, so I stay here."

The conversation at the table swirled about me. Someone would say something and the captain would translate as best he could amid all the racket. I found myself nodding and smiling idiotically, trying to keep in mind all of Vasilyev's many warnings so that I didn't say the wrong thing. How did I like America? What surprised me most about it? Did I get a chance to see a motion picture yet? Was I planning to resume my sniper duties when I returned home? I also thought about the envelope that sat in my pocket, wondering what it was about and who would take delivery from me. This lawyer fellow, whoever that was. I repeated to myself what Vasilyev had said to me, that whatever it was about it didn't concern me. I was just doing what I was told.

At one point, the blond woman to the right of Captain Taylor leaned across him and introduced herself to me.

"Dolores Montgomery," she said, smiling and offering me a hand that felt no more substantial than a rabbit's paw. She smelled a bit boozy. "But everyone calls me Dee."

She smiled to show a row of straight, startlingly white teeth. In her fifties but trying hard to appear much younger, she was thin and attractive in a severe sort of way, with a stony mouth and eyebrows that had been plucked and etched in with pencil. She wore a beautiful evening dress, cut low to show a wrinkly bosom beneath an expensive string of pearls. Her nails were painted red, her bleached blond hair done up perfectly, each strand in place. For the first time since I'd been in America, I felt a bit awkward in my drab military uniform, the cloddish boots, the Sam Browne belt across my chest.

"She wants to know how the women in the Red Army bathe," the captain translated for her.

"*Bathe?*" I asked.

"Yes," he said, that playful look coming to his eyes. "She wants to know how you bathe at the front."

"Tell her, as all soldiers do. That is, if we are lucky enough to bathe at all. Sometimes in a stream or pond. Other times out of water we fill our helmet with."

"Cold water?" she asked.

"Mostly, yes."

On hearing this, the woman raised her penciled-in eyebrows and said something else, which the captain turned toward me and translated. "She wants to know if women are afforded any special considerations for . . ." Here the captain actually gave in to a light chuckle. "Privacy."

"There is no privacy in war," I said.

"You mean to say . . . ," the woman began, pausing, her red mouth curled in an expression of unutterable disgust. "They expect you to . . . right in front of the men?"

"Sometimes it is unavoidable."

"What about—" But then she paused, glanced at the captain and said, "You know. *Our* womanly concerns."

Dragged unwillingly into this absurd conversation, the captain blushed. His pale skin turned pinkish, and the large freckles on his face seemed to darken. Seeing him this way, vulnerable and awkward, I couldn't help but smile with empathy. Then he rolled his eyes, without letting the woman see him.

"We take care of our womanly needs as best we can," I replied to the woman.

When the captain had translated this, she once more raised her eyebrows and exclaimed, "Oh dear. No wonder we couldn't ever get women in this country to fight. We wouldn't put up with such barbaric conditions."

Annoyed by what she said, I replied without thinking, "We Soviet women are not so petty as you American women."

The captain hesitated. "Sure you want me to tell her this? Her husband is an important adviser to the president."

I paused, then said, "No. I suppose not. Thank you, Captain."

He shaped his soft mouth into a frown and cast his eyes back over his shoulder toward the woman behind him. "I apologize for her. She's a fool. But we Americans are not all like her," he said.

"I know."

"Many of us appreciate the sacrifices that you and your troops have made. We Americans are not afraid to fight."

"Perhaps, Captain, it is I who owe you an apology," I offered. "For having said what I did about your country not wanting to fight."

"I know that your comrades are dying while we're still sitting on our hands. But we're not cowards. We're not. We want to fight. We really do. When you go back to the front, please tell your comrades that."

"Of course," I said, feeling bad that I'd obviously hurt his feelings. "How did you lose the arm, Captain?"

He glanced at the empty sleeve. "It wasn't anything heroic. When the Germans invaded Russia, I was in Leningrad. I wanted to fly to England and sign up to fight against Germany. Our plane was hit by Luftwaffe fighters. Everyone else died except for me. I was lucky, I guess. When I got back Stateside, since I couldn't fight, at least I could help in this way, so I enlisted."

"What were you doing in the Soviet Union?"

"Studying Russian."

"Is that how you ended up as an interpreter?"

"I'd studied languages in college. My specialty was Russian. After graduate school, I did some postgrad work in the Soviet Union. After I joined the army, they sent me for further training at a language school out in California. I translate some correspondence and serve as an interpreter as needed. I've gone with Mr. Hopkins to meet with your Secretary Stalin and with Molotov. I'm afraid my Russian isn't very good compared to someone like you."

"No, you speak it very well, Captain Taylor," I said to him.

We chatted for a while, with the captain occasionally smiling modestly at me.

After a while, someone began to clink his silverware against a glass and soon several joined in. I turned and noticed that the president was being helped to his feet. He held up his wineglass.

"I would like to propose a toast to our brave and gallant guest, Lieutenant Levchenko, who has come to us straight from the bloody battlefields on the Eastern Front," he said, the captain whispering a translation in my ear. "We are grateful for her courage and for that of all of her Red Army comrades." Then, smiling at me he added, "I've looked this young lady in the eye and I can tell you, I wouldn't want to be one of those Germans in her sights." Everyone laughed at that and the president sat down. Soon they all began clapping and looking toward me, and some called out my name. Confused, I turned toward Captain Taylor.

"They want you to say something," he explained.

I stood up, feeling uncomfortable speaking to such an august group. I glanced at the captain.

"It's all right," he said supportively. "Just talk and I will help you if you need it."

"I want to thank Mrs. Roosevelt for graciously inviting me here tonight. It is a great honor for me and for my country. I wish also to thank America for its support of us in the war." My gaze then happened to fall on the president, sitting at the end of the table. "And I know that one day soon, Mr. President, your country and mine will be fighting shoulder to shoulder against the Hitlerites. I eagerly look forward to that day."

I sat down and once more they applauded.

Then it was Mrs. Roosevelt's turn to stand up. "I also wish to make a toast. Here's to the student conference, which begins tomorrow afternoon. Let us hope that such international cooperation will lead us into a future without conflict."

After dinner, I asked directions to the toilet, which proved to be just down the hall. When I came out, the man I'd met before, Mr. White, whose pockets were supposedly filled with money, was standing there smoking a cigarette. He was a small, bookish-looking man with glasses, a soft, round face, and a stubby mustache like that worn by Hitler. He nodded at me, and I nodded back, and I was about to return to the dining room when he spoke up.

"*Yurist,*" he said.

I turned toward him. In English, I said, "Please to excuse me," and gestured with my hands, as if to say I didn't quite catch what he said, even though I had. He glanced over his shoulder before saying it again: "*Yurist.*"

So *this* was the contact to whom I was to give the envelope? I reached into the inside pocket of my tunic and removed it. I felt suddenly a cool sensation run down between my shoulder blades, causing me to shiver. Here I was in the home of the most powerful American, our supposed ally, and despite my attempt at ignorance, I knew very well I was doing something fundamentally wrong, as well as fundamentally very dangerous. The man took the envelope and quickly handed me another. "*Vsya vlast sovyetam,*" he whispered to me. A Lenin slogan I had heard growing up from my father: All power to the Soviets. Without another word, he turned and left me standing there. I slid the second envelope into my pocket and hurried back to the dining room.

At the end of the dinner Mrs. Roosevelt said to me through the captain, "It will be a busy day for you tomorrow. Perhaps you should get some rest."

As we got up to leave, Captain Taylor started to accompany us, but Mrs. Roosevelt said something to him, and he nodded and glanced toward me.

"Mrs. Roosevelt is going to escort you to your room. I enjoyed getting to chat with you tonight, Lieutenant," he said, extending his hand.

"The pleasure was all mine, Captain."

Mrs. Roosevelt took me up to my quarters. She led me into a grand room with elegant furniture, a canopied bed, and old paintings on the walls. I could feel the history of the room, as if the old ghosts of America's past still haunted the place. She tried to tell me something about a particular painting, another man with a white wig and knee breeches, but without Captain Taylor I could not understand her. We had to communicate with clumsy gestures and nods, and with the little English I possessed. "Yes, yes," I kept saying, though I didn't understand most of what she was trying to tell me. Someone had already brought my things up and had turned down the bed for me. The room was stuffy in the summer heat, and Mrs. Roosevelt fanned herself, as if to ask me if I thought it was too hot. I nodded, and she went over to the window and opened it up. The night was loud with the sound of crickets, while the sweet odor of roses wafted into the room. She then headed over to the nightstand and picked up a book and handed it to me. She said something in English and then my name and I knew it was a gift she was giving me. It was a small volume in Russian, a book of poetry by Pushkin. There was also a pen and sheaf of paper. Mrs. Roosevelt smiled at me and made a gesture, as if she were writing something on the palm of her hand. I deduced she was telling me that she had seen to this in case I wanted to write.

"Thank you," I said in my awkward English.

Instead of leaving, though, she sat down on the side of the bed and patted the spot next to her, inviting me to come and sit. So I did. She reached out and grasped my hands in both of hers and smiled benevolently at me. There was something about her, a gentleness that put me completely at ease. Then she said something, which of course I didn't understand. She said it again, but I still didn't get what she was trying to tell me. Suddenly she held up a finger, got up, and walked over to the mantel above the fireplace and picked up a framed picture. Returning to the bed, she showed it to me—a photograph of her and the president with a number of children gathered around them. She pointed at each of the children and then touched her chest possessively.

"*Vashi deti?*" I said. "Yours?"

She smiled and nodded, pleased that I had got her meaning. Then she cradled her arms together and rocked an imaginary infant, and pointed at me.

I understood what she was asking, I just didn't know how to respond. How does one explain something as complicated as the death of a child when one didn't share the other's language? I thought perhaps I ought just to shake my head and leave it at that. But Mrs. Roosevelt gave me such a kindly expression, I wanted to invite her into my world, to share my heart's truth with her. I wanted to share my loss with another mother who would understand.

"*Dochka,*" I finally said.

She gave me a puzzled expression, so I removed the small leather case and took out the picture of my daughter and Kolya. I pointed at Masha, said her name, and then touched my chest as she had done. "*Moya dochka.*"

Mrs. Roosevelt smiled and said something else, waiting for me to tell her more.

"*Umerla,*" I said, the word for *died*. Then I put my hands together and lay my head against them and closed my eyes, the universal sign for sleep. "*Umerla,*" I repeated.

Mrs. Roosevelt only frowned.

So I walked over and picked up the paper and pen from the nightstand. Unlike Kolya, I was never much good at drawing things. Words had always been my strength. Still, I tried my hand at sketching a plane sweeping low over the ground. Unfortunately it looked more like a bird than a plane. From beneath its wings I made dots for bullets, which trickled like rain to the earth. The rain-bullets dropped onto a long-haired stick-figure child lying on the ground. I pointed at the child in my crude drawing, then at the picture of my daughter. "Masha," I said, touching my chest as she had done. Then I lay my head on my hands again, to show that she slept. Finally I pointed heavenward. I watched as Mrs. Roosevelt slowly grasped what I was trying to tell her. She stared at me with such a depth of compassion, her awkward mouth furrowed with sympathy. A tear slid down her cheek, rested at the corner of her mouth before she wiped it away. She said something, which I took to mean that she was offering me her sympathy, and I nodded and thanked her. Then she reached out and put her arm around my shoulder and drew me slowly to her, as if I were a child needing comfort. As if I were one of her own children in the picture she had shown me. She stroked my hair and uttered something soothing to me. Though the moment was all quite bizarre, I nonetheless gave myself over completely to her kindness. I had for so long denied myself any feeling, had maintained such a hard shell around me. But it felt good to be in another's arms, to be comforted as my mother had once comforted me. Her gentle touch reminded me, in fact, of my mother's, how she used to hold me when I was frightened or sick. We sat like this for a long time. We needed no words to explain what we felt. I was no longer a Soviet soldier, and she was no longer the wife of the president. We were just two women comforting each other.

After a while, she squeezed my hand and bid me good night.

11

As I lay in bed, I thought back to Masha's death. It was the first time I had permitted myself to think about it. Perhaps because now I was not preoccupied with war, with killing or being killed. Or perhaps it was because of the kindness of Mrs. Roosevelt.

After Kolya had left for the war, Masha and I had moved into my parents' house so that we could all be together, share what little we had in the way of food, which was already growing short. My father kept saying the Germans would be stopped, that they would never get within a hundred kilometers of the Dnieper. Then fifty. Then twenty. Even when the Germans were poised on the outskirts of Kiev, their artillery lobbing shells into the city, he stubbornly refused to accept the inevitable. When we heard the sirens, he wouldn't leave our home to take refuge in the subways. He'd stay there, as my mother and I and Masha rushed for cover. People were already fleeing Kiev, streaming eastward by the tens of thousands, heading for Brovary and Romny, for Kharkov, for the distant Urals, anywhere away from the German onslaught. The railroads had been conscripted for military use, so that left only the roads for civilians. Yet they were clogged with long lines of lorries and horse-drawn wagons, bicycles, and people pushing carts and slogging on foot, their belongings on their backs. My mother tried to get my father to see the light, that we should try to leave before it was too late, but he remained steadfast. "You watch," he said. "Marshal Budyonny will defeat the fascists." Budyonny was the general in charge of the defense of Kiev.

My mother told me to go, to take Masha and leave quickly before the Germans completed the encirclement of the city. She gave me a purse filled with rubles and a necklace made of gold, and she packed some food in a basket. I threw some things in a suitcase, clothes for us, some personal effects, including a pile of poems I'd written. Then I said good-bye to my parents. My father hugged me, as he always did, stiffly, formally, then turned and headed into his study, as if to await the German advance. My mother kissed Masha, then hugged me. "I love you, Tanyusha," she said. When I begged her to come with us, she said her place was beside her husband. I didn't know it at the time, but I would never see my parents again.

By then the Germans had the city nearly surrounded. Only to the east, across the river, was there still a small window for escape, but a window that was growing smaller by the day. Already there was savage street fighting against what was left of the trapped Red Army. I made my way through the city, hoping to slip through the German net and head for Kharkov.

"Where we going, Mama?" asked Masha, in her arms a rag doll she called her baby.

"To safety," I said.

"What of *baba* and *dedushka*?" she asked of her grandparents.

"They have to stay, my love."

"Will they be all right?"

"Yes," I lied.

We traveled by night, hid in bombed-out buildings by day, sometimes coming so close to German troops we could hear their voices. I knew what would happen if they caught us. I would be raped and killed, and my child, as I had heard about other blond, fair-skinned children, would be sent back to Germany to be raised as Aryan.

We wandered south, looking for a way to cross. We chanced upon a family who were crowding into a small rowboat. Though they hardly had enough room for themselves, I begged to let us join them. The father, a burly man named Vidayev, took pity on us and finally allowed us in the boat. We crossed the river under cover of darkness and somehow managed to slip through the German lines. The next day we met up with a farmer driving a team of plow horses pulling a wagon. The wagon was filled with various farm implements, chickens in crates, cord wood, a pile of turnips, a can of petrol, a small piano that his wife played. He had us sit in back and we continued eastward, along the dusty road that led toward Kharkov. The days were blistering hot, the sun beating down on our heads like an iron mallet. But at least we had escaped. At night, we boiled turnips and fried eggs, and slept by the roadside under the warm summer sky, Masha lying in my arms. Vidayev's wife played the piano while seated on the wagon.

Several times during the day, we heard the faraway drone of approaching aircraft. Out of the bottomless blue sky that hung over the steppes, enemy planes would appear on the western horizon, small at first, then growing larger, swarming like bees. Each time the farmer would stop the wagon, and we'd rush to a ditch or small stand of trees at the side of the road and take what cover we could find. Sometimes the only cover afforded us along that skillet-flat landscape was beneath the wagon itself. The planes, Messerschmitts and Heinkels, would buzz overhead, but when they saw it was just a lone farmer's wagon, they'd pass on, heading eastward for more important targets.

We were three days' ride from Kharkov when a squadron of Messerschmitts approached from the north coming in low over the fields. We were caught out in the open. Before we'd had a chance to take cover, they opened up with their 20 mm cannons. I tried to shield Masha with my body. Bullets snapped and hissed and crackled all around us, exploding turnips and showering splinters of wood down upon us. As soon as the planes had passed over, I grabbed Masha. "Are you all right?" I cried. But except for being shaken, she was fine. I breathed a sigh of relief. Yet no sooner had I thought this, than one of the planes broke away from the squadron, which continued on out of sight. This plane banked sharply to the left, then leveled out and came straight for us again.

"Take cover," someone yelled as we scrambled down and hid beneath the wagon.

"I'm afraid, Mama," my daughter whispered near my ear.

"It's okay, sweetheart," I tried to calm her. "Everything will be all right."

The whine of the Messerschmitt's engine intensified, then its twin cannons opened up, strafing us. I could hear the bullets tearing into the wagon, and the *pft-pft-pft* as they bit into the dirt of the road, kicking up little puffs of dust, then the *twong, twong* as they plunked the piano keys. They say you never hear the bullet that is meant for you. I don't know if that is true or not, but I could hear them all around me, hungry for flesh. One of the horses let out with a frantic whinny, then collapsed dead in its traces, blood spurting from its neck. After a while, I smelled petrol.

"Get out," cried Vidayev. "Hurry." We dragged ourselves out from under the wagon and rushed out into a field of sugar beets and lay down. The remaining horse, crazed with fear, was whinnying and dragging its heavy burden down the road, trying to escape. The dead horse was pulled along in the dirt, leaving a trail of dark blood in its wake. That's when I remembered the suitcase filled with all of our things, our clothes, my purse with the rubles and my mother's gold necklace. Also, my poems. I thought it safe then to leave the field and try to recover my belongings before they were consumed in the fire. I instructed Masha to stay there; then I got up and sprinted toward the wagon. By now, though, the vehicle was engulfed in flames, black smoke billowing upward far into the sky. I tried to reach into the back and grab my suitcase, but the heat was too intense and soon I had to give up and turn back.

And what happened next is something I could never understand: off in the southern sky, I saw the German pilot bank again to the left and come back for a third strike. Why? I wondered. Why are you doing this?

I heard a voice calling, "Mama. Mama." When I turned I saw Masha running toward me. "Get down!" I cried, waving her to take cover. But she continued on, her doll jangling in her arms, her thin legs propelling her forward. I rushed toward her. That's when the German cut loose with a burst of cannon fire. I could see the small explosions of dust as they seemed to chase her across the road. Before I could reach her, bullets riddled her body and she collapsed onto the dirt of the road like a puppet whose strings had suddenly been cut. The blood soaked her dress, turning it black as night. I heard someone screaming, but it took me a moment to realize it was I. When I reached her, I picked her up, cradled her in my arms. "No!" I cried. "Dear God, no!" Part of me knew that she was already gone, but another part would not give in to such a strange notion as a world without my child. With my hands I tried to stanch the flow of blood, to keep what little life remained in her. Yet her blood spilled over my useless fingers and down the front of my dress, onto my lap. I glanced up at the sky. This time the plane continued on, receding to a small gray speck in the vast blue. I have never hated anything as I have hated that pilot. All of the other Germans I was to shoot over the course of the war were that one pilot, killing him over and over again.

For a long time, I remember sitting in the road, holding Masha's lifeless body, rocking her, sobbing. When the others tried to tell me that we needed to get going, that we had to move on before more planes came, I yelled at them, howled like a madwoman. When they tried to take her from me, I swore and snarled at them. I wouldn't give her up. I was out of my mind, you see, crazy with grief, and too with the already growing sense of guilt I felt. For having left her to get our things from the wagon. Finally, Vidayev's wife touched my shoulder. "Tat'yana," she said softly, "we must bury your little one." Something about her look calmed me, convinced me of the rightness of her words. After a while, I gave in and surrendered my baby to her. I watched as Vidayev and the farmer used a charred shovel from the wagon to scratch out a shallow grave there in the beet field. We had no shroud, nothing to wrap her in, had to lay her directly on the black dirt of the hole. However, the woman placed an embroidered handkerchief over Masha's face. Before they began to cover her with dirt, I said, "Wait." I wanted a lock of her hair, something to keep with me. The farmer gave me a pocketknife and I hacked off a piece of her hair. I put it in the small leather case I'd had in my pocket, which, along with a few other personal effects, was all that I could say was mine in the world. Then I remembered her doll and ran and got it from where it lay in the road. It too was covered with blood, but I placed it beside her in the grave so she wouldn't be lonely.

And just like that, we moved on, walking on foot. I kept glancing back, watching the newly turned spot of earth, trying to force myself to remember where her grave was, so that in some unimaginable future, an unimaginable Tat'yana Levchenko might return to it, kneel beside her grave, say a prayer for her. But the vast, indistinguishable landscape of the steppes soon swallowed the spot.

Over the next several days as we plodded along, I felt that change in me, a physical sensation, that of my heart or soul or whatever you want to call it, shrivel up and turn to stone inside my chest. A stone as hard as any gem, and just as dazzling. I felt my blood become thick with hatred, with a bloodlust for revenge on those German bastards.

I don't remember much of the next few days. I know only that I hadn't changed my dress, which was caked with her blood, hadn't washed the blood from my hands. It was as if I wanted even that gruesome a reminder of her to hold on to. After several days, we came at last to a small village not far from Kharkov. Somewhere during that time, I'd come to a decision. I decided I would enlist and fight those monsters. Vidayev's wife tried to talk me out of it, to argue that I had a husband to live for now, that he would need me. But I was adamant. Nothing less than the blood of Germans would appease my anger. So I said good-bye to them and went to the recruiting station in an empty factory and signed up to fight.

The next day I boarded a train, a cattle car that still smelled of manure, and with thousands of fellow recruits we headed back east to meet the invaders. One of the political commissars came into our cattle car to explain how it was our job to slow the advance of the southern flank of the German army, to give the Soviet forces time to prepare defenses for Odessa and the Crimea, where, he said, the fascists would be routed and driven from our soil. He told us that ours was a glorious mission in the defense of the Motherland, that we should be grateful that we could offer up our lives for our country. Nearby, I overheard a man say sneeringly, "The fucking German Panzers will tear us to pieces." He was a thin fellow with the blackened hands and stained features of a collier. Somehow what he'd said must have gotten back to the commissar—there were spies and informants everywhere. At the next stop, the man was dragged from the train, brought kicking and pleading out into a field of rye. It was a warm day and the sun beat down relentlessly. The commissar held the man by the hair and yelled that this was how traitors were dealt with. Whereupon he pulled out his pistol and shot the man in the side of the head. A stream of bright red blood gushed out, staining the rye surrounding him. They left his body lying there, and we moved on. I wondered about the man's family, if they would be notified of his death and the manner of it.

The train paused at several junction stops long enough for more recruits to board and for us to be fed a watery potato soup and a bricklike piece of bread. After the first time, though, there were no more hot meals; we were given foul-tasting tins of *tushonka* and sprat fish and cold tea. At one stop we were issued military gear and uniforms. We had to change right in the crowded, weaving cattle cars. The half dozen of us women were shy at taking off our clothes in front of the men. A couple of them whistled or said something as we undressed. But a captain told the offenders to shut up, that he had a sister who had joined to fight, that we were all Soviet soldiers, not men or women anymore.

One of the political officers, a lean man with a shaggy mustache like the tail of a dog, instructed us on the proper use of rifles. He opened the doors, and as we rumbled along toward the battlefront, had us shoot out into the fields, at fence posts and haystacks and road signs. Most were farmers or factory workers with no experience shooting a rifle. They shot nervously, jerking the gun.

"Can any of you sons of whores shoot straight?" the political officer cried.

"I can, sir," I replied.

He looked me over dubiously, then shoved the Mosin-Nagant rifle at me.

"Let's see what you can do, Comrade," he said.

"What would you like me to shoot, sir?"

We happened to be passing a farmer's field with a cow grazing in it.

"Shoot that fucking cow."

"The cow, sir?"

"Yes."

It seemed to me a frivolous waste. Worse, a shameful thing to do.

The farmer would need that cow to survive, especially now. But it was a good lesson to learn about war—that reason and common sense and notions of right and wrong were the first casualties. So I chambered a round, aimed, pictured the cow a Messerschmitt coming in low, and fired. The cow keeled over and dropped to the ground. I turned to the commissar and handed him back the gun.

He smiled at me again, impressed. "Do the same with the Germans."

During the day, I remember looking out the slats in the side of the car as the countryside sped by, at cattle grazing and fields of grain, long, narrow sections of blue summer skies. Here, the earth didn't give the slightest hint that war had begun, that the world as we'd known it had already changed forever. I remembered thinking about Kolya. How I almost envied him, his not knowing about our daughter. For him, she was still a memory of unsullied bliss.

After several days we could hear a faint rumble coming from the east, one that grew louder and louder as we sped forward. At one point Stukas, their distinctive high-pitched whine rending the air, descended on us, strafing us with machine-gun fire. Several soldiers were killed before they'd even gotten out of the train. Finally we stopped and fell out. Only every third solider was handed a rifle. The unspoken assumption being that those with rifles would soon be killed and the others would be there to take up their weapons. The commissar with the shaggy mustache pointed to me and said to the man handing out rifles, "Make sure she gets one."

My regiment was force-marched fifteen kilometers to the Prut River where we were told to dig trenches as bombs exploded all around us. We were all green, all afraid. Even I, who'd thought herself so ready to sacrifice her life for revenge, felt my hands trembling, my stomach knotting with the explosions of the enemy bombs. Despite my sacred anger, I was scared. Across the river the enemy waited, five well-equipped, battle-hardened German divisions along with another dozen Romanian ones. Then their Luftwaffe buzzed overhead, dropping bombs on our position. None of us had any idea what war would be like. I kept wondering if the officer back at the recruiting station had been right after all, that I should have signed up to be a nurse. Certainly shooting a target wouldn't be anything like shooting a real live human being, even a German. When the time came, despite my hatred for the krauts, I wondered if I could actually pull the trigger and kill a man.

Two days later I would get my answer. Ironically, my first kill wasn't a German but a Romanian who was shaving out of his helmet. He was sitting on the far side of the river, behind what was left of a shed. Evidently he thought he was protected, wasn't in the line of fire. Turned sideways, he'd cut himself with the razor just beneath his right ear. I sighted him in, put the man's ear in my crosshairs. However, I hesitated before pulling the trigger. My heart beat faster, my stomach in knots. I felt my hands begin to shake. He was, after all, a person, someone with feelings and a past, loved ones as had I. I realized that this was not going to be anything like shooting a paper target. I found I had to talk myself into it. He is the enemy, I told myself. He's responsible for Masha's death. The bullet caught him at the hairline above his ear. His head exploded. I felt suddenly sick, and I remember leaning over and retching right there in the trench. That was all right, though. Many men became sick with their first experience at killing. Yet I wouldn't permit myself to cry. I didn't want anyone to see such "womanly" behavior. I'm not sure if I felt bad for the man I'd killed or for my daughter. Or perhaps I was feeling sorry for myself, because of what I sensed, even at that moment, the war had done to me. How it would forever alter me.

12

The next morning I rose early and, as Vasilyev had requested, prepared a few words to say at the conference. What I wrote was not, I must say, very original, just the sort of clichés that I thought he wanted from me. About Soviet morale and how the tide of victory was turning, etc., etc. As I wrote, I found myself glancing at the envelope that sat on my writing table, the one that Mr. White—*yurist*—had given me the previous night. Finally I picked it up and glanced at it. What was in it? I wondered. What secret intrigues were Vasilyev and his *chekist* cronies up to, and what were they getting me involved in? I had a strange urge to open the envelope, to see for myself.

But a knock interrupted my writing. Opening the door, I found the woman I'd met at dinner standing there. Miss Hickok. She was solidly built, with broad shoulders, a sharp nose, and eyes that sparkled playfully. She had on slacks and a short-sleeve blouse, exposing muscular forearms that looked as if they'd once milked cows. I was surprised to see her here so early but then remembered her telling me that she actually lived in the White House.

"*Dobroye utro,*" she attempted in Russian.

I smiled at her "good morning" and replied in turn.

She said something in English, then reached out and offered her hand. I followed her upstairs to a room on the top floor, a sunroom, bright and airy. There Mrs. Roosevelt and Captain Taylor were already seated at breakfast.

"Good morning," Mrs. Roosevelt said by way of the captain.

"Good morning," I replied in English.

The captain then greeted me. I noticed that his eyes appeared somewhat bleary, as if he'd stayed up all night translating very small print.

"Would you care for some tea?" Mrs. Roosevelt asked.

"Please," I replied.

I sat across from her, while Captain Taylor sat to my left.

"How did you sleep?" Mrs. Roosevelt inquired of me.

"Very well, thank you," I replied.

The room afforded a spectacular view of the city. To the south loomed the tall obelisk of the Washington Monument, gleaming palely like a majestic god in the sunlight. Beyond, the city stretched out, muscular, green, and lush, with lingering pockets of mist sprinkled here and there. The scene appeared tranquil, almost bucolic, like something out of a painting by Turner. I still found it hard to believe that not a single German bomb had found its way to American soil, that here people could go freely about their lives without looking skyward for the high-pitched screech of Stukas.

"Look," Mrs. Roosevelt said, handing me a newspaper. "You've made the front page of the *New York Times,* my dear."

Indeed, there I was, standing between Ambassador Litvinov and Vasilyev at the press conference the previous day. The photo made me look startled, wide-eyed, like some captured wild animal.

"The *Times,*" the captain added, "is the most important paper in the States. It's read by millions."

Above the photo was a headline.

"What does it say?" I inquired of Captain Taylor.

He smiled sheepishly, one front tooth snagging on his fleshy lower lip. " 'Beautiful Assassin Enjoys Killing Nazis.' "

I felt a little embarrassed at this. "I wish they wouldn't call me that foolish name," I said.

"I wouldn't worry about it, Lieutenant," replied Mrs. Roosevelt with a grin.

"But they make me sound like a cold-blooded killer."

"I don't know how it is in your country, Lieutenant," explained Mrs. Roosevelt. "But here sometimes reporters twist things to sell papers." She glanced across at Miss Hickok.

"We journalists are a disreputable bunch, is what she means," added Hickok, her mouth screwed up into a grin. "We should all be taken out and horsewhipped."

"What else do they say?" I asked.

The captain went ahead and translated the accompanying article for me.

Yesterday during a radio interview at the Soviet Embassy, three young Russian heroes attending the International Student Peace Conference spoke not of peace but of war. Having come directly from the bloody battlefields of the Eastern Front, Staff Sergeant Viktor Semarenko and Anatoly Gavrilov, an official of Komsomol, the Soviet youth organization, discussed the difficulties of fighting the Germans. They described the harsh conditions of the war there—the brutal winters, the lack of supplies, the constant bombing by the Luftwaffe. But it was a mere girl, Lieutenant Tat'yana Levchenko, who stole the show.

Sans makeup and any other feminine accoutrements, Miss Levchenko, who received the Gold Star for bravery, was plainly dressed in an ill-fitting tunic, a long, khaki-colored skirt, and heavy black combat boots. Looking rather masculine in her soldier's garb, the petite woman deftly handled all questions put to her. When asked why she fights, she replied in a resolute voice that it was love of country. Questioned about the wisdom of the Red Army letting women function in combat roles, the spunky young girl shot back, "We must fight!" Miss Levchenko brushed aside inquiries of whether she wore makeup or nylons into battle, calling such concerns "frivolous." Dubbed the "Beautiful Assassin" for having coolly dispatched 315 Nazis, she stated unequivocally that she considered women soldiers the equal of men. "We have more patience." She said she enjoys killing Nazis and takes great pride in her remarkable skill. When not shooting Nazis, Miss Levchenko said she spends her free time writing poetry. The three students will be among those participating in today's international peace conference, one of whose organizers is the First Lady, Eleanor Roosevelt.

"They think I resemble a man?" I asked the captain, self-consciously running my hand through my hair.

"Nonsense," snapped Hickok. "I think you look quite dashing in your uniform, Lieutenant." Her voice was loud and raspy, and she spoke so quickly the captain had a little trouble keeping up with her. "Men," she scoffed. "They only care about what a woman looks like. Not what she thinks or what she accomplishes."

"What did you expect?" Mrs. Roosevelt replied offhandedly, buttering a slice of toast.

"Why, she's a war hero, Ellie, and they're treating her like she's Shirley Temple!"

"Don't knock our Miss Temple," Mrs. Roosevelt quipped lightly. "She's selling plenty of war bonds."

"I'm serious."

"Don't get yourself all worked up, Hick," the First Lady said familiarly. She kept referring to her friend as Hick. "It's too lovely a day."

"They have the gall to criticize this brave woman," Miss Hickok continued, "and the whole bloody lot of them don't have the courage she has in her little finger."

"I know, I know," Mrs. Roosevelt said, trying to placate the woman. "But the article did say some nice things about her too."

"What? Referring to her as 'a mere girl,'" her friend scoffed, shaking her head. "How are things ever going to change with such backward notions?"

Mrs. Roosevelt glanced across the table at me and winked. "As you can see, Lieutenant, Hick has very strong opinions on the subject of women's equality."

"Men are such jackasses," the woman pronounced.

As he translated this last line, the captain smiled good-naturedly at me.

"Certainly you don't mean to include our nice Captain Taylor in that group, do you?" Mrs. Roosevelt offered.

Hickok glanced over at the captain and smiled. "No offense, Captain."

"None taken," he replied, returning the smile to show he held no hard feelings. Somehow during all of this, he had managed to continue translating. He was a very skilled translator. In fact, during my stay with Mrs. Roosevelt, sometimes I would almost forget he was there with us, listening to our conversations, passing on what we said. For long periods of time he seemed to fade into the background, become a mere conduit for the words of others. He was there in the way a waiter at an elegant restaurant was there, ready to serve but almost invisible. In the days and weeks that followed, Mrs. Roosevelt and I would come to share the most intimate details of our lives, and there would be the captain, our go-between, the one who transmitted our thoughts and feelings to the other.

"Well, I wouldn't pay it any mind," Mrs. Roosevelt said philosophically to her friend. "The important thing is that they've recognized her. That's a big step. Would you care for some more tea, Lieutenant?"

"Well, it's certainly extraordinary what you've done for the status of women," said Mrs. Roosevelt's friend.

"Thank you, Miss Hickok—"

I remembered that occasion in the trenches, arguing the same point with Zoya. How what we did in the war would change things for women afterward in the Soviet Union. How it would pave the way for better opportunities, more equal treatment. Now, though, I wasn't so sure.

"Ellie, what was that line you wrote a few years back, about women being shot at?"

"I said that women who are willing to be leaders must stand out and be prepared to be shot at," replied Mrs. Roosevelt.

"Well, I'd say you've certainly been shot at, Lieutenant," Miss Hickok said with a raspy laugh.

"I must confess I wasn't thinking such lofty thoughts when I enlisted," I replied. "It was mostly out of revenge, a hatred for the Germans."

I glanced across at Mrs. Roosevelt as I said this. I could tell by her expression that she was thinking of our conversation the previous night. About what I'd told her concerning my daughter.

"What was her name again?" asked Mrs. Roosevelt.

"Mariya," I said. "But we called her Masha."

Mrs. Roosevelt shook her head. "I'm a peace-loving person by nature. But I think such a thing would fill me with sanguinary thoughts too."

As the captain translated this, he stared curiously at me, not following our conversation.

"We all of us, Lieutenant," Mrs. Roosevelt said, "have our private motivations for doing public good. And, Lord knows, many times they are not very noble reasons. But as Franklin is always reminding me, it's the end result that counts. Whatever the reasons for your bravery, everyone in the world—men and women—are supremely grateful for it."

"Thank you," I said.

"*Life* magazine wants me to write a feature story on you, Lieutenant," said Hick.

"That's a splendid idea," added Mrs. Roosevelt. "I think she's just what American women need to see."

Hick then made inquiries about my life, what I wanted to do after the war, about my poetry. Though she was a bit gruff and opinionated, I liked her. Her confidence. Her independence. The way she was unafraid to speak bluntly, not mince words. I was also struck by the familiar, even intimate way she acted with Mrs. Roosevelt, as if they were best friends from childhood. Once I happened to glance up and catch a look pass between the two. It was the sort of easy, familiar look that sisters might exchange.

"I know that Franklin enjoyed his little chat with you last night, Lieutenant," Mrs. Roosevelt said. "He was quite taken by you. He spoke of your directness."

I was reminded of what Vasilyev had asked me to do. I debated with myself for a moment, then decided it was just a small thing. What harm would it do? Besides, I was a soldier and was only doing my duty. "Your husband is a great friend to my country, Mrs. Roosevelt. We only hope that he remains in office."

"I, on the other hand, pray that he doesn't," she said with a frustrated laugh.

"You don't wish him to be president anymore?" I asked.

"It has certainly been a drain on his health."

She then glanced at her friend. "It's been a drain on you as well," Miss Hickok replied. Turning toward me she added, "Ellie would very much like to get back to her own life. It's been on hold for a dozen years."

"I never minded," Mrs. Roosevelt explained. "I have always supported Franklin's ambitions."

"But it's time to support your own," the other woman said. "You know all the things you'd like to accomplish. Instead of having tea parties, for goodness sakes."

I looked from one to the other.

"So he does *not* plan to run again for office?" I asked.

But just then Mrs. Roosevelt's aide, Miss Thompson, entered the room and spoke to the First Lady. Mrs. Roosevelt said something to Hick, and the two stood.

"They're sending a car for you, Lieutenant," she said. "I have some things to attend to before the conference. I shall see you there."

After they were gone, Captain Taylor and I sat in awkward silence for a moment. Despite the fact that we spoke the same language, I felt suddenly uncomfortable with just him there. I found myself spinning my teacup in the saucer, just for something to do with my hands.

Soon, though, the captain asked, "Who's Masha?"

"My daughter," I replied.

"But you used the past tense."

"Yes." I said, glancing across at him. "She died."

"I'm so sorry."

"Thank you, Captain," I replied.

"Is that why you hate the Germans so much?"

"I suppose the war became something very personal for me. For a long time I did enjoy killing them, just like they said in the article. I'm almost ashamed of admitting that now."

"That's understandable, Lieutenant. How old was your daughter?"

"Three. Just a baby still."

I don't know why, but I reached into my pocket, took out the leather case, and removed the photo of my daughter.

"That's her. Masha," I explained.

"She's very pretty. I can see the resemblance," he said, looking from the photo to me. "Is that your husband?"

"Yes."

"When was he killed?"

For a moment I wanted to tell him the truth, that he wasn't dead, at least not officially, just missing. But then I figured I didn't want it getting back to Vasilyev that I had disobeyed his orders, however silly I thought them to be.

"A month ago I received the letter," I said. Hoping to change the conversation, I asked, "Do you have children, Captain?"

"Me," he said with a startled laugh. "No. I'm not married."

"A girlfriend perhaps?"

He shook his head. "I was engaged."

"What happened, if it's not too forward of me to ask?"

"Not at all. When I enlisted in the army, Becky—that was my fiancée's name—didn't understand why. She thought I had a perfect excuse not to fight and thought I was crazy to enlist. So she broke it off."

"Just like that?"

"Pretty much." He smiled, the flesh at the corners of his eyes crinkling. "It's probably for the best. She's happily married now, already has a daughter."

"She didn't wait long," I offered sympathetically.

"No, she always wanted for us to settle down. A house and a family."

"And you didn't want to settle down?"

The captain shrugged. "When I was a kid, my father was in the service. I was used to moving around a lot. So you see, it was all for the best. For both of us."

"Do you really believe that?"

"Yes. We wouldn't have been happy. I guess I get bored easily," he said.

"You don't look like someone who gets bored easily."

"No? What do I look like?"

"Someone who is very focused. Who has a great deal of patience."

He laughed at that. "I don't think Becky would say I was patient," he said, running his hand over his scalp.

"Where is your family?"

"My parents live in Chicago. My older sister lives about an hour away from them."

"This Miss Hickok," I said. "She is not afraid of speaking her mind, even with the president's wife."

"No, she's quite a character."

"She and Mrs. Roosevelt seem to be very good friends."

"Yes, they go way back. I guess they met when she was covering Mrs. Roosevelt for the newspapers."

"Is Miss Hickok married?"

The captain glanced at me, seemed about to say something, but then said only, "No."

"May I ask you a question, Captain?"

"Certainly."

"In the newspaper, they said I looked masculine. Do you think I look masculine in my uniform?"

He stared at me appraisingly.

"Be honest, Captain."

"For an officer, you're very attractive, Lieutenant."

"Just for an officer," I said, chiding him playfully.

"What I mean is . . ." He stumbled, the freckles over his pale cheeks darkening with embarrassment. "It's just that we don't have any women in the armed forces. I think I would find it hard."

"Hard?"

"I mean, fighting side by side with women."

"You're not one of those who thinks we're only good to cook and clean," I said, assuming a tone as if I had taken offense.

"No, no. Not at all. I only meant, well . . . that I might be distracted."

At last I smiled to show him I was just kidding. "It's all right, Captain. I'll take that as a compliment."

He took out a pack of cigarettes and offered me one.

"That Vasilyev fellow," he said. "Who is he?"

"He's . . . ," I began, but then realized I didn't know who he was, beyond my vague speculations. And I certainly wasn't going to tell this American stranger what those were. "He coordinates my visit here in the States. Like a chaperone."

"Does he work for the Soviet embassy?"

"No. He . . . I'm not sure where he works. Why?"

"No reason," he replied, drawing on his cigarette. "And what is your role?"

"My role?"

"Are they just parading you around for publicity's sake?" he said.

"I suppose you could call it that."

"I take it you don't particularly like America. All of us decadent capitalists." He winked to show that he was joking, at least in part.

"It's not that," I replied. "It's being away from the front."

Smiling, he recited an old Russian proverb: "*Daryonomu konyu v zuby ne smotryat.*"

"Yes, I know—don't look at the teeth of a horse you've been given."

"You should enjoy your time off," he advised.

"War was simple compared to this," I said. "You knew your job. Knew who the enemy was."

"And now you don't know who it is?" he said with a smirk whose meaning I couldn't decipher.

"Who should I consider the enemy, Captain?" I replied, leveling my gaze at him.

"Don't look at me," he said, chuckling. "Come, I should take you downstairs."

13

Vasilyev was sitting in the backseat of the limo that picked me up that morning. It was already unpleasantly warm, the air thick and languid, so I rolled down the window a little. A sweet, not-unpleasant odor of putrefaction slipped into the automobile. Washington, I'd found, was a city built on swamps and dreams, both of which are subject to a slow disintegration. It was just the two of us, so I assumed that Viktor and Gavrilov had already gone ahead to the conference. Vasilyev didn't so much as give me a nod when I got in. He was preoccupied by some documents he was reading. Instead of his usual dark clothing, he was dressed in a cream-colored linen suit with a carnation boutonniere in the lapel. Whatever he was reading, he found the news troubling. He alternately furrowed his brow or exhaled a frustrated sigh, which made the papers in his hand ruffle gently. On the seat between us lay an American newspaper, the same one that Mrs. Roosevelt had shown me earlier. The one with the picture of the Soviet delegation on the front.

Finally he looked over at me and, extending his hand, said, "So?"

I reached into my pocket and withdrew the envelope that the man named White had given me the previous night. He took the envelope and slid it into his pocket.

"Who is this man?" I said. "Is he one of our agents?"

"The less you know, the better. Let's just say that he is sympathetic to our cause." He glanced out the window, searching for something. "Turn left here," he instructed the driver. After a while he said, "Stop."

The driver pulled over to the curb in front of a seedy-looking hotel in a crowded section of the city.

"*This* is where the conference is?" I asked, surprised.

"No," he said. "I shall be right back."

Vasilyev got out of the car and headed into the hotel. I sat there watching people walk by. After half an hour, I saw Vasilyev emerge. He was accompanied by another man. The other was stout, well dressed, with reddish brown hair and a lean, sharp face like a hawk. The two conversed for a moment, then shook hands and parted. Vasilyev got in the car and we continued on.

He turned toward me after a while and said, "How was your big night, Comrade?" I couldn't tell if his tone was mocking or not.

"I enjoyed myself," I replied.

"I am glad to hear that. Was the president there?"

"Yes."

"Did you get an opportunity to talk to him?"

"A little."

"And?" he said, waving his hand in a circle to speed up my reply.

"We talked about the war some. I told him how important a second front was to our troops. He said it was a complicated issue."

"Complicated?"

"He spoke of his Congress. I didn't really follow him. But he said that he would open a second front just as soon as he was able."

"Did he now?"

"Yes."

"And were you able to talk to his wife about his election plans?"

It crossed my mind to lie to him. On the one hand, Mrs. Roosevelt had been kind to me, and I didn't like the idea that I was somehow betraying her trust. Besides, how would he know what we talked about? I was the only one there. I could make up anything I wanted. Yet I told myself I was a loyal Soviet citizen, a soldier that would do her duty to the Motherland. What was more, perhaps Vasilyev was right, maybe it was important to know what the Americans' plans were, how they might affect the war effort. They might be our allies but they weren't dying with us—not yet anyway. We Soviets had to take care of ourselves, I argued to myself.

"She said that she hopes that he doesn't run."

"Really?"

"She is worried about his health."

"How sick is he?" Vasilyev asked.

"She didn't say. But clearly she is concerned about it. And her friend said she wanted to get back to her own interests."

"Her friend?"

"Yes. A reporter."

"What's her name?"

"Lorena Hickok. She lives at the White House."

"What else do you know about her?"

"Nothing," I replied. "Just that she's a friend."

"I see," said Vasilyev, taking out his small notebook and writing down her name.

"Comrade, I will be going home after the conference, will I not?" I said to him.

"Don't worry, you'll be going home soon enough."

The conference was held in a beautiful old hotel that displayed out front flags flying from the various countries represented, and signs in a dozen languages that read, WELCOME, STUDENTS FOR PEACE. Inside, the hotel was decorated with chandeliers and plush carpeting, velvet drapes, and dark oil paintings. Everywhere employees in crisp uniforms and little round hats were scurrying about, tending to the needs of their guests. As we entered, Dmitri approached us.

"Go get the others," Vasilyev ordered him.

We followed the signs, which led us toward a grand ballroom. The room was crowded with people and very noisy, a discordant hubbub arising from all the different languages being spoken. There were student representatives from some fifty nations, as well as diplomats, politicians, reporters, interpreters, and guest speakers. Students had come from as far away as China and Burma, India and Australia, England and France and the Netherlands. Almost all were dressed in the uniforms of their countries.

No sooner had we entered when a number of reporters spotted us and came rushing up.

"Lieutenant," they cried, shoving their cameras at me. They wanted me to smile, to wave at the cameras, and since we hadn't yet found Radimov and the others, they had to communicate with me by hand gestures and a kind of crude pantomime. "Smile," they said as the flashbulbs popped, momentarily blinding me.

After a while, Dmitri appeared moving through the crush of people, with the others from our delegation in tow. Radimov still appeared the worse for wear, his coloring poor.

"We couldn't find Viktor," Dmitri offered.

"What do you mean, you couldn't find him?"

"He was here a minute ago. And then," the Corpse explained, snapping his waxy fingers, "he was gone."

"I saw him talking to some girl from the French Free Forces," Gavrilov added.

"He doesn't speak French," Vasilyev said.

"Comrade Vasilyev," offered Gavrilov, with a fawning smile, "even without words Viktor can communicate with the opposite sex."

Vasilyev shook his head, his lips gathered tightly together in annoyance. "Fools," he lamented. "I am surrounded by fools. Find him! Immediately!"

"Don't worry, Comrade, we'll find him," the Corpse said.

When they were gone, Vasilyev led me a little way apart from Radimov and Gavrilov. "I thought I asked you to speak to him."

"I did," I replied. "Victor has his own mind."

"I told you that there would be consequences."

I felt like saying Viktor was a big boy, that whatever the consequences he might suffer, they weren't my responsibility. But still, he felt like my responsibility. I whispered, "Please don't do anything to him."

Vasilyev stared at me, his anger partially changing into something else. Half of his mouth offered up a smile, but the other half seemed to

remain frozen in its anger, so that the total effect was a decidedly grotesque expression.

"So you don't wish anything to happen to your friend, eh?"

"Please," I said.

"I shall think on it," he said. "Have you prepared something to
say?"

"Yes."

Handing me a piece of paper, he said, "I've taken the liberty of jotting down a few things to make sure you touch upon them in your talk.
Number one: tell the Americans that we desperately need more supplies. Tell them they can send donations to the Soviet War Relief Fund.
We want them to dig deeper into their pockets. Number two: reassure
them that we won't sue for peace."

"Sue for peace?" I said. "What are you talking about?"

"Evidently, the Americans are worried that we are in negotiations
with Germany. That we might cut a deal with Hitler. We need to reassure them we won't do that."

"Is that true? About our cutting a deal?"

Vasilyev pursed his lips and shrugged.

"Finally, I want you to say that it gives you enormous pleasure to be
here. Say it exactly that way: 'enormous pleasure.' Do you understand?"

I had no idea why it had to be this way, just another of Vasilyev's
quirks, I assumed.

"Come, let us go in."

We headed into the auditorium, a large room that was packed with
those attending the conference. A young woman greeted us there.
She led Gavrilov and me up to the front of the room, where, as special
guests of the First Lady, we were to sit right onstage. We were given
headphones so that the speeches could be translated. The stage was
colorfully decorated with flowers and banners, and from somewhere
musicians played something by Mussorgsky. At the podium there was
an array of microphones from various radio stations, as the conference,
we'd been told, was being broadcast across the country and to soldiers
fighting overseas. I happened to spot Mrs. Roosevelt in the wings talking with several people. I recognized one as Miss Hickok. Another was

a Negro woman wearing a long, low-cut gown. The three were chatting amiably. When she recognized me, Mrs. Roosevelt waved and gave me her toothy, infectious grin.

Soon the musicians struck up what turned out to be sections of various national anthems from around the world, including our own "L'Internationale." This was followed by an honor guard made up of student soldiers who bore their respective flags up onto the stage, where they arranged them in a semicircle at the back. Finally, the black woman strode out to the microphone at the center of the stage and began to sing a slow-moving Negro spiritual. She was a striking-looking woman, with delicate features and a commanding presence, and a voice that, when she finally gave herself over to it, soared like a bird in flight. Though I didn't know what the words meant, I felt the hairs on the back of my neck stand at attention as she sang. Quite frankly, though, I was surprised that they allowed such a thing to happen in America. Back home, everything we'd read about the treatment of Negroes spoke only of how oppressed they still were. Like our peasants before the revolution. And yet here was a Negro woman singing before all the world. When she finished, the audience gave her a rousing applause.

Mrs. Roosevelt herself then got up to officially open the proceedings. The voice that translated her words struck me as vaguely familiar, but I was concentrating too hard on what she was saying and didn't really pay it all that much mind. She welcomed the international students and their guests, as well as other dignitaries and representatives to the four-day conference. She spoke about how lasting peace would be achieved only through the cooperation of all the world's nations. It was interesting to see how this plain, soft-spoken, and unpretentious woman suddenly changed right before your eyes into a speaker of great passion and fervor, how she was able to inspire the crowd. She then introduced the keynote speaker, Supreme Court Justice Jackson. This was followed by a number of students who got up to speak. I kept looking around to see if I could spot Viktor, but he was nowhere to be seen. I worried about him, worried that the Corpse and Dmitri would harm him, or perhaps that Vasilyev would ship him back home to be reeducated— and I knew all too well what that meant. Then Gavrilov got up and gave his speech, a lengthy harangue filled with platitudes and clichés, with phony tales of fighting the fascists.

Finally it was my turn to speak. Mrs. Roosevelt introduced me, saying such generous things about me that I felt quite embarrassed. She called me "that brave little soldier" and "the woman with the heart of a lion." On my way to the podium, she gave me a reassuring hug and said something in English that I assumed was wishing me good luck. She must have known how terribly nervous I was. I had never spoken to such a large crowd before. Shooting Germans was easy compared to this. With an unsteady hand, I removed from my pocket the little speech I had prepared.

"To begin, it gives me enormous pleasure to be here," I said. "I want to thank Mrs. Roosevelt and all Americans everywhere for their kindness and support."

Then I read my speech—how the world couldn't rely on the sacrifices of a single country, the need for cooperation with our allies, the necessity for still more supplies and financial support. The fact that we were winning the war, that my comrades would never surrender to the Nazis. I spoke for a while about the importance of opening a second front without delay. I said other things as well. It was not very memorable, I'm afraid. After a while, I looked out and saw a sea of eyes glazed over, of yawns and heads nodding off, and here and there someone glancing at his watch. It had, after all, been a long day, and they had already had their fill of grand words, of martial speeches, of the suffering inflicted by the Nazis. These Americans, I thought, didn't need more empty propaganda, more clichés about fighting and heroism. Unlike us, they hadn't been attacked by the Nazis, and although they were at war, they weren't locked in a death struggle for their very lives. If and when they chose to fight in Europe, they'd be going off to fight in some unclear affair they knew little about and cared even less for. If they were going to fight and die alongside of us they would need the truth, I thought. They would need to be toughened by truth, not puffed up by fancy-sounding illusions. And what was more, if we were going to ask them to die with us, they *deserved* the truth as well. So instead of reading the rest of my speech, I put it away and decided to speak directly from my heart.

"Do you know," I began, "that fifteen thousand of my countrymen are dying each day? Fifteen thousand in a single day! Try to imagine that if you can. Try to imagine how high a pile of bodies that would make. But that is just a number. It's hard to grieve over a number. Better yet, I'll tell you of the time that my unit, after retaking some land held by the Germans, came upon an old people's hospital. When we went inside, we were appalled to find that everyone had been slaughtered by the Germans. The old men had been bayoneted in their beds, the women raped before they were killed. They were harmless old folks. And yet the Germans massacred every last one of them. Try to imagine one of them your grandfather or grandmother. Or perhaps I should tell you of the first enemy I shot. I had expected to feel only joy, as he was part of the enemy that killed my people. But what I felt was not joy. I actually felt sick to my stomach." With this a pall fell over the auditorium. They sat up and stared at me. I heard a low murmur of discord rise from the audience. I saw reporters frantically writing in their little pads. Out of the corner of my eye, I caught Vasilyev lean forward nervously in his chair, no doubt anxious that I would say the wrong thing. But I continued on anyway. "You see, ladies and gentlemen, like most soldiers, I thought killing the enemy would be quite easy," I explained. "After all, they had invaded my country. They had bombed our cities, killed our children, raped our women. My own family was killed by them. Yes, my entire family. Both my parents, my husband. I had a three-year-old daughter named Masha. She was the most precious thing in the world to me. She died in my arms, killed by those monsters. So you see, if anyone had a right to hate the enemy, I did. For a long time, I hated them with all my heart and soul. I lived only to kill them. But I was wrong to give up my humanity in the process. Wrong to make killing the only thing that was of importance to me. If we are to defeat our enemies, to really and truly defeat them once and for all, we must not only defeat them on the field of battle. We must defeat them in *here*," I said, touching my chest. "We must defeat them in our hearts and our souls by not becoming too much like them. That is our most important asset in this struggle. More important than bombs or tanks or planes. That's what makes us different from the fascists. And that's what will help us to defeat them.

In the war and after too. We must hold on to our humanity at all costs. I have heard that you Americans are very brave. I know that you have fought courageously in many wars. And I would like to think you are brave. I would like to think that you will join with me, and shoulder to shoulder we will defeat this common enemy. I ask this of you from the bottom of my heart. Don't let my comrades die in vain. Don't let my country continue to be plundered and burned, our old people killed, our children put to the bayonet before the invaders. Don't let my own child's death be in vain."

I paused for a moment. Then I said, "I thank you, my comrades."

The auditorium was silent as I walked back to my seat. I didn't quite know how my talk would be received, but I studiously avoided looking at Vasilyev. When I reached my seat, I was surprised to hear a thunderous ovation.

Soon afterward, Mrs. Roosevelt and Captain Taylor came over to me.

"My dear," Mrs. Roosevelt said, hugging me, "that was simply marvelous. Why, you had them hanging on your every word."

Patting me on the back, Captain Taylor added, "She's right. That was just great."

Only then did I realize that it had been his voice translating earlier for Mrs. Roosevelt.

"Your adoring fans are waiting for you," Mrs. Roosevelt said to me. Just off the stage, a crowd of reporters was being held at bay by ushers. "Tat'yana," they were calling. "Lieutenant."

Before I left, I felt Vasilyev at my elbow. "I must say, Lieutenant, that you had me a little worried there for a moment. I wasn't sure where you were headed with that. But it was good. Quite good, in fact."

I nodded.

"Rest assured, important people back home will hear of this."

14

hat evening, Mrs. Roosevelt had invited our delegation to a reception at the home of an important senator and supporter of her husband's pro-Soviet policies. She thought it a good idea that we meet him. On the drive over from the conference, Vasilyev, his earlier mood having improved dramatically, sat there humming "Katyusha." When I asked about Viktor, he told me they had found him in the hotel lounge, drunk and flirting with an American waitress. So they brought him back to the embassy.

"And now?" I asked.

"The fool is sleeping it off," replied Vasilyev.

"Will there be the consequences?" I said, referring to our earlier conversation.

"I have to remind myself that I was once his age."

"But Comrade Semarenko is old enough to know better," Gavrilov offered prissily, glancing over at me.

"His only crime is not holding his liquor," Vasilyev stated. "We've all been guilty of that at one time or another."

"If I may be so bold, Comrade, this is not the first time that he has overstepped himself."

"Unfortunately, we can't all be such perfect martinets as you, Gavrilov."

Gavrilov stared at Vasilyev for a moment, not sure whether a "martinet" was a compliment or not. He decided finally it wasn't. "I only try my best to be a loyal Communist," he said, sullenly stroking his goatee. His pince-nez had left red indentations on his nose.

"And we are all deeply appreciative of your loyalty," Vasilyev replied.

"If I err on the side of being, as you put it, a martinet, it is only because of my great love for the Party."

"I was merely joking, Gavrilov. Why on earth do you have to take everything so bloody seriously?"

His feelings hurt, Gavrilov stared out the car's window.

"So nothing will happen to Viktor?" I ventured.

"He will need to know that in the future such behavior won't be tolerated." He reached out and patted the back of my hand. I had not seen him in such a jovial mood in a long while, not since we were back in Moscow when he was showing me about the city. "Let's not worry about him now. Let's try to enjoy ourselves tonight, shall we, Lieutenant?"

The house, which overlooked the Potomac River, was an imposing brick structure, a place that would have comfortably housed half a dozen families back in Kiev. A Negro butler in a crisp white uniform answered the door and led us into a large drawing room, where most of the guests had congregated. Servants floated about with trays of food and champagne and vodka, while strains of Prokofiev drifted through the house. There was a large crowd, mostly civilian but with a number of men dressed in military uniforms. As soon as we entered, Mrs. Montgomery, that same silly woman I had met the previous night at the White House, spotted me and came rushing up. "Hello, hello," she chirped. She held a drink in one hand and planted a wet, boozy kiss on first one and then the other cheek, I guess thinking she was being European.

"Don't they let you wear anything besides that drab old uniform?" she asked me through Radimov. "You must be roasting in that wool."

I simply smiled. Like the previous night, she chattered away. It was apparent that she'd already had too much to drink, which made her tongue wag even more.

"They have some wonderful caviar here," the woman informed me. "I know how you Russians love your caviar and your *wodka*." She pronounced the word with a reverberating *w*.

Vasilyev grabbed three glasses of *wodka* from a passing waiter and handed one to me and to Gavrilov.

"To the Motherland," he said.

Gavrilov, who didn't drink, was able only with great difficulty to gag his down. For me, it was the first of several drinks I permitted myself that night. I decided to take Vasilyev's advice and try to forget about the war, about everything, and enjoy myself for the evening.

"You must be hungry, Lieutenant," Vasilyev said.

"Yes I am, a little."

"I'll get you something. Come, Gavrilov. Radimov, stay with the lieutenant," he said as they headed over to a table filled with food.

While he was gone, several people came up and, through Radimov, introduced themselves and congratulated me on my speech at the conference that day. I hadn't thought it was such a big deal, but evidently it had made quite an impression. I happened to spot Mrs. Roosevelt across the room talking with Mrs. Litvinov. Mrs. Roosevelt looked elegant in a long, sleeveless silver dress with a string of pearls about her neck, her hair done up on her head. She saw me too and eagerly waved me over. Radimov followed closely on my heels.

"I'm so glad you could make it, Tat'yana," Mrs. Roosevelt said. Radimov began to translate but he deferred when Mrs. Litvinov did the honors.

"You look lovely tonight, Mrs. President," I said.

"Why thank you, Tat'yana."

"I listened to your speech on the radio, Lieutenant," the ambassador's wife said to me. "I found it quite moving."

"You brought the war home to us Americans in a way no one has before," Mrs. Roosevelt added. "Franklin was getting calls from all across the country from people who'd heard you. I have some ideas I'd like to share with you later."

Just then Vasilyev arrived with a plate of food for me.

"Good evening, Mrs. President," Vasilyev said to Mrs. Roosevelt, through Radimov. "And how are you, Mrs. Litvinov?"

"Hello, Mr. Vasilyev," Mrs. Roosevelt said, her tone noticeably cool. Mrs. Roosevelt, I could tell, didn't like Vasilyev. I saw it in her eyes, a chilly sort of restraint. She was a woman who spoke much by way of her eyes. When she liked someone, they seemed almost to radiate warmth. But when she didn't, no matter what she said, her eyes told her true feelings.

"What did you think of Lieutenant Levchenko's speech today?" Vasilyev asked.

"I was just telling her I thought it was wonderful, actually."

After a while, Captain Taylor appeared, carrying two plates of food, which he handed to Mrs. Roosevelt and Mrs. Litvinov.

He turned toward me and smiled. "Why hello, Lieutenant," he said, as if surprised to see me here.

Mrs. Roosevelt spoke to him in an aside.

To Vasilyev, the captain said, "Mrs. Roosevelt wishes to introduce Lieutenant Levchenko to some people."

"Certainly," Vasilyev replied. "Comrade Radimov will accompany her."

"If it's all the same with you, Mr. Vasilyev, I wish to use my own interpreter," said Mrs. Roosevelt, through the captain.

"But, Madame President, our two languages have certain nuances. I wouldn't want any confusion about what's said."

"I have every confidence in Captain Taylor."

"As you wish, Mrs. President," conceded Vasilyev, smiling obsequiously. I could tell, however, he took this as a slight.

The First Lady showed me around, introducing me to several congressmen and diplomats and a number of her friends. Secretary so-and-so and this ambassador and that congressman's wife. Being toasted with champagne. Called the "Ukrainian Lion" or the "Russian Girl Sniper" or the "Beautiful Assassin." Asked the same foolish questions I had already been asked many times ("Do you mind getting dirty?" "Do you wear makeup into battle?" "Are women soldiers forced to sleep on the ground?"). Or they would ask me things that exhibited a complete ignorance of my country. "Does everyone live in dorms over there?" one congressman's wife asked. Another wanted to know if the government allowed women to raise their own children or were they taken from us at birth and raised in a nursery.

"No," I said, "we raise our own children, just like you."

For the most part, I nodded agreeably and smiled until my jaw ached. Could these Americans really be such imbeciles? I wondered. I was especially annoyed by the women. I wanted to scream, *You silly prattling fools, don't you know there's a war going on?* Occasionally, though, Mrs. Roosevelt would shoot me a sympathetic look. And once she whispered something to Captain Taylor, who said to me, "She says she doesn't know how you remain so polite."

At one point Mrs. Roosevelt had excused herself, leaving me alone with the captain. We were talking when Gavrilov approached.

"If I might have a word with Comrade Levchenko," he said to Captain Taylor, drawing me aside. Gavrilov seemed a little drunk. His eyes, normally so intense, had softened, become unfocused. He seemed nervous, his mouth appearing to work on saying something that was giving him difficulty articulating. Finally he blurted out, "I have not spoken of this matter before because I did not think it, well, appropriate. But I must say that I find you quite attractive, Lieutenant."

I stared at him, not sure how to take this confession. It seemed so incongruous coming from this normally dispassionate apparatchik, for whom everything was the business of the Party. But of course I recalled that Viktor had confided to me how Gavrilov felt.

"Thank you, Comrade," I replied.

"Perhaps, when we return home we could . . ." Here he paused, stroking his goatee. "Attend a lecture together."

"I don't think that is such a good idea, Comrade Gavrilov."

"But why not?"

"For one thing, I am a married woman."

"But with your husband . . ."

"He's missing in action. Not dead. Despite what Vasilyev would have you believe."

Fortunately, Mrs. Roosevelt rescued me. She appeared suddenly and said she had some people she wanted me to meet. She drew me across the room toward a group of men who were standing in the corner. Through the captain, in an undertone, she said, "These men are very important congressmen, Tat'yana. My husband needs their support for bills related to the war. So work your magic on them."

"Good evening, gentlemen," Mrs. Roosevelt said to the men. "I would like you to meet Senior Lieutenant Tat'yana Levchenko of the Red Army. She's newly arrived from the Eastern Front."

Smiling, I made a stab in my faltering English: "How do you do?" I said.

"It's certainly a pleasure to meet you, Lieutenant," one greeted me, shaking my hand.

"Young lady, I'd say you have an unfair advantage," offered a second, a thin man with a lean, deeply etched face and the gnarled hands of a farmer.

"What is that, sir?" I replied.

"Well, it's plain to see that those poor krauts go sticking their heads out to get a look at you."

They all chuckled at this.

The congressmen and I chatted for a while, about the war, how things were at the front, if I liked America.

After a time, the man with the lined face said, "Young lady, we're spending an awful lot of money on this here war in Europe."

"Senator Pepper," Mrs. Roosevelt explained, "is one of my husband's biggest supporters."

"I'd like to think I am, Mrs. President. But I have an election coming up, and I've stuck this neck of mine out about as far as I can for him," he explained. Then, looking directly at me, he said, "Miss Levchenko, my constituents down in Florida keep asking me what's in it for them to go and fight in somebody else's war, the second time in a generation. What would you have me say to them?"

I glanced at Mrs. Roosevelt and she nodded her approval to speak.

"I suppose, sir, I would tell them this. It's not somebody else's war. It is *your* war, just as much as it is mine. If you think that Hitler is going to stop in Europe, you are mistaken. He didn't stop with Czechoslovakia or the Rhineland or with Poland. And he won't stop with Europe. So the question is, do you want to fight them in Stalingrad or here in Washington?"

"All right," he continued, "let's say we give you everything you ask for. Can you promise that you can hold the krauts at bay until we can get our boys over there?"

"That would all depend, sir," I replied.

"On what?"

"On how fast you can get your boys over there." We held each other's gaze for a moment, and he knew that I was alluding to the immediacy of the second front. "But I can promise you this. That we Soviets are tough. We won't surrender to the Germans. We will fight the invaders as long as we have breath in us."

Senator Pepper slowly gave in to a wide, toothy grin. "I like this girl, Mrs. President. She's got spunk."

"Didn't I say as much, Senator?"

We were about to leave when one congressman, a tall, gray-haired older man with sharp blue eyes, spoke up. He hadn't uttered a word before this.

"Excuse me, Lieutenant," he said. "Have you heard of a man named Krivitsky?"

I was about to say that I hadn't when Mrs. Roosevelt answered for me. "Now, Congressman Rankin, let's not start that."

"With all due respect, Mrs. President, here we are sending the Reds millions of dollars, and they have the gall to come into our country and murder an American citizen, right under our very noses."

"Congressman, that's just conjecture," Mrs. Roosevelt said. "Besides, that's not something the lieutenant would know anything about. Good evening, gentlemen." Mrs. Roosevelt led me away.

Later that evening, feeling a little tipsy from the heat and from having drunk too many glasses of champagne and *wodka,* I told Mrs. Roosevelt that I had to use the lavatory. On my way there, I happened to notice doors leading out onto a terrace at the back of the house, and I took the opportunity to slip outside for some fresh air. I loosened my collar, removed my cap, and took a deep breath of the fragrant-smelling night. It was quiet out here and cooler, the sky speckled with stars like tiny fish scales. In the distance I could see the river, the lights from the far side shimmering off its surface. Farther off was a white stone structure with columns, well lit, seeming almost to glow with a lunar brightness. I was leaning against the cool stone balustrade, thinking of home, when I heard a voice behind me.

"Getting some air?"

I turned to see Captain Taylor standing there.

"Yes," I replied.

"May I join you?"

From his uniform pocket, he removed a pack of cigarettes and offered me one. I took it, and with his right hand he dexterously struck a match with his thumbnail, and I leaned in and cupped my two hands around his and lit my cigarette. I felt a chill at touching his hand.

"Thank you," I said.

"How are you holding up?"

I shrugged. "That congressman," I said, "the one who asked me about the man who was murdered."

"Oh, Rankin. He's on the House Un-American Activities Committee."

"Un-American activities? That sounds rather ominous."

"I guess it does. His committee investigates Communists in America. He and his cronies think you Soviets have spies hiding everywhere," he said, smiling. "You don't, do you?"

I looked at him and replied with a straight face. "Just me," I replied.

The captain laughed.

"And what of that man he mentioned?" I asked. "The one who was murdered."

"The police found this Krivitsky fellow dead in his hotel room. There was a suicide note, so at first they thought he'd killed himself. But later there were some questions about whether he might have been murdered."

"What does this have to do with my country?"

The captain took a long, pensive drag on his cigarette. "Some believe he was a Soviet spy who defected to the West, and then was murdered by agents from your country."

"But for all our differences, our two countries are supposed to be allies, no?"

He turned toward me and ran a hand over his scalp. His mouth formed a faint smile. "Isn't that being a little naïve, Lieutenant?"

I thought how that was the second time I'd been called that in the past few weeks. The other time was by Viktor, when we were aboard ship.

"I may be a lot of things, Captain, but naïve is hardly one of them," I replied.

"Sorry," he said. "But your country and mine have always been enemies."

"We have never fought against you."

"Maybe not openly. But you have to admit that communism's goal is to overthrow capitalism. You want world revolution."

"We want simply what everyone does—enough to eat, a safe place to raise our children," I said. "If you'll recall your history, Captain, it was *your* country who invaded *mine*."

"What are you talking about?"

"After our revolution, it was the United States, along with its western allies, who sent troops into Siberia."

"But what about the Marxist saying: 'The proletariat is the undertaker of capitalism.'"

"We're no one's undertaker. We have never tried to hurt the United States in any way."

"And Molotov's nonaggression pact with Ribbentrop?"

I nodded. "That was wrong, I must admit. But if it were up to you Americans, my country would still be under the repressive tyranny of the czar. You would deny us the basic freedoms that you enjoy."

I found myself, suddenly and instinctively, threatened by what the captain had said and rushing to my country's defense, like some Party zealot, the way Gavrilov would have. Or even the way my father once had. I guess I felt that we Soviets, who'd fought and sacrificed so much for our nation and who'd suffered so terribly under it—*we* had the right to criticize it, but not outsiders.

"I wouldn't exactly call what you have now the sort of freedom we enjoy in America," the captain said.

"Your supposed freedom is not for all of your people," I said. "What of your millions of poor? Or your Negroes? Or what of your Japanese who have been rounded up and put in camps? Do those people enjoy your precious freedoms?"

"All right, all right," he said, raising his hand in surrender. "I can see I'm not going to win this one."

We fell silent for a moment, staring out over the water to the far side.

When I happened to glance at him he was rubbing the sleeve of his missing left arm.

"Forgive me, Captain," I said. "I didn't mean to be rude."

"No, I guess I had it coming."

"It's just that I'm so tired of everyone over here looking down their noses at us. They think of us as godless barbarians. Primitive savages. We had culture a thousand years before your War of Independence."

"You don't have to convince me. I know your country. I studied it. I guess we Americans can be pretty arrogant sometimes. Where's your watchdog?"

"Vasilyev? Oh, he's around somewhere. Spying on me," I said.

"Spying?" he repeated.

"I meant that metaphorically, of course."

"Of course." He paused, then added, "He keeps you on a pretty short leash, doesn't he?"

"He worries that Viktor and I will say something that will cause you Americans to stop sending us guns."

"What could you possibly say to do that?"

"I have no idea," I replied, inhaling deeply on my cigarette. "What is that, Captain?" I asked, pointing at the well-lit monument across the river.

"That's the Lincoln Memorial."

"Ah, yes. We read about your Mr. Lincoln in school. He was a great man, was he not?"

"Yes, he was. He was president during our Civil War and he freed the slaves."

"And yet your Negroes are still not free."

He looked over at me and pursed his lips. "Unfortunately, no. One of our early presidents called it our great and foul stain."

"The Negro woman today, the one who sang so beautifully. What was her name?"

"Marian Anderson. She's quite a famous singer. She's good friends with Mrs. Roosevelt. A couple of years ago, Miss Anderson was supposed to give a concert right here in Washington, but they wouldn't let her because she was black. So Mrs. Roosevelt stepped in and used her connections. In fact, she ended up singing right over there at the Lincoln Memorial. Tens of thousands showed up. Mrs. Roosevelt has done much for the poor and for the working class. And for women too. Some people don't like her because they think the wife of the president should keep out of such things. But I think she's first-rate."

"Yes, she seems to be a very strong-willed woman."

"Are you looking forward to touring with her, Tat'yana?"

"What do you mean?" I said.

"Going across the country speaking about the war."

I stared at him, confused. "I'm afraid you're mistaken, Captain. When the conference is over, I shall be going back home to fight."

"Oh, I was under the impression that you and she were going to tour together."

"No," I said. "May I have another cigarette, Captain?"

As he lit it for me, I happened to look up into his face. The light from the match danced in his eyes, and up close I could smell him— his cologne or hair pomade or sweat mingling into an aromatic fragrance, sweet and musky as fermenting corn. Our eyes met and he smiled at me. He had a smile that was open and generous, that came so naturally to him that it reminded one of a child's, but for the fact that his eyes had a sad, almost wistful look to them. I couldn't help returning the smile.

"There," he said, pointing at me.

"What?"

As if he'd read my thoughts, he said, "You have a nice smile, Tat'yana. You ought to show it more often."

I smiled again, this time exaggeratedly. "You Americans with your grim optimism."

"Isn't it better to be an optimist than a pessimist?"

"Better still to be a realist. One needs to know the world as it is, not as you would wish it."

"And do you know the world as it is?" he asked.

"I suppose I am learning it right now," I said with a toss of my head back toward the party.

"Yes, the complex subtleties of Washington," he replied. "One has to learn one's way around that."

"And have you learned your way around it?"

He shrugged his thin shoulders. "May I ask you something, Tat'yana?" he said to me. "Something personal."

"I'm really not supposed to be talking to you alone."

"Why, because you might say something 'inappropriate'?"

He leaned toward me, staring deeply into my eyes. Then he reached out and touched my face. For a moment I thought that he was going to kiss me.

"I was wondering—"

Just then a voice: "Oh, there you are, Lieutenant." It was Vasilyev. "I was looking all over for you."

Captain Taylor quickly pulled his hand back and used it to rub his face.

"I just stepped out for some air," I explained.

"Good evening, Captain," he said to Taylor with a circumspect nod. "Several people wish to meet you," he said to me, tucking his arm into mine and leading me away.

I glanced over my shoulder at Captain Taylor.

"What did the two of you talk about?" Vasilyev whispered to me.

"We spoke of history."

"History?"

"Yes. Comrade Vasilyev, when the conference is over, I am going home, am I not?" I asked.

"Just as soon as we finish business here. Why do you ask?"

"No reason," I replied. "Have you heard of a man named Walter Krivitsky?"

Vasilyev shook his head. "Should I have?"

"The captain said he was killed by Soviet agents because he was a spy who defected to the West."

"And just how would the captain know such a thing?"

"He said it was in the newspapers."

"Ah, the American newspapers. A bastion of truth."

"Are they any less duplicitous than our own, Comrade?"

Vasilyev leaned in to me and said in an undertone, "I would be a bit more circumspect with my tongue, if I were you, Lieutenant."

15

T hat is wonderful news," exclaimed Ambassador Litvinov at breakfast the next morning.

Secretary Bazykin had just informed everyone at the table that
several hundred thousand dollars had been donated in the past
twenty-four hours to the Soviet War Relief Fund. In front of him were a
number of telegraph cables.

"Here is one from a fraternity at the University of Illinois," said the
secretary. "They have pledged one thousand dollars to our cause. They
cite Lieutenant Levchenko's radio speech yesterday."

"Bravo," the ambassador cried, clapping his hands.

There were six of us at breakfast: the ambassador and his wife, Secretary Bazykin, Vasilyev, Gavrilov, and me. I hadn't yet seen Viktor,
who, Vasilyev had told me, was still sleeping it off. My own head was a
bit dull from too much drink the previous night. I only managed to pick
at my eggs.

"And just this morning," continued Bazykin, "I received a call from
Mr. Hopkins that military recruitment stations across the country have
noted dramatically increased activity. Evidently, the Americans are
signing up to fight in droves."

"Well, it's about time," Vasilyev said harshly. "These Amerikosy have
sat on their fat capitalist asses for far too long."

The ambassador frowned at him and put his finger to his lips.

"Pardon me," Vasilyev countered. "Let us praise the Americans for their newfound support."

As I sat there taking all of this in, my mind drifted back to the previous evening. My conversation with Captain Taylor. The touch of his hand against my face. The personal question he was going to ask me. I wondered what it was.

"Lieutenant. Lieutenant?" a voice called to me.

"Yes, Mr. Secretary," I replied, coming back from my reverie.

"The ambassador was saying that we owe all of this to your inspiring speech yesterday," Bazykin explained to me.

"I fear it might be overstating my influence," I replied with a smile.

"On the contrary, I think you've embarrassed these Yanks into fighting," Vasilyev said.

I thought of what Captain Taylor had said to me, that the Americans weren't cowards, that they wanted to fight but hadn't yet been given the opportunity.

"Perhaps," I offered, "they just needed a little push."

"Whatever it was, my dear," said Mrs. Litvinov, who sat next to me, "we are all so very proud of you."

I glanced across at Gavrilov. He had a sheepish look, as if he was embarrassed by what he had told me the previous night, as well as annoyed at all the attention I was getting.

"I think the lieutenant already has one of the American soldiers under her sway," offered Vasilyev with a wink to the ambassador.

"What is this?" asked Mrs. Litvinov.

"You know that handsome young officer Mrs. Roosevelt uses for an interpreter," explained Vasilyev. "I think he has an eye for the lieutenant."

"Comrade Vasilyev is joking, of course," I countered.

"I'm not so sure," Vasilyev said, rolling his eyes at Mrs. Litvinov. "I caught the two of them out on the terrace together. They were quite absorbed."

The others chuckled.

I felt my face burn with embarrassment. Wanting to divert attention from myself, I said, "Let us not forget Comrade Gavrilov's fine speech."

"You're quite right," replied the ambassador. To Gavrilov, he said, "It was, Comrade, a model of clarity and persuasive rhetoric. And a wonderful reflection of our fine educational system, wouldn't you say, Vasily?"

"Indeed," replied Vasilyev.

While the others were chatting, Mrs. Litvinov leaned toward me and said, "What did you think of Mrs. Roosevelt?"

"I liked her very much."

"I knew you and she would hit it off."

Secretary Bazykin said, "We've received numerous requests for speaking engagements, Ambassador. New York. Chicago. Los Angeles. Sioux City, Iowa—wherever that is," he said with a bemused chuckle. "Several universities and trade unions, as well as a number of American veterans groups who have expressed an interest in having her come to speak."

"Brilliant," replied Litvinov. "It seems all America is quite taken by you, Lieutenant. You are going to be quite busy."

Perplexed, I glanced at Litvinov, then at Vasilyev, who stared somewhat guiltily back at me.

"Busy?" I said to the ambassador.

"You have not told her yet, Vasily?" the ambassador asked.

"No, I haven't had an opportunity, Comrade."

"Told me what?" I asked.

"We've wonderful news," Litvinov said. "Mrs. Roosevelt has asked that you accompany her on a tour of America."

So that's what she had wanted to talk to me about the previous night, I thought, and what the captain had alluded to.

"But, Mr. Ambassador, I was promised that I could return home after the conference."

"We require your presence here for a while longer, Lieutenant," replied Litvinov flatly.

"With all due respect, sir, I wish to return to the fighting."

"Lieutenant," Vasilyev said sharply. "You are a soldier—" But Ambassador Litvinov raised his hand.

"It's all right, Vasily," he said calmly to the other. "The lieutenant is understandably disappointed. As a patriot, she wishes to defend the Motherland in her dire need. We admire your fighting spirit, Lieutenant. Yet your country needs you in a different capacity now."

"But I can best help our country by killing Germans."

"We certainly appreciate all that you have accomplished. But now your country is asking you to perform a service that is equally important. One that will demand no less of a commitment. There are many in the highest levels of the Party who are counting on you. Besides, this could mean wonderful things for your own career."

"I don't care about my career," I said.

"Well, you ought to care, Lieutenant," Vasilyev admonished sternly.

"I won't force you to do this, Comrade," Litvinov said.

"But Ambassador—" Vasilyev interjected.

Once more, Litvinov raised his hand to silence Vasilyev.

"I am going to leave it up to you. I want you to take a few days to think about it. Remember, though, we are all counting on you."

"If I were to accept, what exactly will I be expected to do?"

"Just be your charming self. Give a few interviews, make some speeches about the war in Europe. In short, promote the war effort."

"That's it?" I said. "That's all I have to do?" I thought of the exchange of letters I had made with that man at the White House, the incessant grilling Vasilyev put me through each time I spoke with Mrs. Roosevelt. How they were, I sensed, using me for some clandestine purpose, to find out American secrets. I felt uneasy about all this, felt once again I was being lied to, manipulated. That whatever "service" I was being asked to perform for the Motherland, it was not just about promoting the war, getting the Americans to open up a second front. I thought of all the things that Vasilyev had coached me on, the precautions he'd given me. At the same time, I knew full well that Litvinov's offer that I was free to decline was only an illusion. I had about as much freedom as a caged bird staring out through its bars. I was aware of the consequences were I to decline. Once back home I would be denounced as someone with "individualistic tendencies." If lucky, I would be stripped of my officer's rank, my medals. I'd be hidden away in some boring desk job for the remainder of the war, disgraced; in time, forgotten about. And if I weren't quite so lucky, I would be shipped off to someplace like Kolyma in Siberia to be reeducated, or even, if those in the "highest levels of the Party" watching me were powerful enough, might be tried for treason. I had thought my status as a Soviet hero had protected me, but now I knew better.

The ambassador and Vasilyev exchanged glances.

"Think of it as much-deserved R & R, Lieutenant," he said. "My wife will take you shopping to buy some things you will need. I want you to enjoy your stay here, Lieutenant."

"If I decided to do it, how long would I be gone?" I asked.

"Not long. A few weeks. A month perhaps."

"And then I can return to the front?"

"Of course. You have my word on that."

His *word*, I thought. It was worth about as much as Vasilyev's.

After breakfast, I headed upstairs to my room. As I passed Viktor's room, I heard him coughing in there and decided to knock. I waited, then knocked again. He called out, "Go away."

"Viktor, it's me, Tat'yana."

"I told you, go away."

"I want to talk. Please, let me in."

When he didn't answer, I tried the door and found it to be open.

He was lying on the bed, curled on his side, facing the wall. I sat on the side of the bed.

"How are you feeling?" I asked.

He snorted. "Just great. Couldn't be better."

"I think you were right, Viktor," I said.

"About what?"

"About our not coming here just to promote the war. I think they're planning on using us in another fashion."

"Do you indeed?" he said, with a sarcastic laugh. "For a bright girl, you can be pretty dumb." He turned slowly toward me, wincing as he moved. Then he let out a deep groan. "Jesus," he cursed.

I was shocked to see him. His face was haggard-looking, etched with pain, his forehead damp with sweat.

"Viktor, what's the matter?" I cried. "What happened to you?"

"Huh! Didn't your pal Vasilyev tell you? I thought he tells his little darling everything."

"I'm not his little darling," I snapped at him, surprised that he would accuse me of such a thing. I thought he knew me better than that. "I don't know what the hell you're talking about. What happened to you, Viktor?"

"I'm supposed to say I slipped after having too much to drink."

"What really happened?"

"That fucking *suka* did this."

"Who?"

"The Corpse. He and the other son of a bitch. The filthy whores worked me over good."

"Where do you hurt, Viktor?" I asked, placing my hand on his shoulder.

"Everywhere." He touched his left side gingerly. "I think they broke some ribs," he said, grimacing.

I carefully lifted his shirt. His side was covered with nasty red welts, some already turning black and blue. The skin, though, wasn't broken.

"The Corpse used a lead pipe covered with rubber. Bastard made sure nothing showed through. He's well versed in this sort of thing."

"They did this just because you wandered off?"

"What?"

"They said you wandered off and got drunk."

He laughed again, bitterly this time. "The lying bastards," he hissed. He began coughing. Soon he was hacking pretty hard, spitting up blood. I hurried over to the bureau where there was a washbasin and got him a towel.

"Here," I said, handing it to him. I rubbed his back as he spat blood into the towel. After a while he managed finally to stop, to get his breathing under control. I wiped his mouth, put my hand to his forehead, which was very hot.

"You feel like you have a fever."

He pushed my hand away. "The truth is, they wanted me to spy for them."

"Spy for them!" I cried.

"Vasilyev had wanted me to carry documents back and forth from our agents in the States."

"Why you?" I asked.

"He said the American government was watching the Soviet agents too closely. That they wouldn't suspect me."

"What did you tell him?"

"I told him to go fuck himself. I told him I was a soldier, I wasn't one of his *chekist* pigs."

His head dropped on the pillow, and he stared at the ceiling. I went back over to the bureau, wet a facecloth, and returned and sat on the bed and began to clean him up.

"I'm so sorry, Viktor," I said as I washed his face. "But you have to believe me. I didn't know anything about this. I swear."

He looked up at me, searching my face. "I believe you, Lieutenant. I shouldn't have said what I did."

"Are you going to do what they asked, Viktor?"

He shook his head.

"That could be dangerous."

"What more can they do to me?"

"They could do a lot more, Viktor. You know that."

"Fuck 'em. I'm not afraid of them."

"Don't be foolish."

"If they try any more shit with me, I'll defect."

"Ssh," I told him. Whispering, I said, "You heard how they said the Americans had the embassy bugged." Then I considered the possibility that our own side had it bugged as well.

He said softly, "I will. I don't care anymore. They're as bad as the fucking krauts. At least if we kick the Germans out, we're done with them. These swine, they're here for good."

"Don't do anything you'll regret."

He snickered at that. "Don't worry, I won't. And what of you, Lieutenant? What plans do they have for you?"

"They want me to tour with Mrs. Roosevelt. To talk about the war."

"Is that all?"

I paused for a moment, not sure I wanted to tell him. Finally I whispered, "Vasilyev did have me carrying a message to someone."

"To whom?"

"Someone in the White House."

"The White House. Jesus! So they got you doing their dirty work too."

"I don't think it was anything like that," I said.

"Don't fool yourself, Lieutenant. You're in this up to your eyeballs."

"What else can I do?"

"You can tell them to go fuck themselves, Lieutenant."

After I left Viktor, I went in search of Vasilyev. I was fuming. I wasn't sure what I was going to say, whether or not I should tell him I knew the truth about Viktor's injuries. Perhaps that might only get Viktor in more trouble. But I definitely wanted to tell him Viktor needed to see a doctor. I found Vasilyev in a small office at the back of the embassy. The door was half open and he was on the phone when I knocked. He waved me in, had me sit.

"Yes, Comrade," he said into the phone, his tone the fawning one used with superiors. "Yes, of course. I am well aware of the significance of it. No, Comrade. Rest assured I shall deal with it straightaway."

As he placed the receiver in its cradle, he glanced up at me and said, "What can I do for you, Lieutenant? I am at the moment rather busy."

"I've come to talk about Viktor," I said.

"Ah, yes. Very unfortunate. He's lucky he didn't break his fool neck."

We held each other's gaze for a moment, I knowing that he was lying, he knowing that I knew.

"He needs medical attention," I said.

"So now you're a doctor as well as a sharpshooter."

Vasilyev put his fingers together and tapped his lips.

"Comrade Semarenko's health will improve as soon as he learns to follow orders," he offered. "I told you there would be consequences. He's under the mistaken impression that this is some sort of game. Now if you'll excuse me, Lieutenant."

The conference ran for three more days. I found the speeches by statesmen and politicians and bureaucrats, those in charge of running the war, quite boring. But I did find inspiring those by young soldiers and students, brave men and even a handful of women from around the world who were fighting the Axis powers—members of the Polish Home Army, the Yugoslav partisans, the Free French Forces and the Maquis, the Italian CLN, the Greek resistance, the Norwegian Milorg, the Filipino Hukbalahap. It was moving to hear so many young people devoted to the cause, who knew intimately what it was like to lose a limb or a friend or a loved one.

Each day after the conference, Mrs. Roosevelt had arranged for our Soviet delegation to see various sights around Washington. She'd taken me under her wing, treating me almost like a daughter. A limousine would stop by the embassy, often followed by a small caravan transporting an entourage of reporters, secret service agents, and aides, and pick up Vasilyev, Gavrilov, Radimov, and me. (Vasilyev apologized for Comrade Semarenko's absence, saying that he was indisposed.) We toured the memorials to dead presidents, the zoo, the Smithsonian museums, the Library of Congress, the Capitol, and the National Gallery of Art. At each place the press would take pictures—of us standing in front of the Washington or Lincoln memorials, at Arlington National Cemetery. As we drove about, Mrs. Roosevelt proved a gregarious host, chatting animatedly, pointing out highlights of the capital and providing us with small insights into its history.

"That building there," she said, pointing out the window, "used to be a theater called Ford's. It's where our President Lincoln was shot."

"The assassin was a man named Booth, was it not, Mrs. President?" offered Gavrilov like a diligent student.

"Very good, Mr. Gavrilov," she said.

Plans were made for us to spend a day seeing some of the countryside outside of the city. Shortly before Mrs. Roosevelt was to arrive at the embassy, Vasilyev came to my room and asked me to take a walk with him. We left the embassy and walked down the street to a small park, where we took a seat on a bench. Children were playing on swings, and young mothers were standing about talking.

"The First Lady has asked if you might go with her alone today," he said.

"Alone?" I asked.

"Yes, without the rest of us. She wants a chance to get to know you better. I am going to permit it."

I stared at him, perplexed at this sudden change of heart. Vasilyev, I had come to realize, did nothing without a purpose. Like a chess player, he had an ulterior motive with his every move.

"I thought you didn't want me to be alone with the Americans," I said.

"I have confidence in your discretion. Besides, I think the First Lady would feel more comfortable if it was just you."

He was, I suspected, hoping Mrs. Roosevelt would let her guard down if I was alone with her. The more we became friends, the more likely she'd be to confide in me, to let slip something he considered of importance. It was the beginning of a change in his tactics. From this point on, he was to permit me more and more private access to the First Lady.

"Pay close attention to her," he instructed. "Listen carefully to what she says. I want you to report back to me anything she confides to you."

"Such as what?"

"About her husband. His activities. His upcoming plans. Of course, don't seem to pay it any mind. You don't want your interest to be obvious."

"No, of course not," I said sarcastically, which Vasilyev either didn't catch or decided to overlook.

"And if the opportunity presents itself, make inquiries of this Captain Taylor regarding Mrs. Roosevelt. Her personal life."

"What do you mean, her 'personal life'?"

"For instance, find out about her relationship with this Miss Hickok."

"I don't understand what you are asking me to do."

"Just keep your goddamned eyes and ears open," he said, growing suddenly irritated. "Do I make myself clear?"

I recoiled at what he was asking me to do—betray my growing friendship with Mrs. Roosevelt. I thought of Viktor's warning, that I should just say to hell with them. And yet I was a soldier, and soldiers followed orders, even if those orders went against personal feelings.

More and more I felt trapped: *mezhdu dvukh ogney*. Caught between the hammer and the anvil.

"Quite clear," I replied.

"Make sure you stay clear in your mind, Lieutenant. Otherwise, things could get difficult for all of us."

That day Mrs. Roosevelt surprised everyone by showing up behind the wheel of a sporty-looking roadster, a convertible that had its top down. She wore a straw hat held in place by a white scarf tied over her head, and she waved excitedly as she screeched to a halt at the curb in front of the embassy. Sitting beside her was Miss Hickok, wearing a fedora pulled down low on her head, while in the backseat, bareheaded, was a rosy-cheeked Captain Taylor.

Through the latter, Mrs. Roosevelt said, "Hop in, Tat'yana."

I got in back next to the captain. On the seat between us was a wicker basket filled with food.

"I'm going to show you a little of the countryside," Mrs. Roosevelt called from the front seat.

"You'd better hold on to your hat, Lieutenant," joked Miss Hickok. "Ellie has a lead foot."

We took off with a start. The First Lady proved to be a surprisingly skillful if somewhat daring driver. She expertly negotiated the streets of Washington, shifting the gears and steering like an old hand, though I must say I had to agree with Miss Hickok. Mrs. Roosevelt drove too fast, so that I felt my stomach drop out of me each time she took off from a stoplight or rounded a corner, tires squealing. We sped along the roads, passing cars which, when their occupants recognized our famous driver, honked their horns or waved or called out to us. She would smile and wave back, laughing unabashedly, occasionally even honking the horn in reply. At first I found it a little disconcerting that the wife of the president of the United States would behave in such an undignified fashion. But then I recalled what Mrs. Litvinov had said of her, that she marched to her own drummer. What was more, she seemed to enjoy herself so thoroughly, to revel so completely in riding along the open road, the wind in her face. And viewed in this way, it made me respect and like her all the more. Here was a woman of character and of spirit, a woman very much of the people, a far cry from the dour, anonymous wives of the Soviet leaders.

"Where are her guards?" I asked of the captain.

"She ordered them to stay behind," he explained.

"She can do that?"

"She's the wife of the president. She can do anything she wants."

"Aren't you afraid to be without security, Mrs. Roosevelt?" I called over the noise.

"Oh, I'm not worried," she replied. "I don't think the Nazis would be all that keen on capturing me. Besides, I have the deadliest shot in the entire Red Army in the backseat," she joked.

The morning was bright and crisp, with only a few clouds in the sky to give the vast blue some perspective. The sun felt wonderfully invigorating on my face. In the air I detected the faintest autumnal note, the sweetness of dried leaves and newly cut hay, of things swollen with ripeness. We drove west into gently rolling hills, passing woods and fields burgeoning with wheat and corn and pumpkins, and meadows dotted with cattle and horses grazing, everything so peaceful and serene, unlike the cratered and scorched landscape back home. It felt good to be out of the city, away from reporters and crowds, away from Vasilyev and his claustrophobic control. Perhaps, as Mrs. Roosevelt did, I found it a rare chance to relax and laugh, not be in the spotlight, not have to worry about what I did or said. For well over a year, I had been a target of sorts, first in the crosshairs of German snipers, then in the equally dangerous eye of the Soviet higher-ups or the NKVD, and now with reporters or politicians, all wanting something of me—to smile or say something clever, to project a certain image, to impart wisdom, to be something they wanted me to be rather than simply myself. But with the wind in my face and the landscape sweeping by, I had that exhilarating sense of freedom that comes from being removed from the tedious constraints of others' expectations.

Now and then out of the corner of my eye, I'd catch the captain staring at me. When I looked at him directly, he'd smile somewhat guiltily. I didn't know if he recalled the night on the terrace, how he'd touched my face and was about to ask me something of a personal nature.

Miss Hickok took out a cigar and lit it, and passed it along to Mrs. Roosevelt. The two of them took turns smoking it, like a couple of schoolgirls doing something illicit. They laughed and chatted easily between themselves, occasionally raising an eyebrow or shaking their head at some private joke. The intimacy I had noted between the two before was even more pronounced away from the public eye. I could see that Mrs. Roosevelt was a different person out here—carefree, jovial, a bit of a joker even. The captain didn't even attempt translating what they talked about.

"The president," I said to Captain Taylor, "he does not mind that his wife behaves . . . in such a fashion?"

He looked at me and smiled. "Even if he did, I doubt that he could stop her. She's pretty much her own boss."

"In my country, our leader is not so accommodating with his women," I said.

"I wouldn't imagine your Stalin being accommodating," he said, laughing. "May I share a secret with you? But only if you promise not to tell anyone, or I could get in trouble."

"I promise I won't."

"She doesn't like your Mr. Stalin's mustache."

"His mustache?" I cried. "Why not?"

"She thinks it makes him look sneaky."

"Well, do you want to hear another secret? But you must promise not to tell anyone either."

"You have my word," he said, holding up his right hand.

"I saw him once up very close. And I thought his mustache resembles very much a rat."

"A *krysa!*" he said, chuckling.

At this, I started to laugh too.

"So what's so funny back there?" Mrs. Roosevelt called out to us.

We stopped finally way out in the country, along a deserted stretch of road beside which ran a small river. We got out and headed down toward a grassy spot not far from the water. Captain Taylor carried the basket of food and a blanket he'd gotten from the trunk. He spread the blanket under the shade of a tree, and we all sat down.

"Isn't this just lovely?" said Mrs. Roosevelt, untying the scarf and removing her hat. Handing Captain Taylor a bottle of white wine, she said, "Would you do the honors, Captain?"

While he opened the bottle of wine, Mrs. Roosevelt started serving everyone. She'd brought roast duck and potato salad, green beans and corn bread.

"Try the duck, Tat'yana," Miss Hickok said. "It's fabulous."

"Mary, our cook, makes it for Franklin," offered Mrs. Roosevelt.

The duck did prove to be delicious, as did the sauterne we had for a wine. We ate and chatted and had a delightful time. At one point, Miss Hickok took off her shoes and rolled up her trousers and walked down into the river up to her thick knees.

"Ooh. It's freezing," she called to us.

Mrs. Roosevelt turned to me. "I hate to mix business with pleasure, Tat'yana. But I must ask you. Has your Mr. Vasilyev spoken to you about my idea of touring America to promote the war in Europe?"

I glanced at the captain, remembering his comment that night on the terrace. "Yes, he has," I replied.

"What do you think?"

I paused for a moment to choose my words with care. "It is a great honor, Mrs. Roosevelt, that you want me to travel with you."

She stared at me, and those piercing eyes of hers must have seen my reluctance. "But you don't seem particularly thrilled by the idea."

"It's not that. It's just that I would rather be at the front fighting with my comrades."

"Of course, that's perfectly understandable for someone like your-self. But you see, many here still feel the war in Europe isn't our affair and that we shouldn't get involved. People like Lindbergh and his bunch of Nazi sympathizers. We need something to get us motivated. To get us to fight Hitler with the same tenacity with which we've begun to fight the Japanese. I think that something is you, Tat'yana."

"I am just one soldier, madam," I said.

"But America needs for you to bring the war into our homes and hearts. To give it a face."

"I doubt I could have such an influence."

She reached out and grasped my hand. "I know your warrior's heart lies with your comrades in arms. But you and I must do what we can to get the Americans to open their eyes. Are you with me, Lieutenant?"

Up to this point, I still hadn't made up my mind. But Mrs. Roosevelt was able to make such a persuasive case that I decided then and there that I wanted to do it.

"Yes," I said at last. "I will go with you."

"Splendid," she replied, clapping her hands.

After a while, Mrs. Roosevelt said something to the captain, to which he nodded. He got up and headed down to the stream, where he took off his shoes, rolled up his pant legs, and put his feet into the water.

Mrs. Roosevelt turned toward me and, smiling coyly, said in an undertone, "*Kak*." Then she looked off toward Captain Taylor to make sure I had gotten her point. She had said the word *handsome*.

Up until that point, I don't believe that I had thought of the captain as handsome. Pleasant-looking perhaps. But now, watching him down at the stream, his back to me, the lean curve of his shoulders, I thought, I suppose he was a handsome man.

I smiled shyly to Mrs. Roosevelt. "Yes," I said.

"*Simpatichny*," she replied. Meaning *nice*.

Instead of heading back to the city, Mrs. Roosevelt drove us to a park-like cemetery on the outskirts of the city—Rock Creek Cemetery, the captain explained to me.

"I want to show you a place that's very special to me," Mrs. Roosevelt said as we parked and got out. We made our way to a secluded, leafy grove. We sat on stone benches, Miss Hickok on one end, I on the other with Mrs. Roosevelt and Captain Taylor in the middle. Opposite us was a granite slab atop which sat a large statue of what appeared to be a woman. She was shrouded in a long cape, her eyes closed, in sleep or death, I couldn't tell. Even so, her expression conveyed a profound sadness.

"I come here when I want to be alone," Mrs. Roosevelt told me. "I find it very peaceful."

"The place gives me the willies," said Miss Hickok, only half in jest.

Mrs. Roosevelt told me that the statue was called *Grief.* That it was commissioned by Henry Adams, a famous American writer, she explained, and grandson and great-grandson of presidents, for his wife, Clover, after her death.

"The poor woman killed herself when she learned that her husband was in love with another woman," Mrs. Roosevelt said to me.

"That's so sad," I replied.

"Indeed," said the First Lady, her mouth crinkling into a frown.

"You ask me, I think she was a dumb Dora," Miss Hickok offered blithely.

"But, Hick, she was in love, and her heart was broken," countered Mrs. Roosevelt.

"To kill yourself for some two-timing bastard?" Miss Hickok replied. "No matter how much he broke my heart, I wouldn't kill myself. I might kill him, though," she added with a hoarse laugh.

"You're not a romantic, Hick," the First Lady said with a wistful smile.

Miss Hickok gave the First Lady a critical look. "And you're too much of one, Ellie."

As they spoke, I almost got the sense that they were having a private conversation, one that wasn't about the statue or the Adamses, nor was it one meant for the captain and myself.

After a while, Mrs. Roosevelt said, "There was a poem written about the statue. Let's see if I can remember it.

> "O steadfast, deep, inexorable eyes
> Set look inscrutable, nor smile nor frown!
> O tranquil eyes that look so calmly down
> Upon a world of passion and lies!

"Don't you think that's true, Tat'yana?" Mrs. Roosevelt asked me. "That we live in a world of passion and lies."

"I'm not sure, Mrs. Roosevelt," I said. "I think the world is filled with many who lie. But passion is something that springs from the heart."

Mrs. Roosevelt stared across at the statue. Her normally cheerful demeanor turned suddenly despondent, her countenance as sad and forlorn as if mirroring the face of *Grief*. Her eyes watered, and I thought for a moment she might actually begin to cry. I felt so sad for this kind and strong woman, a woman who'd momentarily let her guard down. Miss Hickok reached out and took one of her hands, the one that had the sapphire ring. Then she uttered something, something that was, I assumed, meant to comfort. When I glanced at the captain for his translation, he gave a faint shake of his head, as if to say this was something not meant for our ears. I sensed at that moment what should have been obvious all along regarding the First Lady and Miss Hickok—that they were much more than friends.

"Would you look at me now," said Mrs. Roosevelt, wiping her eyes with a handkerchief that the captain had handed her. "Acting like a damn fool over a silly statue I've seen a hundred times. I suppose you're right, Hick, I'm too much of a romantic." She stood then, extended a hand to Miss Hickok, and said, "Let's take a walk, shall we? Captain, would you keep Miss Levchenko amused?"

When they were gone, the captain and I were silent for a while, uncomfortable with our having just been a witness to this scene. Even the afternoon had turned melancholy. What had started out as a beautiful autumn day had now become overcast. Dark clouds were gathering, mushrooming into one another like smoke from a bomb, and the air had gotten cooler.

"Looks like we're going to get some rain," he said, looking toward the sky. It was something to fill the awkward silence.

"Mrs. Roosevelt seems rather sad to me," I offered.

"Sometimes. Usually she manages to put up a good front. She was brought up with that British stiff upper lip."

"It must be hard being the wife of the president."

"Yes," he said.

I hesitated for a moment, thinking of what Vasilyev had asked me to do. Then I went ahead and inquired, "Do people know?"

He glanced over at me. "Know what?" he replied, either not getting my point or at least pretending not to.

"About them. Mrs. Roosevelt and her friend."

He sighed. "A few, I suppose. Of course, if it got out it would ruin her. Probably the president too. All she ever wanted to do is help people. That's her whole life, helping people."

"Yes, I can see that. Does her husband know?"

"I'm not sure. But it's no secret that he's had other women. I can only imagine it's been very hard for her. Keeping up her public front as his wife."

"She is a woman who feels things deeply," I said. "And yet, I assume she and her husband are not happily married then?"

"It's what we call a marriage of convenience," he said.

"In my country many get married for such a reason."

"She thinks the world of you, you know," he said.

"And I am very fond of her as well."

He stared at me very strangely then, deep into my eyes in a way I don't think I'd ever been looked at before.

"If her secret got out it would ruin her," he repeated, his stare implying something whose import wasn't quite clear to me.

"What do you mean, Captain?"

"Only that I wouldn't want to see her hurt."

He turned and looked off in the direction of the statue, pursing his full lips. I wasn't sure what he was getting at. Did he worry that I might say something about Mrs. Roosevelt and her friend? I had the strangest sense that he somehow knew about what Vasilyev had asked me to do. I don't know why, but I did. As I stared at his profile, I thought of what Mrs. Roosevelt had said about him. That he was handsome. He was, I thought, and I felt a sudden clutching feeling in my chest, as if a chill wind had blown across my heart. I shivered.

I followed his stare toward the shrouded and mysterious figure *Grief*. Despite the undeniable sadness that the place exuded, I could suddenly understand why Mrs. Roosevelt liked to come here. There was something profoundly calming about it. Though I wasn't particularly religious, I felt a deep spiritual connection to the place. I thought of my daughter, buried in an unknown field half a world away, alone, without so much as a marker to note the spot. Instead of feeling, as I usually did, a sense of panic and guilt and helplessness, I felt oddly at peace right then. I couldn't say whether she was in heaven or not. Didn't even know whether I believed in heaven. I only knew that she was at peace, and because of that, so was I.

"May I ask you something, Captain?" I began.

"Please, call me Jack. We don't need to be so formal. At least when no one's around."

"If you prefer. And you may call me Tat'yana. The other night, when we were talking out on the terrace, you were going to ask me something."

He frowned; then his expression changed as he remembered what it was.

"Oh. I was going to ask you about your husband."

"My husband?"

"Yes. I never hear you speak of him."

"There is nothing to say. He was my husband."

"What was he like?"

"He was a good man. A wonderful father to our daughter."

"You must have loved him very much."

I paused, looked over at him. I recalled the time in the trenches that Zoya said the same thing to me.

"Why do you say that, Captain?"

"Jack," he corrected.

"Sorry, Jack."

"I don't know. I guess because I see you as someone of great passion."

"But you hardly know me," I said

"I'm a pretty good judge of character. You still haven't answered my question."

"Why do you want to know?"

"Just curious," he said.

"We Soviets don't always talk about our feelings like you Americans. We don't wear our emotions on our shirtsleeve, as you put it."

"I didn't mean to pry," he said.

"In my country, things are very different. Life is harder there, and people marry for different reasons besides love."

Even as I said these empty platitudes, I could hear my parents' voices telling me why I should have married Kolya.

The captain smiled condescendingly.

"What?" I said. "You think that is foolish?"

"It just seems wrong to me."

"It has nothing to do with right and wrong," I snapped at him. "It's simply the way things are. Love is a bourgeois Western concept."

"Do you really believe that, Tat'yana?"

"Of course I do," I replied. "Marx said that religion was the opiate of the people. Perhaps in the West, your opiate is love. You sell the notion of love in all of your advertisements so that people buy more automobiles and perfume and pretty clothes. Love is the capitalist engine that drives your economy."

He smiled, shook his head. "I think that's very sad. I feel sorry for you."

"I don't want your pity, Captain," I explained, my pretense of anger trying to hide my insincerity of belief. "Just because one faces the truth doesn't mean one deserves to be pitied. Your fiancée, this Becky, did she want to marry you for love? Or was it simply because she wanted a nice bourgeois life with a big house and fancy things, a washing machine and a vacuum cleaner, and thought you could provide those for her?"

"She loved me," he blurted out, his tone bordering on childish petulance. My question, I could see, stung him, and I immediately regretted having said it.

"Forgive me. I had no right to say that," I offered. "Did you love her?"

"Yes, very much."

"Then you should consider yourself very fortunate."

"Why?"

"I think it is more important to love than be loved. More painful perhaps, but more life-affirming."

"But I thought you just said that love was just a bourgeois concept."

"Even we Communists must have our illusions," I said, smiling.

When I returned to the embassy that day, Vasilyev brought me out into the shed behind the building and "interrogated" me as he had on other occasions regarding my meetings with Mrs. Roosevelt. He wanted to

know in the minutest detail what we had talked about: did she say anything about her husband's attitudes regarding the war, did she happen
to bring up anything about the president's health, his election plans,
whether or not he was planning on traveling overseas. If she mentioned
Mr. Churchill at all.

"No. She didn't talk about any of that," I replied.

"Did she say anything whatsoever about her husband?" Vasilyev
wanted to know.

"She said he liked duck."

"Duck," Vasilyev said, frowning.

"To eat," I explained.

"What of her and Miss Hickok? What did they talk about?"

"Nothing."

"Surely they talked about something?"

"Nothing you would consider important, Comrade."

"I'll decide if it's important or not," he said.

"Miss Hickok thinks Mrs. Roosevelt is a romantic."

"Romantic in what manner?" Vasilyev said, his interest piqued.

"In her views of love."

"And the captain. Did you get a chance to talk to him?"

"A bit," I replied.

"Did he tell you anything about Mrs. Roosevelt?"

I hesitated, with Vasilyev staring at me, waiting. I knew that whatever choice I made, whether I told him the truth or whether I lied, I
would be heading down a path from which I could not return. Yet I
didn't feel I could betray Mrs. Roosevelt's trust in me.

"He avoided talking about Mrs. Roosevelt."

"Did you ask about her?"

"Yes. But he either didn't know anything or didn't want to share it
with me."

"I see," Vasilyev said. "We will have to find a way."

"A way?" I asked.

"To get him to talk."

That evening we had dinner at the embassy, Ambassdor Litvinov
and his wife, as well as Vasilyev, Gavrilov, and myself. We talked about

the upcoming tour. It was to take six weeks and cover some forty cities across America. They'd obviously been planning it out for some time, all without my knowledge. It was an event, said the ambassador, that would change the course of the war. Afterward, as we were drinking our brandies, Litvinov turned to his wife and said, "My dear, why don't you take Comrade Gavrilov and show him our library? I think he would find it of interest." It was a polite way of getting rid of Gavrilov. When they were gone, Litvinov said to Vasilyev and me, "Come."

We headed down the hall, through the kitchen and outside into the cool autumn night. We marched over to the shed and entered it. The ambassador put a finger to his lips to tell us we were to be quiet. Once we were inside, he shut the door and fumbled for a moment, trying to find the light switch. Waiting in the darkness, I distinctly felt the presence of a fourth person, of someone besides Ambassador Litvinov and Vasilyev and myself. I don't know if it was his body heat or a vaguely metallic smell that reminded me of iodine, but I knew that we weren't alone. Finally the light came on.

"Hello, Ambassador," came another voice from directly behind me in the shed. The voice was raspy, and I jerked at the sound. With the sudden illumination, it took a moment for my eyes to adjust.

"How are you, Comrade Zarubin," Litvinov said. "I'd like you to meet Senior Lieutenant Levchenko."

Still squinting, I turned to see a stocky man of medium height, his reddish brown hair plastered down with oil. His nose was blunt and broad, his mouth sullen-looking. He had gray pupils that were dull and lusterless, so that looking into them was like looking into a fog. There was about him something familiar, although I couldn't place him at first.

"I am pleased to make the acquaintance of a true hero of the Motherland," he said, shaking my hand and giving me a little bow. His voice was coarse, his manner both unctuous and brusque at the same time. "I've heard much about you, Lieutenant."

"How do you do, sir?" I replied.

"So, Comrade Zarubin," Litvinov said to the man, "how are things in Tyre?"

Tyre, I thought, realizing he couldn't be referring to the ancient city in Phoenicia.

"They are fine, Ambassador. We are quite busy, of course."

"Is the new man . . . what are we calling him again?"

Zarubin glanced at me, his sharp eyes cutting into mine like an auger. It was then that I realized where I'd recognized him from. He was the man I'd seen Vasilyev with outside the hotel.

"It's all right," the ambassador reassured him. "We have complete confidence in the lieutenant."

My credibility having been vouchsafed, he replied, "Liberal."

"Is this Liberal working out to our satisfaction?"

"Yes, Ambassador," Zarubin explained. "He has good information and is well connected to others that share his sentiments. Feklisov has scheduled a meeting with him next week to continue his training."

"Very good. But proceed with caution. You've heard that the Americans have turned one of ours."

This Zarubin nodded.

Then, glancing toward me, the ambassador asked, "Do you know why we've brought you here to America, Lieutenant?"

I felt like a student taking an exam for which I'd studied but now was wondering if I knew the correct answers. "I think so," I replied somewhat hesitantly, glancing at Vasilyev. "To persuade the Americans to help us more in the war effort. To push for that second front."

He nodded. "Yes, that is certainly one of the reasons you are here. We very much want you to continue those efforts. But there are other, more long-term reasons as well."

The ambassador turned to Vasilyev and used an odd term: *kapitansha*—the Captain's Wife. "Did the Captain's Wife say anything else about her husband?"

"Who?" I asked.

"Have you not briefed her on the significance of the Captain's Wife to our mission?"

Vasilyev glanced at me, then replied, "I have told her only what she needed to know regarding that."

"Well, perhaps it is time." Turning to me, Ambassador Litvinov said,

"Lieutenant, what we are going to ask of you over the next several weeks will have a significant impact not only on our war effort but also on our position in the postwar world. You see, after the war the world will be a vastly different place. Our adversaries will change. We need to be prepared."

"Yet we are fighting Germany now, sir. Shouldn't we be working with America to defeat our common enemy?"

"Of course," Litvinov said with a nod. "But two years ago, Germany was our ally. The world changes. We must look beyond the war, to the future. We cannot afford to fall behind the West."

"Fall behind?" I asked.

"Militarily. America is a very wealthy and powerful country. Until now it has used its great wealth for self-indulgent purposes. Automobiles and phonographs. Now, though, the war has awakened it to the realities of the world. They have embarked on a path that will sooner or later bring us into direct conflict with them."

"But they are helping us now to fight the Nazis," I offered.

"The Amerikosy are throwing us table scraps," Zarubin interjected. "Enough to keep the Germans occupied, but not enough to win."

"I still don't see what all this has to do with me," I said.

"We feel that the Captain's Wife could be very useful to us," explained the ambassador.

"Captain's Wife?" I asked.

"Explain to her, Comrade," Litvinov said, turning to Zarubin.

"Our code name for the president is the Captain," explained Zarubin. "So his wife is the Captain's Wife. She has been very sympathetic to our side," Zarubin continued. "She is an advocate of the proletariat. She has strong connections to the left in America, to trade unions and such. We know, for instance, that her own government has been spying on her for quite some time. Their Mr. Hoover has been keeping an extensive dossier on her activities connected to organizations of the left. He believes her to be a Communist. Even her willingness to sponsor your visit here shows her strong support of the Soviet Union. We feel she might be sympathetic to our side."

"In what way?"

"She has, after all, the president's ear. And he may confide in her certain things. Information that might prove invaluable to us."

"Do you think she is just going to share with us what her husband tells her? State secrets?"

"It might take some persuasion."

"Persuasion?" I asked.

"My dear Tat'yana," the ambassador interceded in a fatherly tone, "we are merely saying that if we were in possession of certain knowledge about her, things she would not want made public, perhaps we could convince her to help."

"What sort of knowledge? What are you talking about?"

"Her friend, Miss Hickok, what do you know of her?" asked Zarubin.

I shrugged. "Not much. She's a journalist. She covers Mrs. Roosevelt. They have long been friends."

"And what is the nature of this friendship?"

"What do you mean?" I said.

"What sort of friendship is it?"

"I don't know. They're friends," I said, a little too quickly.

Zarubin smiled rigidly so that his lips were drawn back over his yellow teeth, baring them like the fangs of a dog about to attack. "Are they intimate?"

"What!"

"Are they lovers?"

"How would I know?" I asked.

"There have been rumors that the two have been involved for some time," Zarubin continued. "Have you seen anything that would lead you to believe this?"

I thought of the quiet familiarity they had around each other, the intimacy with which they had gazed into each other's eyes. I thought too of what Captain Taylor had said to me, how if such a thing got out it would ruin her.

"No," I replied.

"You've seen nothing at all. Not the slightest gesture that would lead you to that conclusion?"

"No. Nothing. Even if they were, I don't see why it should be my business—or *anyone's* for that matter."

"Comrade," said Zarubin, "if we were in possession of such knowledge, it would give us tremendous leverage with her."

"You're talking about blackmailing her," I said. "The wife of the president of the United States. This is absurd."

"Watch your tongue, Lieutenant," Zarubin said. He glanced at Litvinov, then brought his hand up and rubbed his angular jaw. "We prefer to call it persuasion."

I stared dumbfounded at the three of them. My gaze lingered particularly on Vasilyev, hoping to find at least in him some recognition that he realized how preposterous all this was, but he merely pursed his thin lips in an attitude of complacency. It was all so absolutely, so incredibly insane that I didn't know what to say. They were actually considering blackmailing the wife of the president. Threatening her by revealing that she and Miss Hickok were lovers. Had they all gone stark raving mad? I wondered. The entire moment would have been comical if not for the fact that it was so deadly serious.

"So what is it you expect me to do?" I asked.

"I understand she has befriended you," Zarubin said.

"She has been very kind to me, yes," I replied.

"It is important that you continue to gain her confidence. We need someone who is close to her. In her intimate circle. We want you to report back to us anything she says."

"You wish me to spy on her is what you're saying."

"We expect you merely to do your duty, Comrade," replied Zarubin sharply.

"Duty!" I snapped at him. "This," I said, holding up the Gold Star medal on my chest, "proves I've done my duty. What have you done to prove yours, Comrade?"

Litvinov, ever the ambassador, placed his hand on my shoulder. "Lieutenant," he said. "No one is questioning your patriotism. The Soviet Union is deeply appreciative of all that you have done for it. We merely want you to help in a different way now. To learn whatever you can from the president's wife. To continue to befriend her."

"Not befriend her," I replied. "Betray her, you mean."

"Like you, Comrade," said the ambassador, "we are only interested in protecting the Motherland."

"Tell me how spying on her, someone who is trying to help us, is protecting our country."

"There are certain subtleties involved of which you are not aware, Lieutenant," replied Ambassador Litvinov. "For now, it is enough that you watch her closely."

I looked at Vasilyev and asked, "Am I being ordered to do this?"

It was Zarubin who answered. "Yes, Lieutenant. Failure to comply will result in consequences of the most severe nature. Do I make myself clear?"

I paused for a moment, glancing from Zarubin to Vasilyev. Finally, reluctantly, I replied, "Yes, Comrade. Very clear."

From that moment, I was no longer a soldier. I was a spy.

PART III

★ ★ ★

They shall beat their swords into plowshares, and their spears
into pruninghooks; nation shall not lift up sword against nation,
neither shall they learn war any more.

—ISAIAH 2:4

16

t is hard for one who did not live during that period to understand the paranoia, the fear, and the hatred that existed between our two countries, and the lengths to which each side would go to in order to best the other. Over the next several weeks, things with Vasilyev and the shady bunch he worked for grew ever more bizarre, as well as more dangerous. I had seen many strange things in the war, but nothing compared with what I was about to experience. At least since our little meeting in the shed, my eyes had been opened. It would still be a while before I learned the true extent of their machinations, but I knew enough now to realize that my role promoting the war was, if not quite a complete ruse, secondary to their other, more sinister plans, plans that had more to do with fighting the Americans in some future war than fighting our very real enemies now. Viktor, of course, had been right all along.

Nevertheless, I decided I would try to go along with what they wanted, play their game, be the good soldier, at least as much as I was able without completely compromising myself. I figured I owed it to my comrades back home fighting to do whatever I could to help defeat the Germans. Whether that was raising money, increasing the Americans' awareness of the plight of my people, or even trying to persuade the West to open up that second front sooner rather than later. Since arriving in Washington, we had raised more than a million dollars for the Soviet War Relief Fund. Each time I spoke or smiled demurely or agreed to an interview, each dollar I was able to get from the Americans was another dollar to buy guns and bullets, trucks and planes and bandages. I thought of Zoya and Captain Petrenko and my other comrades I'd fought with in Sevastopol. I tried to think only in terms of the Soviet lives I might be saving, the mothers who wouldn't be grieving over children lost, or the Germans I might be helping to kill, even if only indirectly. I figured I could pretend to go along with what Vasilyev and the others wanted me to, if for no other reason than so that I could return home all the sooner to take up the real fight. I told myself that the rest was their slimy business, not mine. I was a soldier. My job was to follow orders.

We began our tour heading north by train. Accompanying Mrs. Roosevelt was a small army of personal assistants, advisers, friends, Secret Service agents, and reporters assigned to cover the First Lady. She brought along Miss Hickock, of course, and Captain Taylor, as well as her private secretary, Miss Thompson, to whom she dictated every morning her daily newspaper column. The First Lady had a train car all to herself and her entourage, while the Soviet delegation and the press corps occupied the car directly behind hers. The train was unlike any I'd ever been on. It was like a hotel on wheels, with a dining car, a lounge car, a smoking car, an observation car, and several Pullman sleepers where at night we slept in private compartments on comfortable beds with windows that looked out on the passing landscape. We had every imaginable convenience, which Gavrilov, in his usual surly manner, referred to as "bourgeois luxury."

Sometimes we would make a brief "whistle-stop" at a station, where the First Lady and I would say a few words from the back of the train to groups that must have heard of our coming. The Americans appeared just as eager to see her as to see me. Like a benevolent queen, she was clearly adored by her subjects. They thronged about her, wanting to touch her, to get her autograph. Some held up their babies for her to kiss. Many called out her name. "Eleanor!" they'd cry. "Over here, Eleanor," almost as if she were a personal friend rather than the wife of their leader. I couldn't imagine anything similar taking place back home, the natural, unrehearsed outpouring of real emotion. Not the sort of staged affairs that occurred in Red Square, where thousands were paraded by Stalin and forced, through the simple mechanism of fear, into obsequious shows of affection. And we certainly had no leaders' wives who would have inspired such respect or love, and certainly none who were so influential. And for her part, Mrs. Roosevelt seemed genuinely to care for "her people," as she referred to them. I marveled at the way she reached out and shook hands, accepted hugs, let them get close enough to look into their eyes, listen with real concern to what they had to say. Her enthusiasm and warmth were incredible. Here, I thought, was a remarkable woman, the model of what a woman could be. Her face beamed, her toothy smile was radiant. The sadness I had seen in her eyes at the cemetery was replaced by passion and joy and love.

At one stop in a small Maryland town, several hundred people, mostly laborers and farmers, had come out.

"Look at all your admirers," Mrs. Roosevelt had said to me through the captain.

"No," I corrected, "it is you they want to see. They adore you, Mrs. Roosevelt."

She smiled kindly at me. "Thank you, my dear. But I'm afraid you haven't met our Republicans yet."

As I watched her waving and smiling to the crowd, the thought that I was going to have to betray her—a woman of such kindness and compassion, someone who had been so considerate of me, so helpful to my country—actually made me sick to my stomach. How could I do this? I asked myself. I thought of what Captain Taylor had told me at the cemetery—that he wouldn't want to see her hurt.

One night on the train, after a pleasant meal with Mrs. Roosevelt and the others, Captain Taylor and I played a game of chess. I'd mentioned to him that I played, so he challenged me. It turned out he wasn't much of a chess player, unlike Kolya. He gambled and played recklessly, lost his queen early, and I was able to checkmate him in short order.

"You're very good," he said to me.

"Not really," I said with a smile.

"Is there anything you're not good at?" he kidded.

After our game, I stepped outside for some fresh air. The evening was cool, the air smelling crisply of autumn, of the fecund aroma of recently harvested crops. It made me think of the fields of the Ukraine, the times my mother and father would take me by train from Kiev to Sevastopol on holiday. I was standing there between cars, staring out at the countryside, when the door behind me opened.

"Good evening, Lieutenant," said Vasilyev.

"Hello," I replied.

He removed his silver case and offered me a cigarette. He lit both of ours, then stood there for a moment silently watching the land pass by.

"It is a beautiful country, is it not?" he said.

I nodded.

"Anything to report regarding the Captain's Wife?"

"No," I replied.

Vasilyev had continued to loosen his previously tight hold on my leash, permitting me more and more freedom with and access to, as Zarubin had called her, the Captain's Wife. Sometimes he would let just the three of us—her, Captain Taylor, and me—take breakfast together in the dining car or stay up late talking with her and Miss Hickok in the First Lady's private compartment. Mrs. Roosevelt had even taught me how to play a game of cards called pinochle. Occasionally, the four of us would play and talk well into the evening. Of course, his goal in allowing me this freedom had nothing to do with friendship and everything to do with the fact that he felt Mrs. Roosevelt would be more likely to "open up" with me if we were alone and I might find out something of interest. Afterward he'd grill me regarding what subjects we had conversed about, if she had mentioned anything of her husband's plans, if he were preparing to travel abroad. I shared with him a few things about our conversations. Not much, and nothing I felt of real consequence, nothing that would do harm to my dear new friend. But I did give him scraps, because I thought if I hadn't he might suspect that I was withholding information. For instance, I informed him once that Mrs. Roosevelt had made a passing remark about Mr. Wallace, her husband's vice president. She'd said Mr. Wallace would likely not be around for a second term. It proved to be a mistake, as Vasilyev interrogated me for an hour about whether she had meant that her husband was going to select another running mate or that he wasn't going to be running at all and therefore Wallace would be free to make his own bid for the presidency. I told him I had no idea, that she hadn't said anything further about it. I also fed him other bits and pieces of my conversations with the First Lady. But mostly I managed to avoid telling him anything of real significance, in large measure because Mrs. Roosevelt and I normally didn't talk much beyond the personal sorts of topics any two women might discuss. Even if Mrs. Roosevelt did allude to something I sensed might be of greater interest to Vasilyev, I carefully chose to ignore it or at least to try to skirt the issue. How would he know what we'd talked about? However, especially when he'd press me for more information, I would become nervous as I found myself ensnared in my own lies. And Vasilyev, the *chekist* well versed in the ways of extracting information from unwilling subjects, was good at ferreting out a lie.

"Did she say anything regarding her and the Hickok woman?" he asked me this evening.

"You mean if they are lovers or not?" I replied sarcastically.

Vasilyev knitted his brows in annoyance, then looked out at the passing landscape. When he glanced back at me his expression had changed. It was almost sympathetic. "If I may give you some advice, Lieutenant. Comrade Zarubin is not someone you want to cross. He has important friends."

"But you can't seriously believe what he suggested," I said to him. "It's all madness. Do you really think Mrs. Roosevelt is going to share state secrets with us, even if we threatened to blackmail her?"

"What *I* think is unimportant," he said. "But if you must know, I do not happen to share Zarubin's opinion. He has, shall I say, unconventional methods. Unfortunately, he has the ear of a higher-up who has the ear of Beria himself. So what I think is irrelevant. But I am in agreement with him that the First Lady can be of use to us, directly or indirectly. As they say in America, there's more than one way to skin a cat."

"Isn't it enough she's helping us raise money?"

"She is also privy to vital information. She shares the president's bed." Then, glancing up at me, he added with a smile, "At least on occasion. Besides, she is vulnerable."

"How do you mean?"

"She is an idealist who believes the best of people. And like all idealists, she is blinded to what's under her nose."

"I think you're wrong. She's one of the smartest women I've ever met."

"I see that you've become quite fond of her."

"Yes, I have."

"That's good. But be careful that your feelings don't cloud your judgment, Lieutenant."

"Rest assured, Comrade, my judgment won't be clouded in the least," I replied. "Did you always know this was to be the real reason for my coming to America?"

"Does it matter?" he said. "Good night, Lieutenant."

He flicked his cigarette into the wind, turned, and headed into the next car.

Now and then we would stop in a particular city and spend the entire day touring it. We made appearances in Baltimore and Philadelphia and Camden, New Jersey. In each city I would make a speech, meet with public officials and reporters, have what they would today call a "photo op" session. At the Aberdeen Proving Grounds, I was photographed shooting a bazooka at an old tank sitting out on the target range. In Philadelphia, I had my picture taken with Mrs. Roosevelt standing in front of the Liberty Bell. At Fort Dix in New Jersey, I sat in the nose turret of a Flying Fortress, pretending to shoot its .50-caliber machine gun at German Messerschmitts while mugging for the cameras. (Vasilyev, of course, continued to remind me to flash my smile. "Show them you are having a good time," he instructed.)

During our tour, Gavrilov's role had been reduced to almost nothing. He would sometimes be called upon to utter a few lines in praise of the Soviet Union's heroic struggle against the Germans, perhaps answer a question or two the press directed his way about the Soviet youth organization Komsomol. But other than that, he'd been told to remain silent, "out of the spotlight," as Vasilyev had put it, because the Americans had come to see the "Beautiful Assassin." Of course this insult stuck in his craw. On the train once, as I was passing between cars, I overheard him talking to Dmitri, with whom he seemed to have struck up a friendship. "The fucking bitch thinks she's movie star." I think too he was jealous of the attention I received from and paid to Captain Taylor. Whatever "feelings" Gavrilov had had for me quickly vanished, to be replaced now by the keenest envy and loathing. He often went out of his way to make cutting remarks about a speech I'd made or something I'd said to a reporter, toning it down only for Vasilyev. It would have done little good to try to convince him that none of this had been my idea, that I didn't seek or want the spotlight, so I let him think what he would.

Viktor had accompanied us also, though he did even less than Gavrilov. He simply smiled woodenly for the cameras, showing off his scar or occasionally mouthing a few words that Vasilyev had written for him—how happy he was to be in the United States, his gratitude to the Americans for their continued support. Ever since the beating he'd received at the hands of the *chekisty,* he seemed to have changed, become complacent and docile, his eyes as vacant as someone anesthetized. Even with me he acted odd, distant and wary. Since leaving Washington I hadn't had much of an opportunity to talk with him. On the one or two occasions that I happened to bump into him on the train or in a hotel lobby, he would give me the cold shoulder, almost as if he considered me the enemy. He would drink with some of the reporters covering the First Lady or play cards with them in the lounge car of the train.

In New York they had arranged for me to make a series of speeches and public appearances at various sites throughout the city—at Astor Place, Cooper Union, Columbia University, Central Park, as well as at factories and plants and union halls, wherever they thought it likely that people would give money. During all of these visits, Mrs. Roosevelt accompanied me, lending me support and encouragement, helping to calm my nerves before I spoke. Our friendship grew, despite the hectic pace of our schedule and the secret task I had been charged with. In front of a large crowd at Columbia, she introduced me. As I passed her to the podium, she whispered, "*Udachi,* Tat'yana." Good luck. During our long trip, with the captain's tutoring, we'd each been trying to learn a little of the other's language. Mrs. Roosevelt would say something like "It is a lovely day," and Captain Taylor would have me give it a try in English. Or in Russian I would say to Mrs. Roosevelt, "I like your hat," and she would try to say, "*Mne nravitsya vasha shlyapa.*" At the Brooklyn Navy Yard, when she was unable to break a bottle of champagne across the bow of a new battleship about to be launched, she turned to me and said, "*Pomogite mne, pozhaluysta*" (help me, please). Along with Mrs. Roosevelt, I had to cut the ribbons at the opening of an aircraft plant on Long Island that had been converted to making P-47 Thunderbolt fighters. At a factory in lower Manhattan we had been invited to speak to workers who built radio compasses and other navigational devices for Allies' aircraft. And always nearby to guard the First Lady there would be policemen, as well as Mrs. Roosevelt's Secret Service agents, men I came to recognize. But soon I thought I noticed other men hovering at the periphery, dark-suited men who reappeared over and over again at our speeches, jotting down notes or surreptitiously taking pictures of us. It was Vasilyev who finally tipped me off as to who they were.

"Do you see those men over there?" he said to me once in a factory in the Bronx. We were giving a speech to workers in a munitions plant and he was pointing at two men standing off by themselves.

"Yes."

"G-men," he said. When I frowned, he explained that they were with the FBI.

Wherever I spoke, looming just offstage would be Vasilyev, watching me carefully, ready to whisper something to me or Radimov, or step in to clarify a statement I had made ("What Lieutenant Levchenko means by that is . . ."), or offer the precise response he wished me to give to a reporter's question: somewhat like an understudy for an unskilled actor who might forget her lines. And he watched too whenever Mrs. Roosevelt or I would say something to the other. Afterward, he would want to know what it was she had shared with me, or what we had discussed over a luncheon with military personnel.

Once Mrs. Roosevelt and I were onstage at Cooper Union, speaking to an audience made up largely of college students. I happened to glance backstage and saw that Vasilyev was talking to someone. It took me a moment to recognize the man as Zarubin, the one I had met in the shed behind the Soviet embassy. After my speech, we headed back to our hotel.

"Let me buy you a drink, Lieutenant," Vasilyev said to me.

We went into the bar and sat down. He ordered whiskeys for both of us. In front of him on the table, he had placed a Russian newspaper.

"Comrade Zarubin has informed me that his superiors are getting anxious," explained Vasilyev.

"Anxious?" I said.

"Yes. They expect some results," cautioned Vasilyev as he nervously downed his glass of whiskey in one gulp and waved to the waitress for another. "You haven't been holding anything back from me, have you, Lieutenant?"

"What do you mean?"

"Don't be coy. Regarding the First Lady."

"Of course not," I lied. "Why would I do that?"

"Misplaced loyalties perhaps."

"You don't have to lecture me about my loyalties."

"Good. It would be unwise to cross Zarubin. His methods are coarse but effective." Vasilyev then slid the newspaper across the table toward me. "There is a very nice article back home about you, Lieutenant. Praising your gallantry."

As I opened the paper, I saw my picture with a headline that read, "People's Hero Welcomed in the States." It was that silly photograph they had taken of me in the tree outside of Moscow. Yet what caught my attention was another article to the right of mine, about another Soviet soldier. He wasn't being praised for his heroism, though. Rather the article was about his recent arrest and conviction for being a *vrag naroda,* an enemy of the people. He had written a letter to his parents questioning the high command's tactics. The letter had been read by Soviet censors, and for this he'd been sentenced to seven years at a re-education camp.

"What do you think, Lieutenant?" Vasliev said to me.

When I looked over at him, I got the feeling that he wasn't so much referring to the article about me as to the one about the other soldier. A kind of warning.

"I wonder who the real enemy of the people is," I said.

"I would think that would be abundantly clear to you by now, Comrade," quipped Vasilyev, downing his second glass of whiskey.

During my stay in New York, I met a number of dignitaries and celebrities. One was the actor Charlie Chaplin, a delightful little man whose silent films had been permitted to be shown in the Soviet Union. Against the strong isolationist forces that held sway at the time, he had supported the United States' entry into the war against Hitler, and he helped raise thousands of dollars for the Soviet war fund. Mrs. Roosevelt had arranged for a private screening of *The Great Dictator,* with Captain Taylor whispering a translation in my ear. I laughed until my sides ached at the slapstick antics of Mr. Chaplin, who played both the role of Adenoid Hynkel, the pathetic dictator of Tomania, with his twitchy little mustache, as well as the part of the Jewish barber. After the film, Mr. Chaplin came up to me and personally thanked me for killing all of those Nazis.

Throughout my tour of the United States, most Americans, despite their naïveté about the war and their general ignorance of or disdain for "Red Russia," treated me rather well. They came in droves to hear me speak. Doubtless it was partly due to their curiosity about such an oddity—a woman who not only killed men but, at least according to one newspaper article, "seemed to enjoy her sanguinary vocation," and was, in their opinion, attractive. Still, they came and cheered loudly and seemed genuinely to appreciate both my and my countrymen's efforts against our common enemy. They dropped their coins and dollars into donation cans. Little girls would come up to me and hand me a dollar and talk to me. Old men would come up and thank me. Afterward various groups would present me with gifts. Mostly they were only of symbolic importance—a bouquet of flowers or some sort of medal, occasionally the key to the city, an honorary degree from some university. But other times it was something of real value. From the labor union of the gunmaker Colt, I was presented with a silver-plated .45 automatic with "Beautiful Assassin" engraved on the side and a single bullet that had stamped on it the number 316 (presumably for the next German I would kill once I returned to the front). And from the furrier workers' union of New York, I received a full-length mink coat. They said it was to keep me warm at the front during the cold Russian winter. I don't know if they thought that we women fighters could wear such things at the front, but I accepted it with gratitude. Afterward, Miss Hickok ran her hand along the coat and said, "It looks stunning on you, Tat'yana." However, after the "show," as I had taken to thinking of each appearance, Vasilyev quickly confiscated it, as he had the gun. "I shall keep these safe for you, Lieutenant," he said with an ironic little smile. My guess was I would never see them again. That the fur coat would end up donning the soft white shoulders of some politburo member's mistress, and the gun, like Vasilyev's cigarette case, would adorn the collection of some higher-up NKVD member.

At every show, the American press flocked around me, as if I were, as Gavrilov had accused me of being, one of their motion picture actresses. Journalists were quite different from the average American: they were prying and meddlesome, tedious in their badgering, usually trying to trick me into saying something I would later regret when I saw it distorted in the newspaper. Whereas the facts of a story in *Pravda* or *Izvestiya* were conjured up by government officials to achieve some predetermined end, in America, I learned, they were manipulated and given shape by the writers' desire merely to sell newspapers. They wanted to know my opinion on all manner of subjects. They would ask what I thought of some recent defeat back home or if I believed Japan would invade Siberia or whether or not the Germans would take Stalingrad. They asked what life was like under communism and how it compared to life under capitalism. They wanted to know what I liked most about America—what were my favorite foods, movie actors, perfume, what items I most wanted to bring back with me to Russia. They especially wanted to know my opinion on various topics related to women, as if I were some sort of expert on all things feminine. One female reporter even wanted to know if Soviet women shaved their underarms. They wanted to know what I thought a woman's role should be in society, if American women should be able fight in the war, if they should be allowed to smoke, wear trousers, work outside the home.

"Let me apologize for the stupidity of my fellow journalists," Miss Hickok offered.

I had, of course, to watch myself during such encounters with reporters, because I didn't want to say the wrong thing and be harangued by Vasilyev. In fact, before each show, Vasilyev would coach me, going carefully over what I was to say, what I was to avoid, and afterward he would be sure to point out my "indiscretions," as he called them. Sometimes he'd give me hypothetical questions that the American press might ask me. "If they bring up the matter of detention camps in our country, tell them you have no such knowledge. Say that we have, as America does, only prisons for the criminal elements." He'd even taken to rewriting my speeches, going over them so that I wouldn't say the wrong thing. Sometimes he would insert words or phrases into my speeches. One time he wanted me to use the word *achievement,* several times, as in "The Allies' great achievement will be in ridding the world of fascism." A number of times he slipped in the word "*ogromny*"—enormous—as he had for my speech at the student conference. "We face an enormous challenge in defeating the Germans." Or, "We Soviets acknowledge an enormous debt of gratitude to the United States for all of their assistance, but we strongly encourage our good friends to open a second front with all due haste." In fact, he used the word in three speeches in a row, so that it seemed rather peculiar to me.

"Why this particular word?" I asked him once as we sat in the lobby of our hotel. It was right before we were to leave for a speech I was scheduled to deliver in Battery Park.

"What word?" he responded, pretending ignorance.

"Enormous."

"I don't know. It just seems to fit."

"But you've used it several times already."

"Have I?" he said with a shrug. "I wasn't aware."

"I shall cut it then?" I offered.

"No. Leave it."

I would shortly learn the word's importance, a word that would become important not just to Vasilyev but to the entire world.

My most important public address in New York came at a big rally in Central Park sponsored by the Russian émigré community of the city. As it turned out, some ten thousand strong had come on a bright, cloudless, autumn morning to hear what I had to say. Actually, to hear what Vasilyev had to say. On the ride over to the rally, he had handed me an envelope.

"That's your speech for today," he said.

"But I've already written my speech."

"Change of plans. Just read it as it's written, Lieutenant," he advised me. "Don't improvise. There will be reporters today from around the world. Everything you say will get back to the Kremlin. So we don't want any slipups. Is that clear?"

I nodded, though inside I felt like saying why not let Gavrilov be his mouthpiece. He'd have enjoyed that.

The late morning sun exploded into a million diamonds off the buildings, and the park was dazzling, green and lush and ornate as an emperor's private garden. With me onstage that day was Mayor La Guardia, as well as a number of other city officials and dignitaries, including the folksinger Woody Guthrie, a thin, gaunt man wearing the plain garb of a peasant and with a cigarette dangling from his lips.

"I've heard a lot about you, Miss Levchenko," he said as he shook my hand. He told me he had even composed a song in my honor, called "300," for the number of Germans I had killed.

"But she's shot three hundred and fifteen," Vasilyev quickly piped up.

Smiling amiably, the man explained, "I wrote the thing when I'd first heard about you. Sorry, but you've been too quick on the draw for me to keep up."

Mr. Guthrie opened the rally with his song:

> Miss Levchenko's well known to fame;
> Russia's your country, fighting is your game;
> The whole world will love her for a long time to come,
> For more than three hundred Nazis fell by your gun.

After Mr. Guthrie finished singing, Mayor La Guardia introduced Mrs. Roosevelt, who talked about the Soviet War Relief Fund for a while before introducing me. Even after having spoken so many times, I was still a bit nervous as I stood behind the microphone gazing out over the sea of faces, and beyond to the park's trees and ponds, and in the shimmering distance the glittering skyscrapers of the city. I suppose it should have been easy enough, just mouthing what Vasilyev had written, but I hadn't had a chance to go over it and so was a little worried.

With Radimov translating, I began to speak. I talked of the need for more American support to defeat the Germans. I called on our "American friends" to understand the "enormous" sacrifice the Soviet people had made to stop Hitler. I spoke of the "tide of war" slowly turning, of the German advance being finally halted, of a new Soviet offensive about to "drive the invaders from our soil." However, despite the optimism, after a while Vasilyev turned the speech into a personal plea for help. "Please, I beg you from the bottom of my heart," I read, "help us. It is not just our fight, but yours as well. We need more assistance from our American friends. Try to imagine the loss of your own dear children to these heartless monsters." At this point in the speech, in parentheses, Vasilyev had written a note to me: "Try to summon up a tear or two here." I ignored it, continued to read. "But Soviet parents take an enormous pride in sacrificing their sons and daughters whom they send willingly to the front to fight the Germans. They gladly forfeit their children to defeat Hitler. I plead to every single American man: join me in the fight for freedom. Don't let a woman do the fighting for you. Be courageous. Stand up for women and children everywhere. Thank you, my friends."

When I finished, I went over and took my seat. Evidently they liked the speech. The crowd clapped and whistled and called out my name, so much so that finally, on the urging of Mrs. Roosevelt, I got up and acknowledged them with a bow, which sent them into another frenzy of applause. Afterward, the press came rushing up, peppering me with questions.

"Lieutenant Levchenko, aren't you throwing down the gauntlet to American soldiers?" one asked.

"Well . . . I suppose I am."

"Are you saying our boys are cowards?"

Before answering, I glanced at Vasilyev, who drew his lips together into a puckery ball of warning.

"No, I didn't say they are cowards," I replied. "You Americans have fought bravely in many wars. But I do think actions speak louder than words."

"What do you mean by that?" another called out.

"Just that war is won by fighting, not by talking. I believe it is high time your troops stood shoulder to shoulder with me rather than behind me."

After Radimov translated this, like a beehive struck with a stone, it stirred the group of reporters into an agitated frenzy. They frantically scribbled in their notebooks and chattered excitedly among themselves. Soon they were calling out more questions, faster than Radimov or I could possibly field them. One yelled something about me saying the Americans were hiding behind my skirt.

Right then, however, Mrs. Roosevelt, as she would do many times over the course of our trip, stepped in to rescue me. Smiling, she said something to the reporters that seemed to appease them, for they all laughed amiably.

As our group left the stage and made our way to the waiting limousines, Mrs. Roosevelt came up to me and said through the captain, "I think you may have struck a nerve, my dear. You assaulted the fragile male ego." Then she laughed.

Just before we reached the street, Captain Taylor leaned in to me and asked, "So how are you?"

I had been so busy for the past several days with appearances and speeches, with running here and there for photos and interviews, I hadn't had much of a chance to talk with him, at least not privately. The last real conversation we'd had had taken place at the cemetery. What time we did spend together involved him mostly translating for Mrs. Roosevelt or for reporters slinging questions at me, or teaching me English. Nonetheless, now and then he'd shoot me a wink when some reporter would ask me an absurd question.

I turned to him and said, "I'm fine, Captain."

"Maybe we can talk later," he said.

On the ride back to our hotel, I sat between Dmitri and Viktor and across from Vasilyev, Gavrilov, and the Corpse. Viktor, I noticed, stared indifferently out the window, his gaze vacuous.

"I think you went a bit too far by saying the Americans were hiding behind your skirt."

"That's not what I said," I replied.

"We want to motivate them, not offend them. Don't stray from what I've written for you," Vasilyev said.

"He asked a question and I answered it. I'm doing my best!" I suddenly snapped at him. My nerves had been frayed from having to be on my toes constantly, having to fawn and smile, say this, avoid saying that, not to mention having to pass on to him whatever Mrs. Roosevelt told me. I had been worn to a frazzle. "If you don't like me doing it, let your lapdog Gavrilov do it."

"There, there," he said, patting my knee. "I think you're just tired. Perhaps you deserve some time off, Lieutenant."

We finally reached the hotel a little after noon. The building was on the West Side overlooking the Hudson, just around the corner from where Mrs. Roosevelt and her group were staying. As we were heading up on the elevator, Vasilyev whispered he wished a word with me and so followed me to my room. I thought he wanted to continue haranguing about my mistakes with the reporters.

In my room, Vasilyev walked over to the window and gazed out. My room was on the fifty-seventh floor, and I got a terrible sense of vertigo every time I looked out, so I usually avoided it.

"It is quite the view from here. Come look."

"I'd rather not," I said.

Vasilyev headed over to a nearby table where there were a bottle of champagne on ice, a fresh bouquet of flowers, a platter of food, and some new correspondence. Each day there appeared various gifts from people I didn't know, as well as letters and cards and cables. Most were from Americans, average people who'd read about me in the newspapers. But there were some from around the world. One was a handwritten letter signed by Charles de Gaulle. Vasilyev picked up a sandwich, looked it over, and sniffed it before taking a bite. He scooped up the packet of mail, began riffling through it. One caught his attention. He opened the envelope and began perusing it, though for what reason, I couldn't fathom, as most were in English. Usually, Radimov would translate those.

"I have to use the bathroom," I said. I went in and shut the door. I turned on the faucet, washed my face. I felt exhausted. In the mirror I saw that my face was drawn, my eyes fatigued. I hadn't been sleeping well, all the moving about, trying to rest in a berth on a train, in strange hotel rooms. I had found all these public appearances and interviews much more draining than I had ever found war to be. Most of all I had grown tired of my role of spying on Mrs. Roosevelt, and trying to avoid passing on to Vasilyev anything that might hurt her.

I stalled in the bathroom, hoping he'd eventually leave. I was exhausted and I wanted to get some rest before whatever it was they had planned for me that evening. When I realized he wasn't going to leave, I finally opened the door. I found Vasilyev seated comfortably in a corner chair, drinking a glass of champagne. He was reading a cable.

"I believe you will find this one of particular interest," he said. He handed me the telegram. In Russian, it said:

Dear Comrade Levchenko (stop) I wish to commend you on your glorious triumphs in the United States (stop) Even now you are helping the Motherland in our Great Patriotic war to defeat the Hitlerites (stop) Respectfully, S.

S, I thought. *Stalin.* I felt something like a piece of ice slide down my spine, the same sort of feeling I'd had back in Moscow on meeting The Man of Steel.

"You've caught his attention, Lieutenant. That's a very good thing."

"Is it?" I said. I glanced at the cable again. Now I was another name in some vast book somewhere, a book that held thousands, perhaps tens of thousands, of names just like mine, whose fates were controlled by him, the master puppeteer. "I think I would prefer he not know who I am."

Vasilyev looked up from his reading, frowned, then let out with a dry cackle. "It is far too late for that, I'm afraid," he said. "Champagne, Lieutenant?"

"You said you wanted to talk."

"Have a seat. You look a little tired."

"I am tired," I said, walking over and sitting on the bed. "I would like to get some rest."

"Indeed, I think you deserve a little R & R," he offered. "Mrs. Roosevelt has invited you to the opera this evening. I think it's a splendid idea. I want you to relax and have a good time. You won't have to wear your uniform."

"What will I wear then?"

"I've taken the liberty of ordering some new things for you. They'll be delivered to your room this afternoon."

"Civilian clothes?" I asked.

"Yes. I thought this way those foolish reporters won't pester you as much. And besides, you are attending the opera, you ought to dress up."

I hadn't worn civilian clothes in well over a year. Of course I had worn my country's uniform with pride. But regular clothes? I wasn't sure how to feel about that.

"Will you be accompanying me tonight?" I asked Vasilyev.

"No," he replied, downing the rest of his glass. "I have some other business to attend to."

"And Radimov?"

"I will need his services. Our Captain Taylor can translate for you."

Our Captain Taylor, I thought. What was he implying by that? Vasilyev poured himself another glass of champagne. He seemed in an odd mood, distracted, content just to sit there.

"You ought to try the champagne. It's not half bad."

"I'd think I would like to rest a little before tonight," I reminded him again.

But he didn't budge. Instead he said, "I believe Captain Taylor may prove to be the key."

"The key?" I asked, looking over at him.

"To unlocking the secrets of Mrs. Roosevelt. I'm sure he knows a great deal about her . . . activities."

I thought of that meeting in the shed behind the embassy, what they had asked me regarding Mrs. Roosevelt. Then I thought of my conversation with the captain at the cemetery, how he'd said that if Mrs. Roosevelt's relationship with Miss Hickok were to be made public, she would be ruined.

"Even if there was something to know about her 'activities,'" I said, "the captain is not a fool. Nor is he disloyal."

"I'm sure you're right. I believe it will take some cleverness on your part to get him to part with what he knows."

"Cleverness?" I said.

"Women have ways of getting men to talk," he said. "Particularly attractive women like yourself."

"What are you suggesting, Comrade?" I hurled at him.

"Just that the captain is quite taken by you."

"Don't be ridiculous."

"Am I? You would have to be blind not to have noticed, Lieutenant?"

I thought of Captain Taylor touching my face that night on the terrace, our conversation at the cemetery, all the times he had stared at me and smiled. The way he would sometimes look at me as he translated Mrs. Roosevelt's words. I knew Vasilyev was right, even if I hadn't wanted to admit it.

"And what is it you wish me to do?"

Vasilyev inspected his nails. "Nothing really. Just don't discourage his attentions."

"You would have me play a whore to get what you want?" I said angrily.

"Relax, Lieutenant," Vasilyev said.

"Don't tell me to relax. I won't do it. I won't!"

I got up and stormed over to the door. I stood there for a moment, debating my next move.

"Just where do you think you would go?"

I stood there, seething, but I knew he was right. Where *would* I go? And even if I managed to escape, I knew they would hunt me down, just as they had Trotsky, Erwin Wolf, Rudolf Klement. I knew they wouldn't let me go, not now, not ever. I was theirs. I belonged to them in the same way as a tractor or a tank, or the fields back in the Ukraine they had taken from the kulaks. It struck me then, in a way it had never quite done before, that I owned nothing, not the clothes on my back, not my medals, not my body or my mind, not even my soul. Everything I was and had was theirs to do with as they pleased. I was just a pawn, to be used and sacrificed when they thought best. Still, I continued standing there for a moment, frozen between anger and fear—fear not so much of what Vasilyev and his bunch of thugs could do to me, but of the unknown, of what lay on the other side of the door, the great, unfathomable gulf that I would be crossing if I made that choice.

"Lieutenant," came Vasilyev's voice from behind me, his tone having softened. "No one's asking you to compromise your precious morals."

"No?" I said.

"No. In fact, I respect your integrity. Please, come and sit down."

Stubbornly, I stood there for another moment or two, staring at the door, knowing that I had already capitulated though not wanting to admit it to myself. Finally I turned and headed over and sat on the bed again.

Vasilyev got up and came over and sat down beside me. The springs groaned under his bulk, and I found myself unwillingly leaning into him. He put his arm around my shoulder and said, "My dear Tat'yana." It was the first and only time I could recall him calling me by my first name. "I can't tell you just how proud I am of you."

I turned toward him, looked into his blood-dark eyes. This close I could actually see my reflection there. Then he leaned toward me and planted a fatherly kiss on my forehead.

"In some ways I look upon you as a daughter," he said. "Do you really think I would ask you to compromise yourself? I'm merely suggesting that you let the captain believe what he wants."

"You mean, lead him on."

"Call it what you will. It won't hurt to be nice to him," he replied, with an ironic smile forming on his lips. "Act as if his feelings are reciprocated."

"And you think this will make him confide in me about Mrs. Roosevelt?"

"It certainly can't hurt. In the presence of a pretty woman men have been known to be less than discreet. There are, shall we say, certain pressures being put on me." I thought of Zarubin, of the ambassador, Vasilyev's bosses. "Are we in agreement on this, Lieutenant?" he said, squeezing my shoulder.

I just stared silently at him.

"Good," he said, standing. "I ought to let you get some rest. You will be picked up around six. Remember: keep your eyes and ears open."

After he left, I paced the room, angry with Vasilyev, with all of them, those dark forces I felt tightening around me, biting into my flesh like barbed wire on a battlefield. Angry too with myself, for having gone along with all of this, for not having opened that door. I desperately wanted someone to talk to, and the only one I could think of was Viktor. Besides a few words in passing, I hadn't really talked with him since that time in Washington. He was on the floor below mine, so I headed down and knocked on his door. He opened it just wearing his trousers, without shoes or socks, his chest bare. I noticed that the bruises along his ribs were beginning to fade.

"Can I talk with you?" I asked.

"About what?" he replied, a wariness to his voice.

"In private."

Before letting me in his room, he glanced out into the hallway to make sure I was alone. He offered me the only chair while he sat on his bed. I noticed there was a half-filled bottle of vodka on the nightstand.

"How are you, Viktor?" I asked.

"How should I be?" he replied evasively.

"Are you feeling better?"

"I probably shouldn't even be talking with you."

"Why?"

He shrugged, as if it were too obvious to need an answer.

"You believe me when I told you I had nothing to do with what they did to you."

"If you say so."

"I didn't. I swear I didn't, Viktor. You have to believe me. Please, I have no one else to turn to."

He stared blankly across at me; then he leaned over and grabbed hold of the bottle on the nightstand. He uncapped it and took a drink. "You look like shit. Here," he said, handing the bottle to me. I accepted it as a kind of peace offering and took a sip.

"So what do you want to talk about?" he asked.

"They've been having me spy on Mrs. Roosevelt."

He pursed his lips, as if he wasn't any longer surprised by anything they did. "And you've agreed?"

"What else could I do?"

"I told you what you could do, but you let them bully you around. What is it they want?"

"I don't know exactly. But they think they can get important information from her. And they are prepared to blackmail her. About her personal life. It's all absurd."

He laughed at this, his scarred mouth knotting his face to one side. Then he took another drink, wiped his mouth on the back of his hand.

"They want me to . . . become 'friendly' with Captain Taylor," I offered, feeling embarrassed even saying it out loud. "They think we might be able to use him to get information about her."

"So what are you going to do, Lieutenant?" he asked.

"I don't know."

"What have you told the American captain?"

"About what?"

"Have you confided in him anything that Vasilyev has asked you to do?"

"No. No, of course not."

"Be careful around him."

"Why do you say that?"

"I just think you should. Don't trust the Americans either."

"But why?"

"Just don't."

I thought of asking him more but decided not to go down that path. At least not right then.

"And what are you going to do, Viktor?"

He shook his head. "I'm not going to spy for that swine Vasilyev, that's for sure. You and I, Lieutenant, we are soldiers. But this is not fighting. This is the usual trickery from those *chekist* bastards. The same ones that carted my father off in the middle of the night. They can get somebody else."

"They'll punish you," I said.

He seemed to want to say something, but I could see that he wasn't fully certain he could trust me.

"I'll play their game. Smile and nod. But when the time is right, I'll make my move."

"Move?"

"The less you know, Lieutenant, the better."

"You can trust me, Viktor."

"It's not that. I figure what you don't know, they can't get out of you." He looked down at his bruised ribs. "They can make a stone talk, those pricks."

I got up and went over to him. I took his face in my hands and looked at him.

"Think about the consequences," I said to him.

"I have."

I shook my head. "Since I can't talk you out of it, at least be careful, Viktor."

"Don't worry. I will. You too, Lieutenant."

17

That afternoon a bellhop delivered my new clothes to my room. Vasilyev had picked out an entire outfit—a crepe de chine dress, a pair of uncomfortable shoes with wobbly high heels, an evening clutch that was no bigger than an ammo pouch, gold earrings, even a new brassiere that pushed up my breasts. The dress was breathtaking, made of a sheer black material, with sequins and gathered shoulders and a daring décolletage. I don't know how or where Vasilyev had bought it, but again, he proved the magician. It fit me perfectly, and when I looked at myself in the mirror I thought, My God, who is that? I felt naked without my uniform, a turtle stripped of its shell. How could I go out looking like this? I considered telling Vasilyev I refused to wear it. The Americans expected a soldier, not some Hollywood pinup girl. I knew, though, that this was exactly Vasilyev's plan, to make me look seductive. But the more I stared at myself, turning this way and that, the more I liked what I saw. I had to admit the fat scoundrel had good taste—the outfit was absolutely gorgeous. Never had I worn anything so fine, not even to my own wedding. For the first time in what seemed like years, I felt sensual, desirable, not like a soldier but like a woman again.

I kept thinking of my conversations with both Vasilyev and Viktor. How the former had wanted me to become friendly with the captain, and how the latter had given me a warning regarding the American. What did he mean by that?

Around six Vasilyev came to my room to tell me that Mrs. Roosevelt's party was waiting for me downstairs in the lobby. Draped over his arm he carried a garment bag.

"Turn around," he said. I did an awkward pirouette in my new shoes. He stared at me for a moment, his dark eyes seeming to frown.

"Is something wrong?" I asked, suddenly feeling like an insecure girl before her first dance.

"No. It's just that you look stunning, Lieutenant," he exclaimed.

"You don't think it's too . . . revealing?"

"Not at all. You're a beautiful woman. That dress is very becoming on you."

He lay the garment bag on the bed and removed its contents. There was the mink coat I had received from the furriers' union.

"Try it on," he said.

I took the coat from him and drew it over my shoulders, then looked at myself in the mirror.

"What do you think?" I asked.

"The question is, Lieutenant, what do you think?"

"It's all right," I said nonchalantly.

Vasilyev chuckled. "Always the obstinate one. Why can't you simply admit that you like it?"

Finally I conceded. "All right, I like it."

"Just one of the many advantages of cooperating," he said. "When you return home, I think you shall find similar benefits awaiting you. They are quite pleased with your work here."

I didn't know what he meant by that, who was pleased or what work I had accomplished. I hadn't really done much except for giving a few speeches and interviews, reporting back to him about my conversations with Mrs. Roosevelt, and very little of what I'd told him in regards to that seemed of particular importance. I could only wonder what he had been telling them back home about me that had so pleased them.

"Lieutenant, some time during the evening," Vasilyev said, "I would like you to bring up the subject of whether Mrs. Roosevelt likes foreign food."

"Foreign food? Whatever for?"

"I'm sure you'll find a way to work it into the conversation. From there it shouldn't be hard to turn the conversation to whether her husband is fond of foreign food."

"What's all this about?"

"Our sources tell us that the president is traveling overseas in the near future. It would be of great value to us if we can confirm that."

"And you think she'll just come out and tell me this if I bring up whether they like foreign food? That's ridiculous."

"Such talk might make her allude to the fact that her husband has plans for travel. And if not, you might quietly broach the subject with the captain. It's possible he'll be accompanying them."

When we reached the lobby, I saw Mrs. Roosevelt, Miss Hickok, and Captain Taylor, along with four or five Secret Service agents in dark suits. They reminded me of our own *chekisty*—silent men with the wary eyes of a cat. Over the past few days I had noticed that their presence had become more apparent, more visible, as if they were suddenly concerned about the First Lady's safety.

"My goodness. You look simply ravishing, my dear," Mrs. Roosevelt said to me through the captain.

"Thank you," I replied.

As we got into the waiting limousine, Captain Taylor said, "You do look ravishing."

I felt myself blush and had to look away. I thought of my conversation with Vasilyev, about not discouraging his attentions. I turned toward him and smiled. "Thank you, Captain," I said.

The four of us chatted pleasantly as we drove through the city, ablaze with lights now as the evening approached.

That night we went to the opera, where we sat in a special box reserved for Mrs. Roosevelt, just above the stage, so close that we could look down and see the actors' facial expressions. Captain Taylor sat between us, so that he could translate, while behind us the two Secret Service men stood guard. The opera, I was informed, was *Porgy and Bess*, by the American composer Gershwin. Before the performance, the captain read the program to me so that I had a basic understanding of the story. Once the opera began, I found I could follow along without knowing exactly what they were saying. The woman who played Bess was my favorite, a large-bosomed soprano with a rich mahogany complexion and a gorgeous voice that resounded through the auditorium. Though the story was about Negroes, I saw not a single black face in the theater. When I mentioned this fact to Captain Taylor, he said, "It's a segregated theater. They don't allow Negroes."

"Given the subject, doesn't that seem hypocritical?" I said.

He conceded a nod, then with a smile added, "They are second-class citizens. Sort of like your kulaks."

After the show, we went out for a late dinner at the Russian Tea Room. I was struck by the bright reds and golds, the gaudy opulence of the place. In some ways it reminded me of the Kremlin.

"I thought you would feel right at home here," Mrs. Roosevelt said. Of course, I didn't reply that this was hardly the sort of place where the average Soviet dined.

Mrs. Roosevelt ordered champagne for the table while Miss Hickok got a scotch. Not far away lurked several Secret Service agents. For a while the four of us talked about the opera.

"Did you like it?" the First Lady asked me.

"Very much indeed," I replied. "But if I may be so blunt, it appears to bring up much that is unflattering about your capitalist system."

"There's plenty of unflattering things to write about in our country," remarked Miss Hickok as she sipped her drink.

"Did not the writer get in trouble with the authorities?" I asked.

"Mr. Gershwin is no longer with us, I'm afraid," replied Mrs. Roosevelt.

"Oh," I exclaimed. I hesitated for a moment before asking, "Was he shot?"

Mrs. Roosevelt and Miss Hickok exchanged incredulous looks, then both broke out in peals of laughter.

"Why, heavens, no," said Mrs. Roosevelt. "He died of a brain tumor. We don't deal with objectionable material like that. People are pretty much free to write whatever they want."

"Even when it's a lie," Miss Hickok interjected. She threw a conspiratorial glance at Mrs. Roosevelt.

"We have something called the First Amendment," explained Mrs. Roosevelt. "It protects freedom of speech."

"Though sometimes I think it might not be such a bad idea if we shot a few in this country," Miss Hickok said, without breaking a smile.

"Oh, stop it, Hick," Mrs. Roosevelt offered with a laugh. "You'll give the poor girl the wrong idea."

All this time, Captain Taylor nimbly translated what we said, hardly stopping to catch his breath. Occasionally, when there was a lull in the conversation, he'd glance over at me and smile.

"The smoked sturgeon is very good, Lieutenant," Mrs. Roosevelt said to me.

A waiter appeared to fill our water glasses. He was middle-aged, with a broad, well-lined face and high cheekbones. He spoke English well, but with a heavy Russian accent. Bowing deferentially to Mrs. Roosevelt, he said something to her, which made her smile. Then he turned to me and said in Russian, "And you are Lieutenant Levchenko, no?"

I nodded.

"I recognize your picture from the newspaper. It is a great honor to meet such a famous countryman," he said, with a little bow.

"Where do you come from?" I asked.

"St. Petersburg," the man replied. "Now they call it Leningrad? Everything there goes by another name now."

"Do you miss home?" I asked.

"The Russia I knew is gone forever. But I have my memories." He stared at me for a moment, then glanced around, leaned toward me and whispered, "Even here one has to be careful what one says. I will pray for your safety, Lieutenant."

His comment struck me as odd.

Mrs. Roosevelt said, "I don't know about anyone else, but I am absolutely famished."

When the champagne arrived, Mrs. Roosevelt proposed a toast.

"*Da blagoslovit vas Gospod,*" she said to me.

"Your Russian is much improving," I attempted in my awkward English. Then, through the captain, I said, "May God bless and keep you as well, my friend."

We conversed pleasantly throughout dinner. At one point Miss Hickok said that perhaps we ought to stop talking and give poor Mr. Taylor a chance to eat some of his dinner before it got cold. As I sat there, I kept looking over at Mrs. Roosevelt. She would smile kindly at me and with gestures inquire if I was enjoying my dinner. I nodded and returned the smile, but secretly I kept thinking about Vasilyev's request. It didn't sit well with me. It seemed one thing to pass on to him what Mrs. Roosevelt freely talked about in a conversation, but quite another to actually conspire to trick her into confiding something she might not otherwise. I felt, in a way I hadn't before, as if I were betraying her trust. And yet, I told myself that it didn't seem to me all that important whether her husband was traveling abroad or not. And, I reasoned, as their allies, shouldn't we know if their president was going overseas?

"Mrs. Roosevelt," I began, "do you like foreign food?"

"Some," she replied. "But I'm afraid my tastes are rather pedestrian when it comes to food. Why do you ask, my dear?"

"Just that you have to travel about so much. And your husband, does he like foreign food?"

"I think being away from home is harder on Franklin than it is on me. Franklin gets tired quite easily, and he's a finicky eater. He prefers plain old American food—hot dogs and pancakes and fried cornmeal," she explained with a chuckle.

"What does he do when he has to travel abroad?"

"His stomach is rather delicate. I'm always afraid he won't eat and he'll lose strength."

I paused for a moment before continuing. "Hopefully, he won't have to travel out of the country for a while."

Before translating this last part, Captain Taylor looked over at me and gave me a searching look. Did he see through my rather crude ploy, or was it simply my own nervousness?

"I only wish that were the case," replied Mrs. Roosevelt.

She didn't elaborate and I decided that if I pressed the issue it would look suspicious. So I decided to change the subject.

"I will miss New York," I offered. "It's a beautiful city."

"It's too bad you didn't have more time to see it," offered Miss Hickok.

We were scheduled to leave in two days for the rest of our cross-country tour.

"You have only the one interview scheduled for tomorrow morning," Mrs. Roosevelt said. "I was thinking that Captain Taylor could give you a tour of the city after that? You could have the entire day. What do you say?"

"I suppose."

"How about you, Captain?" she asked him.

He seemed preoccupied, as if something didn't sit right with him about being asked to act as my tour guide. "I'd be happy to show her about the town if you'd like."

On the drive back to the hotel, we were tired and rode mostly in silence. I sat across from Mrs. Roosevelt, and Miss Hickok beside Captain Taylor. I avoided any sort of eye contact with him, staring out the window at the passing spectacle of New York at night. At one point, though, I happened to steal a glance at Mrs. Roosevelt, whose hand rested on the seat beside that of Miss Hickok. The latter's little finger inched over until it was resting on the sapphire ring on Mrs. Roosevelt's hand. The finger made small circular motions about the ring, rubbing it, caressing it. Watching them, I felt like a voyeur.

It was well past midnight when we reached the hotel. I thanked Mrs. Roosevelt for a wonderful evening and started to get out, but she put a hand on my arm. She said something to the captain.

"She wants me to see you up to your room," he said.

"There's no need for that," I replied.

"She insists. This is New York, not Moscow."

When we reached my room I said, "I'm fine now, Captain. Thank you. By the way, you really don't have to escort me around tomorrow."

"What do you mean?" he asked.

"I sensed that you agreed to take me just because Mrs. Roosevelt asked you to."

"No, I'm really looking forward to it. I just . . . well, never mind."

He stood awkwardly there for a moment.

"Shouldn't you be getting back? Mrs. Roosevelt will be waiting for you."

"I told her I would take a taxi. Is something the matter, Tat'yana?" he pleaded.

"No. Nothing, Captain."

"I thought we agreed that you'd call me Jack, at least when it's just the two of us," he said, drawing his soft mouth into an almost childish pout.

"Of course. Jack."

"What's wrong?" he asked again.

I thought then of Viktor's warning, that I shouldn't trust the Americans any more than I did Vasilyev and his bunch. Despite this, I found myself drawn to Captain Taylor. Something about him that I liked, his smile, his soft mouth, the vulnerability that his missing arm lent to him. He had the sort of looks that made you want to pour your heart out to him.

"Nothing," I said, sighing. But clearly he could see that there was something wrong. Then I added, "At least nothing having to do with you. It's very hard to explain."

"Try me."

I shook my head.

"You can trust me. Whatever you tell me goes no further. I promise."

Trust him, I thought. The captain and I held each other's gaze for several seconds. As I stared up at him, though, I thought about what Mrs. Roosevelt had said about him, that he was a good-looking man— tall and lean, with a sinewy, athletic build despite the missing limb. Those pale lashes, the smattering of freckles. His hazel eyes shimmering with both intelligence and a certain boyish innocence. And he seemed so kind. I wanted to believe I could trust this man, and I felt a wild, almost ungovernable impulse, this desperate desire to unburden myself to him, to seek comfort in his kind aspect. But I said only, "It's just that my life is not my own. What I say or do is not necessarily how I feel. Do you understand what I am saying to you, Jack?"

"I think so, yes," he replied, with an awkward grin. Then before I knew it, he leaned down in to me and kissed me on the mouth. The gesture so startled me that I quickly turned and headed toward my room. "Tat'yana," he called after me. He rushed after me and grabbed me by the arm. "Tat'yana, please forgive me."

"It's all right," I said.

"Are you sure?"

"Yes. Good night, Lieutenant."

My room was dark when I entered, and I had to fumble for the bathroom light switch. Exhausted from the long day, I quickly undressed down to my slip and underwear. I hung the mink coat and the dress in the closet, then returned to the bathroom to wash before bed. I stood looking at myself in the mirror for a moment, my thoughts in complete disarray. You mustn't lead him on, I warned myself. It would only hurt him. And you as well. Then I glanced down at my belly, lowered my slip and underpants, and inspected the knotted scar slithering across the pale skin of my abdomen. I was empty now, a dried-out husk that no longer held even the possibility of life within her. What man would want such a woman as I?

As I walked into the darkened bedroom, I froze. I sensed the unmistakable presence of someone. The corner of the room near the window was dark. As my eyes adjusted, I saw a darker lump seated in the chair. I reached for the lamp beside my bed, intending to use it as a weapon.

"Who's there?" I asked, trying to sound formidable.

Silence for a moment, my breath clawing in my throat. Then a voice said matter-of-factly, "It is I."

Vasilyev. He flicked on the light near the chair.

I set the lamp down. "What are you doing here?" I cried.

"I think you had better put some clothes on, don't you?"

I quickly retrieved the mink coat from the closet and threw it around my shoulders.

"Be careful with that coat or my goose is cooked," Vasilyev joked lightheartedly. On the end table beside him was a half-empty bottle of what looked like vodka. He was holding a glass, and his voice sounded unctuous with drink, his words slurred.

"How did you get in?" I asked.

He held up a key in reply. "Would you care for a drink?"

"I don't want a drink."

"How was your evening?"

"It was fine. I'm very tired. I'd like to go to bed."

"I heard voices out in the hall. Was that Captain Taylor?"

"Yes," I said. "He escorted me up to my room."

"Quite the gentleman. What did you and he talk about?"

"Nothing," I replied.

"You spent a long time talking about nothing," he said. I didn't reply. "This might actually be a golden opportunity."

"For what?"

"If you're alone with the captain all day, he might let something interesting slip about Mrs. Roosevelt."

"I told you already, he's not like that."

"Like what?"

"Disloyal."

"If he brings her name into the conversation, let him talk. Even try to coax him along."

"He's not a fool," I said. "He'll see through what I'm doing."

"Not if you distract him," he said.

"Distract him?"

Vasilyev gave me a look of complicity. "With your looks and charm."

"I told you already, I'm not to prostitute myself for you or anybody else."

"I'm fully aware of your high moral ideals, Lieutenant. But you already have the captain wrapped around your little finger. Simply use it to get him to talk about her. Inquire about her friend Hickok."

He lifted his glass and downed it. Picking up the bottle, he poured himself another.

"Is that all you wanted?" I asked.

"What did you and Mrs. Roosevelt discuss tonight?"

"We talked about the opera."

"The opera? How nice. And Miss Hickok?"

I shrugged. "She seemed to enjoy herself."

I was struck suddenly by the absurdity of the situation I found myself in. Here I was sitting in a strange room in my underwear wearing a mink coat, talking to a drunken man about whether or not the wife of the president of the United States had a female lover. While the world was going up in flames.

"Did you happen to bring up what I asked you to?" he said to me.

I wanted to give him something, a small tidbit so that he felt I was cooperating and wouldn't push me further regarding Mrs. Roosevelt and Miss Hickok.

"Yes," I replied. "She said her husband didn't like foreign food, and when I said that I hoped he wouldn't have to leave the country soon, she said she wished that were the case."

Vasilyev's interest perked up at this.

"Did she say anything else? Such as where he was going?"

"No. Though she seemed to suggest that her husband would have to travel overseas in the near future."

"Doubtless a reference to his upcoming conference with the Boar at Casablanca," he said.

"The Boar?" I asked, thinking of course of my old comrade and nemesis, the Wild Boar, Sergeant Gasdanov.

"That fat little Brit, Churchill," he replied. "He and the president plan to keep us in the dark about it."

"How did you know about it then?" I asked.

"Our sources in the White House."

"That man I gave the packet to?"

"Yes. The conference, of course, is quite secret. They didn't want the Nazis finding out and having Rommel show up unannounced. But we are supposed to be their allies and yet they make plans behind our back. Do you see why we can't trust the Amerikosy?"

"One might well ask what have we done to deserve their trust," I countered.

"The only reason they consider us allies now is that we are fodder for the German Panzers. If it were not for us, Hitler would be having tea right now in Buckingham Palace. Besides, the Brits and Americans have big plans for after the war, plans from which we are excluded." He took another sip of his drink and gazed out the window at the city. There was a certain wistful look in Vasilyev's eyes. "By the way, where did you say Captain Taylor studied in the Soviet Union?"

"I didn't say. But he told me he spent time in Leningrad before the war."

"His name seems vaguely familiar to me. Did he ever say that he worked at the embassy in Moscow?"

"No, I don't think so. Why?"

He shrugged. "I thought I recall that name. Tomorrow, if you get a chance, ask him if he ever worked at the embassy."

He then lifted his glass in the air.

"Here's to my son," he said. "He has been awarded the Red Banner for bravery."

"Congratulations, Comrade," I offered. "You must be very proud."

He nodded absently. Then he finished the drink in one gulp and with difficulty got to his feet.

"Good night, Lieutenant," he said, giving me a little bow. Grabbing the bottle, he made a wobbly line for the door, using his free hand against the wall to steady himself. He opened the door and started out but half turned before leaving. Over his shoulder he said, "Unfortunately, the medal was awarded posthumously."

"Comrade, I—"

But Vasilyev was already out the door.

18

The next morning, before I was to accompany Captain Taylor, I was interviewed by a reporter from the *Saturday Evening Post*. With Radimov translating, we spoke over breakfast in the hotel dining room. The reporter was a woman just a few years older than I, a delicate creature with lovely red hair and fine porcelain features. She wore a dark tilt hat with netting over her blue eyes and a polka-dotted chiffon dress. She was quite pretty. She hadn't done her research, though, and didn't know much about me. She asked the same familiar questions I'd been asked a dozen times already: did I find killing hard, did I mind getting dirty, did I think women were cut out for being soldiers. She wanted me to tell her the story about my duel with the German sniper.

"Weren't you afraid?" she asked.

A photographer accompanied her and took several pictures afterward.

When the interview concluded, I found Captain Taylor waiting for me in the lobby. He had a newspaper in his hand.

"Here," he said, handing it to me. On the front page of the *Times* was my picture, with a headline that he translated for me: "Soviet Sniper Chides Americans: Don't Hide Behind My Skirt."

"Mrs. Roosevelt has already gotten a number of complaints," he explained. "One was from a general at the Pentagon."

"I didn't mean to cause her any problems."

"Don't worry about it. She actually thinks it's funny."

He glanced over at me, a pensive look shading his eyes. The previous night was obviously on both of our minds—the kiss outside of my room. Yet we both tried to avoid it.

"And how are you this morning?" he asked.

"Fine," I replied.

He hesitated, seemed about to say one thing, then changed his mind and said, "I thought we'd start by seeing the Statue of Liberty."

The autumn day was overcast, coolish but pleasant. The city was already teeming with a frenetic activity I was just beginning to get used to. We took a ferry out to see the Statue of Liberty. Up close she was even more impressive than that first time I'd seen her through the mist, her presence more commanding, her visage even more determined. Later we visited St. Patrick's Cathedral, Rockefeller Center with its Radio City Music Hall, then the long ride up in the elevator of the Empire State Building. From the observation deck of the latter, Captain Taylor pointed out sites below.

"You see that island over there? That's Staten Island," he explained, pointing toward the south. "There's Brooklyn and Queens. North, that's the Bronx. And do you see that way off in the distance?" he said, pointing toward the northeast, where a small strip of bluish gray ocean was ringed by land on either side.

"Yes?"

"That's Moscow right over there," he offered with a smile.

"You have very good eyesight, Captain," I said. This made me think of what Vasilyev wanted me to ask him. "Did you ever work at the American embassy there?"

"No. Why?"

"Vasilyev thought he remembered the name Taylor."

"I never made it to Moscow, unfortunately. He must have me confused with another Taylor."

When we were back down in the street, he asked, "Have you heard of the Yankees?"

"It's what they call you Americans, is it not?"

"No. I meant the baseball team. You should see at least one game of America's pastime."

Instead of a taxi, we descended down into the city's subterranean world and got on a subway. Once we were in the stadium, he bought me a hot dog and we sat in the crowded and noisy stands and I watched my first baseball game. The grass was greener and lusher than that of the gardens of Livadia Palace, which had been the czar's summer palace. My father had once taken me to see it when I was a girl.

"Do you see that man out there with the number five on his jersey?" the captain said, pointing to a player running out toward the middle of the green expanse. "That's Joe DiMaggio."

"Is he a good player?"

"The best."

The captain tried, patiently but I must admit unsuccessfully, to explain the game to me. However, the more he tried, the more confused I became. I was used to the simplicity of football, where one had only to kick a ball into a net. Baseball was more confusing than mathematics.

Despite my not understanding the game, I enjoyed myself immensely—the raucous cheering of the crowds, the popcorn and hot dogs, the striking beauty of the fields beneath a gray autumn sky, the way men ran about so carefree and yet with such intensity, chasing the little white ball and sliding along the dirt. I had forgotten that life could offer such innocent pursuits, that everything was not deadly serious. That one could run over a field for no other purpose than the sheer joy of it.

"May I ask you a question about your Mr. Vasilyev?" the captain said.

I looked over at him. "I suppose."

"What's his role here?"

"His role?" I repeated, surprised by the question. "As I told you, to watch over me. To make sure I don't make mistakes."

The captain's hazel eyes bored into me. "Is he with the NKVD?"

Startled by his sudden directness, I didn't quite know how to answer, in part because I wasn't sure myself. But also partly because I wasn't sure what he knew and why he was asking me. Which brought me back to both Viktor's and Vasilyev's warnings about the captain.

"Why would you suggest that?"

"From things I've heard him say."

Trying to remain composed, I replied, "I am a mere soldier. That's beyond my scope."

"But surely you must have your suspicions."

"I've found it's safer for one to keep his suspicions to himself."

After the game was over, we left in the crush of people. The captain grasped my hand, and we rode the surge of humanity exiting the stadium.

"Hold on tight," Captain Taylor called to me over the clamor. "Your Mr. Vasilyev would have my neck if I lost you."

We headed down into the subway again and got on and were propelled into the darkness. The subway car was packed, and we stood pressed against each other. It was only then that I realized he was still holding my hand. His hand was warm and moist, the fingertips, for some reason, smooth as a pianist's. I looked up at him and he released my hand.

"Did you enjoy the game?" he asked, as if to cover his embarrassment.

"Yes. But it's very complicated."

"It takes some time to pick up the nuances," he said.

"Unfortunately, I don't have much time for nuances," I replied.

He glanced at me and smiled. "Well, I'll just have to give you a crash course."

We ended up back where I had spoken the previous day—Central Park. It was late in the afternoon now, the air turning brisk, the sky growing darker with the promise of rain. We spotted a line of horse-drawn carriages parked on the street.

"Have you ever ridden in a carriage before?" the captain asked.

"What, do you think I am royalty?" I said playfully.

He paid one of the drivers, and we climbed up into the elegant carriage. As we rode through the park I thought of those old grainy photos my father had shown me of the czar and czarina riding in a gilded coach to some royal function. We saw couples strolling arm in arm, mothers pushing their prams, people walking dogs, men in suitclothes with their ties loosened, smoking cigarettes after a day's work in one of the city's gleaming skyscapers. It seemed a perfect bucolic setting, like something out of a painting by Constable. As we rode deeper into the park, however, here and there I began noticing these disheveled-looking figures sprawled under bushes or beneath overpasses. Some were riffling through garbage cans looking for food. One fellow in a filthy coat pulled a small wagon filled with what appeared to be rags. They reminded me of those Sevastopolians eking out an existence during the German siege.

"Who are all those people?" I asked.

"The homeless. Those who can't find work," he replied.

"But you are such a wealthy country."

He shrugged. "Yes, it's unfortunate. One of the side effects of capitalism."

"Side effects," I scoffed, thinking of our argument that night back in Washington. "There are those in my country who would point to this as proof that your society is decadent. That capitalism is doomed."

"Things were even worse just a few years back during the Depression. Men who'd lost everything were jumping from the windows down in Wall Street. We had Hoovervilles all over the country."

"Hoovervilles?"

"Ramshackle settlements where the poor lived," the captain explained. "Every city and town had soup lines. People standing on corners looking for a handout. Sleeping under bridges. Many thought capitalism was finished. When President Roosevelt came in he started to put people back to work. Created programs for farmers and young people. Of course, there were those who thought his New Deal just another form of socialism."

"The rest of the world looks at you Americans with great envy," I said. "They don't see this side of your society."

"We have our problems, all right."

"As do we. When I was a a girl, a terrible famine swept across my native Ukraine. People starved to death by the hundreds of thousands. We would see bodies lying in the street. The government tried to blame it on bad weather or on the greed of the kulaks, who they said sold their grain on the black market. Yet the truth is, the leaders were to blame. They secretly wanted to break the spirit of us Ukrainians because we have always been fiercely independent. More than a million died."

"That's awful," the captain said.

"Yes, it was. And we could not even speak about it for fear of being arrested," I explained. "That is one advantage you Americans have over us, that you are free to speak out when you think something is wrong. What did Mrs. Roosevelt call the law that protects your right to speak?"

"The First Amendment. It's part of our Constitution."

"That is a very wise law. To be able to say and write what is in your hearts."

"Somehow I can't imagine you not speaking your mind," he said, a wry smile parting his lips.

"I'm not as fearless as you make me out," I said. "I haven't always spoken up, even when I knew something was wrong."

I paused then, worried that I had already said too much. I thought of all the warnings I'd been given about the Amerikosy. How they weren't to be trusted. How they and the British were working behind our backs. How they were dangerous and would eventually betray us. How in time they, and not the Germans, would be our mortal enemies.

"Mrs. Roosevelt said that you should do one thing every day that scares you."

"That is a very wise idea," I replied. "And what is it that scares you, Captain?"

He smiled at me. "Growing old."

"Really?"

"Yes. I never want to grow old."

"The alternative isn't so good either," I offered, to which he laughed.

"I suppose not. And what of you, Tat'yana? What scares you?"

"Many things."

"I don't believe that for a moment," the captain said.

I thought then of what Vasilyev had wanted me to do—get him to talk about Mrs. Roosevelt. "Why have some called the president's wife a Communist?"

"I guess because of all the work she's done for the poor. She helped workers unionize. Pressured companies for better working conditions. She's been a member of the International Ladies' Garment Workers Union for more than twenty years."

"But she's not a Communist, no?"

"Of course she isn't. She's as loyal an American as there is. She's dedicated her life to helping people."

"Then why are they allowed to say such lies about her?"

"Our freedom of speech works both ways," he said with a bitter laugh. "They've said some pretty nasty things about her."

"Being such a sensitive person, these lies must hurt her feelings."

"She doesn't let on. She's a very private person really. But underneath I think what they say and write about her takes a toll."

"Is she very different in private?"

"A little. She has a temper sometimes. Especially when she thinks something isn't fair."

"But how does she manage to keep her . . . her private affairs private?"

"It's hard sometimes," he said. "As you can imagine she has to be very discreet."

"In your position, you must also have to be very discreet."

The captain turned to look at me directly. He had a partial smile on his face, but his stare was probing, one that made me uncomfortable. "Is that what your Vasilyev wanted you to ask me?"

I stared at him for a moment, speechless.

"What do you mean?"

"I think you know."

He smiled knowingly at me. I tried to overcome my surprise that he had caught me out in a lie. "I don't know what you're talking about."

"No?"

We rode in an awkward silence for a time.

Who was this man? I wondered. And what did he know about me? About Vasilyev and the others?

After a while he said, "You're a very brave woman, Tat'yana. What I don't understand is how you can let that man manipulate you like he does."

It reminded me of what Viktor had said to me.

"I am a soldier. I follow orders."

"That's an excuse. Not a reason."

A light mist started to drift down from the gray sky. It smelled of metal and of smoke, but it left a pleasantly cool sensation on the skin. I could recall in the hot days of fighting, being trapped in a sniper cell for hours, when a rain would suddenly begin. How I loved the cooling touch of rain on my face. The driver stopped the carriage and got down, came around and pulled up the top to keep us from getting wet. Then we started up again.

I sensed the captain's gaze on me.

"Is something the matter?" I asked.

"I wasn't sure I should share this with you or not," he offered, his tone guarded. "But your comrade told me something rather disturbing."

"What did Vasilyev tell you?" I nervously asked him.

"No, not him. Viktor."

"Viktor?" I replied.

He nodded. "If I tell you, though, you must keep this in strictest confidence, Tat'yana. I wouldn't want to get him in trouble."

"Of course. Viktor's my friend." I worried that he had told the captain about his plan to defect. If he had, I knew there would be no turning back for him. "What did he tell you?"

"On the train one night, I bumped into him going between cars. He was bent over, coughing as if he were sick. I asked him what was the matter and he pretended it was nothing. But then he started coughing up blood, holding his side. I offered to go get a doctor, but he got very nervous. Said he didn't need one. When I asked him what had happened, he told me he had gotten into a fight, that he thought one of his ribs was broken. He wouldn't tell me who did it, though. In fact, he seemed very concerned about me telling anyone that we'd talked. Do you know anything about this, Tat'yana?"

I hesitated, wondering if I dare tell him all that I knew. Finally I said, "Those two men who follow us about."

"You mean the two NKVD?"

He seemed to know much more about us than I had imagined.

"Why, yes. They did this to Viktor. They beat him up."

"Why?"

"Because he disobeyed an order."

"What sort of order?"

"I don't know," I lied.

"You don't know? Or you don't want to tell me?"

"It doesn't matter."

"If Mrs. Roosevelt knew, she wouldn't stand for such behavior."

"No, you mustn't!" I said urgently.

"But this is America. We have laws here," he said with that sort of impetuous naïveté that was both so annoying and so appealing. What struck me then wasn't so much that Americans thought they lived by a different set of rules from the rest of the world. It was that they were so confident, like little children playing a game, that there *were* rules at all, that the world was governed by logic, that it was organized around their optimistic wishes. It seemed completely alien to their thinking that there were dark forces beyond their control, chaotic forces that didn't adhere to their sense of fair play.

"We may be in America, but we still are under our government's control," I explained.

Though I wanted to trust the captain, I knew, of course, I couldn't tell him everything—about the spying, about what they wanted to do with Mrs. Roosevelt, about what they wanted *me* to do—not without it all blowing up in my face, without bringing down the terrible wrath of the entire Soviet system on my head. I knew if I confided in the captain all that I knew, I would be setting in motion something I would be unable to stop. It was partly fear. But it had much more to do with the fact that I wanted to do my duty, to be a loyal soldier, to do everything I could for my comrades back home fighting. I was still under the illusion that I could act as they wanted me to without serious consequences, that I could straddle the wobbly fence between what I considered my duty and what were the demands of my own conscience, and that I could return home in a few weeks' time to the moral clarity of the war.

"Tat'yana, if I can help in any way, any way at all, you'll let me know, all right?"

I stared at him, his eyes probing deeply into mine. Then I looked away, out over the park.

When the carriage ride was over, we got off and started walking along the street.

"Are you tired?" he asked.

"A little."

"I thought maybe you might like to go out and listen to some music?"

"Perhaps I should get some rest. It will be a long day tomorrow."

The next day we were scheduled to board a train in the afternoon on our cross-country tour. We were to make a series of whistle-stops and longer stays on our way across country.

"Of course," he said, his mouth turning downward in disappointment. He flagged a taxi and we got in.

As we drove along, I felt this knot of anxiety in my stomach. I thought of our conversation about Viktor, about the captain's asking me if Vasilyev was NKVD. Then I thought of Viktor's warning me about the American. I wondered, too, if I were doing the right thing in lying to the captain about what Viktor and I had been asked to do? Would Viktor really defect? And would they hunt him down as they had so many others who tried to escape from their iron grasp? Then I thought of how when I returned to my room, Vasilyev would probably be lurking there, eager to pump me with questions about what I had gleaned from my time with the captain.

"On second thought, Jack," I said, "perhaps I would like to hear some music."

The captain turned toward me, surprised, a smile lighting up his face.

"Great. I know this nightclub down in the Village."

Even before we entered the place, you could hear the music throbbing upward from the concrete, rumbling through the soles of your feet like distance bombing. Once inside, the noise seemed to grab hold of your spine—this rhythmic pounding of drums and the lusty blare of horns, accompanied by the wild hammering of piano keys. I had never before heard such music. Save for the dance floor in front of the stage, the room was half-lit, with darkened corners where couples sat close, lingering over drinks. A thick cloud of cigarette smoke hung over the room, as well as a pungent mélange of alcohol and perfume and hair pomade.

A band dressed in white coats performed on a stage at one side of the room, while people out on the dance floor writhed and twisted, throwing their arms and heads about, the men twirling their partners around before catching them in their arms. The women threw their hips wildly about and laughed boisterously. There were a number of servicemen in uniforms.

The captain led me through the crowded room to a table in the corner. When a waitress appeared, over the din he called to me, "What would you like to drink?"

"I don't know. What are you going to have?"

He ordered something for both of us.

"So, what do you think?" he asked me, glancing around the room.

"It's quite loud," I replied. "What is this sort of music called?"

"Swing. Boogie-woogie. Do you like it?"

"I think so, yes," I replied. "It makes one's heart beat faster."

He laughed at that. When our drinks came, the captain picked up his glass and said, "*Za zdorov'ye.*"

"*Za zdorov'ye,*" I replied, taking a sip of my drink. It was very strong, burning my throat. But once it landed, I soon felt this delicious warmth fanning out throughout my chest. "What is this called?" I asked, indicating the drink.

"A manhattan," he replied, smiling.

After a while an attractive blond woman in a long blue gown joined the band onstage and began to sing. Her voice was honey smooth yet crackling like a green wood fire. Slowly the music and the drink began to loosen that tightness in my stomach. By the time I'd finished my second drink, the knot had all but disappeared. With my third manhattan, I felt positively wonderful.

"Would you like to dance?" the captain asked.

"I'm afraid I don't know how."

"You never danced back home?"

"Nothing like this," I said, glancing out at the dance floor, where bodies were hurtling around. I had, of course, danced at my own wedding, but it was the traditional *vesilni pisni,* the Ukrainian folk music that my mother had taught me.

"I'm not much of a dancer either," he explained, "but I'll teach you what I know."

"Well, I guess I'm game," I finally conceded.

He grasped my hand and pulled me out to the dance floor. The captain, I found, was being modest about his abilities. He was in fact quite a good dancer, at least compared to me. He moved gracefully, with a practiced step and a natural rhythm that belied his tall and awkward body. Even with his one arm, he expertly spun me about. For my part, I felt clumsy, ungainly as a fish out of water. But he was patient with me, slowly showing me how to turn and what to do as he led me. As I started to get the hang of it, he increased our speed, so that soon he was spinning me around and around. I thought of that time after school when Madame Rudneva had tried to teach me American dancing.

When that song ended we danced another, and then another after that. Despite my earlier reservations, I began to get over my self-consciousness, and the more I danced the more I enjoyed it. It felt good being in motion, the only physical activity I'd had in months.

"Why did you say you weren't a good dancer?" I shouted over the noise.

"Becky said I had two left feet."

"I think she was mistaken."

"She was . . . ," he started to say.

"What?"

"Never mind."

Onstage the blond woman, accompanied by a lilting saxophone, began a slow song, her sultry voice filled with emotion I could sense despite the unfamiliar words.

I could tell that the captain was a little drunk, the way his eyes were slightly unfocused, heavy-lidded, his full mouth partially open. I myself felt a bit tipsy too, my head spinning as he swirled me around the dance floor.

" 'I'm in the mood for love,' " he sang, a little off-key.

I stared up into his eyes.

"That's the words to the song she's singing."

The captain wrapped his one arm around my waist and drew me

gently to him. I felt a little uncomfortable at first, our bodies pressed against each other's. I didn't quite know where to put my right hand so as to avoid the stump of his left arm. Besides, I had not been in a man's arms in such a very long time, it seemed almost unnatural. War had taught me to shun the touch of a man as something filled with threat. Yet as the captain and I danced, my head spinning not unpleasantly from the drinks, the comforting warmth of his hand against the small of my back, I found myself relaxing, easing into him. He moved me across the floor with such effortless grace, with such confidence, I felt something else too, something I had not experienced since the war began. Safe. I felt safe in his embrace. With my head against his shoulder, the music sinking down into my very soul like a balm, the drinks warming my insides, I felt the jagged edges of the world retreat very far away. I inhaled his cologne, the smoke and alcohol scent on his breath, the sour-sweet tang of his body. I must admit too that beyond feeling safe, I experienced another and even more peculiar sensation—the faintest whisper of desire, a language I thought I had all but forgotten. No, I told myself. Don't. But instead of heeding my warning, I actually gave myself over to the sensation. It spoke to me of the fact that despite everything—all that I had lost, the numbing brutality of the war, the deadening of every nerve ending save those for survival—I could still feel like a woman. I held the captain tighter, pressing my body into his all the more firmly, even desperately. I sensed that he too felt as I did, for he started to rub my back in small circles.

"See," he said, his lips against my ear, warm and moist.

"See what?"

"I told you it was easy, didn't I?"

"Well, you are a good teacher," I offered. "What were you going to tell me about your fiancée, Jack?"

He made an exasperated snort through his nose, then he pulled back so he could look at me. "You know I told you she left me because I enlisted? That's not quite true."

"Why did she leave then?"

"The truth is she left me for someone else. He was all ready to settle down and start a family. Could give her the sort of life she wanted."

"Why did you not tell me the truth?"

"I guess I felt like a fool. The funny thing is I think you were right about her. How you said she probably was only interested in the life I could provide for her. And when she found something better she grabbed it."

"It's hard to see into people's hearts. Perhaps she did love you after all."

"I think I fooled myself into believing that."

"Well, it was her loss then," I said. "And you were right as well."

"About what?"

"About love. I don't think it is a bourgeois concept. It's just that I never really experienced it."

"Certainly with your husband," he said.

I shook my head. "No. It was, as you have said, a marriage of convenience."

"I'm sorry."

"I am too," I said, looking up into his face. In the overhead light of the dance floor, his face looked older, more mature, sadder too. The lines around his mouth suggested that this woman had broken his heart more than he admitted even to himself.

The woman singer began another song, and we danced slowly to it, my head naturally settling into the warm crook of his neck. I savored his smell and the touch of his skin, and I wished for the music never to end.

But it did end, of course. When we finally left the club, it was raining hard, the evening air cold and unforgiving. By the time he managed to get a taxi we were soaked. I shivered in the backseat. Jack took my hand in his and rubbed it.

"You're freezing," he said. He brought my hand up to his mouth and blew on it.

At the hotel, we got out, and he escorted me up to the door so that we were under the awning, out of the rain. A uniformed doorman held the door for us, but the captain pulled me over into a corner to one side of the door.

"Thank you for a wonderful day, Jack," I said.

"You're very welcome. I had a swell time too."

Then he reached out and touched my face with his fingertips, five warm points of contact burning my cheek.

"You're beautiful, Tat'yana," he said.

I felt myself blush, my head swirling from the alcohol and from the music still pulsating in my blood.

With a modest smile, I said, "Perhaps you should not say such a thing."

"But why? It's true."

"We're soldiers. Our fates are not our own."

He stared at me in the same peculiar way he had the previous night, an expression that was at once serious and yet with a hint of the mischievous. When I held his gaze, he must have taken that as an invitation, for he suddenly leaned toward me, cupped his hand under my jaw, and kissed me on the mouth. He pulled back a little, staring at me, as if awaiting my response. What I did next surprised me even more than it must have him. I placed my arms around his neck and drew his head down, kissed him back, hard, on the mouth. *Dura*, the thought ran through my head even as I kissed him. Yes, I was a fool, flirting with danger. Nonetheless, I clung to him for a moment, hungrily pressing into him for dear life, as if he were that very same tree I had taken refuge in against the German sniper. All of the previous months of war seemed to overcome me right then and there, and I gave myself over to it. Finally, though, when the moment had passed, embarrassed, I pulled away. Avoiding his eyes I said, "I'm sorry, Jack. We should not have done that."

"Why not?"

"My husband is not dead."

"What?" he cried.

I explained to him how I had received a letter saying he was missing in action. Not dead.

"Then why did you say he was?"

"It's complicated. But I wish not to be unfaithful to him as long as there's a chance that he might return."

"You said you didn't love him, though."

"Yes. But I owe him that much. My heart is not mine to do with what I would."

He seemed about to try to talk me out of it, but then said only, "I'm sorry."

"I am too."

I turned and hurried into the hotel.

19

had a hard time falling asleep and then woke in the morning with a headache, a clapper banging the insides of my skull from those manhattans. When my head cleared enough to remember what had happened the previous night, I tried to blame my behavior on having had too much to drink, the alluring pulse of the music, the fact that I had been so alone for so long. I was a woman, after all, and Captain Taylor, a man, and a handsome one at that. Under the circumstances, my being drawn to him was only natural. And wasn't he as much if not more to blame than I? It was he who wanted to dance, who kept feeding me drinks. It should have been obvious all along that he'd been flirting with me, and yet when he kissed me I had melted into him. Now I lay in bed thinking of him. I ran my fingertips gently over my lips, recalling the sensation of his mouth on mine. Before him, I couldn't remember the last kiss I'd had. I knew it had to have been Kolya, probably at the train station the day he'd shipped out. But I couldn't really summon up what it had felt like. The captain's kiss, however, had been different. In fact, I couldn't stop thinking of him now—how wonderful it had felt to dance with him, his arm around me, the touch of his skin against mine, that odd desire that had risen up inside of me suddenly and fiercely, like a grass fire on the steppes, something unstoppable. I finally had to admit that I did feel something for him. Something very powerful, something I had never felt before.

And yet I hardly knew him. Who was he really? Should I trust him? Or should I heed the warnings of my own side? And how, I wondered, did he know that Vasilyev had wanted me to ask about Mrs. Roosevelt? As much as I was drawn to him, I was also more than a little leery of what he represented.

That morning our Soviet delegation was to join Mrs. Roosevelt for breakfast with a group of women reporters at the Waldorf Astoria. As we drove over, I sat beside Vasilyev, across from the others. Viktor, oddly enough, was dressed in civilian clothes, and I could only wonder what that could mean. He glanced at me but remained oddly silent, the look in his eyes indecipherable.

"Are you all right, Comrade?" asked Gavrilov of me.

"What do you mean?"

"It's just that you look a little worse for wear." At this he smiled.

"Thank you for your concern, Comrade Gavrilov," I replied flippantly.

"A late night with your American officer?"

"He's not *my* American officer. And besides, it is none of your damn business."

"A bit touchy, aren't we?"

Where earlier Gavrilov had merely been petty and annoying, ever since I'd made it clear to him that his interest in me was not reciprocated, he'd become more antagonistic toward me, his comments filled with venom. Doubtless too there was some jealousy regarding Captain Taylor.

"So, did you have a nice day, Lieutenant?" Vasilyev interjected as a means of stopping our bickering. He'd nicked himself shaving and had a small dark scab along his fleshy jawline. I thought about the news regarding his son, the brusque way he'd told me. I wondered if he'd told the others.

"Yes," I replied. "We did some sightseeing, went to a baseball game."

"Did you get home late?" Vasilyev asked.

"He took me out dancing."

"Ah, splendid. I have not danced in ages. I used to rather enjoy it too. And is Captain Taylor a good dancer?"

I glanced at Gavrilov and said, "He is quite a good dancer, in fact." The little weasel glowered at me.

"I'm glad to hear you had a good time. You shall have to tell me all about it later," Vasilyev said.

"The captain is a man of many talents," Gavrilov said, slyly glancing around at the others.

"Why don't you shut up!" I said to him.

"Have I struck a nerve?" he said with a sneer.

"Comrade Gavrilov," said Vasilyev, "the lieutenant went with my full blessings."

"Still, we all must be on guard not to be contaminated by Western ways."

"I have complete confidence in the lieutenant's willpower."

I glanced over at Viktor. I wondered what he was thinking. I was a little worried about him. Was he wondering if Captain Taylor had told me about their having met on the train, their conversation? And if I would keep his plans safe from Vasilyev and the others? He held my gaze for a moment before looking out the window.

"Did you inquire if the captain worked at the embassy?" Vasilyev asked me.

"He said he was never at the embassy."

Vasilyev humphed, then seemed to dismiss the thought with a wave of his hand. "It must have been another Taylor."

At the hotel we met Mrs. Roosevelt, Miss Thompson, her secretary, Miss Hickok, and Captain Taylor. Outside the dining room, the First Lady came up and gave me a hug.

"The captain tells me you had a delightful day in the city," she said.

"Yes, we did," I replied, trying to avoid looking directly at Captain Taylor. Because of what had happened the previous night, I felt awkward around him now. I sensed that he did as well, for he kept his gaze on the First Lady, never once looking at me even as he translated for us. I had a vague feeling that Mrs. Roosevelt sensed something was amiss. She glanced from me to Captain Taylor and back, her brows knitted in a motherly expression of concern. She said something to the captain, and they conversed for a moment. Only then did Captain Taylor look at me.

"She is worried about you and wishes to know if everything is all right," he explained. "Perhaps you and I—"

But before he could finish, I said, "Thank her for her concern. Tell her I'm just feeling a little tired today."

"Well, let's join the others, shall we," the First Lady said, wrapping her arm in mine and leading me into the dining room. "The girls are just dying to meet you."

After we'd finished breakfast, I excused myself to go to the bathroom. When I came out, Captain Taylor was waiting in the small alcove outside the bathroom.

"I just wanted to talk about last night," he said.

"There's really no need, Captain," I replied, attempting to sound blithe about it. When I tried to walk past him, he touched me lightly on the arm.

"But there is, Tat'yana," he offered. "I wanted to say I was sorry."

"I think we both had too much to drink."

"I didn't mean to kiss you," he said.

I stared up at him, feeling the oddest sensation—disappointment.

"You didn't?"

"No. Well . . . yes, I suppose I did." He hoisted his pale eyebrows as he said that, like a white flag of surrender. "What I meant to say is I *shouldn't* have done that. I would completely understand if you wanted someone else to translate. I don't want to make you uncomfortable, and I see that I have."

"You should have thought of that before you kissed me, Captain."

"I know. It won't happen again," he said. "In my defense, though, I didn't know that you were still married."

"Would it have made any difference?"

Grinning shyly, he said, "Probably not."

I shook my head, embarrassed by what I had let Vasilyev talk me into. "I didn't mean to deceive you."

I went on to explain it all—how Vasilyev had wanted me to say my husband was dead in order that it would appear as if I were "available," and that American men would want to sign up and fight to protect me. As I related it to him, it seemed all the more preposterous, as did so much of what I was being asked to do. The captain chuckled lightly.

"I know," I admitted. "It is quite absurd. I am dishonored by it."

"So let's say we just forget about last night, okay?"

With this, he started to turn and walk away. I felt . . . what? *Abandoned*, I suppose is the word. I felt something inside me crack, like a piece of ice that had warmed and broken away.

"Last night I couldn't sleep for thinking of you," I told him. He stopped, turned around.

"Really."

"Yes. Really."

He walked back over to me. He repressed a boyish grin.

"I've been thinking about you a lot lately too," he confessed. "I have something I should probably confess."

"Are you sure that's a good idea?"

"Yes, I think it is. I—"

But right then a voice interrupted us.

"Oh, there you are." I turned to see Vasilyev standing there. I could only wonder how long he'd been there, how much he'd heard of our conversation. "We need to get ready to take the train," he said, looking at Jack. "You'll excuse us, Captain."

Vasilyev had the others take a taxi back to the hotel to pack their things while he and I got in the limousine and headed off in another direction.

"Where are we going?" I asked.

"We have to meet some people," was all he said.

Vasilyev stared straight ahead, his eyes tired and drawn, his thin, hard mouth slightly agape, as if he were winded. It seemed as if he had aged years in just the past few days. Though I didn't trust him, in fact, didn't even like him, I couldn't help but feel sadness for him regarding his son's death. We hadn't talked since that night he'd told me.

"I wish to extend my condolences for your loss," I said.

"Thank you, Lieutenant. Yuri was a good soldier. He died fighting for the Motherland. Any parent should be proud of that."

"Still, I know what it is to lose a child."

He nodded, then smiled wistfully at something that must have occurred to him.

"War was the farthest thing from his nature. Yuri was always a sensitive sort of lad. Loud noises startled him. He liked to play quietly by himself. As a boy, he used to collect butterflies. Had a large collection, all neatly arranged with their scientific names."

"I am very sorry," I said again.

"As am I." And for the first time since I'd known him, he said something negative about the government. "His commanding officers should have been taken out and shot," he said, his jaw set both in anger and in remorse.

We drove for a time in silence. Then he seemed to snap to attention and was all business again. "By the way, Lieutenant, we didn't have the opportunity to talk about your day with Captain Taylor. Did he tell you anything of interest about Mrs. Roosevelt?"

"No," I replied.

"Are you quite sure?"

"Yes."

"This Captain Taylor seems to be infatuated with you?"

"You would have to ask him that."

"Don't be coy. It should be quite obvious to you," he said.

"If he is, isn't that what you wanted?"

"It would have its advantages," he said. Vasilyev leaned over and spoke through the little window that opened into the driver's seat. The driver nodded, pulled the car to the curb, and got out. He walked a little ways away and lit up a cigarette. When we were alone, Vasilyev asked, "And what of you, Lieutenant?"

"What about me?"

"Are you in love with him?"

"Don't be ridiculous. Did that fool Gavrilov tell you that?"

"I am not blind," he said. Reaching out in a paternal sort of way, he laid a heavy hand on my shoulder. "Listen to me, Comrade. I admire you. You are a very brave woman. No one has done more for our country. But you are in a very precarious position. I will do everything in my power to protect you, but I can do only so much."

"Protect me? From what?"

He glanced out the window at the driver standing there.

"You must be careful, Lieutenant. You need to keep your wits about you. Not let yourself get carried away by your emotions."

"I won't be carried anywhere I do not wish to go."

He stared at me, wondering what I was implying.

"Orders have come down from the very highest levels, Lieutenant," he explained. "And there are those who would stop at nothing to achieve their goals. These men you are about to meet, you must give them something."

" 'Something'?" I said.

"Information. I promised them you would find out useful information from your association with Mrs. Roosevelt."

"Why did you do that?" I exclaimed.

"As I said, I am trying to protect your neck. Both of our necks," he said, his hand almost involuntarily touching the knot of his tie.

"Even if she knew anything of importance, which I'm sure she doesn't, she wouldn't tell us," I argued. "It's utter madness to think we could blackmail her into revealing state secrets."

He wagged his head in a gesture of defeat.

"What I believe is irrelevant. Those in power have decided that Mrs. Roosevelt is crucial to our plans, and they will accept nothing less. If we don't give them something, they are going to think you are withholding information—which I myself have my suspicions about. Be that as it may, you must give them something of interest about the First Lady."

"Such as?"

"Tell them at the opera the other night you saw her and that Hickok woman holding hands."

"That's absurd. I am a soldier," I said. "I refuse to stoop to such a thing."

"Don't get high and mighty with me, Lieutenant. You must throw them a bone to keep them satisfied. Otherwise . . ." He fell silent, rubbing his chin in thought. "Listen to me carefully. They may ask you about a certain project the Amerikosy are working on. A project of the highest secrecy. They might want to know if you've heard anything about it from Mrs. Roosevelt or Captain Taylor."

I couldn't stifle a laugh. "If it's of such secrecy, they surely wouldn't confide it to me."

"That doesn't matter. Tell them you recall that Mrs. Roosevelt mentioned a scientist who met with her husband. A man named Szilard."

"Who is he?"

"That's immaterial. Just say that Mrs. Roosevelt mentioned that this Szilard fellow had met with her husband. Make it sound as if it were a passing remark. Do it in such a manner that it doesn't seem rehearsed. Is that clear?"

"They're fools if they believe such a story."

"They are and they will. It's important that we convince them we are making headway. Remember the name: Szilard."

Vasilyev then rolled down the window and called to the driver, and he got back in and we continued on.

We came to a stop in front of an apartment building on the East Side of the city. It was not quite dilapidated, but it was older and a little run-down, like one of those bland, sprawling Soviet-style apartment blocks that had sprouted up in every city during Stalin's modernization period. We entered and headed up by the elevator, walked down a hallway and stopped in front of a door, upon which Vasilyev hammered with his meaty fist three quick strikes followed by a longer fourth—*dah-dah-dah . . . dahhh*—the first notes of Beethoven's Fifth. From behind the door a man's voice, vaguely familiar, said the word "antelope," and Vasilyev responded with "leopard." When the door opened, I saw the man named Zarubin, the person I'd met at the Soviet embassy in Washington.

"Welcome, Comrade," said the stocky, red-haired man to Vasilyev, shaking his hand. "And you, Lieutenant Levchenko."

It was a tiny apartment—a narrow kitchen, a small sitting area, a bedroom I could see through a doorway. In the kitchen I saw a fat, unshaven man in a sleeveless undershirt preparing something at the stove. He wore a shoulder holster. The place smelled of boiled meat and cabbage, and of the bodies of men living in close proximity. As I passed by the bedroom, there were at least two other men in there. One had headphones on and was tapping out a telegraph message. I was led into the sitting area, where another man, nattily attired in a dark suit and tie, waited. He stood as I approached.

"Lieutenant Levchenko, I would like you to meet Comrade Semyonov," Zarubin said. This Semyonov fellow shook my hand. He was a short man with thinning hair and a pudgy, too-eager face, dark little eyes that flitted anxiously about like sparrows.

"It is a pleasure to meet you, Lieutenant," offered this Semyonov. "Please, sit." The man in the undershirt appeared from the kitchen, carrying a tray with a teapot, cream and sugar bowls, cups. He wore no socks and his undershirt was yellowed, bulging with his belly. As he bent over to put the tray on a small table in the middle of the room, his holster hung down. In it was a bulky Tokarev pistol.

"You want some tea?" Zarubin asked, in his usual gruff manner.

"No, thank you," I said.

"Your pictures hardly do you justice, Lieutenant," Semyonov said, smiling obsequiously. With a nod to the man in the undershirt, he indicated that he wished to have him pour some tea. He was soft-spoken but with the precise movements and the meticulous manners of someone who had grown up attended by servants. Semyonov didn't ask Vasilyev if he wanted any tea. When the man was finished pouring the tea, he headed into the bedroom and shut the door. I could hear him conversing with the others, though I couldn't make out what they were saying.

Semyonov made small talk with me for a time—about the weather, our impending trip, if I had found New York to my liking. Now and then he would glance over at Vasilyev, who sat quietly in a chair near the window. A look seemed to pass between them that at first I couldn't put a name to, other than that they knew each other. After a few minutes of polite talk, Semyonov glanced at his watch and decided it was time to get down to business.

"Comrade Vasilyev tells me you have become quite good friends with Mrs. Roosevelt?"

"I suppose we have. I like her very much."

"Excellent. What have you and she discussed?"

"I have already told Comrade Vasilyev everything."

"But now I wish you to tell me."

"We talked about many things."

"Comrade Vasilyev has told me that she said her husband was planning on traveling. Did she say to where?"

"No. But as I have already told him, I got the sense that it was abroad."

He leaned forward and carefully poured some milk into his tea, followed by three perfectly rounded spoonfuls of sugar. He picked up the cup by the saucer and with the spoon made cautious circles in it, tapped the spoon, then placed it on the saucer and took a sip.

"Do you think she has Communist sympathies?"

"I do not know, Comrade. She certainly supports our struggle against the Nazis."

"And what of this Captain Taylor? What sort of terms are you on with him?"

"Terms?" I said.

"Are you intimate with him?" he asked, staring levelly at me.

"No, of course not," I said, too quickly, so that my tone rang hollow even to myself.

"But you are quite friendly with him, are you not?" he asked.

"We are friendly, yes," I replied coolly.

"Have you been able to elicit from him any information regarding Mrs. Roosevelt?"

"Nothing of consequence."

"In regards to her personal life, did the captain say anything about that?"

I shook my head. "No. Nor would he. He is quite loyal to her."

"I see," said Semyonov, glancing over at Vasilyev. I could see an expression flitter across the latter's face. This one I recognized as a look of annoyance but also one of consternation. I could now tell that Vasilyev had a bitter antipathy toward this man. Also, that if he didn't quite fear him, he regarded him with caution, the way you might a wasp very near your hand.

"This journalist friend of hers, what is her name again?" Semyonov said, snapping his fingers impatiently and tossing a sideways glance at Vasilyev.

Vasilyev supplied the name for him: "Hickok," he said.

Turning back to me, he asked, "Have you been able to discern the exact nature of this friendship between Mrs. Roosevelt and this Hickok woman?"

"No," I said.

"Are they lovers?"

"How would I know that, sir?"

"Certain . . . ," he said, gesticulating with his hands, searching for the right word, "gestures of affection. Things they might say to one another in private."

"I know only that they are close friends," I replied.

I decided, then and there, that that was as far as I would go down the path of betraying my friendship with Mrs. Roosevelt. I wouldn't say any more than that, even if they were to threaten to do to me what they had to Viktor. And even then I felt a terrible sense of betrayal twisting in my stomach.

Finally Semyonov said, "In your conversations with Mrs. Roosevelt or Captain Taylor, has the word *Manhattan* ever been broached?"

"As in the city?" I asked.

"No," he said. "As in a certain project the Americans are working on."

With this I recalled, of course, my recent conversation with Vasilyev. What he had instructed me to do.

"I don't believe she mentioned any such a project, but . . ." I paused for effect.

Semyonov took the bait. "But what?" he asked eagerly.

"There was something, I recall. Yes, Mrs. Roosevelt mentioned someone visiting her husband. A scientist, I think it was."

At this both Semyonov and Zarubin sat up, their interest piqued.

"Do you happen to remember the name?" Vasilyev asked, playing his part.

"It was an unusual name," I said, furrowing my brow, as if I were trying to recall it. "I think she said it was Szilard."

"Szilard?" asked Semyonov, barely able to contain his satisfaction at hearing this news. "Are you certain?"

"Yes, I'm quite sure," I said.

Semyonov glanced at Zarubin and nodded. Then he turned his gaze back to me, studying me for a moment as he took a sip of tea. Any fool should have been able to see through my pathetic lie. But they had so convinced themselves that their scheme would work, they were ready to believe anything. They had been trained in the Communist system, which warped their sense between what was real and what they were told to believe.

"Make sure to alert Kharon of this development," Semyonov instructed to Zarubin. From the coffee table he picked up a manila envelope and set it on his lap.

"May I inquire what all this is about?" I asked.

"You don't have to concern your pretty little head with the details, Lieutenant," Zarubin interjected. "Suffice it to say, the Americans and their British lackeys might be developing a new sort of weapon. We don't know much about it. What we do know, however, is that the Americans are pouring tremendous resources into it and that they have done their utmost to keep it a secret from us. Our code name for it is—"

A split second before he could utter the word, it came to me like a blindingly bright flash, like one of those brilliant flashes the world would very shortly see—the infernal explosion of light followed by the blackening mushroom cloud unfolding ever upward toward the heavens, an image later imprinted on all of our mind's eyes.

"Enormous," I blurted out, glancing at Vasilyev as I said it.

"Why, yes," Semyonov said, surprised, also looking toward Vasilyev.

"That's why you repeatedly used the word in my speeches," I said. I could only guess that they'd used the word in my speeches as some sort of code, to inform our agents here and those back home of our progress.

"The less you know, Comrade, the better," Zarubin advised me.

"We hope to learn whatever we can about Enormous from whatever sources available to us," said Semyonov. "We feel that Mrs. Roosevelt might prove instrumental in this."

"Assuming for a moment she's even aware of this secret project," I said. "What information do you hope to gather from her? She's not a scientist."

"But she might have overheard her husband talking about meeting someone like this Szilard fellow," Semyonov said. "Even if we can confirm they have actually begun work on it, this would be of great assistance to us."

"And you expect that Mrs. Roosevelt will share this with us?"

"As I have already mentioned to you, Lieutenant," Zarubin interjected, "we hope to be able to persuade her."

"Blackmail, you mean?"

At this, Semyonov opened the manila envelope and removed its contents. They appeared to be a group of photographs. He extended them toward me.

"What are those?" I asked.

"Go ahead. Take a look."

I leaned forward and picked them up. As I began shuffling through the pictures, I felt sick to my stomach. They were black-and-white photos, some grainy and from a distance, others quite clear and sharp, as if the person taking them had been just a few feet away. Some were of Mrs. Roosevelt alone, but most were of her and Miss Hickok. They showed them standing together, walking side by side, in various settings. In one they were strolling hand in hand, somewhere in what appeared to be a rural area, or at least where there were trees and shrubs and grass in the background. In another they were embracing. In the background of this photo I spotted first one headstone and then another and soon realized they were in a cemetery, and then I realized that the cemetery in question was the same Rock Creek Cemetery to which Mrs. Roosevelt had taken me. In yet another photo, several people were seated at a restaurant which proved, on closer inspection, to be the Russian Tea Room. They were close-up shots. One of the captain, another of me. How had anyone taken them, I wondered, without us noticing? Then I recalled the waiter who'd struck up a conversation with me. Had he somehow taken these pictures? Others showed the captain and me at the baseball game, getting into a taxi, riding in the carriage in Central Park. Just when I thought their little show was over, Semyonov handed me one last picture. It had been taken out of doors, during a rainy night, the black water glistening in spots off the pavement. The quality of it wasn't particularly good. It showed a woman and a man, both in uniform, standing together under some sort of overhanging cover. They were kissing. That much was clear. If I had not known the two participants in the photo, their identities would have remained anonymous. But I *did* know them: it was Captain Taylor and me. My God! I thought. The bastards had been spying on us all day.

"What is the meaning of this?" I cried, feeling a little as if I had been violated.

Semyonov just stared at me while Zarubin had a thin, crooked little smile pasted on his face. I glanced over at Vasilyev, to see if he was part of this, but he wouldn't meet my gaze.

"Are you still contending that the captain and you are not intimate?" Zarubin stated.

"You had no right."

"The fact of the matter, Lieutenant, is that we had every right," Zarubin said to me.

"I won't stand for this."

"You will shut your pretty mouth and do as we tell you," Zarubin commanded.

I got up, started for the door. Before I reached it, however, the fat man in the undershirt stepped out of the bedroom and blocked my way. He stood there with his arms folded over his chest.

"Come and sit, Lieutenant," Semyonov called to me. "There's no need for any of these dramatics."

I hesitated, then turned and walked back and sat down.

"Good. Are you sure I can't interest you in some tea?"

"I don't want your damn tea," I spat at him.

"Very well. We want you to continue to monitor the activities of Mrs. Roosevelt," Semyonov explained. "Work to gain her confidence. Get her to trust you. I want to know everything she says, particularly regarding her husband and his plans. Also, I would encourage you to capitalize on your relationship with this Captain Taylor."

"Capitalize?" I scoffed.

"It's obvious his interest in you is more than professional. We would not be opposed if you were, shall we say, receptive to his attentions."

"You mean you want me to sleep with him," I said.

"You are free to use whatever means to find out information from him," Semyonov said.

Zarubin chuckled. "He wouldn't be the first man who let himself be led around by his cock."

I felt my jaw knotting. I hated these men with a passion, as much if not more than I had the Germans. At least the Germans I'd faced had been soldiers. They'd fought and died bravely. These men were lackeys, cowards who hid behind their influence.

"Comrade Vasilyev will keep me apprised of your progress," Semyonov said. "And do not, I caution you, mention the American project to anyone. Do you understand?"

I stared at Semyonov, then Zarubin before saying, "I understand."

Semyonov then reached into his inside coat pocket and removed what appeared to be a letter of some sort.

"Here," he said to me, handing me the envelope, which was sealed yet had no address on it. "We would like you to deliver this to our contact in Chicago."

"Why me?"

"The Americans are watching us very closely. It's too dangerous to go by the usual means. They won't expect you to be carrying anything. Keep it on your person at all times. These are very important documents. You mustn't let them fall into the wrong hands. Someone will be in contact with you. His code name is Larin."

"Larin?" I said.

"Yes. That is all for now."

With this, Vasilyev stood and gave a perfunctory nod to the others, and I followed him to the door. Just before we left the apartment, Semyonov called, "Remember, Comrade Levchenko, you are still a soldier. You are merely fighting a different enemy now."

20

I woke to the rhythmic swaying of the train, the remnants of a dream snaring me like barbed wire. In the dream a mustachioed man with soulless black eyes asked if he could trust me. I couldn't utter a word. My mouth seemed frozen. Finally he said, "If I can't trust you, you are worthless to me." Only when I woke did I realize who it was. Stalin.

We were headed for Chicago, hurtling through the night. For the past several days, Mrs. Roosevelt and I had been giving whistle-stop talks along the way, in small towns and villages where people came to hear us. Sometimes, as we had in Pittsburgh, we spoke in a large auditorium, followed by a dinner with local dignitaries. Often I would be interviewed by the press. At each event, they would sell war bonds and ask for donations for the Eastern Front. At a stadium in Cleveland before a baseball game, I gave a short address, for which I was given a rousing ovation. Afterward, Mrs. Roosevelt turned to me and, through Captain Taylor, said, "I think we just bought you another tank."

I lay in my berth in the dark, thinking even darker thoughts, the rails beneath me clicking away the miles. I almost had the feeling that each mile was bringing me closer and closer to some uncertain but equally unavoidable destiny. I thought about what they were asking me to do—to spy on Mrs. Roosevelt, to use Jack Taylor to get information, to be a courier of secret documents.

Ironically, they had so little faith in me they were spying on me at the same time they were the Americans. Otherwise what was the significance of the pictures of me and Captain Taylor? Why had they followed us around? What were they hoping to learn? Were they going to blackmail me too? Or did they think I was betraying them to the Americans and planning on using the photos as evidence against me once I was home (though, of course, I knew if they wanted to arrest me, they didn't need *any* evidence). Since the meeting with Semyonov and Zarubin, I'd found myself looking over my shoulder, wondering if someone was watching me. Snapping my picture. And now that I suspected I was a target of their interest, I had taken care to keep my distance from the captain. I didn't want to draw him into this morass any further than I already had. I was polite but formal with him. Once or twice when we chanced to be alone for a moment, I would excuse myself, thereby avoiding any sort of contact of a personal nature. I think he sensed my coolness toward him, and several times over the preceeding days, he would glance at me with an expression both confused and hurt. If only I could have told him all that was going on behind the scenes. I pondered my options. I could go along with them and betray Mrs. Roosevelt and Captain Taylor. Or I could disobey them and risk everything—my reputation, my freedom, perhaps even, as Vasilyev had put it, my own neck.

A couple of nights earlier on the train, I had gone into the club car for a drink. It was crowded with people, White House staff and reporters covering the First Lady. I saw Viktor seated at a table playing solitaire and drinking vodka.

"Can I sit down, Viktor?" I asked.

"Suit yourself," he said, without looking up.

"I need to talk to you."

"So talk."

"Someplace private."

Finally he glanced up at me. He stood, and I followed him outside between cars.

"So what's going on?" he asked.

I explained to him in general terms what Semyonov had wanted me to do. I didn't tell him, however, about Enormous. I felt the less he knew, the better. For both of us.

Viktor humphed. "Those fucking *chekist* whores," he said. "So what are you going to do, Lieutenant?"

"I don't know."

"Come with me."

"Defect?" I said. "How can I do that? That's madness, Viktor. You know it as well as I do."

"What's madness is staying with them and doing their bidding."

"Where would I go?"

"I have some friends here in America who would take us in for a while."

"You know what they'll do to you if they catch you," I said.

"First they will have to catch me," he said, smiling. He grasped my hand and added, "Don't let them do this to you. Come with me."

I shook my head. "I don't know. I must think on it."

"Don't think too long on it."

That was two days earlier. Since then, I'd found myself contemplating his offer. I knew it would be unimaginably difficult trying to break free from the iron grip of the Soviet secret police. I knew they would come after anyone who tried it, hunting them down, even if it took decades. But I also considered something else, something I hadn't really thought of before—what I felt for Jack Taylor. I could no longer deny that I felt something for him, something very powerful. And I was pretty certain he felt the same way for me. However, I hadn't seen Viktor the previous night at dinner. The day before we'd made a stop near Toledo, Ohio, and now I was worried that he'd already made his move without me.

That morning at breakfast, I met with Vasilyev. He was already eating, stuffing his face with food, washing it down with gulps of coffee.

"Do you want something to eat?" he asked.

"Just coffee," I said.

A black waiter happened to be passing by, so Vasilyev got his attention and said, "*Kofe*," and pointed to me. When his cup was refilled he took out his flask and spiked it liberally with whiskey. Between forkfuls of food, he said to me, "They want you to bring up a name the next time you speak to Mrs. Roosevelt."

"What name?"

"Fermi."

I shrugged.

"He's actually quite famous. Won the Nobel Prize."

Since the meeting with Semyonov, I had been passing along notes of my conversations with the First Lady to Vasilyev. Mostly I tried to steer Vasilyev toward topics that might on the surface appear of interest to Semyonov but in actuality were really quite benign—what Mrs. Roosevelt felt toward the labor unions, whether she thought her husband was going to run for office again, some sudden issue regarding the president's health. I once told him that Mrs. Roosevelt had said in passing that her husband had recently called in his entire cabinet for an urgent midnight meeting. With this, Vasilyev's ears perked up. It was, of course, a complete falsehood. I fabricated what I could, evaded where I was able, anything I could do to protect my friend the First Lady. Whether he suspected this or not—my guess was on some level he did—I could only imagine on his end that he also elaborated and falsified enough to keep Semyonov and Zarubin thinking that we were making progress. My attitude toward Vasilyev had changed a little. I still didn't trust him, but I looked upon him no longer as the evil architect of all this but as someone who also had to follow orders, who was being pressured to do what he was told. I even felt a bit sorry for him. He seemed to perform his job now with a perfunctory indifference, as if he were just going through the motions. I wasn't sure if it was the fact that he disagreed with Semyonov and his plans, or if he had been so devastated by the death of his son that his mind was preoccupied. He had also taken to drinking more than he had. Before he had always managed to carry it off. Now he sometimes got quite drunk. Once in the dining car, he was slurring his words so badly that Gavrilov and Dmitri had to help him back to his berth and put him to bed. He would take down what I told him without seeming to have the slightest interest, his thoughts drifting elsewhere. And now it was an amorphous "they" who wanted to know this.

"This Fermi is an Italian national," he continued. "Up to this point Italian nationals couldn't move about the country. However, the president just gave the order declaring them no longer enemy aliens. We know too that this Fermi has recently moved to Chicago, and we believe he is conducting experiments there with other scientists, which might be connected to Enormous. See if you can work his name into the conversation."

"And just how would I go about doing that?"

"Use your head. You can say something to the effect that you read about him in the newspaper. See if she bites at it."

I told him I would try.

"I see you've been rather aloof with Captain Taylor," he said.

I shrugged.

"What is it they say?" he offered with a smile. "Honey catches more flies than vinegar?"

"I am not your damn whore," I cursed.

"Ssh," he said, glancing around the dining car. "I'm simply trying to protect you. You don't want to end up like Viktor."

"What do you mean? What happened to him?"

"Ah," he said. "Your friend was called home suddenly."

" 'Called home'?" I said, startled at the implication.

"He returned yesterday, accompanied by Comrade Shabanov." That was the one we called the Corpse.

"What's going to happen to him?"

"He was warned. It's out of my hands now. If you don't want to share his fate, you had better be more cooperative."

That evening in the dining car, I was invited to join Mrs. Roosevelt, Miss Hickok, her assistant Miss Thompson, as well as two other women I had not previously met, and, of course, Captain Taylor. Mrs. Roosevelt and one of the two women, a Mrs. Smythe from England, spoke of refugees streaming into the West from Eastern Europe.

"We have to do something about these poor people," Mrs. Roosevelt said. "Especially the orphans. Why, it just breaks your heart."

They spoke of ways of helping the displaced people, how to involve the Red Cross more, sending packages of food, getting their two countries to allow more refugees to immigrate. While they spoke and the captain translated, I felt his eyes on me. At one point during a lull in the conversation, he whispered to me, "Is something the matter, Tat'yana?"

"No, why do you ask?" I said, pretending not to know what he was getting at.

"I just had the feeling that something was wrong."

Mrs. Smythe turned to me and said, "You must have seen your share of refugees, Lieutenant Levchenko."

"Indeed," I replied. I suddenly recalled Raisa, the young girl Zoya and I had rescued in the sewers of Sevastopol. I remembered that Zoya had said that some orphans from the Crimea were sent to Canada to live.

"Mrs. Roosevelt," I said, "how would one go about finding a Ukrainian girl who entered Canada?"

I briefly told her about Raisa, how we had found her living in the sewers, how she had been evacuated with other orphans.

"What a touching story," added Miss Hickok. "You must let me tell it for you. People would love to hear it."

"I would like to find out if she is all right," I said.

"That would be like finding the proverbial needle in a haystack," replied Mrs. Roosevelt. "But I'll have Tommy look into it."

Miss Thompson, her secretary, made a note of it.

After a while, I thought about what Vasilyev had wanted me to do. I felt awkward doing this, using my friendship with Mrs. Roosevelt in this manner, but I considered gleaning information regarding some scientists to be less intrusive and far less of a betrayal than ferreting out details about her personal life.

"Speaking of refugees, Mrs. Roosevelt," I said. "I recently read an article about a man from Italy. A scientist by the name of Fermi . . ."

Late that evening, I was having a cigarette between cars. The night was calm, the midwestern sky ablaze with a million stars. As we passed through small villages and hamlets, I'd see a light on in a window, occasionally the figure of a woman standing at a sink. In some ways, I envied these women, their quiet lives so far removed from all the chaos in the rest of the world. I imagined children asleep, a husband sitting at the table reading the newspaper. They would retire into the warm certainty of each other's embrace. Had my own life ever been so peaceful, so reassuring?

At that moment, the door clanged behind me and I turned to see Captain Taylor step out into the night.

"Hi," he said.

"Good evening, Captain."

"Back to being so formal, I see," he offered with an ironic smile.

"I think it's preferable that we maintain a certain professional distance."

"Is it because I got out of line with you the other night? I already apologized."

As I looked up at him, I thought of our kiss, that wonderful, blissful kiss that had so confused and yet so thrilled me. "It's just that I've had a lot on my mind lately."

"Because of your husband?"

"No. Well, perhaps that too."

"May I ask you a question? If you didn't love him, why did you marry him then?"

"It's a long story."

"It's a long war," Jack Taylor said. He gave me a mock-serious look, which softened into a smile. He took out his pack of cigarettes, offered me one. As I inhaled, I glanced out at the passing countryside.

"I guess in part I married him because it was what everyone expected of me. My parents. Kolya. I guess even I did."

"But you don't seem to me someone who is easily talked into something she doesn't think is right."

He looked at me with an expression that suggested he was referring to more than just my marriage.

"I was young. I let myself be convinved it was the right thing to do. When the war came, I saw my husband off at the train station. It sickens me to confess this, but the truth is I felt a certain relief at his going. I even secretly hoped he wouldn't return. Then I would be free. I know you must think I am a terrible person for such a thought."

He shook his head. "No. Just honest."

"When I got the letter saying he was missing, I felt somehow I owed it to him to wait and find out if he was alive or dead. Out of guilt or loyalty, I cannot say."

We both fell silent for a while. I considered heading inside then, but I remained there, staring out over the darkened landscape.

"Jack?" I began. "What were you going to tell me the other day? You said you had something to confess."

"Oh," he said. He turned and stared at me, his eyes searching mine. Then he reached out and touched my cheek. "I was going to tell you that . . . well, that I love you."

I pulled back from his touch. "You mustn't say that."

"But why? It's the truth."

"It doesn't matter if it's the truth or not. There are other things to consider."

"Such as?"

"Duty. Loyalty. Honoring one's word. When I married Kolya, I vowed to be faithful and I have."

"I admire that. But you shouldn't confuse loyalty with love. What's in here?" he asked, touching the middle of his chest.

"What do you mean?" I said.

He leaned toward me so that our faces were only inches apart. "What do you feel? For me, I mean."

"I . . . I like you, Jack."

"Is that all?"

"I like you very much, in fact."

He kissed me lightly on the mouth, then withdrew and stared into my eyes, a challenge of sorts.

"I thought you said you weren't going to do that again."

"I lied," he said, smiling.

"You are courting danger, Jack. In more ways than you know."

"I know."

This time it was I who put my arms around his neck and kissed him, kissed him so hard that our teeth rattled against each other's with the force of our desire. I felt his tongue slide into my mouth, felt his hand reach up and cup my left breast, felt myself yield to him. As we kissed, I sensed the night rushing by like something from a motion picture, frame after frame, the earth moving beneath our feet. Everything dissolving away save for his mouth on mine, his body pressing into me, his smell and taste and the feel of his warm skin against mine. I felt almost dizzy with desire, with wanting him.

I wondered if I should tell him what I felt. That it was more than simply liking him. And too I suddenly had an inexplicable urge to unburden myself to him completely, to confide in him all that Semyonov and Vasilyev wanted me to do. But I warned myself it would be dangerous, for both of us. Instead I said only, "We have to be careful, Jack. We are being watched."

"What do you mean, watched?"

I hesitated, trying to figure out how much I could share with him without giving everything away and having it all blow up in my face.

"If I tell you, you must promise me you won't say anything to anyone," I told him.

"That all depends on what it is."

"No, you must promise first. You must swear to me that you won't say anything."

"This sounds serious."

"It is."

"All right, I promise."

I took a deep breath to quiet my pounding heart. "There are people who are spying on us. They've taken photographs of the two of us."

"Who has?"

"Soviet agents."

"You're kidding," he said, frowning.

"No, it's true. I saw the photos with my own eyes. They must have had us followed that day in the city. They were pictures of the two of us in the park. At the baseball game. Even kissing."

"Those bastards," he said, slamming his hand against the metal railing.

"Maybe it was intended to scare me. I don't know."

"Are you in danger?"

I thought of telling him about Viktor, what had happened to him. Maybe it wasn't too late to help him. Maybe he was still in the country yet. Also, I thought of telling him that they had pictures too of Mrs. Roosevelt and Miss Hickok. But I realized that it would place him in an untenable position, of having to choose between his loyalty to Mrs. Roosevelt and his promise to me.

So instead I said, "I don't know. Perhaps."

"Let me help you," he said.

"There's nothing you can do."

"Maybe there is. I have a friend who works for the State Department. He might be able to help us. And if not, at least he would know who would."

I was struck by the way he said *us*. I hadn't thought of my being part of an *us* in a very long time, perhaps not ever. I considered this proposition for a moment, but then I quickly realized if I did this, there would be no turning back. I would set in motion forces that would be irrevocable, and I wasn't ready for that. At least not yet.

"No."

"But why not?"

"Please, don't do anything. Not yet anyway. I need to think it out first."

That's when I heard the train door open a second time. It was Dmitri.

"The boss wants to speak to you," he said to me, glancing suspiciously at Jack.

"Good night, Captain," I said.

Vasilyev was seated in his private compartment. He had his spectacles on, and he was reading a telegram when I entered. He was coatless, his tie loosened and askew.

"Have a seat, Lieutenant," he instructed me, his tone somewhat curt.

When he finished reading, he removed his spectacles and puffed his cheeks with a sigh that was both weary and annoyed. He gazed toward the window, though I couldn't tell whether he was looking out at the night or the dark reflection of his own hulking image.

"The son of a bitch" he cursed.

"Who?" I ventured.

"Zarubin. He's got me by the balls and he's squeezing hard."

"What does he want?"

"He's losing patience. He wants concrete information and he wants it now."

"Tell him I am doing my best."

"Unfortunately, your best is not good enough. Did you bring up the name with Mrs. Roosevelt?"

"I did, yes. She said that her husband had had a visit with him."

"Did she say anything else? When they met? What they talked about?"

"No. Just that he visited the White House."

Rubbing his jaw, Vasilyev glanced at me dubiously. Of course, all of this was pure fabrication on my part. I had brought up the name with Mrs. Roosevelt, but aside from having heard of him in passing, she said nothing about him. If there was more to it than that, she wasn't saying.

"Semyonov will be pleased to hear this," he said. "Did you know about Viktor?"

"Did I know what?"

"That he was planning on defecting?"

"No."

"Would you have told me if you had?"

"He didn't tell me."

"Did he mention any names to you? Contacts he might have had here in America?"

I shook my head.

"You didn't tell him about Enormous, did you?"

"No. Of course not."

"Because if you had, they will get it out of him," Vasilyev said. "So I advise you to tell me the truth now."

"I *am* telling you the truth. I didn't say anything to him."

"Semyonov is very upset over this Viktor business. He thinks you were in on it. I had to persuade him you knew nothing about his plans. But when they get him to talk—and they will, believe me, they will—

and he says you knew of his plans or that you told him about the project, I won't be able to protect you."

"If Semyonov doesn't trust me, let him send me back now," I said.

"I wouldn't call his bluff if I were you. Right now, he thinks you are valuable. If you cease being of value to him, he will send you back. And that isn't something you would like, believe me." He paused for a moment, then said, "Apparently, this Captain Taylor is not who he claims to be."

"What?" I said, trying to sound nonchalant. "What do you mean?"

"For one thing, his name isn't Jack Taylor."

"How do you know that?"

"The only Captain John or Jack Taylor in the military is stationed in San Diego. He's in his forties, married, and has three children."

"There must be some mistake," I said.

"There's no mistake."

"I don't believe you."

Vasilyev didn't change expressions, just continued to stare at me.

"Who is he, then?"

"That's what we're trying to find out. In the meantime, be careful with him. And don't let your emotions cloud your thinking."

That night I lay in bed, considering what Vasilyev had told me. I tried to pass it off as just another one of his lies, intended to keep me from falling in love with Captain Taylor. Perhaps to keep me from doing what Viktor had planned on—defecting to the West. Despite this, I couldn't help but wonder what it meant if it was true. If he wasn't Captain Taylor, who was he? Why had he lied to me? Was he, like Vasilyev, just using me? I tossed and turned in my berth for the longest time. Finally, I threw my robe on and got up and headed outside for some air.

Now and then I would see a small silent town rush by or the glossy shimmer of a river meandering along the railroad tracks. I thought of my daughter. No doubt because of my having mentioned the girl Raisa earlier to Mrs. Roosevelt. In a rush, I recalled the softness of her skin against my cheek, the sweet yeasty odor of her breath as she kissed me, the shape of her mouth. She seemed suddenly so very close to me, as she hadn't in so very long, and before I knew it I felt the tears running down my cheeks. Masha, I whispered. My little *krolik*.

We arrived in Chicago the next day. I gave a speech at a large auditorium at the University of Chicago, a speech that Vasilyev, or someone at least, had written for me. Afterward, I met with the press, and that was followed by a dinner with dignitaries in a large hotel ballroom. Several times during dinner I chanced to meet the gaze of Captain Taylor. He would smile at me and I would find myself smiling back. I thought about our meeting on the train, his declaration of love. I thought too of my own unexpressed feelings for him. What I felt for the captain confused and frightened me, and yet it also made my heart rap fiercely in my chest. I was in love for the first time in my life. But then I would start to think of what Vasilyev had told me about him. That his name wasn't Taylor. I told myself that Vasilyev was lying, just trying to manipulate me, as he always was. Still, I had an uneasy feeling about it.

During dinner, I excused myself to go to the bathroom. I was looking into the mirror when I heard someone say, "*Vy lyubite ego?*" It was Mrs. Roosevelt. I don't know where she picked it up, but she was asking me, "Do you love him?"

"Whom?" I replied. But her smile told me she saw through my pretense.

"Captain Taylor," she said. Then she touched my uniform right above my heart and asked again. "*Vy lyubite ego?*"

Finally I confessed. "*Da,*" I said, nodding my head and giving in to a smile.

At the news, Mrs. Roosevelt's face lit up with delight. She said something to me, which I knew was a form of congratulations. Then she hugged me the way my mother had when I told her I was getting married to Kolya. With gestures, she somehow managed to ask me if Captain Taylor knew how I felt. I shook my head.

She said something in English and raised her hands, palms skyward, obviously inquiring why I hadn't told him. I didn't know how to answer that, not only because of the language barrier but also because I wasn't sure myself.

Back at the table Mrs. Roosevelt said something to the captain, and with a frown, he translated for me.

"Mrs. Roosevelt wishes to know what you plan on doing regarding what you and she talked about."

"Tell her that I shall have to give some thought to that," I said, glancing over at the First Lady. She gave me a conspiratorial grin. Then she said something else.

"She says not to think on it too long," the captain translated for her. In an aside, he asked me, "What did you and she talk about?"

"It was private," I replied.

Sitting there I felt what I'd often felt since being asked to spy—a gnawing sense of guilt over my betrayal not only of Mrs. Roosevelt's friendship but of those feelings I had for the captain too. One part of me wanted suddenly to tell Jack everything, come completely clean with him. I had also reconsidered his offer of help, though I wasn't thinking of me so much as Viktor. I thought perhaps of asking the captain to use his contacts to find out if Viktor was still in the country, and if so, maybe the American government might be able to help him, maybe even offer him asylum. But another part recalled the warning Vasilyev had given me, that Jack Taylor wasn't exactly who he claimed to be, that I needed to keep my emotions under check. That part of me remained cautious, wary of confiding anything to him. Dare I trust him? I wondered.

Still, near the end of the dinner I tore a piece of paper from my notebook, jotted down a message, and slipped it to the captain when no one was watching: "We must talk. Come to my room tonight. Please."

That night in my room, I waited anxiously for the captain to appear. I wondered just exactly what I would tell him about Viktor, and what and how much of the rest of it I would confide in him. When a knock on the door finally came, my heart jumped and I ran to it and threw it open.

"Jack—" I started to say but stopped short when I saw a stranger standing there. He was a tall, thin man, middle-aged, with thick glasses from beneath which cool blue eyes stared out at me. Before I could say anything, he shouldered his way past me and closed the door behind him. "I am Larin," he said. "You have something for me." From my suitcase, I retrieved the envelope Zarubin had entrusted to me and I gave it to this man. He took it and shoved it into an inside pocket of his coat. I was glad to have it taken off my hands. However, I'd hardly given it over to him than he took out another envelope and handed it to me.

"In San Franciso, you are to deliver this. His code name is Kharon. He will be in touch with you regarding further instructions."

Instead of taking the envelope, I held my hands up, almost in a gesture of surrender. "No," I blurted out.

The man frowned. "What?"

"I don't want any part of this."

"You don't have any choice."

"I can refuse," I said.

At this, he grabbed my wrist and squeezed it hard.

"Let go. You're hurting me."

"I'll do more than that, you *shlyukha*. If you know what is good for you, you will take this and do as I say."

Finally I accepted the envelope and he turned and left without another word.

I stared at the letter I held. I felt myself being sucked down into a whirlpool of deception and subterfuge, of code names and secrecy, and I had no idea what I was doing or how I could stop it. I was a soldier, I told myself, and soldiers took orders. And yet I knew that what I was doing was wrong. If not wrong between nations, at least wrong because of the betrayal of friendship. I hid the letter in my suitcase. Not five minutes later, another knock sounded at the door.

Through the door, I said in English, "Yes?"

A familiar voice replied in Russian, "It's me."

I quickly opened the door, and without thinking threw my arms around Jack Taylor. I was never so happy to see anyone.

Surprised, he said, "I came as soon as I could. Are you all right?"

"Yes," I replied, then changed my mind and said, "No."

"Your note sounded urgent. What's the matter?"

"I have been doing a lot of thinking. There is something . . . what I mean is . . ." I paused for a moment, wondering why exactly I had asked him here. I started to say something about Viktor, stopped, started again, this time about Vasilyev and what he had warned me about the captain, then, before I knew it, I began to cry. Soon I was sobbing.

The captain came over, put his arm around me, and held me.

"It's all right," he said soothingly, rubbing my back.

"I'm so . . . sorry," I blurted out. "I'm so terribly sorry."

"What are you sorry for?"

"For what I've done to Mrs. Roosevelt. To you."

"It's all right," he said, stroking my hair. "Everything will be all right."

"No, it . . . won't be all right," I uttered between sobs.

"Tat'yana, whatever it is it can't be that bad."

"It is."

He lifted my chin so that I was looking up into his face. His hazel eyes shone with such tenderness and concern.

"Tell me about it."

Instead of saying anything, though, I kissed him on the mouth. I kissed him with all of the pent-up sadness and frustration, anger and bitterness and heartache that the war had filled me with. Kissed him too with the desperation of one who had feared that there was nothing left inside her soul save hatred. But mostly I kissed him because I knew then, as I had never known in my life, that I loved someone. That line from Tsvetaeva that Madame Rudneva had read to me so long ago appeared suddenly in my mind: *Ah! is the heart that bursts with rapture.* My heart then did seem to burst with a kind of rapture I had never known.

"I love you, Jack," I said.

He didn't say anything at first. Just smiled that soft, rumpled smile of his. Then he kissed me back.

I don't know who made the first gesture after that, but in a moment our uniforms were shed, and we stood naked before the other, as innocent and yet as frightened as children. When I looked at the stump of his left arm, he frowned, embarrassed, and said, "I'm sorry."

"No, you mustn't think that," I told him, recalling the young burned soldier back in the hospital in Baku, who had been so worried that his beloved would no longer think of him as handsome. And how I had lied to him and said she would. Now though I wasn't so sure it was a lie. I touched the stump gently, ran my fingers along its bumpy knots, its sharp recesses and contours. When I put my lips to it and kissed it, he shivered like a little boy who is ticklish. "Look," I said, showing him my own scars. He kneeled before me. With his fingertips he traced the long, rough scar that sliced across my stomach.

"I love you, Tat'yana," he said, looking up at me. When he placed his warm, soft mouth against the scar and kissed my skin, I trembled and clutched his head so that I wouldn't fall, pressing him tightly against me. I thought of telling him what the scar meant—that I could never have children—but right then it didn't seem to matter. He was all that mattered, and I was all that mattered to him. We existed in our own little world, a world where nothing else mattered. He kissed me again, lower, and I cried out his name, the passion blooming in me like a flower lifting its head toward the sun. When we made love, he gazed deeply into my eyes, a murmur resounding in his throat as he entered me. "I love you, Tat'yana," he said.

"I love you, Jack."

Afterward, we lay in bed, spent, indulging in that sweet drowsiness following lovemaking, when the body is emptied of passion but the heart is even more filled with love. We lay side by side, touching each other, gazing into each other's eyes. I wanted never to leave that bed, that room, that moment, for I knew a security I had never known before.

"So did you really want to tell me something?" he asked. "Or was that just a ruse to get me up here and seduce me."

"Can I trust you?"

"Yes, of course."

"But how do I know I can?"

"I love you. And you love me. That should be enough of a reason."

"What I tell you might place you in an awkward position."

"I told you, you can trust me. Whatever it is. I promise."

So I went ahead and told him about Viktor, that I feared something terrible had happened to him.

"Remember you asked me what order he had refused, and I said I didn't know. Well, that wasn't true. They wanted him to do certain things."

"What kind of things?"

"To act as a spy."

"A spy?" he said.

"Yes. They wanted him to carry information between Soviet agents."

"What happened?"

"He refused. I think Viktor was planning to defect. He even wanted me to come with him. I don't know what happened. Perhaps they found out about him. I am worried about what will happen to him."

"I could make some inquiries. See what I can find out."

"But only if you can do it discreetly."

"I'll talk to my friend in the State Department." He looked at me, waiting. "And what about you?"

"What about me?"

"You said you were sorry. For what you did to Mrs. Roosevelt. To me."

I hesitated, still wondering if I should tell him everything, every last despicable secret I had been witholding. You see, I had gotten so used to lying—to Vasilyev, to Semyonov, to Mrs. Roosevelt, to the captain, but most especially to myself, I suppose that it had become almost second nature to me. I realized that it was what the Soviet system had fostered in the hearts and minds of its people: that deception, if practiced long enough, becomes its own truth.

"It is very complicated, Jack. They lied to me. Vasilyev and the others. About why they wanted me to come to the States. They told me I was here to promote the war. But their real reason was that they wished for me to spy too."

"What did they want you to do?"

Though I was still suspicious of who Jack Taylor was, I decided to trust him. I explained everything to him. How they wanted me to find out things about Mrs. Roosevelt, hoping to use it to blackmail her.

"That's crazy," Jack cried.

"Yes, I know. These men are very crazy. But also very dangerous."

I went on to tell him that they had taken pictures not only of us but also of Mrs. Roosevelt and Miss Hickok, how they were prepared to use them to "persuade" her to cooperate.

"What did they expect to get from her?" Jack asked.

"Many things. Whether her husband was going to run for office again. If he was planning on meeting with Churchill. Most important, they hoped to obtain information about a secret American project."

"What sort of project?"

"A new weapon which you Americans are evidently working on. It's called Manhattan. Have you heard of such a project?"

"No," he said, frowning. "But then again, why would I?" As he stared at me, his expression slowly changed, and there came over his eyes what I thought of as a certain glimmer of understanding. He smiled. "So that's why you asked about those scientists?"

I nodded.

"I thought it was odd. So just what do *you* have to do with all this?" he asked.

"I told them nothing of consequence. I swear. And nothing about her and Miss Hickok. She is my friend. I would never hurt her. But to keep them off my back, I decided I would have to give them things, lies, half-truths, something that would occupy them. For instance, I told Vasilyev that Mrs. Roosevelt said her husband had met with one of those scientists."

He laughed at that. "Very clever. And how did *I* figure into your plans?"

"You?"

"Yes. Isn't that what *this* is all about?" He said *this* with a wave of his hand, indicating us, our relationship, what we had just done.

"No. No, of course not. I mean, they wanted me to but . . ."

"But what?"

His face took on an aggrieved, almost pouty look.

"Is that why you slept with me?" he asked, his tone turning petulant.

"No," I replied, reaching out and touching his face. "I did so because I wanted to. Because I love you."

"Am I supposed to believe that?"

"Yes. You must believe me. I never wanted to do any of this. I wanted only to help defeat the Germans. That's why I agreed to come. The rest . . . well, they lied to me. They lied about everything."

He was silent for a moment, pondering all I'd confessed to him. Finally he said, "Well, we have to do something then."

"What do you mean?"

"I can't let them get away with this. They're stealing military secrets. I'm a soldier too. I have my own loyalties."

"But you promised. You said I could trust you, Jack."

"Yes, but I didn't know it was this. My God. They're spying on us."

"If you tell them, you could be putting me in danger."

"What would you have me do? I can't sit back and do nothing."

I shook my head.

He rolled onto his back, put his hand behind his head, and stared at the ceiling. "What do you want to do, Tat'yana?"

"I don't know. As I said, Viktor had tried to talk me into defecting."

"Do you want to defect?"

I shrugged my shoulders. "It's all so sudden. I can't even think straight."

"It would be very tricky because of your position. You're too well known. And our government might not want the trouble it would cause with your government. But, on the other hand, if your life was in danger, they might consider that. Or if Mrs. Roosevelt knew about this, she could pull some strings, I'm sure."

"But she would be very disappointed in me. For what I did."

"You didn't mean to. They forced you. I'm sure she'll understand."

"Don't do anything just yet," I said to him. "I need time to think about it."

"All right. But we will have to come up with a plan, and soon too."

We lay quietly there for a while. Finally I asked, "Were you always called Jack?"

"Since I was a kid."

"Who were you named after?"

He stared at me, knitting his brows in confusion.

"What's this about my name?" he said.

"Nothing," I replied. But then I found myself saying, "Vasilyev said that you weren't who you say you are."

"Who did he say I was?"

"He didn't. Just that I needed to be careful with you."

He turned toward me and touched my cheek. "You don't believe him, do you?"

"No." Then for emphasis, I added, "No, of course not."

"Because if you can't trust me, who else are you going to trust?"

"I do trust you," I said.

"Good. Because we're going to have to trust each other. I should probably go." Before he left, he leaned over the bed and kissed me. "I love you," he said.

I was going to say something like how being in love with me wasn't a good idea, that he shouldn't count on me, that I wasn't free to give myself completely to him. But instead, I said the only thing that seemed to matter at that moment. "I love you too."

21

Over the next week, before everything was to collapse like a house of cards, I gave myself over completely to being in love with Jack Taylor. I say "gave," as if I had some actual choice over the matter. The fact is, I fell in love so fully, so wholly and unconditionally, I couldn't have stopped myself if I'd wanted to. And I didn't want to. Despite still not trusting him completely, I surrendered to my feelings. I was inexperienced in the ways of love, a novice when it came to the intricacies of passion and touch, of the way the gaze of a lover seemed to ignite one's soul. Whereas with Kolya, my choice had seemed a surrender, with Jack it felt like liberation, the way a prisoner must feel whose cell door was suddenly thrown open after years of confinement. I loved his hazel eyes, the soft fullness of his lips, his earlobes, the boyish cowlick at the top of his head, the hard plane of his stomach. I loved the way his missing arm made him appear so vulnerable, so delicate and fragile. I loved the way he would whimper when he entered me, and the way afterward he would run his long fingers through my hair. We made love with the lights on, savoring the other's naked body. Jack touched me in ways I had never been touched.

We pursued our passion with a recklessness that both startled and yet made me feel, for the first time ever, alive, vibrant, like the woman I was always meant to be. We behaved rashly. We threw caution to the wind. We ran to each other's embrace every moment we could, this despite being always in the reflected glow of the First Lady, as well as the fact that Jack and I were both conscious of being spied upon by Soviet agents. (Besides Dmitri, there were now two other *chekisty* who suddenly appeared, sinister-looking men we first took notice of in Chicago and later on the train. The two lurked at the periphery, pretending to read an American newspaper but eyeing us clumsily from a distance.) But knowing they were there, we were usually able to elude them. We conspired to find moments alone and capitalized on those. Late at night on the train Jack would slip into my berth. Or if we were staying somewhere, he would come to my room after everyone was asleep, take me in his arms, and make love to me. Once, after giving a speech at the University of Chicago, I excused myself to use the bathroom. Jack followed me and we slipped into an empty science classroom for our tryst. Giggling like children, aroused by the fear of being caught, we tore at each other's clothing and made frenzied love behind a table filled with beakers and Bunsen burners. Afterward, I had to appear at a press conference. Vasilyev leaned toward me and indicated that one of the buttons was missing on my tunic: "You're getting rather careless, Lieutenant," he said, but more a caution rather than an admonishment.

In restaurants we held hands beneath the table. With my boot, I would rub his leg, and over dinner our gazes would meet as I found myself counting the seconds before we could be together again. Whenever we were standing in an elevator his hand would brush my leg, and I'd feel a tremor of desire ripple through me. We sent each other missives declaring our love for each other. In one letter he wrote, "To my precious beloved, always and forever, J." In bed we would talk about our "future," as if we actually had one. The things we would do, the places we would go, conjuring a distant, faraway place on the horizon in which we were together. Though, of course, I think we sensed on some level that we didn't have a future. We had only now, these few stolen moments to share, but this fact seemed only to kindle our passion.

For her part, Mrs. Roosevelt seemed to know about the captain and me, and implicitly gave us her blessing, with a wink or nod of understanding. Occasionally she even arranged for us to be together, like some matchmaking aunt. She would send us off under the pretense of Captain Taylor continuing my tutelage of English. "You need to work on those irregular verbs, young lady," she'd say, giving Miss Hickok a knowing look. Or sometimes she would glance at me and smile that crooked, adorable smile of hers. Once at a dinner for a veterans group in Des Moines, she leaned toward me, squeezed my hand, and said, "*Ya rada za vas*" ("I'm so happy for you").

And I was never more happy in all my life, and yet, never more afraid. Yes, I was afraid. I had not been afraid in the war, not of German bullets or bombs, but I was afraid now. Before, you see, I had nothing to lose. Now I had everything to lose. I was happy. I was in love, and love makes a person very vulnerable. It made me want to cling to life with a fierce determination. I didn't want to lose this feeling, one I had been waiting for all my life. I worried constantly. I felt every moment, most especially during those glorious ones in which I was in his embrace, that something bad would befall us, felt this looming sense of impending disaster. That Vasilyev or Semyonov would find out that I had been lying to them, that they would realize I was no longer their pawn to be manipulated as they saw fit, and have me sent back home. I feared they would view me no longer as a Hero of the Soviet Union, but as an Enemy of the People.

Several times, Jack tried to convince me I should defect, that it was my only choice.

"I contacted my friend at the State Department," he told me once as we were having coffee in the dining car. Outside the window, the overcast day lay suspended over the bare, ocher-colored plains unfurling to the hazy gray of the autumnal horizon. At the other end of the dining car I spotted those two men, the new *chekisty* who had begun to watch us. One was squat and powerfully built, with a broad face; the other thin and wiry, with a small, sharp nose like a chicken's beak. "I told him about your case."

"What did he say?"

"He spoke to some people in the OSS."

"What's that?"

"They deal with this sort of thing," was how he explained it. "There's a chance my government could offer you political asylum."

"But I'm not sure yet."

"What are you not sure about? It's not as if you have a lot of options, Tat'yana," he said, his hazel eyes fixing me in their stare.

"It's just that I'll be leaving everything I know—my home, my country."

"You're tired of doing their dirty work, right?"

"You know that I am."

"And you don't want to end up like Viktor."

"But if I choose this path, there's no turning back." I looked outside at the landscape rushing by. With a wave of my hand toward the window, I said, "Could you leave all of this, Jack? Your home. Everything you loved."

"I know it's hard. But we're running out of time. Besides, I can't just stand by and pretend I don't know what I know. What Vasilyev and the others are trying to do. And you can't play it both ways."

"I'm not playing it both ways."

"No?" he said. "Sometimes I almost think you're playing me too."

"How can you think that!" I cried, a little too loudly. The two *chekist* officers at the other end of the dining car looked up.

"Ssh," he warned me.

"Why would you say that?" I whispered to him.

"You lied to me about all of this at first," he said. "How can I trust that you're not still working for them and just using me?"

"I'm telling you the truth, Jack. You know I love you."

"Do you?"

"Of course I do. How can you doubt that?"

"Then prove it. Leave them."

I closed my eyes, my head spinning at how fast things were moving.

"What about us?" he pleaded.

"Us?"

"If we're going to have a chance to be together, you have to defect. It's the only way."

"Jack, even if I decided to stay in America, do you think they," I said, rolling my eyes toward the two *chekisty*, "will just let me go?"

"We can protect you."

"We?"

"The American government."

"You don't know these people. They won't give up. They will hunt me down and find me. Whether it takes a year or ten years."

"I'm willing to do anything to be with you. To risk everything. Are you willing to do the same?"

"You know I'd do anything to be with you, Jack." I paused to sort out my thoughts. "Just give me a little more time to think about it."

"All right, I'll give you until we reach San Francisco. And then I'll have to act."

In the meantime we agreed I would continue to provide false information to Vasilyev. I decided I had to trust Jack Taylor, so I removed the letter from my coat pocket, the one I'd gotten back in Chicago. I glanced at the two *chekisty* before I handed it under the table to Jack.

"What's this?"

"A man back in Chicago gave it to me. I'm to give it to someone in San Francisco."

"Why didn't you tell me about it sooner?"

I pursed my lips. "I wasn't ready to yet."

"This man in San Francisco, his code name wouldn't be Kharon, would it?" Jack said.

I stared at him in surprise.

"Yes. How did you know that?"

"My friend who works in the State Department. He told me."

He slid the letter into his pocket. Before he got up, he squeezed my hand under the table, then stood and left. One of the two *chekisty* got up and followed him.

Over the next few days, things began to escalate, to spin out of control. My own side, I got the feeling, had stopped trusting me. When we stayed in a hotel, sometimes I would notice one or another of the *chekisty* outside my hotel room. I sensed the desperation of Vasilyev too. For example, one time he had me come to his hotel room.

"They are worried that you have become too emotionally involved with the captain."

"I thought *they* wanted me to get close to him."

"Close, yes. But not to the point that you've lost your loyalties."

"I haven't lost my loyalties."

"Let's hope not, for your sake."

"Is that why you've begun posting someone outside my room?"

He ignored my question.

"Do you get the sense the captain knows more than he's letting on?"

"He's just a translator. That's all he is."

"When you are with him, try to feel him out about Enormous."

"You're wasting your time, I tell you."

"That's an order. And not from me but from higher up." He ran a hand across his face. "Lieutenant, I would warn you not to think all your medals or status will protect you. Because if you try anything, you'll find just how unimportant they are. One more thing. Inquire of the captain if he was ever in Moscow."

"I already did. I told you he wasn't."

"Ask him again."

Shortly after this last conversation with Vasilyev, our train pulled into Denver, where we were going to stay for a few days. We were to attend a rally, give a few speeches. In the evening after one such event, Jack Taylor slipped into my hotel room.

"I've missed you," he said, kissing me urgently on the neck. We hadn't been able to be together for two whole days, and our hunger cut us like a well-honed blade.

"Did anybody see you come in?" I asked. As I spoke I was already fumbling with the buttons on his jacket, as he was tugging at my Sam Browne belt, trying to get it off my shoulder. Our need was so strong we were willing to take any risk.

"No," he replied. "I love you."

"And I, you, my dear."

Afterward, we lay in each other's embrace. I ran my fingers over the scars of his missing arm, then placed my lips against his skin and kissed him.

"I have the letter you gave me," he said. "No one can tell it was opened."

"What was it?"

"A list of names. But they were all in code. They're connected to something called Enormous. That's code for our weapons project, isn't it?"

I looked away from him momentarily and actually considered lying to him. I knew that I had reached a point of no return. That if I told him what I knew and my side found out, they wouldn't bother with sending me home to go through the façade of a trial. They would just take me out in the woods outside the Kremlin and put a gun to the back of my head.

"Yes," I conceded. "That's the term they use for your project."

Jack stared at me in amazement. "My God," he exclaimed. "This is unbelievable. They have the names of a couple of dozen scientists working on it. Do you think you could try to find out from Vasilyev more about this Kharon fellow?"

"Vasilyev might get suspicious. Why do you want to know about him?"

"If our government knows who this Kharon is, they might be able to crack the entire Soviet *rezidentura* in the United States."

Rezidentura? I thought. There was the word I'd first heard Vasilyev mention on the voyage over.

"What is *rezidentura?*" I asked.

"A Soviet spy network here in the States."

"And how would you know of such a thing?"

He stared at me. Behind his eyes I could almost see his darker thoughts. I considered the prospect that he was, as Vasilyev had warned me, someone other than whom I thought.

"My friend told me," he explained.

"The one in the State Department?" I said.

"Yes. My friend also said if you're going to defect, the government will expect something in return."

"In return?"

"That's the way these things work. You do something for them, they do something for you."

I was soon to learn all about the quid pro quo of espionage.

Jack traced his long fingers down my belly, where it stopped at the scar. As he kissed my ear, he said, "And you'll need to give Vasilyev something too. So he thinks you're still working for him. The next time you meet with him, I want you to say that Mrs. Roosevelt spoke of a man named Oppenheimer visiting with her husband."

"Oppenheimer?" I said.

"Yes. He's a scientist. He's very important to the work on that bomb project. That should keep your bosses happy for a while."

"But if this scientist is so important, why would you want to give away such a secret?"

"It's not really a secret anymore. Your people already know about it. But it'll convince them that you're still playing along."

"And just how do you know all of this?" I asked. Before he could answer, I said, "From this friend of yours in the State Department?"

He stared at me, probably suspecting that I knew he was lying.

Instead of replying, he began to kiss me, my mouth and neck and breasts. As I lay there, letting him make love to me, staring at the ceiling, I felt something in the back of my mind, not the kindling of passion but a kind of low droning noise, like a Messerschmitt coming in from a long ways off. I kept trying to bat it away, but it kept returning. *Why would he be in possession of such important information?*

He must have sensed that my mind was not on our lovemaking.

"What's the matter?" he asked.

"When you were in the Soviet Union, did you ever get a chance to visit Moscow?"

"I told you already. No," he replied, attempting once more to arouse me. "Why? What's all this about?"

I wondered if I should continue or just drop the entire thing and savor his body against mine.

"Vasilyev said the only Captain John Taylor in the army was in San Diego. That he was married and had a family."

Jack smiled. "Now how would he know that?"

"I don't know. That's just what he told me."

"And you believed him?"

"No, I didn't say I believed him."

"Well, obviously he's wrong."

Jack got up then and walked over to where his trousers lay on the floor and picked them up. I watched his naked body—tall and slender, the muscles taut, the tight curve of his buttocks—a body I had come so quickly to know and to love as I had never known and loved a man's body. He removed his wallet and brought it over to the bed. He began taking out pictures of himself, his family, his sister, throwing them on the bed for me to peruse. He even had one of him standing before the Hermitage Museum in Leningrad.

"There," he said. "What more proof do you want?"

"I don't need any proof."

"It seemed like you did."

He lay back on the bed. He took up my hand, brought it to his mouth, and kissed it.

"You have a choice, Tat'yana. You can believe me. Or you can believe him."

"I believe you," I replied, though that droning sensation in the back of my head continued unabated.

"Good," he said. "I want to ask you something."

"Yes?"

"What do you want to call our first child?"

"Our first what!" I asked, shocked at his question. And yet I found myself smiling. "Aren't you getting a little ahead of yourself?"

"I like to plan ahead."

I thought of telling him I couldn't have children, that I was an empty shell of a woman. But I didn't want to spoil the moment—for him or for me. Right then, I even let myself pretend that there was such a possibility. I imagined our child walking between us in a park, holding each of our hands.

"If it's a boy," I said, "I suppose we ought to call him Jack."

He smiled and kissed me gently.

———

From Denver we headed north to the small town of Laramie, Wyoming, a place whose streets were filled with bowlegged men wearing cowboy hats. I had seen cowboys only in the rare silent picture shows they played back home. I had thought they were just more of the American myth. The First Lady and her guests had been invited to a rodeo. We watched men with leather pants ride horses that tried to throw them off or rope cattle and tie the helpless creatures' hooves together.

"Have you ever seen anything quite like this, Tat'yana?" Mrs. Roosevelt asked me. I was seated on the other side of her from the captain, and she had leaned forward to say this. She smiled at me, but there was something about her smile, a kind of reserve, a certain diffidence I had never encountered with her before. I wondered if Jack Taylor had told her about what I had been doing for the past several weeks now. And I felt the shame of my betrayal spread over my face like a hot draft from a fire.

That night we stayed at a lodge that had a large Indian tepee out front and the heads of animals in the dining room, their glossy gray eyes staring woefully at us while we ate. Later I was in my room, waiting for Jack, when I heard someone knock. I rushed over and threw open the door only to find Vasilyev slouching against the door frame. The disappointment must have shown on my face.

"Were you expecting someone else?" he asked coyly. He let himself in and walked over and sat in the chair near the window.

"What do you want?" I asked.

He stared at me, giving me a look whose precise meaning I couldn't interpret, though it was, I knew, in the general nature of a warning.

"Here," he said, dropping an envelope on the table in front of him. "You are to deliver this to Mrs. Roosevelt."

I walked over and picked up the envelope. On it were words in English.

"What does it say?" I asked.

"Private and confidential."

"What is this about?"

"A message. For her eyes only," he said. "So give it to her when you are alone with her. And be sure to wait for her response."

"Her response?"

"Yes, she is to give you a reply." He then got to his feet and headed toward the door. Before he left, he said, "They are getting very impatient. I don't know how long I can keep them at bay."

For a long time I debated about what to do, wondering if I should open it or not. Finally I decided to call Jack's room, see what he thought.

"I have to see you," I said. He told me to come right up. I checked the hall, and after seeing no one lurking anywhere, I sneaked off to his room.

As soon as I entered he embraced me and started to kiss me.

"No, wait," I said.

"What's wrong?"

"I have to show you something first." I handed him the envelope and explained what Vasilyev had instructed me to do.

"Do you know what's in it?" Jack asked.

"No. But he said I was to await her response. What do you think we should do?"

"I think we should open it."

I hesitated, then finally agreed. The letter was brief, just a few sentences, which he translated for me.

> We know about your relationship with a certain female reporter. We have incontrovertible evidence of your "activities," and if you don't cooperate with us, we are prepared to expose you. Indicate your willingness to discuss the matter by giving your assent to the bearer of this letter.

It wasn't, of course, signed.

"Those bastards," Jack cursed. I snatched the letter back from him, and in my anger I was about to tear it up, when he stopped me.

"Don't. We might need this as proof."

"Of what?"

"Of your government's attempt to blackmail the wife of the president. It might help strengthen your case for being granted asylum."

"But I would not wish her to know of this . . . of my part in it."

"She's going to have to know," he said. "I can't let this go on any longer, Tat'yana. You have to make a choice. Right here, right now."

I looked at him and nodded. "I have already made my decision. I wish to defect."

He approached, threw his arms around me, and hugged me. Then he leaned back, stared down into my eyes. "I'm going to have to consult with Mrs. Roosevelt about this."

"Are you going to tell her of my role in it?"

"I don't see how I can't. But I'll only tell her what I absolutely have to. Then we'll have to see how she wants to handle it."

I cringed at the thought that Mrs. Roosevelt, a woman who had been so kind to me, who had befriended me, would now know of my deception and duplicity.

"She will be very disappointed."

He nodded, pursing his lips. "She's also going to be your most important ally."

22

Over the next couple of days as the train sped westward on the final leg of our cross-country trip, I stayed mostly in my sleeper compartment, feigning illness. Jack had come up with this plan, so as to buy us some time. That way, I could say I hadn't yet had a chance to deliver Vasilyev's letter to Mrs. Roosevelt. Out my window, I watched as the flat, endless plains gave way first to towering mountains, some already snowcapped, followed by brown, desiccated deserts, then more mountains, and at last, the green abundance of California. I lay there thinking about Jack Taylor, about the possibility of a life with him, about all that was soon going to change for me. Wondering if I could actually go through with defecting to the West. Once, as if sensing my conflicted state of mind, Jack Taylor stopped by to see how I was doing.

"I heard you were sick," he said loudly, playing along with our ruse in case one of the *chekist* officers was within earshot.

"I'm feeling a little better." Then in a whisper I asked, "Did you talk to Mrs. Roosevelt?"

"She's been busy," he said, somewhat evasively, I thought. "Listen, I have to go. I'll check back with you later."

Before he left, I said, "Jack."

"Yes?"

"You do love me, right?"

He smiled, reached out and stroked my cheek. "Of course I love you. How could you doubt that?"

Finally we arrived in San Francisco. I was to give a couple of speeches, make a tour of the city, meet with some reporters, before having a final gala dinner. After that, Vasilyev had informed me that we were to head home by way of an American merchant ship bringing lend-lease materials through the Persian Gulf. We arrived at our hotel, which was in the downtown part of the city, near the water. I went up to my room and took a long bath. I was lying there in the hot water, thinking about everything, when there was a knock on my door.

I threw my robe on and answered it. Dmitri was standing there.

"The Boss wants to see you," he said.

"What's he want?"

"I don't know. But he's in one of his moods, so you better get a move on."

I quickly got dressed and followed him to Vasilyev's room. When I entered, I saw Gavrilov sitting on the bed, his back to the wall. Prior to this, Vasilyev had usually excluded Gavrilov from our most private conversations, but now he sat across from me, staring at me with that smug expression of his. On his lap he held a briefcase. Vasilyev was seated on one of two wing chairs overlooking the city below.

"Have a seat," Vasilyev told me brusquely. I sat opposite him. "I trust you are feeling better, Lieutenant?"

"A little."

"Did you get a chance to deliver the message to Mrs. Roosevelt?"

"Yes," I lied.

"And?"

"She didn't say anything."

"What do you mean, she didn't say anything?"

"She just read the letter."

"She didn't give you any response at all?"

"No."

Vasilyev and Gavrilov traded glances. I realized then that Gavrilov was in on all of this too, just as Viktor had guessed. He wasn't just a student representative, a Komsomol member. He was one of *them*.

"Do you still have the letter you received in Chicago?" Vasilyev asked.

"Yes, of course."

"Give it to me."

"I don't have it on me. It's in my suitcase in my room."

"Bring it to me later," he said. "Did you inquire of Captain Taylor if he were ever in Moscow?"

"He said he wasn't."

"Do you think he's telling the truth?"

"How would I know that?"

With a nod to Gavrilov, he said, "Show her."

From the envelope on his lap, Gavrilov removed what I could see was a photograph. He leaned across the bed and handed it to me, a thin little sneer drawing his face into a rigid mask.

"I knew I'd seen him somewhere before," Vasilyev commented.

I glanced at the photo. It was a little fuzzy and had been taken from some distance. It showed two men emerging from a building. I didn't recognize the first one, a heavy, middle-aged man with a light-colored suit and a fedora. The other was younger and slender, also dressed in civilian clothes. Despite his clothing and the fact that he had both his arms, there was no mistaking that it was Jack Taylor.

"Do you recognize him?" Vasilyev asked.

I looked across at him. "Of course. It's Captain Taylor."

"Do you recognize that building?"

"Should I?"

"You were there," Vasilyev said. "That's the American embassy in Moscow."

"So?" I said, trying to act as if this information didn't come as something of a surprise.

Gavrilov said, "Has love blinded you to his deception?"

"Go to hell," I hurled at him. "That could be any building."

"But it's not," Vasilyev replied. "The captain lied to you when he said he was never in Moscow."

"So what? Perhaps he forgot. Perhaps he merely made a visit and overlooked it," I said, though I was starting to get that buzzing sensation in the back of my head again.

"No, he wasn't visiting, and he surely didn't forget. He worked there," explained Vasilyev. "The man with him is Robert Fowles. He's a well-known agent of the Americans. A spy. As is your Charles Pierce."

"Who?"

"Captain Taylor. His real name is Charles Pierce. Or at least that was the name he used on his visa back then."

"I don't believe you," I snapped at him.

"Stop behaving like a schoolgirl with a crush," said Vasilyev harshly. "Charles Pierce is an OSS officer. He worked in Moscow and later in New York translating cables the Americans had stolen from us."

I recalled then Jack telling me his friend had contacts in the OSS. Still, I fought to keep my doubt from being displayed on my face.

"How do I know you've not made this all up?" I said.

"Pictures don't lie," Gavrilov added.

"What have you told him?" Vasilyev asked.

"What do you mean?"

"About what we are doing? About what we know regarding Enormous?"

"I haven't told him anything."

"You're not working for the Americans now, are you?"

"No! Of course not."

Vasilyev's eyes searched mine, trying to ferret out a hint of falsehood. "You had better be telling the truth."

"I am telling you the truth."

"Has the captain told you anything I should know?"

"Nothing of importance."

"The American is only using you," said Gavrilov. "He doesn't love you."

I wanted to strike his thin weasel face. "And what would *you* know about love?" I flung at him.

"All right, enough," Vasilyev said. "Comrade Gavrilov will be giving the rest of the speeches."

I looked at Gavrilov, who raised his eyebrows self-righteously, as if to say he'd won.

"It makes no difference to me," I replied. But the truth was I was wary about what this sudden change implied.

"You will speak to the press only under my direct supervision and with Radimov doing the translating," Vasilyev continued. "And you are to cease having any contact with the Americans."

"The Americans?" I asked.

"Yes. *All* Americans. Including the captain. Is that clear?"

"You don't wish me to talk to Mrs. Roosevelt?"

"That's correct. No contact."

"Won't they think that's strange?"

"It doesn't matter what they think anymore. You will be going home shortly."

"Home," I said.

"Yes, that's what you wanted, isn't it?" offered Vasilyev.

I felt a churning sensation begin in the pit of my stomach. I wondered what was going on. If they had gotten Viktor to talk, perhaps he'd told them I had been considering defecting. Or maybe they had somehow found out about my conversations with Captain Taylor. Or what was the other name Vasilyev said? Charles Pierce. It did cross my mind that they had somehow bugged a room I'd been staying in and had listened to our conversations.

"Why the sudden change?" I asked.

"It's just the way it will be, Lieutenant," Vasilyev said, staring at me. "Do I make myself clear?"

"Yes. Will I be returning to the front?" I asked.

"In two days we sail for Dudinka."

"Siberia?" I exclaimed. "I thought we were headed for the Gulf."

"A change of plans."

Dudinka, I knew, was a port on the Arctic Sea. It provided supplies for the nickel-producing town of Norilsk, made infamous for its labor camp. Back home, people spoke of "going to Norilsk" as one might say "going to hell."

"I warned you, Lieutenant," Vasilyev said. "Now it is out of my hands."

When I left this meeting, I headed back to my room. I lay on the bed, staring at the ceiling, my thoughts in complete disarray. What was all that about? I wondered. Did Vasilyev know about my plans to defect? Why had he suddenly ordered me not to have any contact with the Americans? And he was obviously worried I had told the captain something about what we had been doing. But then I thought about the picture he'd shown me regarding Jack. How he'd said he was really someone called Charles Pierce, an American spy. Could I believe him? I wanted to think that Vasilyev was lying just to manipulate me, but why had Jack denied being in Moscow? Could I trust him? Or was he just using me, as Gavrilov had said? I found myself ensnared in a web of treachery and deception, with seemingly no way out. I couldn't trust anyone, it seemed.

After a while, someone knocked on the door.

"Who's there?" I asked.

"It's me," came Jack Taylor's voice.

I opened the door a little but not wide enough for him to enter.

"Are you going to let me in?" he asked, smiling.

"I'm not supposed to talk with you anymore."

"What?"

"Vasilyev's orders. I'm not supposed to talk to Americans."

He frowned.

"You're not serious, are you?"

"It doesn't matter what I feel," I replied coolly. "Those are his orders."

"What's really the matter?"

"I told you."

"There's obviously something else going on, Tat'yana."

I stuck my head out and glanced down the hall both ways, to make sure no one was watching us. Then I said, "Come in quickly." After I'd shut the door, I said, "I think Vasilyev suspects us."

"What did he say?"

"He asked me about Enormous. If I had said anything to you about it. And he ordered me not to talk to you anymore."

"Did he say anything else?"

"That we would be sailing to Siberia. Not the Middle East."

Jack ran his hand over his face, rubbing his jaw contemplatively. "Jesus. Do you think they got Viktor to talk?"

"I don't know." I stared at him, remembering the picture of him and the other man coming out of the American embassy. "Why did you lie to me?"

"What are you talking about?"

"You said you hadn't been to Moscow."

"It's true. I haven't."

"I saw a picture."

"Picture?" he said. "Of what?"

"Vasilyev showed me a picture of you and another man. You were coming out of the American embassy."

"That's impossible."

"Stop trying to deny it, Jack. I saw it with my own eyes. It was you."

He took a deep breath. "All right. I can explain."

"You can explain!" I said with a caustic laugh. "How convenient."

"I can."

"What else did you lie about?"

"Nothing. I swear."

He leaned toward me and tried to kiss me, but I turned my head.

"No," I said. "Do you know a Charles Pierce?"

"What?" he said, feigning ignorance of the name. He quickly and adroitly recovered, but I saw a momentary flicker of acknowledgment in his hazel eyes, enough to tell me I had hit a nerve. "Who's—"

But I cut him short. "For God's sakes, stop lying to me, Jack. Or Charles or whoever the hell you are."

"I'm not lying," he pleaded.

"Yes, you are. Tell me, who is Charles Pierce?"

He seemed about to continue with his denials, but then he suddenly changed tactics and said, "All right. Let me explain."

I laughed at that. "You can explain away all of your lies."

"Please, Tat'yana. I love you."

"Do you take me for a complete fool?" I said, turning and heading over to the window. "Damn you . . . ," I said, not knowing whether to call him Jack or Charles.

He followed me over and put his hand on my shoulder. "We don't have time for this now, Tat'yana."

I spun around. "We don't have time for the truth, you mean. You made me believe you. That you loved me."

"I do. You have to believe that."

"I don't have to believe anything," I cried.

"I understand how it must look to you."

"Look to me! You lied to me."

"We can talk about this later. Right now, Mrs. Roosevelt wants to see you."

"I don't know if I want to see her."

"Why not?"

"I told you, I'm not supposed to talk to Americans. They might be watching me," I said. "Besides, I don't know if I want to go through with it anymore."

"What?"

"I'm not sure I want to defect," I said.

"You don't have any choice," he cried.

"One always has a choice."

"If you go home, they'll punish you."

"I don't care anymore."

"If you don't care about yourself, what about us?"

"How can I believe there was ever really an 'us'? That it wasn't just another one of your lies?"

"It wasn't, I swear. I love you."

"I don't even know who or what to believe anymore. You Americans are as bad as our side."

"Before you make up your mind, please, just talk to Mrs. Roosevelt. It's very important."

I shook my head. I wasn't sure what I wanted to do, whether I wanted to go back home and perhaps be denounced as an enemy of the state, be sent to a camp, or worse. Or take the chance of defecting. Both paths seemed equally unappealing and equally fraught with peril now.

After a while, I said, "All right. I'll talk with her."

"She's on the eighth floor."

We headed over to the door. He started to open it, but I said, "Wait."

I poked my head out and saw one of the *chekisty* just down the hall. He was leaning against the wall, smoking.

"I will go distract him," I whispered to Jack. "When he's not watching, slip out of the room. Tell Mrs. Roosevelt I shall be there as soon as I can."

I headed down the hall and struck up a conversation with the *chekist* officer. It was the stocky one. I stood on the far side of him so that he wouldn't see when Jack Taylor left my room. I asked him if he had a cigarette. He hesitated for a moment, then took out a pack, an American brand, and gave me one and lit it for me. He had a broad face, with high cheekbones and small liquid eyes. I asked him where he came from, and he replied Sverdlovsk. He wasn't much for words. As we spoke, I saw the captain slip out of the room and disappear down the hall. Then I thanked the man and told him I was going down to buy some cigarettes at the front desk and did he want anything. He shook his head.

Mrs. Roosevelt sat in a high-backed chair in a small sitting area over near the window, with Miss Thompson across from her. The First Lady seemed to be dictating something to her secretary. Without stopping what she was saying, when she saw me the First Lady indicated that I have a seat, which turned out to be one of the two twin beds in the room. The captain stood off to one side, glancing at me from time to time. When Mrs. Roosevelt was finished, Miss Thompson shut her pad, stood, said something in English to the First Lady, and then left the room. Mrs. Roosevelt remained silent for a moment, staring out the window, lost in thought.

Finally, turning toward me, she said, "Captain Taylor has briefed me on what has been going on, young lady. And your role in it." Her tone was businesslike, restrained, even aloof. "I understand the pressures that were placed on you, Lieutenant. You were a soldier and you were simply following orders. That's what soldiers do. However, I can't say that I'm not sorely disappointed in your behavior."

"I am very sorry, Mrs. Roosevelt," I pleaded. "You have been a dear friend to me."

"As I thought you had been to me."

"I didn't mean for any of this happen. And I never meant to betray our friendship."

"But betray it you did, Tat'yana. I feel very hurt by what you've done. You betrayed not only me, you've betrayed the United States of America. An ally of your country against the Germans."

Tears suddenly sprang to my eyes and streamed down my cheeks. In a moment I was sobbing. I felt a burning shame at what I had done to this good and decent woman who had shown me nothing but kindness.

"Please . . . forgive me," I said, between sobs.

Mrs. Roosevelt got up and came over and sat down next to me. She put her arm around my shoulder and hugged me to her, as she had done that first night when I stayed at the White House.

"It's all right, my dear," she said soothingly. "I suppose we will all soon be living in a world where we won't be able to trust one another. Though I shall be very loath, indeed, to have to live in such a world. Still, I am proud of your accomplishments in this war and shall always value your friendship."

"Thank you, Mrs. Roosevelt."

"The captain tells me you're in trouble with your own side and that you wish to defect."

I shrugged. "I'm not sure anymore."

She glanced across me at the captain.

"Well, if you're going to ask for political asylum, you will have to make up your mind pretty quickly, I'm afraid," Mrs. Roosevelt explained. "You're slated to leave the day after tomorrow. I've spoken to my husband about all of this, and he informs me it will be a very sticky situation. Your Mr. Stalin will no doubt be quite upset if you jump ship, so to speak," she said with a sad smile. "However, I made it quite clear to Franklin that you may well be in danger if you return to the Soviet Union, and he assured me we can work something out. It all depends on how much your side expects in return. Of course, you know that if you defect, there's no going back."

"I know."

"So what's it to be, Tat'yana?"

I took a deep breath, looked at Captain Taylor, then back at Mrs. Roosevelt.

"I will defect," I said.

"Very well then. We'll have to work quickly. We don't have much time. Certain arrangements will need to be made for your being granted asylum." She gave me a last hug, then stood. "I have a meeting. I suppose you two have lots to talk about." Before she left, she leaned over and grasped my hands in both of hers. "I wish you all the happiness in the world, Tat'yana. And I forgive you."

I thanked her and then she left.

That was the last time I would ever see her.

Captain Taylor and I remained silent for a moment. Then he came over, sat beside me, and took my hand.

"I'm sorry," he began.

"I don't even know what to call you. Is that your real name, Charles Pierce?" I said to him.

"Yes," he said. "Let me explain."

He went on to tell me how he'd gotten into this "spying" business. How since he'd been good at languages, they'd recruited him before the war to spy on the Soviets. He told me how he had worked in Moscow as an American agent. That the United States had feared that the Soviet Union would sign a treaty with Nazi Germany, which, of course they did, and which would allow the Germans to focus all of their might on the Western Front. That he had worked in the embassy reading and translating cables the Americans had intercepted. He told me how his government had received incontrovertible evidence of my government running an extensive spy ring in the United States well before the war, that it had infiltrated high levels of American industry, government, and now even in the development of this secret weapons project.

When he was finished explaining, I paused for a moment. Then I said, "Just tell me one thing. Did you get involved with me just to find out about the spy network?"

"No."

"Tell me the truth."

"All right. At first I did. But later it had nothing to do with my job."

"How am I supposed to believe that? Or anything you tell me?"

"I love you, Tat'yana. You have to believe me."

I didn't know what to say.

"So who are you really?"

"Charles Pierce is my real name. But most people called me Charlie."

"Charlie."

He smiled at me, that smile that could soften my heart. "I'm still the same person."

"Are you?"

"Yes."

He put his arm around me and kissed me on the lips. "I love you," he said again.

And suddenly all of my fears and doubts and worries simply crumbled. I had a choice to make in this as well.

"I love you too," I replied.

As I headed back to my room, I saw the familiar figure of Vasilyev standing outside my door.

"Where were you?" he asked.

"Out for some fresh air."

"I thought I told you to stay away from the American."

"I shall be returning home shortly. And you can do whatever you want to me then."

"And they will, Lieutenant. Believe me, they will."

"I am going to bed."

I unlocked the door and pushed past him, yet he followed me in.

"By the way, this just came for you," he said.

I turned to see him holding out a letter to me.

"What is it?"

"You might want to read it."

He handed me a letter that had already been opened. It was on official military stationery. My heart stopped for a moment as I thought it was going to confirm what I already knew in my heart—that Kolya was dead. Before I read it, I felt the guilt well up in me again. He had tried to be a good husband, had certainly been a better one to me than I had been a wife to him. And yet, as I began to read the letter, I found myself thinking, No, this can't be. This is wrong. The letter said that Kolya was in a hospital in Leningrad, recovering from wounds suffered in battle.

"What is the meaning of this?"

"Meaning?" Vasilyev said, furrowing his brow. "Just that your husband is alive."

I stared at him, wondering if this could actually be true. Even then it occurred to me that it was only another one of his deceptions, a trick intended to keep me under his control.

Vasilyev gave me that avuncular smile of his.

"Why, I thought you would be pleased," he said. "This will give you something to look forward to when you return home."

23

I was up most of the night, and now as morning broke, I lay in bed, thinking about the various revelations of the previous day. Vasilyev informing me that the captain was actually someone named Charles Pierce. My emotional meeting with Mrs. Roosevelt, followed by the equally emotional one with Jack—I still couldn't bring myself to call him Charlie, if that was his real name. And on top of everything, receiving the letter informing me that my "dead" husband wasn't actually dead.

I picked up the letter from the nightstand and read it for what must have been the sixth or seventh time. It said Kolya was in a hospital recovering from his wounds. But alive. I kept wondering if the letter was real, or if it was just more of Vasilyev's trickery. I wouldn't have put it past the *chekisty* to do something like this. Perhaps Viktor had told them that I'd considered running off with him, and this was their way of ensuring that I'd go back to the Soviet Union. They knew how to play upon both my loyalty as well as my guilt. *This will give you something to look forward to when you return home*, Vasilyev had said to me. And yet, what if it were true? I wondered. What if Kolya *were* alive? Though I didn't love him as a wife, didn't I owe him something? Wasn't I at least obliged to be there for him, to tell him about the last moments of our daughter's life? Didn't he deserve better than for me just to vanish without a word, to bring shame on him, as of course my defection would back home. And more than shame, I knew there was the very real possibility that my actions would bring harsher consequences to bear on him. Should he pay for my actions?

I was thinking about these thoughts when my phone rang.

"It's me," came the captain's voice. "I tried to come by, but one of your secret police is watching your room. It would be better if you met me."

I thought of telling him then about the letter, but I decided to hold off.

"Where do you want to meet?" I asked.

"Take the elevator down to the third floor. Make sure that the man outside doesn't follow you though."

I got dressed but then threw on my bathrobe over my clothes. I stuffed the letter in the pocket of my tunic. I didn't put my shoes on but rather wrapped a towel around them and left the room with them under my arm. I passed the *chekist* officer, the thin, bony one, who was slumped against the wall, smoking a cigarette and pretending to read a magazine.

"Do you know where I can get some clean towels?" I asked him.

He glanced up, surprised that I spoke to him. With his thumb he pointed at a cart halfway down the hall. I thanked him and walked on. As I passed the elevator, I quickly hit the down button, but continued on to where a Negro woman with a cart was cleaning rooms. With hand gestures I indicated that I wanted a clean towel, which she gave me. I glanced back over my shoulder to see the man still leaning against the wall. I walked slowly back toward my room, trying to time my passing of the elevator just as it arrived on my floor. Luckily the doors opened as I reached the elevator, so I was able to slip in and push the button before the man could follow me. Once safely ensconced, I removed my robe and put my shoes on.

The captain was waiting for me when I got off. He leaned in to kiss me. He must have felt me stiffen a little, for he said, "Is everything all right?"

I nodded.

"Come, we have to hurry," he said, taking my hand and leading me down the hall. We entered a room where two men dressed in dark suits waited.

"These men are going to help you," he said to me.

He told me their names, though I don't recall what they were, and besides, they were no doubt as phony as Jack Taylor's had been. I do recall that they said they were from the Federal Bureau of Investigation. One of the two did most of the talking. He was middle-aged, good-looking in an austere sort of way. He was all-business, never smiling once. He told me how that evening Mrs. Roosevelt was to hold a press conference in the lobby of the hotel, where she was going to officially thank the Soviet delegation for coming to America. Then we were to gather for a final dinner and reception, which was to be attended by a large crowd. He told me that during the meal I was to excuse myself to go to the bathroom. But that I was to make sure to leave my handbag and coat at the table, to indicate that I would be returning. In one of the stalls of the bathroom there would be a bag waiting for me. It would be filled with civilian clothes I was to change into, as well as a wig. When I left the bathroom they would be waiting to take me away in a car.

"Where will I go?" I asked.

"We can't divulge the details," the dark-haired man explained. "But you'll be brought to a safe place. You'll stay there until our government issues a statement saying that you've defected and have requested political asylum."

"Then what?" I asked.

"There'll be some name-calling on both sides. We'll denounce your country for spying; then your side will issue denials and will probably lodge a formal complaint against us, demanding your return. Both countries will beat their chests for a while, but we don't believe either side will push it too far. I doubt your Mr. Stalin will want to risk endangering our lend-lease program. Behind the scenes, our government will be working with yours to broker a deal. But that won't concern you. After a time it should all blow over. At least publicly."

"What will happen to me?"

This man looked at Charlie and furrowed his mouth into a cautionary *O*.

"You'll have to go into hiding, of course."

Though I already knew the answer, I still asked, "What for?"

"You will have caused your government much embarrassment. Besides, you know too much. So they'll come after you. But we can protect you. We'll give you a new identity, set you up someplace with a new name and a job. But before all that, we're going to want to interview you."

"Interview me?" I asked.

"We're going to want to know everything you know about the Soviet spy network in America."

"I don't really know that much."

"We're still going to want to talk to you." He glanced at Charlie, as if he considered this a subject that should already have been explained to me. "If you wish us to help you, Miss Levchenko, you're going to have to play ball with us. Do you have any questions?" the man asked.

"No, I do not think so. Oh, there is one question. Will I be able to write to anyone back home?"

"No," he said.

"Not even family?"

"Sorry. You will have no contact at all with anyone from your past. Do you understand?"

I had the sensation of a large steel door slamming shut behind me, leaving me completely, utterly alone.

I nodded. We stood and shook hands. And just like that I'd left one world and entered another.

"I'd like to officially welcome you to the United States of America, Miss Levchenko," the man said.

Charlie led me out of the room. I was silent, my thoughts occupied. As we walked down the hall, he said to me, "Are you sure you're all right?"

From my pocket, I took out the letter about Kolya and handed it to him.

"What's this?" he asked.

"Read it."

He stopped and read it slowly, then shook his head. "Well, you know it's a fake," he said.

"Yes, it could be."

"Not could be. You *know* it is. They're trying to manipulate you. Trick you into returning home."

"I've considered that."

"Don't you find it just a little too coincidental that it happens to come now?"

"I don't know what to think."

"You're not considering going home, are you?"

I shrugged.

"But that's crazy. If you return, you'll be in danger. They just want to get you back home, Tat'yana. Can't you see that it's a trick?"

I nodded. "But what if it's not a trick? What if the letter is true, and my husband is alive?"

"Your returning home isn't going to do him any good, and it will only jeopardize yourself."

"It might endanger him if I don't go."

"You don't know that."

"But I do," I said.

"You said you didn't love him."

"He's still my husand. I owe him something."

Charlie's face took on a wounded expression. He stared at me, then reached out and grasped my left hand.

"What about us, Tat'yana?"

"He will need me."

"*I* need you," he said. "I love you."

"And I love you too," I replied.

"Then stay here. After the war we can be together."

Charlie leaned into me and kissed me, at first tentatively, then putting his arm around me, he kissed me with a passion that bordered on desperation. This time I found myself yielding to his kiss. I knew I loved Jack or Charlie or whatever his name was. Knew I loved him as I never could or would love Kolya. Still, I was confused, torn between my love for one man and my loyalty toward another.

"I will have to think about it," I said.

"You don't have time to think about it," he replied. "Those men back there are making plans for your defection. Once we move forward on this, there's no turning back."

"Just give me a little while. Not long. Please."

Charlie wagged his head in disappointment.

"All right," he finally said.

"I'll call you with my decision."

When I returned to my room, the *chekist* officer was no longer out in the hall. Perhaps he had gone off in search of me. I paced my room for a long while, thinking. Would I choose loyalty and duty over love? The past over the future? My homeland over America? At one point, I found myself at the window, looking out. The autumn morning was sunny and clear, with a sparkling view of the ocean extending beyond the city's buildings. It was the sort of bright, expansive day on which I had married Kolya, hardly five years earlier, though it seemed like a lifetime ago now, as if I were already an old woman looking back on my life and on the choices I had made. I tried to imagine my husband for a moment, alive, lying in a bed, thinking of me and Masha. I wondered if he had gotten any of my letters, if he knew she was dead. When I told him, for him it would be as if she just died that very moment. I thought of how we would grieve together over our loss, how I would hold him and try to comfort him. And when he'd recovered enough, I knew exactly what he would say, knew the engineer in him would strive to find a solution to our problem. He would tell me something about how we would have more children, just as Zoya had. But then I would have to tell him about that as well, and how there was to be no answer to our childlessness. Sadness and grief and our memories would have to be the bonds that united us as we grew old together. Then I thought about Charlie, how he made me feel, how light and airy my heart felt in his presence, and I wondered if I could give him up just because of my obligation toward Kolya. Finally, I picked up the phone and called Charlie's room.

"It's me," I said.

"Have you made a decision?" he asked.

I paused for a moment, then said, "I have, yes."

He was silent on the other end, waiting like a man on trial for his verdict. "For God's sakes, Tat'yana, tell me!"

"I wish to defect."

He gave out a nervous little laugh, then said, "That's wonderful news, darling. I love you."

"I love you too."

"In the meantime, be very careful. Don't say or do anything that would give them the slightest indication of what you're planning. I'll meet you in the lobby at five for the press conference."

A little before five there was a knock on the door. Expecting Captain Taylor, I was about to open it but at the last moment decided to ask who it was.

"It's me, Vasilyev," came the reply.

"What do you want?"

"We are to meet Mrs. Roosevelt downstairs for the press conference."

"You're early. I'm not finished getting ready."

"A change in plans."

"Come back in a little while," I said.

"Open the door, Lieutenant," he commanded in a voice that made me sense something was wrong.

I hesitated, a bad feeling working in my stomach like bile. I thought of not unlocking the door but then figured that that would only make me look all the more guilty. So I went ahead and opened it. Vasilyev was standing there, accompanied by the heavyset *chekist* officer.

"Where did you go earlier?" he said, entering my room.

"I had to get some clean towels."

Vasilyev poked his head into the bathroom, glanced around.

"Put your coat on," he commanded. There was something inflexible in his voice.

"I told you, I'm not ready."

"You look fine. Get her coat," he said, snapping his fingers to the other man, who went over to the bed and got my military tunic.

We got on the elevator, but instead of heading down, it started up. My stomach continued to churn.

"I thought you said we were going to the press conference."

"In a while. They want to have a little chat first."

"Who?"

"Some people," was all Vasilyev offered. "You look a little tired, Lieutenant."

"I didn't sleep well."

"It has been a long and strenuous trip for all of us. You'll have plenty of time, however, to rest during our voyage home. Let's hope that the seas are calm."

He glanced at me when he said this.

We got out and headed down the hall until we stopped in front of a door. I knew then that something was terribly wrong.

"Who's in there?" I asked.

Vasilyev turned to me. "I tried to protect you, Lieutenant," he said, his voice restrained. "But you wouldn't listen. Now it is out of my hands."

I turned and bolted, running wildly down the hall. I hadn't gotten more than half a dozen steps, though, before the secret policeman caught me, grabbing me roughly around the waist. He yanked me off my feet as if I weighed no more than a pillow. I screamed and he quickly covered my mouth with a meaty hand that smelled of tobacco. I tried to bite him, but he pressed my mouth firmly, painfully shut.

"Don't be a fool, Lieutenant," Vasilyev advised. He got close up to my face and whispered, "Your only chance is to cooperate with them. Give them what they want. Do you understand?"

The man dragged me into the room and someone else shut the door behind me. There I saw several other men. Gavrilov and Dmitri helped drag me over and force me into a small wooden chair. Next, they bound my legs to the chair with pieces of rope and my arms behind my back so that I couldn't move. The rope dug painfully into my flesh.

"Bastard," I cursed at Gavrilov.

"If I were you, you traitorous whore, I would shut my mouth," he hurled back at me.

I started to scream for help but one of them put a gag over my mouth and tied it so tightly behind my head I thought I couldn't breathe.

From behind me, I heard a familiar voice say, "Not too tight. We don't want to leave any visible bruises."

I turned my head to see Zarubin standing there.

"How are you, Lieutenant?" he said in that gritty voice of his.

He walked over and pulled up a chair and sat down in front of me, leaning toward me so that his knees almost touched mine.

"That doesn't look very comfortable," he said. "If you promise not to scream again, I will have it removed."

I stared into his dull gray eyes. Though I hated him, I finally conceded a nod.

He motioned to one of the men behind me, who undid the gag and removed it. Then Zarubin leaned back in the chair and crossed his legs, as if he intended to be there for a while.

"So. Tell me what you and the captain talked about this morning."

"I didn't see the captain this morning."

Zarubin took a weary breath and blew it out noisily through his nose. "We know you did. So stop lying. How much have you told him concerning Enormous?"

"Nothing."

"Don't test my patience, Lieutenant. What did you tell him about what we know?"

"I told you, nothing."

He sighed again, then gave a nod at the heavyset man. "Just don't touch that pretty face of hers," he instructed.

The *chekist* officer grunted, and I felt a sharp blow in my right side that exploded upward into my chest, forcing the air from my lungs. I tried to curl into the pain, but the rope held me fast. For a long time, I couldn't breathe, the pain was so savage, so overwhelming. Slowly, though, the pain lessened and I was able to draw air into my lungs again.

"Don't force my hand," Zarubin said. "We know you talked to him about it. What did you tell him exactly?"

"Nothing."

"And they told me you were intelligent."

He gave another nod to the man, which was followed immediately by another blow to my side. This one was harder than the first, slamming into me so hard it rocked the chair I was sitting on. I heard something snap, felt a red-hot stabbing pain in my side. Each time I took a breath it felt as if someone were sticking a fork into me.

"I am going to ask you once more, Lieutenant," Zarubin said. "And I want you to think very carefully before you answer. Did you talk about Enormous to the captain?"

I thought of lying, telling them anything, just so that they'd stop, but I sensed that if I lied I would be making it only harder for myself, because I wasn't sure what they knew already.

"No, I didn't talk to him about that."

Another nod, another blow to my side. I felt sick with the pain.

"What of your plans with Viktor?"

"I had no plans with Viktor."

Zarubin shook his head. "We already know you were going to defect with him. We know that much. So stop trying my patience."

"I thought about it, yes."

"With whom was he working?"

"I don't know. He didn't tell me any names."

I flinched even before the blow struck my side. My head spun with the pain. I thought I would pass out.

"We have all the time in the world, Lieutenant," Zarubin said. "Was he working with the captain?"

"What?"

"Viktor. Was he working with your American lover?"

I slowly looked up at him. It was the first time it had occurred to me that perhaps the captain had been working with Viktor as well as with me.

"I . . . I don't know."

"Did you tell the captain anything about our *rezidentura*? About Comrade Semyonov or myself? Or about our contact in the White House?"

"No. I swear I didn't."

He gave another nod, and I was struck again, this time on the left side. Spasms of pain rippled through my body. I leaned over and vomited on my lap.

Zarubin smiled, seeming to enjoy this. He took out a handkerchief, leaned forward, and gently wiped my mouth. Leaning in so close that I could smell his aftershave, he said, "Did you tell the captain the names of the scientists who are cooperating with us?"

Between paroxysms of pain, I said, "How . . . would I? I don't know . . . who is working with you. I only know those Vasilyev . . . told me to bring up with Mrs. Roosevelt."

Zarubin appeared about to give the order to hit me again but Vasilyev said, "She's telling the truth. The only names she knew were those I supplied her with."

Zarubin stared at Vasilyev, as if annoyed with him for cutting short his fun.

"You are in serious trouble, Lieutenant," Zarubin said, but he kept his eyes trained on Vasilyev. "And that trouble might spill over to those closest to you."

I lifted my head to look at him. "What are you talking about?"

"I hear that you received a letter informing you that your husband is alive." He stared at me with his dull gray eyes. "That's wonderful news. Though it would be unfortunate if he had to pay for your acts of disloyalty."

"He had nothing to do with this," I said to him. "You leave him alone."

"That is entirely up to you."

"I didn't want to come here. I wanted no part of this."

"Still, you betrayed your Motherland."

"Go to hell, you bastard."

Zarubin pursed his lips. "I think the whore might need a bath," he said. "Take her and clean her up."

They untied me and dragged me roughly into the bathroom. There I saw that the tub was already filled almost to the top with water. It was one of those clawfoot tubs, so the water was very deep. The slender policeman held my legs while Dmitri grasped my arms, and the heavyset man had his arm wrapped around my neck in a headlock. They lifted me into the tub and forced me down into it, fully dressed, my back toward the water. It was freezing, and I shuddered as soon as cold water came in contact with my skin. I realized right away they weren't intending to wash me, and I started to kick and thrash about, trying to get free, the water sloshing over the edge onto the floor, splashing against the wall, the three of them struggling in the narrow space to subdue me.

"Are you ready to talk, Lieutenant?" said Zarubin from the doorway.

I didn't answer.

The heavyset man grabbed me by the hair and pulled my head backward into the water. I tried to pull away, but he held me firmly, painfully by the hair. Looking up through the undulating surface, I could see the muscles in his face straining, his eyes red and bulging. I wanted to scream but of course I couldn't. My lungs burned, my head seemed as if it would explode. Just when I thought I would lose consciousness, he yanked my head out.

I coughed and spat out a mouthful of water.

"Is your memory coming back, Levchenko?" said Zarubin.

I struggled to catch my breath, trying to ready myself for another dunking.

"Again," Zarubin commanded.

Once more the man plunged my head beneath the water. After what seemed like hours, he yanked me up again.

"Ready to talk?" Zarubin said.

I just stared at him.

"Again."

"Wait!" I heard a voice cry.

It was Vasilyev. He had pushed by Zarubin and now stood in the confined space of the bathroom.

"She doesn't know anything," he said.

"That's what we aim to find out," countered Zarubin.

"I'm telling you, she doesn't."

Zarubin ignored him. "Again," he commanded.

The man was about to dunk my head when Vasilyev yelled, "Stop it!" The heavyset man paused, looking over at Vasilyev. I followed his gaze to see that Vasilyev had pulled a gun out and was pointing it at the *chekist* officer.

"Let go of her," he directed. "She's telling the truth."

"Comrade, I would strongly advise you not to interfere," Zarubin warned.

"Get her out of there," Vasilyev said. When they didn't obey, he turned the gun on Zarubin. "Now!"

Zarubin nodded toward the others, and they lifted me out of the water. I struggled to get to my feet, but my uniform was drenched and it weighed on me like a suit of lead. Oddly, though, I no longer felt cold, nor did I feel the pain in my sides as intensely.

"You had better think about what you are doing, Comrade," Zarubin said to Vasilyev.

"Shut up." Then turning to me, Vasilyev said, "Get out of here, Lieutenant. Quickly."

Our eyes met for a moment, and everything I had thought or felt about him suddenly changed.

"Thank you, Comrade."

"Go!"

I pushed past him and out into the room. I started for the door, but someone slammed into me, driving me into the wall. When I turned I saw that it was Gavrilov. I wheeled about and struck him flush in the face as hard as I could with my fist. He continued to grapple with me, so I hit him again, several times. Finally he relinquished his hold on me and dropped to the floor, coughing. Then I turned and fumbled with the lock before opening the door and rushing out of the room. As I started to scramble down the hallway, I heard what I thought was a single gunshot coming from behind me, inside the room. Vasilyev, I thought.

I rushed to the elevator but decided at the last moment not to risk it and continued on for the stairs. By this point I heard someone calling after me. "There she goes."

I flew down the stairs, taking them two at a time, my waterlogged shoes making squishy sounds as I ran, water spraying all around me. I thought how I would be an easy trail to follow. I tried to fall back on my sniper training. What would I do if I had been spotted? How would I slip away? Somewhere above I heard their footsteps and their cries. When I came to one door, I started past it so that the trail of water would lead them away, then I quickly backtracked and opened the door and ran down the hallway. Here at least the carpeting deadened the sound of my steps and the trail of water wasn't quite so obvious. I ran wildly, not really knowing where I was headed. When I came to another door and another set of stairs, I glanced back over my shoulder to see if they were following. For a moment at least I had eluded them.

I entered the stairs and rushed headlong down them, trying not to trip on my soaked trousers. Of course I couldn't read the floor numbers on the doors and had to keep going until I thought I had come to the lobby. I opened the door and ran over to a phone booth. I went in and closed the door and dialed the operator.

"Captain Taylor," I said. The woman on the other end said something to me in English, and I repeated, "Captain Taylor."

The phone rang several times. *Please, be there*, I pleaded. I was about to hang up when he finally picked up the phone.

"They know everything," I blurted out.

"What?"

"They know everything. They tried to kill me and now they're after me."

"Where are you?"

"I'm hiding in a phone booth in the lobby. Come quickly."

While I waited for him, I watched the lobby through the glass door of the phone booth. I thought of Vasilyev, what he had done for me. After all my doubts about him, after all our arguments and conflicts, he had sacrificed his life to save mine. I was thinking about this when I saw Dmitri and the heavyset *chekist* officer come rushing into the lobby, looking around. I quickly ducked down and tried to hide. I thought how in some ways I had come full circle. As I had when I was a sniper, here I was once more hiding from my enemies, trying to avoid their detection. Only now my enemies weren't the Germans. They were my own countrymen.

I was cowering like this when the door flew open.

"Jack—" I began but stopped when I saw the heavyset one looming over me. He grabbed my arm roughly and yanked me upright, then pulled me out of the booth. "If you scream," he whispered hotly in my ear, "I will kill you, you bitch." He took one arm, Dmitri the other, and they led me along. Then I saw Zarubin standing there, a look of outrage on his face.

"If you make a scene, Lieutenant, I promise you, your husband will pay dearly," he said to me. "Come along quietly and nothing will happen to either of you. You will return home to a hero's welcome and a grateful nation. You have my word."

"Your word," I scoffed.

"Just keep your mouth shut and everything will be all right."

They quickly escorted me through the front door and outside to a waiting limousine. The skinny one was standing there, holding the door open. I didn't see Vasilyev or Gavrilov in the car. I don't know why, but I knew then, as assuredly as I had ever known anything, that the letter about Kolya was a fake, that he was dead, or at least that he had not been found. And I knew too that I would not return home to a hero's welcome, that I would rot in some prison camp or be dispatched with a bullet to the back of my neck.

Just before I was put into the car, I heard a voice call out in Russian: "Stop!"

I turned to see Captain Taylor, surrounded by half a dozen men in dark suits, as well as several uniformed policemen. They came rushing up to us. Charlie stared at me. "Are you all right?"

I nodded.

"What the hell did they do to you?"

"Captain," Zarubin interrupted, "this is not your concern."

"Lieutenant Levchenko has asked the United States for political asylum."

"My government will be extremely displeased at this action. Lieutenant Levchenko was invited as a guest by your Mrs. Roosevelt. And now she is going home as a Soviet citizen."

"But she has asked for and been granted asylum."

"I think you are mistaken."

"Why don't we ask her?" Charlie said.

Zarubin turned and tried to usher me into the car.

"Hold it," cried Charlie. "Do you want to go with these men, Lieutenant?"

I looked at him. "No. I don't."

Charlie grabbed my arm, but the two *chekisty* wouldn't relinquish their hold on me.

The dark-haired man, the American I'd spoken to earlier, said something to Charlie in English, and then in Russian Charlie translated to Zarubin, "We have the authority to take her into protective custody. Now stand back."

"You are going to be in a lot of trouble, Captain."

"Not as much as you if you don't let her go."

Zarubin looked from Charlie to the other men surrounding him. "Release her," he commanded the Soviet agents. Staring at me he said, "I hope you appreciate the implications of your decision, Lieutenant."

"I know what I'm doing, Comrade," I replied.

As Charlie took my hand and started to lead me away, Zarubin called, "You haven't heard the last from us, Lieutenant."

We headed inside, and Charlie brought me up to his room. Once he shut the door, he put his arm around me and held me. "You're shivering," he said. I hadn't even been aware of it. "Let's get you out of those wet things," he said to me. While I undressed, he got me a blanket. When he saw the bruises on my side, he cried, "Those bastards. I've a good mind—"

"I'm all right, Charlie," I said, putting my hand on his cheek.

"Are you sure?"

"Yes," I replied. "I'm just tired."

He wrapped the blanket around me and led me over to the bed, where he pulled the covers back and we lay down together. I remember how I couldn't stop shivering, as if I could never get warm, but after a while I slowly felt myself relax. It felt so good to be held by him. Safe, comforting. Everything—the war, my personal losses, the business with the *chekisty*—all of that seemed to fade far away, and it was just Charlie and me in that room. Nothing else seemed to matter. I had no idea what would happen after that, what my life in America would look like, but for that moment at least I felt I was someplace I was supposed to be. Charlie and I didn't talk much that night. We just lay quietly in each other's embrace, savoring the brief time we had together.

"I love you, Tat'yana," Charlie said to me.

"And I love you, Charlie," I replied.

Despite all the death I had seen and been a part of, despite the fact that I had convinced myself the war had left me an empty shell incapable of feeling anything other than anger and hatred, here I was, in love with another human being. It all felt so strange and incomprehensible, yet so wondrous at the same time. I thought of what Mrs. Roosevelt had said, how we had to do something each day that frightened us. Perhaps this was the thing that frightened me the most, permitting myself to love again. And I thought once more of that line from Tsvetaeva: *Ah! is the heart that bursts with rapture.*

After a while I let myself go and I drifted off to sleep in his arms. I slept for a long time.

EPILOGUE

When the old woman had stopped talking, Elizabeth looked up, her neck stiff from being bent over for hours. She noticed, for the first time really, that night had slowly given way to dawn. To the east, the sky was a lighter blue, thin and diaphanous as gauze, the air on the porch having grown uncomfortably cool. Some time during the night the old woman had gone and gotten Elizabeth a blanket to throw about her shoulders. A single lamp cast a fine, pale light like dust over everything. Elizabeth glanced across at Tat'yana Levchenko, who was staring intently toward the dawn. She appeared almost in a trance, her gaze that of one hypnotized. She didn't seem to be aware of Elizabeth's presence. Her eyes were tired, her face haggard. But there was in her look a certain expectancy, a solemn concentration, as if the dawn would bring something she'd been waiting a long time for.

Elizabeth hesitated saying anything, like someone reluctant to interrupt a sleepwalker near a cliff. Softly Elizabeth finally ventured, "Tat'yana." When the woman didn't seem to hear her, she offered louder, "Tat'yana, are you all right?"

Gradually, almost grudgingly, the old woman came back from wherever it was she'd been. Her eyes slowly adjusted, and she sighted in on Elizabeth, bringing to bear on her the same sort of cool intensity she would have had looking through the scope at those doomed Germans half a century before.

"Ah! Where did the time go?" the old woman said.

Elizabeth wondered if she meant by this more than the previous night.

"What happened after you defected?"

"They gave me new name, new identity. I had to move about several times."

"Because of the Soviet agents?"

"Yes. I was told they were getting close," replied Tat'yana Levchenko. "The Americans were afraid they would find me. Finally they moved me out here."

"Did you fear they would find you?"

The old woman stared at Elizabeth. "I was certain they would."

"Even after all these years?"

"You don't know those people. They were not the sort to give up. They were . . ." Here she paused, searching for the right words, and, not finding them in English, she fell back on her mother tongue. "*Bezdush-nye.* How you say, without a soul."

"What was it like to feel yourself hunted all those years?"

"Like an animal, I suppose. Each time I see stranger in town, I fear it's one of them. That they find me at last. Once these two young men come to my door. They are dressed in suits. Strangers don't come here. I was home alone, so I went and got Walter's rifle. I open door with gun in my hands, ask them what they wanted. It turned out they were those religious people. Mormons. I scared those poor boys half to death."

With this the old woman let out a dry cackle, which made Elizabeth laugh too.

"And you thought I was KGB?"

"Yes. But . . ." Here the old woman paused, waving her hand before her face. "Does not matter anymore."

"Did you ever hear from Mrs. Roosevelt?"

"I received letter. Many years ago. After her husband had died. After the war too."

"What did she say?"

"She asked how I was. But she spoke mostly of her husband. How surprised she was at the pain she felt at losing him. That she cared for him much more than she ever realized."

"Did you ever write back?"

"No, I couldn't."

"And your husband?"

"You mean, my first husband?"

"Yes. Did you ever find out if he had lived or not?"

"No, I never find out."

"Do you think they were trying to trick you into returning to the Soviet Union?"

"Who can say?"

"Did you ever hear from anyone else from home? Zoya?"

"No. It wasn't permitted. I could have no contact with anyone from my past. It was as if my previous life had never happened. It was suddenly gone—like *that*," she said, snapping her fingers.

"That must have been hard."

The old woman shrugged. She seemed to be distracted again, stared vacantly out the window.

"What happened to Vasilyev?"

Tat'yana Levchenko pursed her lips in thought. "I do not know. But I owe him my life."

"Why do you think he helped you?"

The old woman shrugged. "I think he was good man at heart. Like many of us who suffered through those times, he lived two lives. The one he needed to survive and the private one. The private one finally won out."

Glancing at the photo on the wall, Elizabeth asked, "Did you tell your husband about your past?"

"No."

"He knew nothing about what you did during the war?"

"He knew it was something I didn't want to talk about. And he respected my wishes. Only because he's dead I am talking to you now."

"Did he know about your daughter Masha?"

"He knew I had been married before. That I lost my family in war."

"And what of the captain?"

Elizabeth saw the old woman's mouth harden, as if she'd just jabbed herself with a needle while sewing. Even after all these years it was evident that his memory was still very much with her.

"He died."

"Oh, no," Elizabeth exclaimed. "How?"

"He had to fly to Moscow for meeting. As interpreter. The war was almost over. On the return trip plane he was in ran into bad weather. They think it crashed into the sea. They never found any bodies."

"But you had a chance to spend some time together?"

"Not very much, unfortunately. I had to go into hiding and he had his work. We did have one night, though."

"Would you mind telling me about it? If it's not too personal."

The old woman smiled ruefully. "Everything I've told you is personal. What can one do that is more personal than to kill another human being? Back in Washington I was interrogated by American agents. They want to know what I knew, about Soviet spy network, about project called Manhattan and how much our side knew about it. I was shuttled from place to place, trying to keep one step ahead of *chekist* agents, who, it was known, had orders directly from Stalin himself that I was to be silenced. The last night Charlie and I had together was in hotel room in Washington. Mrs. Roosevelt had arranged for us to spend night together. We made love and later we lay in each other's arms. We spoke of our future together, our life after the war. How we would get married. The places we would go, things we would do. He spoke of children again as he had that one time, and I just smiled and pretended it was something that would happen. I could not bring myself to tell him the truth."

"Do you think if he'd lived you would have gotten married?"

"Who can say?"

"Oh, how very sad," Elizabeth exclaimed.

The old woman nodded. "But it was long time ago."

"And Walter? Did you love him?"

"We had a good life together."

"That's not the same as loving someone."

"My mother was right when she said one can learn to love."

"So you were happy?"

Tat'yana Levchenko smiled. "You Americans and your happiness. Let's say that I was as happy as one can be who has seen so much sorrow. I consider myself very fortunate. America has been good to me. I had full life. I have no complaints." She paused and glanced over at the photo of the young blond woman on the bookshelf. "I have wonderful daughter too."

Elizabeth followed her gaze over to the photo. She assumed it had to be her husband's daughter.

"Was that his child?"

"His?" she said, frowning. "No. Both of ours."

Elizabeth frowned. "But I thought—"

"We adopted her."

"I see. What is her name?"

The dog happened to wander in then, its nails clicking on the floor. It put its muzzle on the old woman's lap and stared expectantly up at her.

"Do you have to go out, old girl?" the woman asked, petting the dog. With difficulty the old woman got to her feet and shuffled off toward the front of the house, the dog following on her heels.

She was gone for a while. Elizabeth stood, stretched, her muscles aching from sitting so long. She went over and picked up the photo of the young woman and stared at it.

When the woman finally returned, she was carrying something. She handed it to Elizabeth. It was a small black leather book, frayed with age. Opening it, Elizabeth saw that it was a notebook, the yellowed, brittle pages filled with words and numbers. There were what looked like poems and random thoughts and journal entries separated by dates. As she read along, she realized it was Tat'yana's private notebook from the war, which included the log of her kills. At the back there was a single photograph wedged among the pages. Elizabeth removed it and stared at it closely. It showed three people, two adults and a child standing between them. The man was thin, with a serious expression, the woman pretty, dark-haired, the girl blond, perhaps two years old.

"That was us before war," Tat'yana Levchenko said. "Kolya and Masha and me."

"Your daughter was a very pretty child."

"Yes, she was."

Elizabeth turned back to the photo on the shelf.

"And your other daughter. What is her name?"

"Raisa," the woman replied.

Elizabeth stared at her in surprise. "Raisa? Not—"

"Yes. That Raisa."

"Oh, my God. How did you find her?"

"Why don't I make us some tea and I shall tell you all about it," the old woman offered.

"Yes. That would be nice."

ACKNOWLEDGMENTS

This novel is, first and foremost, a work a fiction. However, like almost all historical fiction, it combines the work of the imagination with real people and real events. In the novel, much of the fighting that is reported as having taken place during the siege of Sevastopol is based on fact. I tried to remain faithful to what is known not only about the fighting on the Eastern Front, but also to what was taking place in America during this early part of the war. My main character, Tat'yana Levchenko, does bear some striking similarities to an actual female Russian sniper of World War II, Lyudmila Pavlichenko, and yet, despite those similarities, Tat'yana is solely a creation of my imagination. Her thoughts, feelings, and actions are independent of any actual people.

Regarding Eleanor Roosevelt, I tried to remain faithful to what is known— or at least to what can be reasonably inferred by those more knowledgeable than I—about her personal life. At times I did consciously telescope or rearrange time sequences in her life as well as in the larger historical context of America during the war. For example, exactly when Enormous—the Soviet term for the Manhattan Project—was known to Soviet operatives working in America may have been premature by a few months, but certainly by late 1942 Soviet agents were on the trail of our atomic bomb project and already infiltrating it with spies. Also, I eliminated or combined some of the Soviet agents that were heavily involved in spying for atomic secrets.

The following books proved to be invaluable for research regarding the war on the Eastern Front: *Russia's Heroes* by Albert Axell; *Heroines of the*

Soviet Union, 1941–45 by Henry Sakaida; *War of the Rats,* by David L. Robbins; *Stalin's Other War,* by Albert L. Weeks; *Treasonable Doubt,* by R. Bruce Craig; *The Sword and the Shield,* by Christopher M. Andrew and Vasili Mitrokhin; *WW2 People's War: An Archive of World War Two Memories,* developed by the BBC; and *Women in War and Resistance: Selected Biographies of Soviet Women Soldiers,* by Kazimiera J. Cottam. Regarding the extensive network of Soviet spying in America before, during, and after the war, *The Venona Secrets* by Herbert Romerstein and Eric Breindel was of enormous help to me in understanding just how extensive the Soviet spy network was in America. Regarding the life of Eleanor Roosevelt I am indebted to Blanche Wiesen Cook's wonderfully frank but impressive portrait of Mrs. Roosevelt, *Eleanor Roosevelt, Vol. I, 1884–1933,* and her relationship not only with Franklin but also with her lifelong friend Lorena Hickok.

I would also like to thank several organizations and individuals for their help in writing this book: the staff of the library at Fairfield University, who provided me with much-needed research materials, in particular Jonathan Hodge; Eastern Frontier Society and Steve Dunn for allowing me the time and quiet on Norton Island to work on the book; and Linda Miller, in the Department of English, dear friend and supporter in everything I do. I would like to thank my neighbors and good friends, Rita and Art, who often fed my body and nourished my soul when I most needed it.

My editor at William Morrow, David Highfill, is a writer's dream of an editor and advocate, who not only supported and encouraged me in the writing of this book but also pressed me again and again to make it better.

Finally, and most important, I wish to acknowledge my ongoing gratitude to two dear friends and longtime supporters of my writing, my agents, Nat Sobel and Judith Weber, who continually amaze me with their penetrating insights into my writing, both when it works and when it doesn't, and with their emotional support to help me carry on with it. Thanks for more than a quarter of a century.